Heartache

Lynn Johnson left school with no qualifications. With determination and hard work, she ended her career as a Human Resources Manager with a large County Council. Born and raised in Stoke-on-Trent, she now lives in Orkney with her husband and six cats. Lynn is a member of the Romantic Novelists Association.

Also by Lynn Johnson

The Potteries Girls

The Girl from the Workhouse
Wartime with the Tram Girls
The Potteries Girls on the Home Front
A New Day at Paradise Pottery
Heartache For The Tram Girls

LYNN JOHNSON
Heartache *for the* Tram Girls

hera

First published in the United Kingdom in 2025 by

Hera Books, an imprint of
Canelo Digital Publishing Limited,
20 Vauxhall Bridge Road,
London SW1V 2SA
United Kingdom

A Penguin Random House Company
The authorised representative in the EEA is Dorling Kindersley Verlag GmbH.
Arnulfstr. 124, 80636 Munich, Germany

Copyright © Lynn Johnson 2025

The moral right of Lynn Johnson to be identified as the creator of this work has been asserted in accordance with the Copyright, Designs and Patents Act, 1988.
All rights reserved. No part of this publication may be reproduced or transmitted in any form or by any means, electronic or mechanical, including photocopy, recording, or any information storage and retrieval system, without permission in writing from the publisher.
No part of this book may be used or reproduced in any manner for the purpose of training artificial intelligence technologies or systems. In accordance with Article 4(3) of the DSM Directive 2019/790, Canelo expressly reserves this work from the text and data mining exception.

A CIP catalogue record for this book is available from the British Library.

Print ISBN 978 1 83598 114 6
Ebook ISBN 978 1 83598 117 7

This book is a work of fiction. Names, characters, businesses, organizations, places and events are either the product of the author's imagination or are used fictitiously. Any resemblance to actual persons, living or dead, events or locales is entirely coincidental.

Printed and bound in Great Britain by Clays Ltd, Elcograf S.p.A.

Look for more great books at
www.herabooks.com | www.dk.com

'The value of family and friendship, near and far, knows no bounds.'

Chapter One

October 1913

Ruth was almost ready to leave for her friend Dottie's wedding. She had taken her pale lemon dress down a few days earlier. The high-waisted dress with three-quarter sleeves complemented her dark brown hair. Carla and Ruth had agreed to arrange each other's hair. She had prepared a small suitcase with everything she needed. There was nothing else to do.

She was now sitting in the front room which had, in recent months, become Mother's bedroom. The illness which had caused her mother to take to her bed had worsened and she needed constant care. Today being a Saturday, Ruth was waiting for Father to get home from the potbank where he worked so that he could take her place. Her eyes filled as she watched her mother, propped up with pillows, trying to smile as she asked Ruth questions about the wedding. She knew it was unlikely her mother would see her only daughter married. She turned her head away before Mother caught sight of the tears that threatened.

The sound of the hooter going off, warning that the shift was over for the day, gave her the excuse to jump up and glance through the net-covered windows. It looked like a fine day, thankfully.

'Father'll be home very soon,' she said, surreptitiously wiping her eyes so her mother wouldn't see.

'Fancy that. One of you three girls getting wed. You're all so grown up now. Proper young ladies.'

Ruth leaned over and gave her a hug as she felt the strength of feeling her mother put into it. She squeezed her back. 'It won't feel the same. Not having her just around the corner.'

'All things end sooner or later, Ruth.'

Ruth heard the back door open and took hold of Mother's hand, patting it, gently. 'Father's home.'

'Kiss me – before you go, Ruth.'

Ruth looked at her keenly. 'Are you feeling all right? Do you want me to stay?'

Mother smiled and her bottom lip shook momentarily. 'No dear, I wouldn't hear of it. You go to the wedding. I'll not have you missing it for the world.'

'Everything all right?' said Father as he walked in and gave Mother a peck on the cheek.

'Of course. I'm just telling our Ruth to enjoy herself and that I have a splendid doctor to look after me while she's away.'

Ruth gave her one last kiss before heading to the kitchen to pick up her suitcase, hat and coat. As she was ready to leave, she peeped around the door to the front room to see Father sitting in his chair beside the bed holding Mother's hand, unable to take his eyes off her. Quietly she let herself out of the house and hurried down to Hesse's Stores, a few doors away, where Carla lived.

–

Mrs Hesse, Carla's mother, was serving in their shop and immediately walked through into the back to shout Carla, who appeared, complete with her own suitcase, seconds later.

'Isn't it exciting. I can't believe it's come so quickly. The first of us three to get married. Can you remember the covenant we made when we were at school, Ruth?'

'Of course I can.' Ruth held up her hand as if swearing an oath, which it was, to them at the time.

> *We, Ruth Latham, Dottie Scott and Carla Hesse, do solemnly promise at each of our marriages the other two will be bridesmaids. Signed Ruth, Dottie and Carla.*

'Have you still got your copy?'

Carla grinned and nodded. 'Of course.'

Mrs Hesse interrupted. 'Now have you got everything, Carla?'

'I have. And give Dottie our good wishes.'

'Will do, Mother.'

Carla kissed her and headed for the door just as it opened. It was Carla's brother, Bertie, short for Albrecht, reflecting their German parentage.

'You off now, girls?'

'We are,' said Carla. 'And we are young ladies, if you don't mind. One of us is getting married today.'

'Give Dottie my best, won't you?'

Ruth watched Carla's face soften. Carla and Bertie were close; there was just the two of them. They were never far apart. Although Walter and Bertie were older, they would often join the girls. They liked to think they protected their sisters and the girls allowed them to think that.

They made their way quickly to Dottie's house in Gordon Street. The front door was open and the noise, deafening. Dottie had three sisters, two of whom were excitable bridesmaids and a brother who marched about the house pretending to be in charge.

Dottie's mother herded Ruth and Carla upstairs to the girls' bedroom so that the three of them could help each other. She did her best to keep the rest downstairs until called for.

'Thanks, Mrs Scott. We won't be long,' Ruth called as Dottie's mother closed the door behind her.

Carla carried the veil borrowed from one of their friends, to lay it out on one of the beds. 'Let Ruth help you, Dottie, for goodness' sake,' she muttered.

Dottie was struggling to fasten the little pearl buttons, climbing up her back like a silver snake. Ruth smacked her hands away. 'Dottie, you'll rip those buttons off if you keep pulling them like that. Let me help you.'

'How do you feel, Dottie, love?'

'Strange. I can't believe that this time tonight I'll be Mrs Spilling.'

'And you'll be sleeping with Donald,' reminded Carla with a saucy smile.

Dottie's face turned pink. She covered her cheeks with her hands. 'I hope I don't put him off when he sees me in my shift.'

'He'll fall in love with you all over again,' said Ruth. 'There, your buttons are all done up.'

Dottie rubbed her hands, grinning at her friends. 'And where would I be without the pair of you? Sit down, Ruth and I'll put your hair up.'

At that moment, Mrs Scott opened the door. 'Are you three nearly ready?'

'Almost done,' said Dottie. 'You can let Brenda and Linda come in now and we'll fix their hair too.'

Mrs Scott walked onto the landing and called the two other bridesmaids, who appeared in seconds. 'Now, listen, it's an important day for your big sister, so I need all of you to be on your best behaviour.'

Tears welled in Mrs Scott's eyes as she stared at Dottie, who would, in a couple of hours' time, no longer be just her daughter. The room fell quiet. Mother and daughter hugged each other, and the rest of the group joined in. Mrs Scott excused herself. The two youngest, Roy and Eliza, who had followed Brenda and Linda upstairs, stood open-mouthed staring at Dottie before grabbing each other's hand and following Mrs Scott out of the room.

Dottie and Donald had been walking out for more than a year. She was the only one of the three that had a gentleman friend. Ruth had been too busy looking after her mother while Carla was kept busy working in Hesse's Stores. Ruth was sure Dottie would feel strange talking through her innermost thoughts with someone who wasn't part of their shared past. That's what she had said to Dottie when Donald first asked her out. Ruth remembered what Dottie had replied. 'If you love each other, you'll share much more with him than you ever did with us. You two have never been close to a man and I don't mean that in a nasty way.' Now Ruth thought about it, Dottie had sounded quite knowledgeable about the subject.

'I wish my hair was brown with soft curls, like yours, Ruth. You can do so much more with it. Donald likes my mousy hair just the way it is. And you've styled it so beautifully, I can hardly believe it's mine.' Her fingers touched it gently as she turned towards the mirror to admire it yet again.

Carla threw a cushion at Dottie just as Mrs Scott walked back into the room, frowning at first, but then giggling. 'Girls, please get a move on.'

'Mother, sit down; you're making me nervous,' pleaded Dottie.

'Dorothy, I am your mother and I am allowed to worry.'

Ruth combed through Carla's hair and pinned it up. She looked taller now.

Mrs Scott wandered over to Ruth. 'How's your mother, Ruth?' she whispered.

Feelings of guilt for straying from her mother's bedside returned in an instant. 'Not good.' Ruth swallowed hard. 'We can't leave her. Father's looking after her and he'll stay with her tonight like he always does. Walter will take a turn to give him a rest.'

Mrs Scott took Ruth's hand in hers. 'They'll look after her. Don't worry. They're good men.'

'Sometimes it's so hard. I have to force myself to go into her room. I can't bear to see her like this.'

'That's because you love her so much. She couldn't wish for a more caring daughter.'

'It's nice of you to say so, Mrs Scott.'

She patted Ruth's hand. 'I tell as I find. You're a good girl, Ruth. Whatever you choose to do with your life, I'm sure she'll be very proud of you.' Mrs Scott raised her voice again. 'Now then, girls, remember to pick up your flowers on the way out.'

The bridesmaids followed Mrs Scott's instructions and were soon ready to leave. Ruth checked herself in the mirror in Mrs Scott's bedroom for one last time. She had never felt so good and if she felt like this wearing a bridesmaid dress, how much more overcome would she feel wearing a wedding dress and being the centre of all the day's events – if she ever found the right man.

They all trooped down the stairs where Mr Scott was waiting. Ruth watched his face as he saw Dottie and heard him clear his throat. He held out his arms to her, and she walked into them.

'No tears, darling,' Ruth heard him say. She watched as Mrs Scott joined them and that was the precise moment that Ruth felt her own tears rise – not because of the emotion of the moment – but because it was likely that her own mother would not be there to see her married.

–

Donald, handsome as ever, dressed in his sergeant's uniform of the Territorial Force. His friends from the Territorials, together with drivers from The Potteries Tramway Company where Donald worked, had arranged a guard of honour. A trumpet played as the happy couple walked through as man and wife.

Once the formalities were over and the wedding party arrived at the Scotts' house for the wedding breakfast, the celebrations began, led by a proud but bemused-looking Mr Scott.

'Now then, everyone, I want yer to pick up a glass on yer way in and we shall all drink a toast to our lovely daughter and her husband, Donald,' said Dottie's father in a loud and possibly inebriated manner.

Donald beamed. 'I'll second that – Father.'

Ruth had never seen Donald looking so – so jolly, probably from a pre-wedding whisky or two. Ruth couldn't take her eyes off Dottie as she stood, head held high in the front room of her mother's house, looking a picture of happiness as she welcomed each guest to join her, during her first hours as Mrs Spilling.

'You'd best take care of my daughter, Donald Spilling. Otherwise I shall—'

The plans Mrs Scott had for Donald if he failed his new wife remained undisclosed. He swept Mrs Scott off her feet and planted a huge smack of a kiss on her cheek. Dottie couldn't take the smile off her face. She clapped her hands in delight at seeing her usually staid mother losing control in her own house.

Around twenty-five guests crowded into the terraced house on Gordon Street, relations, friends, and friends from work. It was a community of people who would probably spend most of their lives in Stoke-on-Trent, knowing each other better than they knew most of their own families.

—

As the evening drew in, Ruth and Carla changed into their outdoor clothes and said their goodbyes. They walked home, arms linked, hearing the sounds of their boots echoing on the pavement. Carla giggled.

'What's so funny?'

'We talked about this moment loads of times when we were young – about getting wed – but now it's actually arrived. I believe I won't be able to look Dottie in the eye. What with her being married and… you know what happens in the bedroom once the door's closed.'

Ruth could feel her face reddening. 'She's married now.'

'Yes, but she's the first one of us to sleep with a man. Doesn't the thought of one of us doing that make you feel odd? Everybody knowing what you're up to?'

Ruth hadn't thought about it in that way before, but Carla was right. Now that she'd mentioned it, Ruth couldn't get the idea out of her mind. 'We're adults now, Carla. We're expected to take things like this in our stride.'

The trio of friends had been born within six months of each other, living only a few streets apart. Even now, at the grand age of twenty, they were never at a loss for things to talk about. But Dottie had moved her belongings and clothes down to Donald's parents' in Leason Street, in Stoke, behind the station and Dottie would travel back to her job in Burslem each day. Opportunities for the friends to get together would be so much less. Donald wanted to look for somewhere to rent as soon as possible, but wanted to remain in Stoke because of his job with the PTC. Dottie had already confessed to her friends that she would be too embarrassed to live under his parents' watchful eyes for long.

'A penny for them?' Carla smiled.

'I was thinking how much we'll miss Dottie.'

'Especially you. She's been such a help to you over the past years.'

Ruth nodded. After Mother had become bedridden and forced to move her bed downstairs into the front room, Dottie and Carla had organised themselves to sit with her, allowing Ruth some time to herself each day.

'I'll miss her most as a friend, but I have to admit, the pair of you have been so good at helping me look after Mother. I will always be grateful.' Ruth sighed. 'This is the start of everything changing, for all of us, isn't it?'

'Everything changes, Ruth. It's down to each of us to make sure we keep in touch. We were lucky because we were in and out of each other's houses every day because we live so close. We have to make sure we stay in touch with Dottie wherever she lives, so she still feels she's one of us. Promise?'

Ruth slapped her hand on top of Carla's. 'I promise.'

Chapter Two

November–December 1913

Ruth strode along the street, hugging her coat around her. November had brought in heavy rain and a biting wind. She wished she had remembered her gloves, but it was too late to think about that now. She had shopped for groceries and had turned towards home.

Since Dottie's wedding, Mother had slowly got worse, and it was rare for Ruth to leave the house. Carla called past most nights after the shop had closed. Recently, Carla's mother had stepped into Carla's shoes in the shop so Ruth and Carla could spend time together. The Hesses were good people.

Then Mother succumbed to pneumonia, something that everyone dreaded. The doctor had told them that pneumonia often followed when patients were already unwell. There were days when Mother could barely speak and all she seemed to want to do was close her eyes, as if any light was just too much.

Throughout November, Mother had grown worse. Carla called round every day, keeping the family supplied with all their needs and giving Ruth a chance to get some rest. They were tough days and nearly broke the whole family. Without asking, Carla brought round sandwiches and a fruitcake, or some such, so they didn't have to think about such mundane matters. A kettle was regularly on the boil. Sometimes Ruth and Carla just sat there, each deep in thought.

Today, Frank, Ruth's elder brother, and his wife, Joan, supervised Mother, freeing Ruth from the need to rush. Instead, she took deep breaths and slowed her pace, moving her heavy bag to the opposite arm as her mind focused on her mother's condition, now declining day by day.

When she arrived home, she was told the doctor had called and that they should prepare themselves for the worst.

—

Ruth barely left her mother's side during those dark days, apart from giving Father time to spend alone with her after getting home from work. Mostly, he sat on Mother's bed. Sometimes he lay next to her, cradling her. They held hands, their love obvious. Ambitions came in many forms, and the love of a good man must surely be at the top of every woman's list.

Frank called regularly on his way to his own home, and would often stand with Walter by their mother's door, their faces haggard but not wanting to show their pain. Ruth would put her arms around them. The feel of their bodies comforted her just as she hoped she was passing comfort to them.

Carla called round after the shop had closed. 'How's your mother today?'

'She's getting worse, Carla. I look at her and I want it to stop and then I feel so guilty because I know the only way it'll stop is if she...' Ruth couldn't go on. 'I hate to see her like this, Carla. As if the neurological disease wasn't bad enough, she had to go and get pneumonia too.'

'It's natural that you don't want to see her in any more pain, Ruth. You mustn't feel guilty.'

'I can't help it.'

'You're not the only one going through what you are feeling right now, but you will get through it. I promise.'

'Will we? I've never been this close to... losing... someone.'

At that moment, Walter walked into the kitchen, his eyes red and watery. Carla went straight to him and put her arms around him.

He said, 'She wants to see yer, Ruth,' before burying his head on Carla's shoulder.

Again, Ruth shook her head, reading the real message Walter was attempting to pass on – their mother hadn't got long. Ruth put her hands to her cheeks, burning her palms. 'I don't think I can.'

Carla reached out and brought Ruth into her embrace too. 'You can, Ruth, because your mother has asked you to.'

Ruth stared into Carla's face.

Carla nodded. 'You can do it.'

Slowly, Ruth walked towards the door without looking back. She reached the bed and stared at her mother. This was likely to be the last time Ruth would see her alive. She knelt beside the bed and picked up her mother's hand, stroking it gently. Mother opened her eyes slowly and a smile spread across her face.

'Ruth, my dearest.'

'Oh, Mother!' She bit into her lip to stop herself from crying out. Mother tightened her grip on Ruth's hand.

'Now don't you go worrying about me, duckie. I shall watch over you.'

'I don't think I can carry on without yer.'

'Dear Ruth.' Mother slowly moved Ruth's hair out of her eyes. 'You can – and you must. You're bound to get on. But, darling, I fear you've spent so much of your life looking after me, you've forgotten how to have fun and enjoy yourself. For your sake and to put my mind at rest you should find a young man as good as your father, just like Dottie has. I couldn't wish for anything more for my beloved daughter.'

Ruth sniffed and gave a wobbly smile. 'I'll try. I will try.'

'I'm sure you…'

Then, Mother started coughing and lost her grip on Ruth's hand.

'Sorry, Miss Latham, I need to check on your mother.'

The doctor had arrived again. Ruth hadn't heard him come in. She rose painfully and moved out of his way. He checked Mother over, her eyes closed now.

He moved back towards the door. Ruth heard his quiet voice. 'If you would like to say your goodbyes, please come now.'

It was over; only the sound of quiet sobbing remained.

Mother died on 12 December of pneumonia brought on by her long-standing illness and even though it was expected, the hurt was just the same.

–

Carla appeared at the funeral that morning with two cakes she had freshly baked. Ruth, Carla and Carla's mother made piles of egg, cheese and ham sandwiches. The food for the wake was laid out in the kitchen and covered with clean tea towels. Little was said, but companionship and friendship filled the kitchen.

With the help of the other two, Ruth hoped she would be strong enough to get her family through the day ahead. The men had carried Mother's bed upstairs to the small bedroom to be stored for the time being and had prepared the front room for the coffin, allowing those who wished to pay their final respects. The curtains at the front of the house were closed until after the funeral, according to the custom.

Ruth dressed in appropriate black attire and welcomed the mourners into the house, leaving their wreaths and flowers on the doorstep and filing past the coffin before the lid was closed for the last time.

Upstairs in Ruth's bedroom, the mood was sombre.

'Why do so many funerals take place in winter when everywhere is so cold and depressing?'

'I suppose it gives people something to talk about instead of the funeral,' returned Carla, shrugging, her eyes red and swollen. The two gave each other a hug before making their way downstairs to a kitchen full of mourners.

'I shall think of you, *meine lieber Freundin*.' Carla smiled. 'My dear friend.'

Ruth mainly kept her black coat for special occasions and funerals, ensuring she always had something smart to wear. It was thick enough to keep out the cold on this crisp December day, although she couldn't stop her body from shaking.

Father, Frank and Walter carried the coffin with the help of the undertaker's assistants to the hearse waiting outside. Then, headed by Father and Ruth, followed by Frank and Joan, Walter and Carla, Donald and Dottie, and the rest of the mourners, the cortege began its slow journey to the chapel on Hamil Road, through the Holmorton Estate. Many people along the route removed their hats as the coffin passed. The weather was kind, cloudy but dry, but the sun shone briefly as it stopped outside the chapel. The men assigned to the task took their places to complete the journey into the chapel for prayers and hymns, including Mother's favourite, 'The Lord is my Shepherd'. Ruth heard whimpers and sniffs around the chapel, and the sound brought tears to her eyes as she reflected on her mother's life.

Surprisingly, Ruth couldn't cry and how guilty that made her feel. She had attended several funerals in the past and always the tears were ready to fall. Today, she stared unblinking at the coffin. It was as if she was still taking strength from her mother, who guaranteed to be there when she was most needed.

Ruth found her mother in her thoughts nearly every hour of every day following the funeral. The woman they had lost who had always been there for them. The little things she would do for them, without being asked. Noticing a tear in their clothes almost before they did. Buying her a new hat for Easter as a surprise. Buying a bag of sweets when Ruth had done well at school, particularly in arithmetic, the worst subject Ruth could think of until, eventually, she became top of the class. Listening to Mother singing before she was taken poorly the first time. Mother had an answer for everything, but made it appear as if Ruth had discovered it for herself.

—

Christmas Day loomed and the whole family came together in Dartmouth Street for this, the first Christmas without the most important person in their family. No one felt like celebrating. Ruth and Joan had cooked a small chicken and boiled potatoes, but nobody's heart was on eating. Ruth didn't blame them. Anyone with an empty belly could reheat the food later.

Frank and Joan were sitting at the table, talking while the rest of the family tried to avoid using the front room, until so recently Mother's sick room. Ruth confined herself to the kitchen to clear everything away, relieved to be on her own. She couldn't believe that it would be so hard to spend time with her family.

Ruth closed her eyes to dispel her tears, her heart thumping in her chest. Seeing everyone together in Dartmouth Street had brought it home to her just how much of a woman her mother was. When they weren't all together, it was easy to pretend Mother was upstairs or out shopping. Today, that wasn't possible. Nor would it be at any family celebration in the future. This was what the future would be like – forever.

Mother had been behind Ruth going to the Wedgwood Institute to learn shorthand and typing. She could obtain qualifications in the evenings when Father or Walter could look after Mother. Then she might get an office job or go to college to train to be a teacher. Working-class girls like her didn't go to university, but with three wages coming in each week, it was something her mother had hoped for. Luckily for Ruth, her brothers weren't interested in university.

Then, Mother's illness came along and put paid to all their dreams.

If only Mother were here. The last words Mother had spoken came into her mind. *I shall watch over you.*

Perhaps she was. Ruth hoped so.

Chapter Three

January–February 1914

Ruth cleaned the house from top to bottom during the weeks that followed, preferring to keep busy rather than think of the woman she would never see again, standing at the scullery sink or complaining when the men left their dirty washing by the back door. Over and over the floor she went, followed by the dusting, as if by doing so she was cleansing her soul and caring for her family.

In the last few days, she had caught Father and Walter in conversation – a conversation that would cease immediately on her arrival and would turn to football and their favourite team, Port Vale. One thing she had concluded was that she would not stay at home looking after the family. She was too young for that.

Neither of her brothers wanted to work in the potbanks. Walter was studying for mining exams, in particular, the shotfirer's qualification, essential if he was to fulfil his ambition to become a pit deputy at the colliery one day. Mother had been none too pleased when she heard of Walter's plans; the shotfirer prepares, positions and detonates explosives to break up rocks in the mine. An important job. Using too much explosive or not surveying the area properly could lead to a collapsed seam or tunnel.

Although Mother trusted Walter more than anyone, she still worried about him.

Her brother Frank's ambitions seemed to lie in other areas. He just wanted a job. Father had wanted him to train as a mould maker and follow in his footsteps. But Frank said he'd done enough schooling, and he wanted to earn some money. Frank's love of cricket was high on his list of priorities. Joan, his wife of three years, put up with it. They only lived around the corner from Joan's family in Smallthorne. When Frank was playing cricket, Joan could visit her mother, brothers and sisters and friends. The one thing they both had in common was a love of children. They had two, Douglas, who was born on their first wedding anniversary, making him two years old, and Ruby, just coming up to six months. Frank often joked he was building his own cricket team.

With Walter and Frank's father-in-law both working at the Sneyd Colliery, Frank asked them to help him get a job there, too. It was better money, especially if you could become a face worker.

Joan was a nice person and friendly, but she tended not to have much to do with her father-in-law, Walter or Ruth. She would do anything to help you, but she could be distant.

Mother had always talked about ambition and, although she had wanted to study, it hadn't been possible. For her, babies had come along quickly. She loved her family but had advised Ruth, in later years, that she must think of herself and lay out her future so that when the time came, she was ready.

Ruth remembered the day she realised her mother needed round-the-clock care. There were only a few weeks left at school, and Ruth had been planning to get a job. Mother's body had been letting her down more often. She couldn't go out on her own for fear of falling. Around the house, lifting anything heavy was usually possible, but Mother had begun to drop things. Ruth became increasingly worried that Mother might scald herself when cooking or lifting the kettle.

The day after she left Park Road School for the last time, Ruth announced she was taking over the care of her mother. Father agreed, but Mother objected, as Ruth knew she would. Ruth was as strong-willed as her mother, and nothing was going to stand in her way.

'But I can't let you give up your future, Ruth. It's not right that you should shoulder such responsibility.'

'Why, Mother, isn't that what you did when you gave birth to us?'

'That was our choice. You children may have come along a little sooner than we expected, but you were all much loved. You giving up everything now, when you've worked so hard, is too much. I don't want to be the one to stop you.'

'You won't be, Mother.'

'You are a darling girl.'

Ruth shook her head and pulled herself back into the present. She had been cleaning without a break since early morning. Thinking about her family and friends helped to pass the time. She stopped for a bite to eat at dinnertime and resolved to sort out her working life as soon as possible – after tea tonight would be a good time to start.

—

Once Ruth had cleared up the dishes after tea, she waited for a break in the conversation between Father and Walter.

'Can I have a word with the pair of you? It's about work.'

'Of course you can, Ruthie.' Father was the only person she allowed to call her by that name.

'I have decided that I am going to get a job. I worked hard for my qualifications, and I want to make use of them.'

'Don't you think it's too soon...' Walter's voice trailed away, showing thoughts of their mother still affected him.

'No, I don't think so.'

'If that's what you want to do, I'll not stand in your way. But you've no experience, so dunner build your hopes up too much. Starting wages on the pots are very low and you'd have to get a job locally in Burslem, which dunner give yer much choice.'

'Yes, I realise that, but I must try. I want to get office or clerical work. I don't mind starting at the bottom, but I want to start.'

'Me and Father have talked about paying you a wage – the same as you would have got at work. You can then stop at home and look after...' Walter paused, as if he realised he was digging himself into a hole.

'It's not the money, it's the work I want.' Ruth glared at her brother, who was sensible enough to shut up.

'I wouldn't want you to do that. You've got education and you should use it. Walter can look after himself,' said Father. 'Your mother would turn in her grave, God rest her soul, if you dunner make the best of your skills.'

'I am certainly going to do that, and I want to ask you both a favour. Will you ask at work if there are any opportunities I can apply for in the offices?'

'Yes, sis, I will, but I wouldn't be too hopeful as there are few women working in the pit offices at the moment.'

'Same for me, Ruthie. I will ask tomorrow. I'll go to the wages office; one bloke there plays cricket for Cobridge, so we have summat in common. It might help. My father always told me, "It's not what yer know, it's who yer know," when it comes to getting a job.'

'That's given me an idea,' said Ruth excitedly. 'I'm going to ask Donald if he knows of anything that might be going at the PTC or in Stoke.'

Ruth gave them both a big hug. In bed that night she was happy and excited, but realised getting a job wouldn't be an easy task.

—

It was fresh and windy when Ruth and Carla set off to walk down to the centre of Burslem. They were off for Sunday tea with Donald and Dottie in their new house. To save money, Ruth had suggested that they only catch the tram between Burslem and Stoke. Moorland Road was a nice steady slope down, making walking easy, although it seemed steep and never-ending when walking in the opposite direction.

They were lucky. A tram was waiting at the stop, and they boarded immediately. They alighted in the centre of Stoke and walked down Campbell Road to Dottie's new house.

Dottie greeted her two friends, and they were soon sitting around the range, warming their feet and drinking tea.

'Donald's had to work today, but he'll be back at half past four – in time for our tea. He wasn't due to work, but another driver didn't show up, so they woke us up at six this morning.'

'Does that happen very often?' asked Ruth.

'It's the first time since we've been married. Donald usually gets plenty of notice when his shifts change and wasn't very pleased. He had wanted to spend the morning on the allotment—'

'Is that what you call it, then?' interrupted Carla with a big grin.

Dottie blushed, but her calm reaction surprised Ruth. Only later did she remember her friend had worked on potbanks for a long time and was quite familiar with that type of humour.

Dottie regained her composure and continued with her story. 'I don't really understand what must be done during winter, but whatever it is, it's very important. He's still helping his father on *his* allotment. He loves his gardening, and I love the vegetables.'

The three girls broke down in laughter and the conversation took a more personal turn.

'Let me show you around the house.'

The three friends walked and talked. Ruth was surprised how everything seemed to match, but nothing was new, Dottie said, except for a pair of curtains she'd made. All of their furniture was second-hand. When they had finished, they returned to the kitchen.

'You've done well to get everything so nice so soon,' said Carla.

'Thank you. We were lucky that the previous tenants had looked after the house.'

'How did you find it?' asked Ruth.

'The woman in the reception at the PTC found it. She knew somebody who knew somebody else and they knew the rent collector. Donald went to see it and agreed to rent it straight away. He met me outside Mintons and told me all about it, and we walked past it a few times. It looked ideal.'

'Your Donald chose well. You don't think it had anything to do with the allotments?'

Dottie laughed. 'I think that may have had something to do with it, but we both realised that living with his mother was difficult. My mother always said, "Two women can't share the same kitchen."'

The subject of work came up. 'I've been at Mintons since November and love the job. What are you planning to do, Ruth?'

'I want to work in an office, that's why I took those subjects, but I was naïve in thinking qualifications would make up for a lack of experience.'

'But you have experience of life, Ruth. Think about it. You've looked after your mother and the rest of your family for – how long is it?'

'Seven years.'

'There you are. That's your strength. You can teach anyone to type, to lithograph plates or to work in a shop, but you can't teach responsibility, dedication and commitment and that's what all bosses want. All those years you looked after your family count for something, don't they?'

'You're right. But I can't tell them unless I get an interview.'

'You don't need to,' said Carla, chipping in.

'Think about the people you know who can speak for you, just like your father did for Bertie,' said Dottie. 'That's the way it is in the pottery industry.'

Carla added, 'My father was disappointed when Bertie said he wanted nothing to do with the shop. In fact, we had a bit of an argument as Father thought he was building a business he could pass on to his son and give him a good start in life. Instead he told us he was going to apply for an apprenticeship at Royal Edwards, one of the best potbanks in The Potteries. Mr Latham helped by talking to my father about how good it would be. Mr Latham's support got him the apprenticeship right after leaving school, and look at him now, a time-served mould maker.'

'He'll always be a good earner as a mould maker, and my father is so proud of him.' An idea came to Ruth. 'Do you think Donald knows anybody at the PTC who might know of any jobs in the office?'

'I don't think so, but we can ask him at teatime.'

–

The kettle was singing to itself when Donald walked into the scullery, shouting that he was home while changing his boots. He opened the kitchen door, smiling.

'Hello. Have I interrupted some juicy gossip?'

'No, dear, we were just talking about work. You have a wash and I'll put the tea out. You must be hungry.'

The four had lots to talk about over tea. They had nearly finished eating when Ruth broached the subject of jobs. 'Donald, do you know of any office jobs going at the PTC?'

'Why? Do you want one?'

'Yes, I do.'

'Can't say as I do, but I can ask Mrs Langley at reception. She knows everything. She's the one who found us this house. Miss Simmons deals with office jobs, but I've not spoken to her.'

'You mean Daisy Simmons?'

Donald shrugged. 'Dunner know her name. It's only surnames in the offices.'

'It is Daisy,' said an excited Carla. 'Her mother comes into the shop and I'm sure that's where her daughter works.'

'I'll ask my mother. If it is the same person, she lived opposite to us and used to look after us when Mum and Dad went out. She was nice as far as I remember. You could try her first.'

'Thank you for that.'

'I'll have a word when I next go up to Mother's and let you know.'

By the time Ruth and Carla left Dottie's, it was getting dark. The skies had cleared, and the temperature was dropping. They walked slowly from Moorland Road to Hesse's Stores, chatting about the afternoon but, in her excitement, Ruth found it difficult to concentrate.

–

Just before tea on the following Sunday, there came a knock on the door. It was Donald and Dottie, bearing good news, together with a bag of sprouts from Donald's allotment.

'I spoke to Mother this morning, and we decided it would be a good idea to speak to Miss Simmons directly. Luckily for us, Daisy was visiting her parents, and I told her everything about you.'

'What did she say?'

'She wants you to write a letter to her enquiring about typing jobs. She seemed definitely interested and said she would send you a letter arranging an interview.'

'An interview at last!' Ruth could hardly contain her excitement.

'Remember, Daisy likes to do everything correctly, so you still need to impress her, and that starts with the letter in your own handwriting. You have such a beautiful hand – you can show your typing skills off when you get there. Just because our parents are friends doesn't mean she'll show any favouritism.'

'What should I wear?'

'Something formal and plain. White blouse, dark skirt and a jacket will do just fine. A bit like a schoolteacher.'

'By the way, you might want to know that Peggy Thompson works there, in the offices.'

'Peggy Thompson! Great that's all the news I need.'

'Yes, and she's a typist too.' Carla pulled a face. 'Mother says Mrs Thompson's always going on about what an important job Peggy has and how they couldn't do without her. Anyone would think she ran the place, Mother says. She's also got a young man who works there; he's the head mechanic and very important, she says.'

She dragged her mind back to the present to find the others looking at her. 'I will not let Peggy Thompson decide which jobs I can or can't apply for. It's not right. Besides,' Ruth paused, 'she might not be so bad now she's grown up. You never know…'

As Ruth's voice faded away, she glanced at Donald. The look on his face didn't suggest that Peggy was any better liked now than during her school days.

Donald sniffed. 'I wouldn't bank on it, Ruth. The last thing I want is to put you off getting a job, but most blokes keep out of her way. At the moment, she seems to have her claws well and truly into Stan Bristow in the garage.' His eyes went to Carla. 'Yer mother's right, he's a mechanic, and a decent bloke, but he isn't the main man even if Peggy would like to think he is.'

Ruth nodded. So be it. If anything, the information she had gleaned had made her more determined than ever to try for the job – and hang the consequences – while feeling sorry for the unknown Stan Bristow.

Donald and Dottie stayed talking for half an hour. Donald and her father chatted about gardening and cricket, although neither of them knew anything about the other's pastime.

After tea, Ruth ran upstairs and sat at the little table in her room. She took out an old exercise book and drafted the letter – the most important letter of her life. When she was happy, she copied it down in her neatest hand, twice. She chose the best one and placed it in an envelope. She would post the letter after she had read it to Carla.

When she returned from posting the letter the following day, she had the house to herself. How wonderful life was becoming and then immediately tears came to her eyes. Here she was getting excited and her mother wouldn't be there to witness it.

She blew her nose on the handkerchief she carried in her pocket, knowing she had to accept that it was time to plan her future rather than dwell on the past.

–

Ruth wasn't the only one with good news that week. Frank had applied to Sneyd Colliery and had just learned that he had been successful. To say he was rather chuffed would be an understatement. He was waiting for a letter to tell him when he could start, but knowing that it was all settled was just what he needed. Initially, he would be a surface worker but, with some experience under his belt, he hoped to become a face worker.

Yes, thought Ruth, the Lathams were doing rather well. Frank wore a smile all evening.

A letter inviting Ruth for an interview arrived by return of post and she made sure she arrived a good ten minutes early. Being late was not an option for something so important. She had time to stroll through the churchyard, stopping periodically to stare up at the huge church that dominated the entrance to the town of Stoke.

For the briefest of moments, she wondered why she'd put herself in this position. Why couldn't she be like most of the other girls she knew and get a job on a potbank? Some would say she had ideas above her station with no experience to draw on.

Sitting on a bench, Ruth practised how she could respond to their questioning.

She left the churchyard and crossed the road, calmer now. She really wanted this job. The interview would soon be over. Walking along Bowstead Street, she followed the single tram line to the depot. Then she turned onto Woodhouse Street and reached the door of the PTC. The building surprised her; it looked more like a fancy house than an office.

After straightening her coat and adjusting her hat, she took another deep breath and pushed the door open. She found herself in a large entrance area, with ceramic tiles on the floor and inlaid in the centre was the coat of arms of the company. A small set of stairs on the right led up to a door marked *Private* and a much larger and grander staircase led up to the first floor. To her left there was a sliding window with frosted glass. Beside the window was a shelf on which sat a wooden plaque containing the word *Reception* in bold letters, followed by *Mrs Pearl Langley* in smaller letters. A bell stood beside it.

The window opened with a flourish and a woman's head appeared.

'Good afternoon. How can I help you?'

'I've come for an interview with Miss Simmons.'

'She's expecting you. Take a seat, please. Miss Simmons will be down in a few minutes.'

'Thank you,' said Ruth, nodding politely.

Mrs Langley closed the window and Ruth turned towards a seat in the corner next to a sideboard, on top of which was a model tram in the red and cream colours of the PTC. It looked perfect and so detailed.

Before she had time to sit, she heard footsteps on the large staircase – it must be Daisy.

'Good afternoon, Miss Latham. I'm pleased to meet you. I'm Miss Simmons and I'm the secretary to the managing director. Come with me.'

Miss Simmons crossed to Ruth, they went through a door marked *Private* and she motioned for Ruth to follow her down a long corridor, which she did with alacrity. They met no one. Their shoes echoed on the tiled floor.

Miss Simmons opened a door partway along the corridor and beckoned Ruth into a small room in which there was a desk with a chair on each side and a typewriter similar to the one she had used in her night class. Beside it lay a sheet of paper, a sheet of carbon paper and a flimsy sheet. Were they going to have a chat, or would she be expected to type something there and then? She hoped not. She hated people watching her.

'This will be a formal interview, Miss Latham, so you must treat it as such.'

'I understand.'

'Now then, I have a hand-written report which needs typing up. I need a top copy for my boss, and a copy for the files. You have approximately a quarter of an hour to type it. Accuracy is most important, so bear that in mind. If you finish before I come back, you must remain here until I collect you.'

She *was* going to be tested. Damn! At least Miss Simmons wouldn't be looking over her shoulder.

'I understand,' said Ruth, taking a breath.

'Make yourself comfortable and I'll leave you to get on.'

When Ruth looked at the hand-written note, her eyes opened wide. She doubted she would finish early, struggling to decipher crossed-out words and misspellings. And it had to be right the first time, given she had only one sheet of paper. Surely Miss Simmons wouldn't have produced a report like this? The mistakes were probably deliberate and she must be on her guard as she worked through it.

She skimmed through the words to get a general drift of the contents, then picked up the sheets and fed them into the typewriter. Any mistakes would be identifiable at a glance. How many would be allowed? Immediately, she cursed herself for thinking that way. Hadn't Mother always told her to believe in herself? Typing was her best subject, after all. Ruth shuffled in her chair to get comfortable and began.

It was no time at all when the door opened and Miss Simmons walked in.

Ruth felt a rush of excitement bordering on confidence. She had just that minute finished. She could barely take her eyes off it, desperate to see no missing capital letters or incorrectly spelt names.

'Have you finished?'

Ruth nodded and, not knowing what else to say, added, 'I haven't had time to finish checking it. I hope it's all right.'

'I'm sure it will be.' Miss Simmons closed the door and sat in the seat opposite. 'Sorry about the test. We ensure that when girls say they can type, they can. You have certificates, I believe?'

'Yes, I have them here.' Ruth reached into her bag and drew them out with pride.

'A merit for your typing.' Miss Simmons nodded, impressed. 'What speed did you attain?'

'Forty words per minute.'

'But not so well on the shorthand, I see.'

Ruth shook her head. 'It's my weakest subject, but I've been practising since the class finished.'

'Why do you want to be a typist, Miss Latham?'

'I believe that typing is a skill that is needed in all offices and, to be honest...' Ruth looked Miss Simmons in the eye. '...it was something I could train to do while looking after my mother. She had been ill for a long time. She passed away before Christmas.'

Miss Simmons nodded. 'Do you have any other family?'

'Yes, two brothers, both older than me.'

Miss Simmons smiled. 'I see – and you don't want to spend your life at their beck and call.'

Ruth returned the smile. 'I wouldn't put it quite like that, but...'

'Don't worry, I understand. So, Miss Latham, what tempted you to apply for a post when you admit you don't have any experience?'

Ruth felt her face burning. It sounded audacious when Miss Simmons put it like that, but she pushed on with the lines she had memorised last night.

'I believe I can offer you a good typist who is not afraid of hard work. I believe I'll be able to do better as I gain experience and I'm willing to take on whatever work you wish me to do. I believe a little maturity would be helpful too.'

'So – if you were successful, when could you start?'

The suddenness of the question made Ruth jump. 'Erm... I... I could start as soon as you need me.'

'How about next Monday?'

'Monday?' The word came out as a squeak, but Ruth was sure her eyes glowed. 'I would be very happy to.'

'Good. Just what I want to hear. The office staff begin at eight o'clock and work until half past five. I'm afraid the pay isn't good for a junior typist, but if all goes well, you can expect an increase once you have proved yourself competent.'

Ruth didn't know what to say. This was entirely unexpected, having tried so hard – and now to be told she could start next Monday was a miracle.

Chapter Four

February 1914

With a good deal of elbow-grease yesterday, Ruth's black shoes had come up a treat. She arranged her dark brown hair in a roll at the back of her head. Her dark eyes, eyebrows and eyelashes needed no colour to increase their boldness. As far as clothes were concerned, she wore the same dark skirt and white, long-sleeved blouse, feeling its smartness would give her confidence. After all, they had worked well at the interview. She donned the same jacket, looking in the mirror and turning this way and that, to make sure everything was perfect.

Overall, her glance in the mirror was extremely positive and a thrilled Ruth marched off to catch the tram to Stoke for her first morning as a junior typist with the PTC.

She had been waiting around ten minutes when her eyes lighted on a tram in the distance making its steady way along the lines. She could make out the bell tinkling as it drew to a gradual halt in front of her.

The conductor stepped off the tram to allow passengers to board, his hands holding his money bag close to his side as he waited. She deliberately sat towards the back so she might watch him as he moved along the tram. He passed the time of day with each of his passengers, even if it was a mere sentence about the weather. At one stop, the conductor jumped down from the platform and sauntered around the tram to have a word with the driver, whose job must be very lonely as he stood in his cab, waiting for the bell to ring so that he could drive on. From what she could see, the men appeared good friends, and it caused her to smile. If the rest of the employees at the PTC were as friendly, she would have an enjoyable job. She wondered if she would get to know any of the drivers or conductors once she was working, or would she be cocooned in the offices?

Ruth sat back and relaxed as she waited for the tram to pull up in the centre of Stoke. How nervous she had been at the interview. Today's nerves would be about getting to know people and hoping she did nothing wrong on her first day. She followed the same route as the day of the interview. She walked into the PTC reception and tapped on the window.

Pearl glanced up with a smile. 'Morning, Miss Latham.'

'Morning, Mrs Langley.'

'Daisy told me you were starting today. Congratulations! You'd best come through, then.'

She moved to open the door and stood to one side as Ruth entered her office. 'As you can see, this is my little empire, for my sins.' Pearl turned towards her desk, waving her arms. 'You can call me Pearl most of the time. We use formal address only when bosses are present.'

'And I'm Ruth.'

Pearl grinned. 'You'll be working in the typing room with two other ladies. Daisy will be down in a moment and she'll take you up there to meet them. You can introduce yourself to some of the other staff as you go. If you meet too many, you'll not remember their names any road. They're a good bunch here – in the main. But, now and again, there'll be a bit of trouble – usually in the wages office if the men don't get as much as they were expecting.' Pearl laughed. 'Still, that won't be your problem.'

At that moment, Daisy appeared. Smiling, she held out her hand. 'Pleased to see you again, Ruth.'

Ruth beamed back. 'Likewise, Miss Simmons.'

'Now first things first,' said Daisy. 'We ladies call ourselves by our first name, unless one of the bosses is around or there are visitors about. So do the younger men, but some of the older men still like to call us Miss or Mrs. They say as they can't get used to having ladies working here.' She looked towards Pearl, who nodded in agreement.

'Here's your clock card. Make sure you clock on and off when you leave or enter the building, unless you're going out on business, which is unlikely in your case, otherwise you won't get paid and we wouldn't want that,' Daisy continued. 'This other card will give you free travel on our trams, so make sure you have it with you.'

Ruth's eyes lit up. The journey from Burslem to Stoke was quite long, so not paying fares would be a tremendous bonus.

'Right… I think that's all down here. Follow me and I'll take you up to my office.'

Daisy led the way out of the reception and along the same corridor where she had taken her typing test. Daisy paused at the door opposite. 'Lavatories are here when you should find yourself in need of one.'

They came to a flight of stairs to their right. 'If you continue along this corridor and turn to the right, you will come to the wages office run by Mr Blakeman. It's on the ground floor because that's where the wages get paid out every week. I'm sure you'll be able to find that office for yourself. It's always busy on Fridays! Next to wages, there are a couple of interview rooms where we can eat our dinners. We're not allowed to eat at our desks. Now we're heading upstairs. This building used to be St Peter's Rectory and these are the old servants' stairs. We try not to use the main stairs unless absolutely necessary.'

Their footsteps rang as they climbed to the next floor, where Ruth found herself in a long corridor with numerous doors, each one with name plates that currently meant nothing at all to her.

'The names on the doors will help you find your way about the place initially. It's so easy to forget when you first start,' Daisy murmured as she opened the door marked *Secretary*.

It surprised Ruth that it was Daisy's job on her door rather than her name. Could that be because she was a woman and not so important?

'So, Ruth, this is my office and you can come to see me any time if you have a problem.'

Ruth's eyes wandered to the other three doors, each with name plaques attached. Daisy's eyes followed.

'Ah… These are the most important people in the company. Mr Taylor is our managing director. The top man, you might say. Then we have Mr Perkins, the assistant manager and next to him is Mr Simpson, our company secretary. I work for all of them and I also pass work through to the typing room, the next door along. That's where you'll work with two other ladies – more of them in a minute. Next to them are the four cashiers. A lot of their work is done with the clerks in the depots.'

Daisy opened the door marked *Typing Room* and walked straight in. 'Good morning, ladies.'

Ruth followed and found herself in a room with four desks, each with a typewriter, and a table holding baskets and a range of files. Two rows of desks, facing the same direction, reminded her of her schooldays. Two women, one looking very familiar, sat at the two desks on the left-hand side.

Ruth groaned inwardly – she would share an office with Peggy bloody Thompson. She closed her eyes and took a deep breath. She was better than that and forced a smile.

'I'd like you to welcome Miss Ruth Latham, who has started with us today as a junior typist. I hope you'll make her feel welcome and show her around. Ruth, can I introduce Peggy Thompson and Cissie Lowndes, our two shorthand typists. Peggy sits on the front row and you, Ruth, will sit in the second row with Cissie. I'm sure they will both make you very welcome. For the moment, Peggy will sort you out with a pile of envelopes to type up from our address book. We shall send out posters to our customers later today. I shall need the envelopes by dinnertime. I'll leave you in their capable hands now, Ruth, and I'll speak to you again later.'

'Thank you, Miss… Daisy,' Ruth stammered at Daisy's retreating back.

'Hello, Ruth. You can start by taking your coat off and settling in,' said Peggy, coming over to Ruth's desk armed with a pile of envelopes and a slim volume holding names and addresses. 'I remember you from Park Road School.'

'Yes, I remember you too.'

'You used to hang around with Carla Hesse and Dottie Scott. Dottie's done well for herself, landed a fine man and her own house too. He's one of our drivers.'

'Yes, Peggy, I know, we're still in touch.' Ruth wondered where the conversation was going.

'I heard you were both bridesmaids at her wedding.'

'Yes, it was a very nice day.'

'Dottie's mother is friendly with Daisy's mother, so no prizes on how you got the job.'

Ruth shook her head, Peggy hadn't changed since their school days. 'I'm sure Daisy is very professional.'

Cissie had stopped work and was staring at them, mouth wide open.

'How is that handsome brother of yours?' There she goes, determined to have the last word. 'We were very friendly at one time. Very friendly.'

Ruth was quiet for a moment and was about to speak when Cissie intervened. 'Come on you two, leave the reunion until dinnertime, or else we'll get in trouble.' Peggy gave Cissie a stern look.

'Give him my best and tell him he's too late. I have a man of my own now.'

'Good for you. I'm pleased to hear that.'

'Can't stop here talking all day – you've got work to do.'

Ruth was shown to the desk on the right-hand side of the office, in front of a window. She was sitting directly behind the biggest typewriter she had ever seen. Its use would undoubtedly be revealed to her.

Peggy picked up some files and left the office. Ruth took the opportunity to find out a bit more.

'Do you enjoy working here, Cissie?'

'I do. Daisy's good to work for, and Peggy's fine as long as she gets her own way.'

'How long have you worked here?'

'I started eighteen months ago. Peggy had already been here for over a year.'

Peggy returned, and the conversation died.

Peggy was taller than Ruth and very slim. With her fair hair and blue eyes, she had grown up to become quite attractive. Cissie was mousy, but Ruth soon found she was anything but mousy in nature. She was pleasantly plump, and it only took Ruth one day to confirm that she enjoyed a good laugh. In fact, Peggy and Cissie couldn't have been more different in both looks and personality.

Ruth settled into her seat and glanced at her typewriter. It looked more modern than the one she had used during her evening class and the one she had used during the test. The keys were not so clunky, so her fingers didn't ache as she typed her envelopes.

–

It was mid-morning and Ruth could wait no longer – she had to use the privy. She remembered passing some on her way up to the typing room. She just needed to retrace her steps.

She found the stairs easily enough but, once at the bottom, she couldn't think which door to take. She selected one and arrived at a door marked *Private*.

Pleased to have found it on her own, she was about to enter when a young man came out. Ruth didn't know who looked most embarrassed. She swore her cheeks were on fire, as were his.

In a hushed voice, and without opening the door, he whispered it contained three lavatories. And she would be best knocking before entering if she didn't want to be put into a similar situation in the future. She waited until his footsteps died away and then knocked on the door and listened.

Silence.

She found three doors – one for ladies, and two for gentlemen – after passing through the door marked *Private*. There was nowhere to hide from the embarrassment of meeting a man when needing to relieve herself. Hurriedly, she locked the door marked *Ladies* and went about her business, praying all the while she would meet no one and leaving as quickly as she could.

–

The heels of her boots echoed as she climbed the steps towards her office. Unfortunately for Ruth, as she appeared at the first door, who should come out but the man who she had met downstairs. Of all people!

Ruth's eyes locked on his as a grin spread across his face. 'If it isn't the little lady I met just a few minutes ago. I never thought to bump into you again so soon.'

'Well, now you have.'

Ruth turned and was about to open the typing-room door when he put a hand on her shoulder. She jumped. He removed it as swiftly as he had put it there. The door he had come out of had the words *Cash Office* painted on it in gold lettering.

'Is it a coincidence, do you think? Or could it be fate?' He placed the papers he was carrying to his chest as if protecting his heart.

'I must go.' She tried to pass, but he moved in the same direction.

The door to the cash office opened again as a second man appeared, this one much older and wearing spectacles.

'Don't you think you should be at your desk, Mr Wilson? And what d'yer think you're doing with this young lady?'

'Sorry, Mr Routledge. I was attempting to help her. I thought she looked lost.'

'Good morning, young lady. Are you new to this establishment?'

Ruth nodded, sure her face was scarlet.

The man lifted his eyebrows. 'And are you lost, Miss…?'

Ruth looked at Mr Wilson, who gave a quick nod of his head.

'Latham. Yes, I was. It was… good of… Mr Wilson to help me.'

Mr Routledge turned back to Mr Wilson and spoke in a dry voice. 'As you appear to be in a helpful mood, perhaps you can introduce Miss Latham to your colleagues. And then she will not have to rely on your good self. Heaven knows why, given that the typing room is only next door. Good day, Miss Latham.'

'Come in, then, Miss Latham,' said Mr Wilson. He opened the door to the cash office and three heads lifted at the same time.

'And what have we here?' said the man nearest to her.

'I found Miss Latham looking lost. It's her first day, so I helped her. Obviously, Mr Routledge agreed, for it was his suggestion that I introduce her to you layabouts.'

'Trust you, Jim. If anyone can find pretty young ladies wandering round the PTC, then it would be you.'

'First you need to introduce yourself,' said Jim with a grin. 'We can't keep calling you Miss Latham, now, can we?'

With all eyes on her, Ruth wanted to get out of their office, happier to have Peggy's attention than the grinning faces of the young men. 'I'm Ruth and it's my first day in the typing room, which I have just been told, embarrassingly, is next door,' she said, forcing a smile.

Each of them came forward to say hello: Jim Wilson, whom she had met, Tom Walton, Brian Bertram and Dickie Smith, with Jim appearing to be the youngest.

'Thank you for your introductions, but I really must go.'

She muttered a quick thank you and backed out of the office before scurrying to the door she was looking for. She burst in, banging the door closed behind her, and leaned heavily against it. Luckily for Ruth, Peggy was out, but Cissie nearly jumped out of her skin.

'What on earth—'

Ruth clapped her hand across her mouth. Poor Cissie's eyes were like saucers. 'I'm so sorry, Cissie. I didn't mean to scare you.'

'Tell me what's going on and I might forgive yer.'

Ruth flung herself down in her chair. 'I went downstairs to visit the… *privy*…' she whispered.

'So?'

'I met a gentleman coming out. Well, I'm not sure he was a gentleman.'

Cissie nodded, seemingly unimpressed.

'He was a bit… forward.'

'You mean he nearly saw you going to the…?'

'Well… yes.'

Cissie burst out laughing. 'I'm sorry, Ruth. We should've told you. It's not very private. I don't think the PTC has grown used to employing women and their associated problems.'

'I think it would've been gentlemanly to pretend not to see me.'

'Who was it? Describe him.'

'Mr Routledge called him Mr Wilson.'

'So you've met our resident playboy. Jim likes a laugh, but there's no actual harm in him. Mr Routledge is his boss.'

'Will he get into trouble?'

'Knowing Jim, it'll be like water off a duck's back.'

–

At twelve o'clock, Peggy rose from her seat and turned to face Ruth and Cissie. 'If it's all right with you two, I need to go for an early dinner, but I'm sure you'll cope without me.' She gave one of those smiles Ruth remembered from school, the sort of smile which really meant, *I don't care if it's all right or not.*

She picked up her hat and coat, followed by a shopping bag, and disappeared through the door.

Cissie turned to Ruth. 'So you know Peggy from school.'

'Yes. We were never on good terms. Her family had a bit of a reputation, shall we say. She took a fancy to one of my brothers, but he wasn't interested, so she took it out on me. Bumped into me on purpose, knocked me against the wall, tripped me up from behind. Childish stuff really… but you know how it is with kids. Anyway, that was a long time ago. I hoped she'd forgotten about it.'

'The likes of our Peggy have long memories, Ruth. I should keep my head down for a while. Let her get used to the idea of you working here.'

Ruth nodded. 'That's what I hoped, but it rather depends on her, doesn't it?'

They each continued to work, concentrating for the moment on the individual jobs Peggy had given them out of the in-tray before she left. Daisy had scribbled the initials of the typist to be allocated the work — no doubt to ensure fair distribution.

'Have you brought your dinner with yer?' said Cissie after a while. 'When Peggy returns, I'll take you down to the dinner room and we can have our meal together and get to know each other.'

'Yes. Daisy said there were a couple of interview rooms downstairs that we could use.'

'The bosses don't allow us to eat in the offices. They are afraid of the smell and that we might make too much noise. I think you had your typing test in one of them. It's pretty grim. It was the place where Charlie used to print the tickets in the old days, but now we have them pre-printed, so Daisy and Pearl claimed it for our use.'

'Who's Charlie?'

'You won't have met him yet. He's in charge of the ticket store and rarely comes out. No one's allowed in there, except his assistant, Gerald. The tickets are the same as money, I'm told. We call him Dracula, because he only comes out of his tomb occasionally.'

They laughed.

'If you see him and he talks about racing pigeons, don't join in or else you'll be there all day. Apart from his work, they're the only things in his life. He lives on his own and never married. Lived with his mother until she died.'

Ruth bent down to retrieve a sandwich and an apple out of her bag. 'I might take a walk around the town to get my bearings. Never been shopping in Stoke.'

'Really?' Cissie's eyebrows shot up.

'Yes, we do most of our shopping in Hanley or Tunstall.'

'You get off as soon as you like and dream of the day when we have a canteen for our use.'

Ruth did as Cissie suggested. She took in a gulp of air, glad to be outside even if the weather was set to drizzle. She had completed her first morning.

'Thank goodness you've finally appeared!'

It was a man's voice. Ruth turned sharply to see Jim Wilson leaning nonchalantly against the wall, smoking a cigarette, which he immediately flung onto the path before flattening it with his shoe. Then he grinned.

She gave him a faint smile. 'Hello, Mr Wilson.'

'Well done. You've remembered. Call me Jim.'

Ruth flushed. 'You made me look stupid… Jim.'

The grin disappeared. 'I'm very sorry. I didn't mean to, Ruth.'

'It's my first day and I'm only a junior. I want them to see me at my best.'

'Then I am most definitely sorry for upsetting you.' He bowed his head. When he lifted it again, his face was full of contrition.

Ruth couldn't help smiling.

He grinned back. 'There, that's better. You should always wear a smile. It suits you.' After a momentary pause, he said, 'Where are you going?'

'For a walk. I don't know Stoke all that well.'

'Would you like some company? I could show you where to find anything you need.'

'That's very kind of you. But perhaps another time? I just want to wander about, Jim.'

He looked disappointed and shrugged. 'Then it's my loss. I hope to speak to you again. And by the way, Ruth...'

'Yes?'

'You have a lovely smile.'

Ruth couldn't stop her smile broadening as she walked away. She agreed with Cissie. He *was* a playboy. But he was nice!

—

Towards the end of the week, Daisy came down to the dinner room to eat with her typists and, not one to miss out, Pearl invited herself too.

'I thought it would be nice for us to get together and have a natter. We're a bit spread out at work and we're very busy. So, how're you getting on, Ruth?'

'Fine, thank you, Daisy.'

Daisy smiled. 'Good, good. And what about work?'

'I'm enjoying it. Lots to familiarise myself with.'

Pearl folded her arms under her ample breasts. 'I'm sure you'll enjoy it even more when you get your first pay packet, I shouldn't wonder.'

Ruth laughed. 'I'm sure I will,' she said, tucking into her rolled-up oatcake with cheese filling. The Potteries staple of oatcakes and cheese was her favourite dinnertime meal. At home, she would have it warmed up with the cheese melting inside. Here at work, she had to be content with it cold – but it was just as good.

'Are you going out anywhere this week with yer bloke, Peggy?' asked Pearl, taking a large bite out of her oatcake.

'Hope so. It's been over a week now and I've only seen him once.'

Pearl grinned and turned to Ruth. 'Peggy's walking out with Stan from the garage, although not so much recently.'

Ruth noted the sudden frown that appeared on Peggy's face.

'He's been busy.'

Peggy sniffed and turned to Ruth. 'And what did you do before you came here?'

'I took care of my mother for a long time after she became bedridden. She died in December last year.'

'That was so kind of you, Ruth.' Cissie placed a warm hand on Ruth's shoulder.

'Really? And then you thought you'd have the skills to work in an office, did yer?'

It was plain that Peggy knew more about her than Ruth knew about Peggy. Ruth was just about to open her mouth when Daisy spoke up.

'I believe Ruth will make a fine typist for us and may have the skills to go even further. She attained merits in her evening classes.'

Ruth looked a little embarrassed at being the centre of attention. 'Cissie, where did you work before you came here?'

'I worked at Mintons as a shorthand typist, but the pay here was much better, so I jumped at the chance. I've been here a while now and I do like it.'

'Do you like shorthand?' Ruth smiled.

'Not really. I'm not very good at it.'

Daisy shook her head. 'Nonsense, you're very good, and your speed will pick up with use.'

Cissie pulled her face. 'It's the reading back that gets me. Do you like it, Ruth?'

'I haven't had chance to use it, except in class.'

'I can make sure that both of you get plenty of practice.'

They all laughed. Daisy turned back to Ruth. 'You live with your family, don't you, Ruth?'

'That's right.'

Daisy looked up at the clock. 'It's been lovely to spend some time with you and get to know a bit more about you, hasn't it? We must do it again soon. Now, we should really get back to our work.'

Ruth reflected as she started typing a short report that Daisy needed by the end of the day. Tomorrow, Peggy would show her how to set up the wide carriage typewriter used for the depot summary sheets and Pearl would show her how to deal with the post coming in and going out, and the intricacies of the stamp book. She would certainly be busy.

—

It took about forty-five minutes to get home and at the end of her first week, Ruth was looking forward to Sunday. Carla met her outside of the shop and walked the rest of the way home with her. The two friends prepared the tea comprising meat pudding with potatoes and carrots, followed by fruit crumble. It wouldn't be long before the rhubarb was ready for picking. That was the good thing about crumble. It could make a substantial pudding with just about any fruit. And, with two grown working men in the house, keeping them fed was hard work.

'You're happy with the job, then?' said Carla, watching Ruth's face carefully.

'Yes, I am. They seem a good group. I hope Peggy changes her attitude. But I doubt it, somehow.'

Carla shook her head. 'She always wanted to be top dog, or should I say top bitch, if you know what I mean.'

'And she gets jealous easily enough.' Ruth laughed. 'Perhaps she'll grow out of it.'

'Ruth – she must be twenty-three or -four by now. How long does it take to grow up?'

'Don't forget, it's Peggy we're talking about.'

'God help us.'

They laughed. 'Ignore her, Ruth, and stand up for yourself. Bullies don't like being challenged. Peggy bullied all of us girls and gave Bertie and Walter sleepless nights, too. In the end, we called her bluff, and she moved on to other people.'

'When did all this happen?'

'It was the year after we left school. Peggy had been making suggestions to Walter, which were not ladylike. When he refused, she said she'd tell her father Walter had taken advantage of her. But the four of us visited Peggy on the way home one night in November and let's say she didn't trouble us again.'

'Nobody told me nothing.'

'You were busy with your mother and had enough to worry about. Anyway, enough of Peggy. Have you spoken to the man you met in the privy since?'

'Only for work matters when I return his typing. He's very formal when the other men are about and their boss's office has a door directly opening into their office, so they're all on their best behaviour.'

'At least you meet men. All I see is women moaning about the price of everything, always trying to get a bit knocked off. The only men we see are usually on their way home from work and stopping off for their cigarettes and tobacco.'

'Never mind, Carla. Mr Right is out there for you – you've just got to find him!'

Like pigeons returning to the loft, her father and brother arrived just in time for tea, from wherever they had been – ensuring they didn't get asked to do women's work.

Chapter Five

June–July 1914

At dinnertime on Monday, Ruth made her way to her favourite bench overlooking the flower beds of the graveyard of St Peter's Church. It was a pleasant place to walk when the weather permitted. Yesterday was Midsummer's Day.

Someone had left a copy of *The Sentinel*, which Ruth browsed through. She scanned the headlines and there was an interesting article on women's suffrage and on the sports page there was a report on all of the local cricket matches and speculation that some Stoke players would represent the county in the Minor Counties competition. She decided she must ask Frank if he was one of them.

She left the paper for someone else to read and crossed the road. She walked along Bowstead Street, where she bumped into Jim heading in the opposite direction. She smiled politely, and he grinned back.

'Ah, my favourite typist. You're heading back, I see.'

Ruth couldn't help responding to his lightness of mood. 'That's right. You're quick today.'

'You bring out the best in me, Ruth.'

She felt a hotness in her cheeks, as if she was flirting with him. Before Mother was taken ill, she was just getting used to the idea of boys and watching Carla and Dottie gave her some ideas, which she never got to try out because of nursing her mother. Flirting was a fresh experience.

'To ensure you have a continuing effect on my better nature, would you consider accompanying me to the pictures on Saturday?'

'Me?'

'Why does that surprise you?'

'I… I don't know. I mean, I didn't expect it.'

Today was Monday, and she'd have plenty of time to think about it. She felt something building up inside. From what she had seen so far, he could be rather charming. She couldn't see any harm in it. 'Very well, Jim. I'd be happy to come with you. Which one?'

He nodded and Ruth was positive there was a certain amount of relief in the nod. Perhaps he wasn't as sure of himself as he made out.

'I'll find out what's on and leave you a message at work.'

'But keep it to yourself. I'll never hear the end of it.'

'I should like you to know that I'm a much sought-after escort.'

'Then, you won't mind keeping quiet about it, will you?'

He gave a salute and continued on his way.

Ruth could hardly contain herself. A gentleman asking her out to the pictures! Would it be right to go with such a man, unaccompanied? Walking out with a man for the very first time. How she wished her mother could be here – to talk to – to guide her, because she didn't know what she wanted. She could hardly ask her father!

Her initial panic subsided, replaced by excitement. It came on so quickly. The more she thought about it, the more her body responded. For the rest of the afternoon, she had a smile on her face that wouldn't go away and she found she didn't care a jot what anyone else thought!

Jim was true to his word. He left a note in the bottom drawer of her desk the next day. She didn't recognise the handwriting and opened it quickly. It was short and to the point.

> *Hanley. Burton & Dunn. Half past six, Friday.*
> *Meet you there. Can't wait. J.*

Ruth gave a quick glance around. No one was looking. Then she pushed the note into her bag and carried on typing. It was only one outing and may amount to absolutely nothing.

Jim was waiting as agreed outside Burton & Dunn's. A little group had gathered, although they didn't appear to know each other. It seemed to be a regular meeting place.

'Hello, Ruth.'

Jim had been standing close to the shop, but his height gave him away. He moved forward and took her hand. 'It's good to see yer. Glad you found my note.'

'It's pleasant to be out on a nice evening like this.'

'Hm. Perhaps we should have gone for a walk instead of being cooped up in a picture house.'

'No, I'd like to see a film. I rarely got the chance when Mother was ill and I had evening classes to go to.'

They walked towards the Empire just a few minutes away.

Together they entered the gloom of the picture house and Jim led the way to their seats at the end of a row towards the back. As darkness descended, Ruth felt a flash of expectation run through her. She tried to concentrate on the film but was all too conscious of the man sitting beside her. He really was good-looking. She was smiling as he sent a grin in her direction and grasped her hand. She turned away, unable to look at him as her heart flipped over.

—

Ruth told nobody about her visit to the pictures, but word had got out. Jim vowed it wasn't his fault his mates in the cash office had worked it all out for themselves. Ruth decided there was no point in remaining quiet if the cash office lads were going to blab, so she went straight into the typing room and told them. Actually, she felt quite pleased with herself.

'You're a dark horse and no mistake,' said Peggy. 'Going out and not telling any of us. You've only been here five minutes.'

'A girl has to be careful,' giggled Cissie.

'We're her workmates and if she can't tell us…'

'I didn't want to say much. It'll probably come to nothing.'

'I'd tell yer about my Stan, wouldn't I, Cissie?'

'Suppose so. But you haven't mentioned him in ages, Peggy. I thought it was over between you two,' said Cissie.

Peggy's face flushed. 'Well, it isn't. We're taking our time, that's all.'

'Jim and I are going to Hanley Park Fete straight from work. There's a huge floral display and the military band with soldiers and their black horses. It should be spectacular and I can't wait.'

'How marvellous.' Cissie beamed.

'He's vowed to take me out to lots of places.' Ruth smiled directly at Peggy, as if daring her to speak. 'He's very thoughtful.' Ruth felt embarrassed about the way she was trying to outdo Peggy. It wasn't normal for her.

Peggy sniffed again and stood beside her desk for a moment. It was obvious she was trying to think of something to say.

'Just be careful, Ruth. The investment Jim is making will have to pay dividends for him, if you get what I mean?'

Peggy sounded so sincere in that moment, a hint of doubt flashed into Ruth's mind. She dashed it away quickly. She knew him better than that. 'He's been nothing but a gentleman.'

Peggy laughed. 'Jim, a gentleman? I don't think so. I've warned yer now, so if you *do* get into trouble then at least I tried.'

Ruth was speechless as Peggy walked out of the office without a word. Ruth stuck her tongue out at Peggy's back. Childish again, but she couldn't help it. Peggy always got her hackles rising and Ruth always seemed to be the one who suffered.

—

A whole new world had opened up for Ruth. She closed her eyes and sent up a little prayer, hoping her mother was listening. 'Mother,' she whispered, 'I think you'd be thrilled if you could see me.'

The evening with Jim turned out to be every bit as good as she had expected. It was about nine o'clock when the heavens opened and the crowd ran for cover. She found herself with Jim sheltering in a doorway, soaked to the bone.

He turned towards Ruth, a smile playing on his lips, and softly kissed her. Ruth responded naturally. It felt good but strange to have a man's lips capture her own. Her stomach churned and she could barely breathe.

A clap of thunder broke the mood and returned her to reality.

When he pulled away, she could see his waistcoat was damp where she had leaned against him, and they both laughed.

He smiled. 'I didn't realise you were so wet.'

Ruth smiled back at him. Now she understood what Peggy meant and felt she had given Jim some dividend from his investment, but how much more would he expect?

They walked up Piccadilly to the tram stop. The rain had stopped and, despite the potbanks, the air was pleasantly fresh. They said nothing about what had just happened.

–

The following Saturday, Jim wanted to pick her up from home. Ruth wasn't ready for Jim to meet Father. It was too soon. In her eyes, it gave their relationship more importance than it warranted. He was rushing her. Taking control. He persisted.

'It's not right that you should make your own way there, Ruth. I've never asked a young lady out and not picked her up from home. Won't your father want to give me the once-over?'

'That's what I'm afraid of.' She was smiling when she said it, trying to make light of the situation.

'What if I promise to be on my best behaviour?'

'No. Not yet.'

He looked annoyed, but seemed to respect her wishes. It didn't appear to make any difference to their relationship, but she doubted if that was the end of the matter.

—

The Sunday morning brought good news for the family. Frank and Joan were expecting their third child in March next year. Ruth was so pleased for her brother and it made a change to receive good news.

In the afternoon, Ruth was meeting Jim for a walk around Burslem Park. The weather was sunny and warm and they both delighted in being outside, enjoying the freedom it brought. Jim looked smart in his Sunday best suit and hat.

They walked in silence until they neared the bandstand where a group of people had gathered.

'What have we here?'

'Let's have a look,' said Ruth, curiosity getting the better of her.

They joined the back of the crowd and could just make out a woman standing on a box, talking to the group of mainly women surrounding her. Ruth recognised the green-and-purple rosettes and sashes worn by the two ladies who looked to be in charge.

'It's the suffragettes campaigning for the vote. They come here regularly to the bandstand.'

'We'll leave them to it, then,' said Jim, turning away.

Ruth snatched at his jacket. 'No, don't go. Don't you want to hear what they have to say?'

'Not really. I suppose we could listen to them – if you're so interested.'

'Of course I am. It's important to all women. Men should be interested too.'

A young woman with auburn hair wandered through the crowd, smiling. She handed Ruth a pamphlet. Ruth smiled back and was about to thank her when Jim snatched it away and tore it in half before throwing it on the ground.

'Jim! What're you doing?' Ruth glowered.

'They're posh women campaigning on behalf of posh women. You don't want to be bothered with them, Ruth. They're trouble.'

Ruth bent to pick it up, shocked by Jim's response. It wasn't like him.

The woman handing out the pamphlets had stopped on hearing Jim's comment.

'We are members of the Women's Social and Political Union and we're campaigning for all women. Perhaps if you read our pamphlet, you might discover more about what we do, sir.' She held out a new pamphlet to Ruth. 'Here, have a clean one. I'm sure it'll be easier to read,' she said, glancing at Jim. Then Ruth recognised the woman. It was Constance Copeland from the big house. Ruth didn't know her well enough to speak to.

Ruth bit her lip. Miss Copeland was obviously posh, but the woman standing on the box delivering a speech was neither posh nor pauper, but somewhere in between.

'We could stay and listen, Jim. I'm interested.'

'You don't want to get involved with troublemakers, Ruth.'

'I believe the young lady would like to know more.' Miss Copeland smiled sweetly.

'It has nothing to do with you. Come on, Ruth.' Jim's face looked stony.

As Ruth and Jim continued on their way, he turned their conversation to the possibility of war, something the newspapers had been going on about recently. Then the conversation turned briefly to family and children and whether they were important in a marriage. Ruth didn't want to talk about it and changed the subject.

Jim accompanied her home, but she didn't invite him into the house. She offered an excuse that she had a lot of things to do, but would see him at work tomorrow. To be truthful, a wave of disappointment had washed over her as she considered his actions. She had thought he was enlightened, but his behaviour today had been – at best – disappointing. Ruth walked down to Carla's for a chat and to tell her about Joan's pregnancy. She was greeted by a smiling Carla who had identical news about Edith. She was expecting her first child in March 1915.

—

It was Monday evening and Ruth checked the drivers' rota in the Stoke depot office to see if Donald was working. He was, which meant Dottie would be on her own. She knocked on the door and Dottie answered. They walked through to the kitchen and Dottie made a cup of tea.

'Ruth, have you got any plans for the holidays?'

'No. Being the new girl, I'll be working throughout the Potters' holidays. The trams have to keep rolling.'

'I know. Donald always gets one week off for his Territorial camp. The bosses support the men who wish to go, but they don't get paid. A lot of the men would rather have a week's work and the money it brings. He has worked extra shifts to make up his wages. He gets something from the army.' Dottie topped up their tea. 'How are things going with your young man?'

'That's what I wanted to speak to you about.' The smile disappeared from Ruth's face.

'What's up, duck? Things not going well?'

'Yes and no.' Once Ruth began, she couldn't stop. She talked about her attractions to Jim, that they had kissed and how much she'd been tempted by him.

Dottie hugged Ruth. 'It's perfectly normal to feel the way you do about him. I felt the same way about Donald. Do be careful. He sounds like a man of the world. You would be wise to stand your ground. There are men around who would take what they want and then dump you as soon as look at you. I'm not saying Jim's like that because I don't know him well enough. Weakness could lead to a child changing your life forever. Ensure he's the right one, but regardless of what he says, you need to save any intimacy for after marriage.'

How mature Dottie sounded, and, of course, every word she uttered was true. Ruth took a deep breath. If that had been all she was worried about, Ruth was old enough to decide what she had to do for herself.

Dottie narrowed her eyes. 'I don't think that's uppermost in your mind, is it?'

Ruth shook her head. 'I'm sorry to burden you with my troubles, Dottie, but you're right. It's not the only problem I have with Jim.'

'I thought so. Here, I'll top up our tea and you can tell me what's really troubling you.'

Ruth recounted the story of yesterday's walk and the incident with the suffragette. Her face burned as she spoke of it. 'It wasn't just his attitude to the suffragette that bothered me at the time.' She returned her cup to the saucer. 'I couldn't believe he could be so... so objectionable. He was a different person... as if he was, somehow, my guardian. My own father wouldn't treat me in such a manner.'

Dottie looked incredulous. 'That's definitely a problem, Ruth. He clearly doesn't like the idea of women having summat to say for themselves, and trying to control what you read or who you talk to is wrong. You stood your ground, and it looks as though the suffragette got the measure of him too. She's probably used to dealing with that sort of behaviour from men. But watch him. If he's like that now, then what might he be like once you are married? You might have to fight your corner. He's likely to treat you as a possession, and expect you to be grateful. At the moment, he's using words to impose his ideas – how long before they become fists?'

'I don't like to admit it, but I think I've made a mess of the situation. His attention flattered me, and I really didn't think any further than that.'

'I think you've found the answer you're looking for, Ruth. You know what to do.'

A few moments passed, and Ruth washed her face under the scullery tap and patted it dry. 'There, that's better. I can face the tram home now. There was one other thing I was going to tell yer. That suffragette looked familiar, and it took me a while to work out who she was.'

'Do we know her?' asked Dottie.

'Yes, she's Constance Copeland from Holmorton Lodge. She's older than us and never went to our school – too common for the likes of her, I suppose. Anyway, she's the one who went to prison for throwing a rock through the window of a government building in London.'

'Of course, I remember now,' said Dottie. 'It's a funny house, to be sure. So grand, but surrounded by all those new terraced houses. The potbank owner who built it used to own all the land our estate was built on right up to High Lane, but he had to sell it to pay debts. The people there now bought it almost derelict. Mother said they spent a fortune on it and it's really bonny inside. She knew the cook.'

Ruth grinned. 'That's something I've learned.'

Ruth returned from Dottie's with a lot to think about. She wondered whether to call on Carla, but it was getting late and she had already decided about Jim.

—

Ruth woke up the following morning after one of the best night's sleep in a long time. She lay on her back staring at the ceiling thinking of all that had happened the previous day. She hadn't changed her mind about anything, so there was no point in prolonging the situation. At the first opportunity, she would slip over to Jim's office and ask him to meet her outside at lunchtime.

—

Ruth was waiting on the steps outside, getting slightly more anxious as the minutes passed. They couldn't talk outside the PTC and so had decided on a walk through the churchyard where they could talk unheard.

At that moment, Jim appeared.

'Now then, Ruth, what's up? I hope it's important. Old Routledge's got his eye on me. I said I was busy, didn't I?'

That was a good start. Somehow, she didn't feel so bad about ending things with him any more. Unfazed, she returned his greeting and suggested the walk. As they strolled through the gravestones, she went over in her mind what she wanted to say.

She sat on a bench away from the main pathway and motioned for him to sit beside her. They both eyed the two trams making their way back towards the PTC depot. Ruth wondered if Donald was driving one of them. She took a deep breath. 'There's no easy way to say this, Jim, but I've decided that I don't want to see you any more.'

His mouth fell open. Ruth doubted anyone had said that to him before.

'I'm sorry... Are you really finishing with me, Ruth?'

'I rather think I am, Jim.'

'But you can't – I thought we were fine. I mean, what's brought this on?'

'If you have to ask, then we're not fine, are we?' Somehow, his show of surprise made her more determined than ever.

'I don't understand. You'll have to tell me or else I won't know what I've done—'

'I don't think that I'm ready for a relationship with a man as mature as you are. You have expectations which I definitely cannot fulfil.'

'So it's your fault?' He stared at her, confused.

That goaded her even more. 'It's nobody's fault, Jim.'

'Was it about what happened in Hanley Park? I'm sorry if I was forward, but we've been out together a few times now, and I thought you were ready.'

'Ready for what?'

'A bit of fun. You know.'

'It's quite a big thing to take for granted, Jim. Don't you agree?'

She gave him time to answer.

'In my experience, most young ladies would be grateful. You won't even allow me to meet your father.'

'Thank you for that information,' she said, putting up a hand. 'No, Jim, don't interrupt. You need to hear what I have to say. I didn't like your attitude towards that suffragette. I was shocked at the way you spoke to her and also your attitude towards me for daring to have an opinion of my own and expressing it.'

His head went up and there was genuine confusion on his face. 'What? Are you saying that the reason you want us to finish is that I told a suffragette to mind her own business?'

Ruth said nothing.

'You are, aren't you?' he snorted. 'I told you the suffragettes were just campaigning for votes for posh people and the likes of you aren't important to them. What do you think would happen if women get the vote and they disagree with their husbands? How can a man be in charge of his own house and family when his wife has her own ideas about what should happen?'

'That's it. That's just the point I'm trying to make. You seem to think it is your right as a man. I'm afraid I can't agree with that and if we disagree about something as fundamental as that now, what's it going to be like if we marry?' Her voice raised as she grew more and more angry. 'Supposing children come along and the house is full of wet washing? You're working twelve hours a day and there's no tea for you because I haven't had time. You'll say it's all my fault.'

'Now you're being melodramatic, Ruth. You're making a lot of assumptions there. Who says I would want to marry you? You've been reading too many romance books and they're giving you ideas. All the men I know are happily married and they don't have any trouble with the wives. It's all this newfangled stuff about getting the vote that's making women forget their place – in the home.'

Ruth forced herself to remain calm and spoke quietly. 'It isn't "new-fangled". Women have been fighting this war for years.' She pursed her lips. 'Jim, I may have had some doubts at the start of this conversation, but you've just argued, most eloquently, about why I don't want our relationship to continue. We can be civil to each other at work, and that's all.' She got to her feet.

Jim stood up. 'There are plenty more fish in the sea and grateful ones too. I was never sure about you, Ruth. You seemed quite happy to accept my money to go to the pictures, but I don't consider one kiss in a doorway in Hanley Park much recompense.'

Ruth closed her eyes, shaking her head. With one last glance, she said, 'Goodbye, Jim.' She turned on her heel and walked away, reckoning she'd had a lucky escape.

Chapter Six

30 July–5 August 1914

Ruth and Carla were sitting at the kitchen table in Hesse's Stores. Carla had been reading *The Sentinel*, and she looked at Ruth. 'It seems there'll be no stopping this threat of war in Europe. The Austrians have been shelling Belgrade. Do you think we'll fight?'

'Lots of people say we won't. I hope they're right. What does your family think about it?'

'Probably the same as every other family. They don't want to see their son going off to fight and possibly get killed.'

At that moment, Bertie entered the kitchen. Edith had got a headache and had gone to bed. It was too nice of an evening to stay indoors, so Bertie suggested the three of them go for a walk.

'I'm looking forward to Wakes Week. Bit of money in my pocket. Let's hope the weather stays like this.'

'You got anything planned, Bertie?'

'No. I'll have to see what Edith wants to do, and I suppose that'll mean spending time with my in-laws. It usually does.'

'You don't sound very pleased by that prospect?'

'Ruth, I love Edith so much, but I can't say the same about her mother and sisters and I don't think they hold me in very high regard, either. I feel sorry for Mr Wren. He has to put up with them all the time. I dunner think I could do that. Thank the Lord.'

'Me and Ruth are thinking about going to Longton Park on Sunday because we don't have the luxury of a holiday, like some people. You're welcome to come along with us. We're going to ask Dottie and Walter, so it'll be the old gang together again.'

'For one last time,' Bertie said thoughtfully. 'We might be at war next week and me and Walter are the right age for the army.'

'You and Walter wouldn't volunteer, would you?'

'We may not have any choice. Everyone's mobilising their men, and that's a lot of men. We've got the Empire to defend, so if we join in, they'll be asking for volunteers. I may have been born in Germany, but I don't think it influenced me at the age of two. I'm as British as you are. If war comes, I'll fight for my country, Britain, if I have to.'

'What do your mother and father think?'

He shrugged. 'Nothing really, as long as it doesn't affect the shop. Don't get me wrong, they still consider themselves German, but they've been here so long they think they're more British than German now. Father doesn't see any problem and Mother thinks what Father thinks.'

They were quiet for a few moments and then Bertie laughed to himself. 'You know how we've always spoken German at home? It'll come in useful as I can say "I surrender" in both sides' languages.'

When they returned to the shop, they made plans for Sunday afternoon. Bertie said he wouldn't be able to come. He wanted to stay with Edith. Ruth would ask Dottie if she wanted to join them, too. Donald would be away at his annual camp, so Dottie would have the choice of visiting parents or having a jolly afternoon with her friends.

—

Ruth put on her Sunday best and walked down to the shop. The atmosphere differed totally from how it had been two days earlier.

Carla was ready and waiting, but her mother looked worried. 'Are you sure you'll be safe? There's a lot of bad feeling out there.'

'But Mother, no one outside of these streets knows anything about me. I'll be as safe as Ruth. Now, don't worry, we'll be back before six o'clock.'

Mrs Hesse hugged her daughter and the two young women set off for their afternoon in the park. They walked down into Burslem and caught a tram through to Longton. They were to meet Dottie outside the main gates to the park.

Dottie was waiting as planned.

The day was sunny with a gentle breeze and the seating around the bandstand proved quite a sun trap, heavy with the scent of summer flowers in full bloom. They listened to the music and chatted away during the breaks.

Ruth had read an article in *The Sentinel* which said Russia held the key to peace, and yesterday it was reported that Russia was mobilising. It was looking increasingly likely that Britain would be at war with Germany soon. Cheers went up at the end of the tune and a startled Ruth jumped. She must have fallen asleep. She hoped nobody had noticed. It wasn't very complimentary to the performers.

'You fell asleep. Me and Carla thought you needed your rest, so we've been sitting here listening to the music.'

'How long was I asleep?'

'Only a few minutes during the last piece of music,' replied Carla.

The conductor announced they would play three patriotic songs in keeping with the times and they would be their last tunes for the day. He thanked everyone for attending, then, turning to the band, he raised his baton.

At the end of the concert, a man jumped onto the bandstand and, in a loud voice, announced the Territorial Force's mobilisation and immediate orders to prepare for service.

Ruth's heart sank. She looked at Dottie, who gave a weak smile. 'Do you want to go home now?'

'No, I want me money's worth. Donald's at camp. It'll take him a while to get home.'

The first tram to come along went straight past the queue waiting at the tram stop, full to the gunwales, but Ruth, Carla and Dottie boarded the next one. Dottie left the tram outside of the depot in Stoke and the others continued on to Hanley and Burslem.

In Hanley, there seemed to be two separate demonstrations going on. One group urged the government not to get involved and seemed fairly peaceful while the other demonstration was rowdy and urged the government to stand fast and help France and Russia stop the Germans.

Ruth and Carla looked at each other but didn't speak. As the tram passed another group of protesters, a man on the tram rose and raised his arm in the air.

'Bloody Germans! Buggering up our holidays. They could have had the decency to wait. Wait till we get at them. We'll learn them to pick on Little Belgium.'

The audience greeted this enthusiastically.

Carla's face grew pale. Ruth didn't blame her. The shouting was becoming increasingly venomous. She reached out to hold Carla's hand. It was cold.

An older man, wearing pince-nez glasses, shouted, 'Fancy going to war over a piece of paper signed seventy-five years ago designed to stop the French pinching the newly independent Belgium. Ironic, isn't it?'

'You're one of them bloody peace-mongers. Shut up and sit theeself down.'

The rest of the tram clapped, and both men sat down, having had their say.

Then it was the turn of two women talking in the seat behind them.

'It's been awful trying to get back. I suppose it's the start of what'll happen from now on.'

'What d'yer mean?' said her friend.

'They've already re-directed some trains and begun moving soldiers around. The train we were due to come back on stopped at a place called Stowford Halt. Never heard of it, have you?'

'No.'

'It's somewhere near Macclesfield. We was told to get off, and we had to wait nearly an hour before they sent another one to bring us back to Stoke.'

'How tiring for you.'

Ruth was feeling sick when they descended from the tram in Burslem and walked up Moorland Road towards Bowden Street in order to get some fresh air. They arrived at Hesse's Stores around seven o'clock to be greeted by a tearful Mrs Hesse and concerned Mr Hesse and Bertie. *'Wo bist du gewesen? Geht es dir gut? Hattest du irgendwelche Probleme?'*

'*Beruhige dich, Mutter, bitte sprich Englisch für Ruth.*'

'Sorry, Ruth, I was so worried.'

Ruth and Carla told the family what they had seen and heard.

Only now did Ruth notice that Carla's hands were shaking as she laid them on the table. Carla noticed Ruth's gaze. 'I suppose it's the shock. Maybe things will get back to normal before long. Our neighbours are all very nice. They wouldn't turn against us. After all, they've known us since Bertie was a youngster – and I was born in this house.'

'People round here won't stand for no nonsense. And you've got plenty of friends. I'm sure you'll be safe enough.'

'I suppose we'll have to see what tomorrow brings.'

'Are you worried, Carla? Tell me the truth,' begged Ruth.

'I probably wouldn't be telling the truth if I said no. When the newspapers arrive at the shop, I can't help seeing the headlines. We've been following all the reports. It's too late to stop a war now. We shall have to pray whatever happens doesn't last long.'

—

On Monday, Ruth and Peggy arrived at work on the same tram. It was so quiet compared to normal. How different the towns looked when there were no kilns being fired. This was the origin of the holidays. The bosses carried out maintenance when the kilns were cold. They didn't start new firings unless they could finish them on time, and they didn't leave any decorated ware unfired during the week before the holiday. Workers emptied each kiln, let it cool, and then performed maintenance.

'It looks a different place with so few of the kilns belching out smoke,' said Peggy.

'Yes, I'd forgotten what it was like,' replied Ruth.

'You'll enjoy the holiday. There is not as much work as normal. Most of the bosses aren't working and we should have some time to talk about what's happening.'

'Yes, I'm worried too.'

'Everybody is, but my father thought that Sir Edward Grey's speech was encouraging,' said Peggy. 'It seemed to offer the possibility that England would stay neutral.'

'My father thought it meant the opposite,' said Ruth. 'He said that Sir Edward told everyone why we didn't have to take part, but at the end said we would help our friends.'

'Confusing, isn't it?'

The tram pulled up at the depot stop in front of St Peter's churchyard, and the two young women alighted and thanked the conductor. They walked up Bowstead Street on the right-hand side to avoid trams moving in and out of the depot and opened the door into the offices. It was surprising to talk to Peggy without having an argument. It just goes to show that when faced with a common danger, petty local squabbles aren't as important.

All day the talk was about the possibility of war and some of the preparations people had seen or heard about. Dinnertime came round soon enough and Ruth popped round to check on Dottie and ask her if Donald was back. This proved unnecessary when Pearl appeared and handed her a note from Dottie, explaining Donald's recall the previous day and that he was back home waiting for orders.

–

The next day, Ruth arrived on her own and made her way to the typists' room. As she passed the cash office, she heard them talking and joined them. Both Peggy and Cissie were there along with Pearl.

'I heard that some men who are in the Territorials were sent straight back home when they got to their annual training camp on Saturday and told to be prepared to join their units,' said Pearl.

'Yes, that's what happened to Donald Spilling,' added Ruth.

At that moment, Henry Blakeman, from wages, came in. Everyone said good morning, and the conversation continued.

'I told Mr P, on Friday, that we employ at least twenty reservists and to my knowledge about the same number in the Territorials. Looks like you ladies will be driving trams shortly instead of those typewriting contraptions,' said Henry, who for once was not sucking on his pipe. Whatever Henry smoked, it was vile. Most of the lads said it was dead rat or horse droppings – or both.

The group laughed, but Ruth could see the concern in their eyes.

'Good morning, everyone.' Mr Routledge entered the room. They were about to return to their desks, but he asked them to remain. He had some news. 'I have just learned that Germany has invaded Belgium. So it looks as if we will join this war after all.'

There was a stunned silence in the office while everyone digested the information. Everybody knew this meant war. Ruth thought to herself no matter how much you prepare yourself for bad news, it still comes as a shock when it happens, like the day her mother died.

The rest of the morning and early afternoon passed without further news. Everyone she met seemed deep in thought.

Ruth was handing some typing over to Cissie for correction. There was a disturbance in the yard and Peggy, nearest the window, peered out and saw several men gathered together.

'What's going on...' asked Cissie, but before she could get her words out fully, Pearl burst through the door.

'It's happened.' She was waving a copy of *The Sentinel* and red-faced. 'Listen, "The King of the Belgians has made an appeal to His Majesty the King for diplomatic intervention on behalf of Belgium. His Majesty's Government are also informed that the..." It says the ultimatum will expire at eleven o'clock tonight.'

There was silence as they were joined by the cashiers and Mr Routledge.

Meetings went on most of the afternoon. Before they left that evening, Mr Routledge asked everyone to write down how they could be contacted if required. Only one or two people had access to a nearby telephone, so it would be by telegram, Ruth assumed.

Like many people, Ruth got little sleep that night.

–

When Ruth woke up the next morning, it was to find the country was at war with Germany. She had prayed before she went to sleep that, somehow, there would be a last-minute reprieve. But no such luck. She had slept only intermittently and felt groggy. She would be glad when she got to work. At least she would have something to take her mind off the world around her. How must

Carla and her family feel this morning? To wake up to the knowledge that she and the rest of her family were on different sides of the war that seemed to involve the whole of Europe.

When Ruth got into work on that Wednesday morning, the place was a hive of activity. She went to her desk and both Cissie and Peggy were there already hard at work, having been called in at six o'clock.

Even before the ultimatum expired, the British government began full mobilisation. Henry Blakeman told her that all twenty reservists employed by the PTC had received their mobilisation documentation and twelve of them were working on the late trams. Several Territorial volunteers who had taken their annual holiday to attend their training camps had received their orders.

'You're a friend of Dottie Spilling, aren't you?'

'Yes, Henry. Why?'

'Donald wasn't working yesterday evening, so it's likely he will have had his papers at home sometime last night. He's been called back to his regiment.'

'Oh no! Poor Dottie.'

At dinnertime, Ruth rushed over to see Dottie and hammered on the door, but there was no reply. The woman across the street told her that Donald had left for the army and Dottie had gone to see her mother.

Around lunchtime, *The Sentinel* published a special edition confirming recent events and detailing the number of reservists and Territorials in The Potteries recalled to arms. The impact on the post office and the police seemed severe, as they employed many ex-soldiers.

By the time Ruth got home she was exhausted. She had typed and retyped lists of drivers, conductors and other staff who had been mobilised, in addition to the normal duties of the day. The latest edition of *The Sentinel* contained a chilling advertisement headed *Your King & Country Need You*, an appeal to every single man between the age of eighteen and thirty to volunteer for military service. She read the newspaper from cover to cover, surprised at the speed at which everything was happening.

She immediately thought about Walter and Bertie, followed by Jim, Tom, Dickie and Brian, and countless others, all under the age of thirty. She prayed vehemently that none of them would actually volunteer.

Chapter Seven

7–11 August 1914

By Friday, it seemed the country had gone mad. Ruth dressed quickly and made her way downstairs. Father was sitting in his chair by the range staring glumly at – Ruth wasn't sure. He must've seen her shadow move through the room. He sighed.

'Hiya, Ruth.'

'Oh, Father, where on earth do we go from here?'

'God only knows. I just hope as them in charge know what they're doing. Yesterday I went to Burslem at dinnertime. The numbers of protesters had grown and now everybody hates the Germans. I feel sorry for people like the Hesses. They'll get it in the neck, I've no doubt.'

'Poor Carla. She's worried how far it'll go. If people stop using the shop, they'll go out of business.'

Her father nodded. 'They've been here so long they're almost as English as we are. I don't suppose they'll have any trouble. People will remember they are German and when people are angry and want revenge, they don't ask for paperwork.'

Ruth sat at the table to eat her toast.

Father sighed and shook his head. 'God help us all,' he said. 'You know what's worse for me now, our Ruth?' His face wore a strained expression. 'It's not having yer mother here to talk to. She may have been ill for a long time, but we could talk about anything and she would make me feel we could get through it.'

Ruth got up and placed her hand on top of his, which was gripping the arm of his chair, his knuckles white.

'But her's gone and we've got to carry on without her.' He looked directly into Ruth's eyes. 'This is a strange world we're entering now. All we can do is hope it doesn't last.'

Reluctantly, he got to his feet. 'We'd best get off to work. There's nowt we can do about it; we'll have to take what's coming.'

There was a banging on the front door as Ruth cleared the table of empty dishes when tea was over. 'I'll see who that is.'

She set the used crockery down and hurried to stop the insistent banging. It was Carla. Her face was white and her teeth chattering.

'Come in, Carla. What's happened?' said Ruth as she pulled Carla inside and closed the door sharply.

'The police have been to our house,' Carla panted, barely catching her breath.

'The police?' Ruth covered her cheeks with her hands. 'Why? I mean, sit down, and tell us what's going on. Is everybody all right?'

Carla took a deep breath and nodded. 'He came into the shop about six.'

'Who did?'

'Sergeant Birchall from Burslem Police Station. I didn't want him hanging around in the shop where everybody could see him, so I took him upstairs and went back down again. The shop was empty. I closed up so as I could go back up to find out what was going on. When I got up there, Sergeant Birchall was asking Father lots of questions about his private life, and about being German. He asked Father where he was born, how old he was, and whether he was a naturalised British citizen. So many questions, Ruth. And they wanted proof of nearly everything he said. It was horrible, but Father, to his credit, answered their questions calmly, although I noticed his fists were clenched. Sergeant Birchall said it was a "friendly visit" but it didn't sound friendly to me. Father remained calm. The sergeant said the police had been ordered to collect details from all aliens in the area and make them fill out a form with their details.'

'Sergeant Birchall's a good man, Carla. Me and yer father have known him for donkey's years. He'll see yer right,' said Father.

'That's terrible, Carla. You were born here. You're English.'

'Yes, but Mother, Father and Bertie were born in Germany and that makes them aliens now. According to the law, me and my family are on different sides in this war, Ruth. God, what shall I do? We've only been at war a few days and look what's happened.' Carla's eyes filled. 'I thought we'd be all right because we've got friendly neighbours and they're good to us, but after what we heard on the tram, I'm worried it'll all change. Everybody round here knows we're German, and I expect I'll be treated in the same way.'

'I'm sure your friends will be on your side. What does Sergeant Birchall think you should do?'

'He said we should lie low and keep out of trouble. He was very interested in speaking to Bertie.'

'Where were Edith and Bertie during this?'

'At her mother's. She persuaded him to take her there as soon as he got home from work.'

Ruth and her father glanced at each other, frowning.

'What's wrong?'

'The paper says that men of military age will be interned.'

'Sergeant Birchall said that was likely, but the army want full internment, and the government want something different, so he said to sit tight and make sure Bertie doesn't do anything silly.' She gave a shuddering sigh. 'Anyway, I'll go now.'

'I'll walk you back.' Ruth hurried to get her hat and coat.

'Want me to come with you two girls?' Father got to his feet.

'No, we'll be all right, Father. There's been no trouble round here.'

He pursed his lips but nodded his agreement.

They let themselves out into the street, first Ruth, then Carla, who couldn't help but look furtive as she glanced around her. A few people were out chatting with one another. As they walked swiftly towards the shop, they caught the words 'war', 'Germans' and 'bloody politicians'.

'I feel a bit of a ninny getting you to walk home with me, Ruth.'

'You didn't ask. I volunteered. Best be safe than sorry.'

Seconds later, they arrived at Carla's and shot inside.

'Ruth! What're you doing here?' asked Mr Hesse, who stood up when they opened the kitchen door.

'Carla's just told me everything. I'm so sorry for the way you've been treated, Mr Hesse.' Even *he* looked pale.

'The sergeant was only doing his job, Ruth.'

'It's good of you to take it like that.'

At that moment Bertie walked in. 'Are you lot all right—'

He looked surprised when he saw Ruth, but Carla spoke up, telling him Ruth had been her protector tonight.

'Where's Edith?' asked Mrs Hesse quietly.

'She's going to spend the evening at her mother's. I'm going to fetch her back home later. She's really nervous about what's going on. I thought it best to let her stay what with her being pregnant.'

'My father said that things were frosty at work, Bertie,' said Ruth.

'You can say that again. People have been staring at me, or giving me a wide berth. It's as if I've suddenly grown two heads.'

'The police were here earlier,' sighed Mr Hesse.

'What for?'

'Quizzing your mother and me about being Germans.'

Bertie drew in a breath.

'They said it was a "friendly visit", Albrecht, and I took it as so. No point in looking for trouble.'

Ruth decided this would be a good time to leave the family to talk. It was the first time she had heard Bertie being addressed by his German name – Albrecht – for a long time, a sure sign Mr Hesse might be feeling more anxious than he was letting on. 'I'd best get off home now,' she murmured.

Mrs Hesse rolled her eyes. 'And I've never even offered you a cup of tea to say thank you.'

'It's fine. I wanted to see Carla home, even if it's only a few doors away.'

'Then please stay for a cuppa.'

Ruth smiled. 'How can I refuse?'

Bertie went to get changed out of his work clothes while Mrs Hesse made the tea, clearly feeling the need to do something.

—

Just over half an hour later, there came a banging on the front door. 'Seems to be a busy night tonight,' said Mr Hesse firmly. 'I'll go.'

Bertie was the first to go after his father, followed by Carla and Ruth. The light was on in the shop and Mr Hesse was talking to someone by the front door. Ruth looked at Carla as she moved towards her father.

'Someone's daubed the shop windows with red paint. It's as if they had thrown the paint and let it run down the glass like blood. They've painted "Germans go home" on the shop door,' said a pale Mr Hesse.

Ruth recognised the man Mr Hesse was talking to. He lived on Bowden Street. He had been on his way to the pub when he turned the corner into Dartmouth Street and ran smack into the culprits, two of them, dressed in black and wearing black caps and masks.

Ruth had never felt so useless before. This couldn't be happening. Not here in Burslem. Where would it end?

A few people came out of their houses to see what was going on, mostly apologetic, calling the perpetrators hooligans and vandals. But these were the people who knew the family – and there were many, many more who didn't. But one thing that people discovered fairly quickly was that the enemy was living in their town.

–

Monday came around all too quickly. The words on everyone's lips were about the government's call to arms. Thousands of men answered the call, joining the army to fight the Germans. Today's *Sentinel* still ran the large advertisement encouraging men to 'Rally around the Flag', which had appeared on the first day. Dottie said Donald had reported to his barracks on the Tuesday war was declared. That's all she knew. She would make time to visit Dottie again in the next day or so.

Peggy arrived at work at the same time as Ruth and they walked up the stairs together, passing the time of day and very little more. As they neared the door to their office, Ruth said, 'Did you do anything exciting at the weekend?'

Peggy gave an aloof smile. 'Me and Stan spent some time together. He wanted to see me on Sunday an' all, but I said no. I don't want him thinking he only has to ask. A girl's got her pride.'

'I see.' Privately, Ruth felt sorry for Stan. He probably didn't know where he stood if Peggy was telling him she loved them being together, and then the next minute she was pushing him away, just so that he knew she was in control.

In the office, Jim was talking to Dickie, Tom and Pearl.

'Jim was just telling us about his holiday in Blackpool. Sounds fun,' said Pearl.

Ruth glanced at Jim's handsome, tanned face wondering if she'd been a little hasty in sending him on his way. Something inside her stirred, but it was too late now.

The conversation turned to the war.

'I can't see as how the odd few Germans could make any difference to who's going to win the war,' said Dickie, shrugging his shoulders. 'There's a bloke down our way what's been here nigh on thirty years. I don't see him deciding to bludgeon somebody to death because he's suddenly remembered he's German.'

'I, for one, think that when it comes to war, you can't trust nobody,' said Jim. 'It only takes one person to shoot a man. How can you trust them when they're on the other side?'

'You can't trust 'em, Jim, that's the whole point. And anybody who says otherwise is a fool.'

As one, they turned towards the door. It was Peggy speaking, but she was looking at Ruth.

Ruth sat upright in her chair, a lump in her throat. She didn't like where the conversation was heading. Surely she wouldn't have any cause for telling everyone about the family of Ruth's closest friend. What could she hope to gain?

Ruth's eyes glued to Peggy's and detected a slight glint.

'We all know that Ruth and me went to Park Road School. Our paths crossed briefly, didn't they, Ruth?'

Ruth frowned. 'Briefly.'

'But long enough to get to know each other – and our friends.'

Ruth nodded. 'We knew many people, from Park Road and from round about, what with so many terraced houses being built. But that was years ago.'

'I can see you don't want me to carry on, Ruth, but I think your fellow workers here at the PTC deserve to know, don't you? I'll have to do it because I doubt you'd tell them otherwise.'

Ruth's face grew cold. Not for herself – but for Carla. She didn't know many people who worked at the PTC, but one would be enough if they were a blabbermouth like Peggy.

This conversation was turning into a nightmare.

'What are you talking about, Peggy?' Jim said.

'I'm talking about the Germans, aren't I, Ruth?' Peggy stood, hands on hips now, keenly watching all their faces.

At that moment, the door opened. It was Mr Routledge, but Peggy was too far into her tale to stop now.

'Ruth's best friend is a German!'

–

'What's going on here?' bawled Mr Routledge.

The rest of the room was silent. Ruth closed her eyes so she didn't have to look at anyone.

'I think you should get back to work – or start to work if you haven't already done so.'

Dickie, Tom and Jim returned to their desks. Pearl scuttled out of the room, leaving Ruth and Peggy with Mr Routledge.

He shut the door. 'Now then, ladies, I don't know who's responsible for this performance, but you are all here to work. The country's in enough trouble without you bringing it into the PTC. I don't care who started this outrage, but I suggest you get back to work.'

With that, Mr Routledge glanced at Ruth. 'Miss Latham, could you come with me?'

Ruth bit her lip. Why had he picked her out instead of taking Peggy to task? She was the one who had been talking. This wasn't fair. She followed him to his office.

'Come in, Miss Latham, and close the door behind you.'

Ruth did as he asked and then came to stand in front of him.

'You may sit, Ruth.'

Ruth had been staring at the floor until this point, but she quickly raised her head. He wasn't smiling, but his face didn't look as stern as she was expecting.

'Now, then, would you like to tell me what exactly was going on when I walked into the cash office?'

Ruth swallowed. 'Peggy and I were at the same school briefly and she lives nearby, so she knows a lot of the people I know.'

He nodded for her to continue.

One of my friends, she was about to say, but changed her mind. 'It's true. My best friend *is* German. Well, not strictly. She was born in England, but the rest of her family is German. I've known them all my life. You can ask Miss Simmons; she knows them too.'

He sat up. 'I see.'

'They are a lovely family, Mr Routledge. They own Hesse's Stores on the corner of Dartmouth Street. It was their shop that had paint thrown at it.'

'I see, and Miss Thompson thought she could help spread the word around, did she?'

'I believe so, sir.'

'Ruth, I think you had better get back to work. It would seem that your friend has more than enough to deal with without PTC employees getting involved.'

'You... won't say anything to Miss Thompson, will you? I don't want to—'

'I will not have this behaviour in these offices. I will have a word with Miss Thompson to make sure she understands this is not acceptable behaviour. But I won't involve you. In fact, you can send her in now.'

Ruth trudged back to the typing room. Immediately, Peggy and Cissie stopped talking.

'Mr Routledge wants to see you, Peggy.'

Peggy looked pale as she set off.

'What did he say?' whispered Cissie.

'He said it sounds like my friend has more than enough to deal with.' Ruth began to type, leaving Cissie in no doubt that the conversation was at an end.

—

Since Peggy had returned from Mr Routledge's office, the typing room had been deathly quiet. She hadn't said a word and had handed work out without explanation. Ruth felt sorry for Cissie, who had little idea of what had gone on between the two of them. What Cissie knew was that, once again, Peggy was not thrilled.

In the late afternoon, Daisy appeared with a couple of hand-written reports which she gave to Cissie and Peggy. As she came to Ruth's desk, she stopped.

'Ruth, would you mind coming with me? I have need of your shorthand skills until the end of the day. If you please?'

Ruth smiled at Daisy. 'Of course. I'll bring my pad and pencil.'

'If you're doing anything that needs to go out tonight, pass it over to Peggy.'

Ruth felt mortified that Daisy should tell her to pass on her work to Peggy. In the circumstances, it was sure to get her back up. But Peggy smiled as she took the small bundle of papers from Ruth.

Ruth followed Daisy along to her office and slipped into the chair opposite Daisy, holding her writing pad in one hand and pencil in the other.

'It's all right, Ruth. You can relax. I wanted a private word with you. Mr Routledge has told me about the skirmish earlier.'

Ruth laid the pad and pencil on the table.

'I'm not wanting to pry, Ruth, but I gather this is about Carla and what happened to the shop?'

Ruth nodded. 'It's awful for them, Daisy. I was there when the shop got daubed in paint.'

'It must've been terrible. They've not had any trouble before, have they?'

'None. It's because of the war. She's very upset. Her brother. You remember Bertie?'

Daisy nodded.

'Bertie's likely to be taken in by the police any day now, but he's done nothing. His wife's terrified about what might happen to him.'

'Why is that?'

'They're intending to intern all German men of fighting age.'

'In today's newspaper' – Daisy pushed it across her desk to Ruth – 'they only mean men of fighting age who are reservists in the German Army. Bertie would be safe.'

'That's a relief.'

'How are the rest of the family?'

'Mr Hesse seems all right. The police have been to question him, but apart from filling in some forms, that's all. Mrs Hesse doesn't know whether she's coming or going, to be honest.'

'And this is only the start of the war. God help us all. Give Carla and her family my best wishes. And you needn't worry, I won't tell anyone, but if there's anything I can do…'

Ruth nodded. 'I will. And thanks, Daisy.'

—

That evening, Ruth returned home from work and noticed a small group of women outside the shop talking. They stopped and watched Ruth open her front door. Surprisingly, Peggy Thompson was there too. She ignored Ruth's friendly greeting.

Ruth stepped inside, taking off her coat as she entered the kitchen.

'Hiya, Father. Any idea what's going on outside? There are a few women gossiping. Has something happened?'

Father lifted his head. 'No idea. There were some people out there when I got home half an hour ago.'

'They were talking until they saw me and then stopped. One of them was Peggy Thompson.'

'If a Thompson's involved, then there's no knowing what them women are up to,' Father muttered. 'Two women at work told me that someone was arrested on our street today. They didn't know the reason.'

'I'll go down to see Carla after tea to find out how they're coping.'

—

After tea, Ruth made her way down to Carla's. She walked down the alley because the shop's door would be locked by now. She knocked on the back door. The curtain at the kitchen window upstairs twitched to one side, and Carla's head appeared. She waved and disappeared – to reappear at the door moments later.

'It's you, oh, thank God. Come in. Quickly!' She pulled Ruth through the door and checked no one had followed her.

'What's happened, Carla?'

'They've arrested Bertie!'

'No. What for?'

'For being German, why d'yer think?' Carla's voice came out harshly. She covered her face. 'I'm sorry, Ruth. I don't know what to do.'

Ruth entered the kitchen to find Edith sitting on the settee, sobbing. 'I'm so sorry, Edith. When did this happen?'

It was Carla who explained. 'Edith says that two policemen must've been waiting outside for him to get home from work tonight. They followed him into the shop and asked questions, similar to those Sergeant Birchall asked Father. Only this wasn't a friendly visit.'

Ruth nodded.

Edith took over. 'They said they would have to take him in for questioning. That he was an enemy alien because he was born in Germany. I told them he hadn't had his tea but they wouldn't listen.'

If it hadn't been so distressing, Ruth might have chuckled at Edith's concern for Bertie's belly.

Then Carla spoke. 'One of the policemen said that an enemy alien of his age was a threat to this country. They didn't care how long he'd been here. They needed proof that he had become naturalised as a British citizen, otherwise, they'd have to arrest him.'

Ruth closed her eyes. How would she feel if similar had happened to Frank or Walter? She sat beside Edith and took her hand, giving it a rub. She didn't know Edith very well, but it seemed the right thing to do.

Ruth hoped, for all their sakes, that the police would find Bertie had done nothing wrong and would let him go. It would only add to the gossip if word of his arrest got out.

Mrs Hesse had appeared while Carla was speaking.

'Two of my regulars came into the shop after the police had gone. They said how sorry they were for what had happened and if there was anything they could do to help let them know.'

'That's good of them. I'm sure your friends will support you, Mrs Hesse.'

Carla let Ruth out through the back door shortly after that. She plodded back to number 32, hoping very much that Mrs Hesse's 'regulars' meant what they said and weren't after finding out yet more gossip.

Ruth shook her head. Damn it! Is this how it's going to be from now on? Not knowing who you can or can't trust?

Three days had passed since Bertie had been arrested, and every morning, he was the first person on Ruth's mind. Where was he now? How was he getting on?

It was much to her relief when Carla came rushing round that evening to tell them the police had let Bertie go. Apparently, Mr Hesse had visited the police station and proved Bertie's legitimate entry to England and his continued residence since the age of two. Of course, that meant he could not have served in the German Army or its reserve.

'So you see, it's all sorted now,' said Carla, happy that her news was good for a change.

'It's marvellous and if the war's over by Christmas like people are saying, we shall all be back to normal soon.' Ruth smiled. She imagined they would all sleep soundly in their beds tonight.

—

The beginning of the next week wasn't much better as the Lathams gathered for tea.

'It was Bertie's first day back at work and he had a rough time of it,' said Father, out of the blue.

Walter and Ruth looked startled. You could hear a pin drop.

'Why – what happened?' asked Ruth.

'We started work as usual this morning and everybody was giving him the cold shoulder, poor bloke. Everyone had heard that he'd been arrested because he was German.'

'Not poor Bertie as well as the shop.'

'I stood up for him but they said as I should be careful who my friends were. I said they should know better when they've worked with the lad for ten years. In the end, they left us both alone, but I dunner think as they'll let it drop from the way they was talking.'

'How horrible. He's done nothing wrong and now look at him – all because he had the misfortune of being born where he was.' Ruth shook her head. 'Whatever next.'

'Most of the blokes kept out of Bertie's way. Some sent him to Coventry. Nobody said a word to him until dinnertime. At knocking-off time, one boss came down and took him away. I heard as they told him not to come to work for two weeks and let the whole thing blow over. Course, there'll be no pay neither, poor bugger.' Father shook his head. 'They said it was for everyone's safety.'

When Ruth went to bed that night all she could think of was the baby Edith was carrying and praying that the war would be over before its birth.

Chapter Eight

September 1914

The war was on everyone's lips over the next three weeks. It was Friday afternoon and there seemed to be a lot of rowdiness in the cash office. Even Peggy appeared to be smirking at the noise from down the corridor, although she said nothing, probably because she didn't know what was going on.

'I'll bet the lads have been down the Red Lion now they've been paid. Shame on them for drinking away their hard-earned cash,' Cissie tutted.

Ruth listened but couldn't make out any actual conversations going on. Surprisingly, Mr Routledge hadn't stopped it.

The door was flung open and Pearl shot in, eyes bulging, her hand covering her heart and her breaths coming in quick gasps. Ruth stood up quickly and offered Pearl her seat.

'Whatever's the matter, Pearl? Are you all right? You look like you've had a shock.'

'Is it anything to do with the cashiers? They've been making a hell of a noise since dinnertime,' said Peggy.

'Oh, it is. You'll never guess. Oh, my word… I dunner think as I can talk, girls.'

Ruth rubbed her hand across Pearl's ample back. 'Take deep breaths, Pearl, else you'll be in danger of collapsing, never mind talking.'

Pearl leaned back, took two or three deep breaths – and looked calmer. She swallowed. 'I needed to go to the you-know-what, I got someone from wages to cover for me so as I could come up and tell yer. I thought yer might already know, what with you three being the nearest.'

'The nearest what? For goodness' sake, Pearl, tell us,' muttered Peggy.

'It's a good job I came to see yer if yer didn't already know. Not that I'm one for tittle-tattle, you—'

'Pearl!' all three shouted at the same time.

Pearl put her hand up to stop the noise. 'I've come to tell yer that three of the cashiers went into town at dinnertime. It was unusual because if they're out together, it's usually the pub they go to.'

Peggy was about to erupt.

'And?' Ruth said quickly. Pearl would only impart her news when she was ready.

'Dickie, Tom and Jim have only gone and enlisted.' Her face was nearly purple.

Nobody said a word.

Pearl looked at each of them, waiting for their surprise, shock, laughter – anything that showed they understood what she was saying.

Still nothing. Ruth, Peggy and Cissie had frozen.

Pearl looked triumphant that she had been the one to pass on such important information. 'I was passing Mr Routledge's office, and I heard them and he said, "What, all together?" – just like that. I've never heard him so shocked. I suppose I'd best get back to reception. I said I was only popping to the you-know-what.' She hurried towards the door. 'Daisy probably knows, but I might just pop along to make sure.'

Once Pearl had gone, Ruth, Peggy and Cissie stared at one another. 'Well, I never,' retorted Cissie.

Ruth couldn't think. It couldn't just be a passing thing. Jim surely must have put a considerable amount of thought into joining up. Nobody in their right mind would just go along and say they wanted to enlist purely on a whim?

–

It was a long afternoon. Ruth couldn't concentrate. She had three attempts at typing the same letter. Ruth ripped out the paper and was about to crunch the lot together when Brian walked in.

'Ruth, what's that paper done to yer?'

'This typewriter has got a mind of its own.' Carefully, she removed the carbon and threw the remaining paper into the bin.

Brian walked over to Ruth and sat down beside her. 'What's up, Ruth?'

'What do you think about the others enlisting?'

'I'm proud of them. If they want to do their bit for the country, so be it. But I'm married and we've another child on the way. I've got responsibilities. How could I enlist? It would be selfish if I did.'

'I didn't know you was expecting another. When's it due?'

'Before Christmas.'

'I understand, Brian. As this war progresses, more and more men will have to make that decision.'

'Unless they introduce conscription and then we'll have no choice.'

'Let's hope it doesn't come to that.'

Brian said, 'I'll do you a trade – make us a cup of tea and I'll give your typewriter a good talking to!'

—

Ruth walked steadily into the PTC offices from her dinner on the following Monday. Peggy was still in there when she got back. Ruth smiled at her. Peggy looked unimpressed and retorted, 'I'm glad one of you two is back. I've been waiting ages.'

'Where's Cissie?'

Peggy shrugged. 'Beats me. See you later.' She strode out, banging the door behind her.

She must've met Cissie in reception on her way out, because Cissie appeared moments later.

'What's up with Peggy now?' she said, hanging up her coat.

'No idea,' said Ruth. 'To be honest, I don't care. There are far more important things going on in the world without taking care of what I can and can't say to her.'

Daisy walked in. 'Have you had your dinner, Ruth?' When she replied that she had, Daisy said, 'Good, come with me, please.'

Automatically, Ruth picked up her writing pad and pencil, and followed her. She was surprised when Daisy stopped outside Mr Routledge's office and knocked.

'Enter. Come in, you two, and sit down,' he said, leaning back in his chair. 'Now then, Ruth, your work has been very satisfactory since you started here. How do *you* feel about it?'

Ruth looked from Mr Routledge to Daisy, who nodded, encouraging her to speak. 'I'm fine. I've enjoyed it – I still enjoy it.'

'Daisy reminded me that you have a certificate in bookkeeping.'

'Yes, I did an extra night at evening class to get it. I thought it might be useful.'

'Because of that, we have a better job for you.'

Ruth sat upright. 'I don't understand.'

'I want you to move to the cash office, starting immediately. The three gentlemen leaving at the same time have put us in a difficult situation. We think you have the potential to be a good clerk, maybe even a senior clerk, Ruth. How do you feel about that?'

Ruth stared from one to the other, unable to believe her ears.

'If the war should suddenly end, you'll have your old job back.'

Daisy smiled. 'And I'd welcome you back in a heartbeat. Do you want to think about it?'

'I don't need to – of course I'll do it. I accept.'

'Good,' said Mr Routledge. 'Daisy will go with you back to your office and tell Peggy and Cissie while I tell the three musketeers. I want you to start tomorrow, so you have time to pick up as much as you can before they leave. Daisy's assured me she'll cope with two typists for the next two or three weeks. I have someone else starting in the cash office tomorrow, someone who has experience, so you won't be on your own.'

Once they were in the corridor, Daisy gave Ruth a huge smile. 'I'm so excited for you, Ruth. Congratulations.' Daisy hugged her. 'Now let's break the news to the other two, shall we?'

–

Daisy entered the office almost at the same time as Peggy. She must have been waiting for her to return from dinner.

'Peggy, have a seat. I've an announcement to make.'

Daisy looked calm and authoritative as she waited for Peggy to take off her coat and sit at her desk.

'As you're aware, the lads joining up mean we're short of workers for the cash office.'

Ruth glanced at Peggy, sitting straight-backed with a smile of anticipation on her face.

'As Ruth has a bookkeeping qualification, we've asked her to move to the cash office immediately. I'm sure the pair of you will cope admirably without her for a few weeks. Any questions?'

Peggy looked as if she was about to burst a blood vessel. In a matter of seconds, she changed from a fresh complexion to bright red, to sallow grey. Ruth honestly thought she was going to complain and tell Daisy why she and Mr Routledge had made a terrible mistake.

All was quiet. Daisy thanked them all for their hard work, and without hesitation, left the office.

Daisy had broken the news firmly and killed any sign of complaint stone dead. Ruth thought she would do well to walk in Daisy's shoes in the future. But she couldn't help thinking she'd given Peggy another reason to dislike her.

Chapter Nine

September–October 1914

Ruth was at work bright and early on the Tuesday morning. Even so, she walked into her new office to find the lads sat at their desks watching Mr Routledge, who was talking to a woman she hadn't met before. The silence was – surprising. Ruth hadn't heard the cash office so quiet.

She walked in, smiling. 'Good morning, Mr Routledge,' she said, and turned her eyes towards the woman standing beside him and nodded.

'Right, then, it's time for formal introductions now that you're both here.' He introduced Ruth first, followed by the woman standing beside him. 'This is Miss Molly Delaney. We are very pleased to get her. She's just moved to Stoke from Liverpool where she worked in the offices of the Liverpool Corporation Tramways. You'll be able to tell us how we're performing from what you know, Miss Delaney.'

Molly grinned. 'I'm used to doing all sorts where I come from and I'm glad I got this job.'

Ruth, surprised by Molly's accent, had to concentrate very hard to understand her new colleague.

'I'm from Liverpool. Probably take a while before yer can understand me. That's why I'm best working in the office rather than on the actual tram. I came from County Mayo with my husband when we got married, so when I get excited, you will hear a mixture of Scouse and Irish.'

'I'm sure we'll get used to it, Miss Delaney. After all, our own Potteries dialect can be very difficult to understand. Miss Delaney, you can work with Mr Wilson and you, Ruth, can work with Mr Smith. Pick up everything you can about how things are done, where things are kept. Everything.'

The men all got to their feet. 'Why don't I have a young lady to look after, Mr Routledge?' asked Tom, with his lips turned down at the corners.

'If we can find one before you leave, Mr Walton, I will likely be as pleased as you. Mr Bertram is promoted to senior cashier and will supervise the operation of the office. Everyone else will be new and this department is the most important in the company. Mr Bertram's experience will be invaluable to you all.'

'Congratulations, Brian,' said Dickie, reaching out to shake his hand.

'The gentleman in the corner, Mr Blakeman, is the wages clerk and also responsible for payment of suppliers. The gentleman next to him, Mr Wainwright, will help Mr Blakeman in the wages department. Mr Degg, who is not here, has been put in charge of what we call the "milk run". That covers the collection and delivery of cash and other items, including tickets to the depots and collection of cash from the trams as required.

'Now, Mr Wainwright, you have worked here for three years as an office boy and latterly you have taken on more responsibility. This is now your chance to further develop your skills. I'll leave you to organise the details, Mr Bertram, and then we can get to work.'

Ruth was thrilled at the opportunity, but as it came closer to dinnertime she was relieved when Brian said she could have her lunch from one o'clock until two with Molly for this week. He winked when he said it because Peggy always had twelve o'clock until one. It was good to know that she wasn't the only one to feel the sharpness of Peggy's tongue.

—

Ruth was sitting at the kitchen table practising her shorthand. She had been told that it was like any language. If you don't use it, you forget. She knew that Carla, Bertie and their parents tried to speak German at home in private for the same reason. They had always done this since she had known them.

Father and Frank had a cricket match that afternoon. They didn't play competitive matches on Sundays, but they allowed friendly matches against other local teams. Ruth doubted very much that her competitive father and brother treated any match as friendly. This afternoon it had been showery and about half past four Ruth heard the back door go and Father walked in.

'Did you win?'

'Nah, the rain stopped the match. I doubt there'll be much cricket left this season, and whether there'll be any cricket next year's anybody's guess.'

'Where's Frank?'

'I left him talking to the captain of the other side. I don't know if Joan and him will call in, but I think not as Mrs Clement has got the kids and Frank and Joan will have a full innings to themselves.'

'Father, don't be so coarse.'

'When you're married with kids, you take the opportunity when it comes.'

'So, was I a rained-off cricket match?'

'You might well have been. It's not for me to say.'

Father and daughter laughed.

'Have you had your tea?'

'Yes, it seemed such a shame not to, as two of the wives had made a lovely spread. Joan stayed up at the pavilion, helping to clear up and do the dishes. I think you'll be the only one eating tonight, Ruth.' Father went to the kitchen and drank a mug of water and came back. 'I was talking to our wicketkeeper.'

'You mean the man that cuts the grass?'

'No, you know who I mean, the bloke with the big gloves on.'

Ruth like to tease her father about cricket. She understood the rules and actually quite liked to watch, but only when the weather was nice.

'As I was saying, Greville told me the bosses have agreed to let Bertie return to work tomorrow. I think somebody from the company was seeing him today. Greville said that he doesn't know what sort of reception the lad'll get. A lot of the men'll probably not speak to him, but I'll keep an eye on him.'

'I'm popping round to see Carla to tell her about my promotion to cashier. Is it all right to mention Bertie?'

'No, Ruthie, best leave it until she tells you – we dunner want them to think we've been talking about them.'

—

Ruth and Molly split their time with Jim, Dickie and Tom, checked and tidied cupboards and, importantly, learned how to deal with the steady stream of cash passing through the office.

Jim, Dickie and Tom left the PTC on Tuesday, 15 September, after a little congratulatory party in the cash office – no alcoholic beverages, only sandwiches, and two enormous cakes made by Pearl. When asked where she managed to lay her hands on the quantity of ingredients needed, Pearl said, 'It's best not to ask.'

These men weren't the first to go from the PTC and probably wouldn't be the last. Ruth watched as they moved around the people who came to see them off. Watching their faces changing, she thought it was only just sinking in. It may have been a party to everyone, but to those leaving, it was all too real.

Dickie and Tom saw her looking at them and came over.

'I'll miss you two,' she said, smiling. 'I know people have to fight, but I'll be sorry to see you go. Do you know where you're heading for tomorrow?'

'We've got to report to Cannock Chase. It's a big camp, still in Staffordshire, but in the south, near to Birmingham. That's all we know.'

Jim left his goodbye to Ruth to the very end. They walked towards each other, meeting somewhere in the middle of the room.

'So, Ruth, we meet to say our goodbyes. Who'd have thought it? When I think back to those days we had not so long ago?'

'We just weren't the right people for each other, were we?'

Jim flushed.

'Once you're in uniform, the women will come flocking.'

He grinned. 'Of course they will.'

His bottom lip quivered, and Ruth realised he wasn't joking. He was saying things that people like her expected him to say. But it wasn't the real him yet. She felt a tear run down her cheek and quickly snatched it away.

He kissed her hand in one of those bold, flamboyant gestures of his. She didn't pull away.

Then they were gone. Life at the PTC would be very different without them.

–

Daisy and Mr Routledge had been busy. A third cashier, Madge Butler, started towards the end of September. She'd worked at the Co-op cash room so was acquainted with handling cash and paperwork.

Daisy got a newly qualified shorthand typist from the class at the Wedgwood Institute. Iris Philpot looked even younger than she was. Ruth had a quiet word with Cissie to keep an eye on things in case Peggy took it into her head to bully the girl.

For the first time in PTC history, female staff at the head office outnumbered the men.

On the whole, there was great camaraderie between them all. Lots of banter going on at dinnertime and, as many of them were single young women, the talk of men was high on the agenda. For many, it helped to take their minds off the danger their loved ones were facing while for others it was showing them a new kind of friendship away from the home.

Chapter Ten

December 1914

It had been three months since the women cashiers had started and they had settled in. Brian was a good boss, and they all worked well together. The one thing that had changed was their relationship with the depot clerks.

Until now, the clerks in the cash office and the depot clerks had always been men. Along with Brian and Henry, it had been a proper boys' club with plenty of banter. Since the cashiers had left for the war, the depot clerks rarely came to Stoke unless they had to. The clerks didn't like having their mistakes pointed out by a woman. Only Andrew, the Stoke depot clerk, seemed to accept them.

It came to a head when Molly found mistakes on the cash sheets for Goldenhill. Dennis Laycock, the depot clerk there, made it plain he didn't like the idea of women working and resented them pointing out any errors in his work. It culminated when Molly returned several cash sheets to Goldenhill, which contained many errors. Dennis must have caught the next tram out of the depot and came into the office with all guns blazing.

'What is the meaning of this? Where's Mrs Delaney?'

Molly stood up. 'I'm Mrs Delaney, I returned your sheets, Mr Laycock.' Molly stared him straight in the eyes.

'You had no right to. There's nowt wrong with them sheets. I can understand them.'

'Mr Laycock, I've been doing this work in Liverpool for the last two years. I know mistakes when I see them.'

'I told everyone it was a silly idea to employ women.'

Molly said nothing.

'You aren't used to figures and you burst into tears if anyone speaks to you.'

Molly still said nothing.

Dennis was catching his breath when Mr Routledge and Brian entered the office.

'What is the meaning of all this shouting. Calm down, please,' ordered Mr Routledge. He called Molly into his office along with Brian and Mr Laycock. A few moments later Molly walked out and returned to her desk, her demeanour clearly indicating she didn't want to talk.

Raised voices continued for a few minutes and then the door opened and the three men emerged.

Mr Laycock had to have the final word and spoke up making sure everyone heard him. 'Mr Routledge, if you employed men like you should, it would've been sorted out. Two minutes and a fag's all it'd take. Conner speak to women. That's all I'm saying.'

Molly rose from her seat and said in a steady voice making sure everyone could hear. 'If I'd have been a man I'd have flattened you. It's your lucky day. Good day, Mr Laycock.'

Mr Laycock's mouth fell open, as did Ruth's, and she quickly smothered a laugh.

Mr Routledge apologised to Molly in particular and assured all the cashiers that they were doing a fine job, but perhaps it would be better in the future if Brian dealt with all the depot clerks.

'I'm sorry Mr Routledge, but I disagree. Mr Laycock will feel he's won and that wouldn't be right,' said Ruth.

A clearly embarrassed Mr Routledge quickly assessed the situation and realised that this wasn't the time or place for a battle with anybody.

—

It was getting closer to Christmas and the cashiers suggested to Mr Routledge they would like to put a small Christmas tree in the office and maybe a few decorations, which they would pay for themselves. They just wanted a bit of colour to lift their spirits. After a few days and no doubt several discussions, it was agreed that they could put up a small tree and a handful of decorations. Madge seemed to have persuaded Mr Routledge that it would be a good idea. So, for the first time in its history, the PTC offices had their Christmas tree.

Madge made the decorations after work, and the following morning, Brian came into the office and exclaimed, 'Bloody hell. It looks like Burton & Dunn's in here.'

'Away with yer, Brian. It is nice, and what we agreed,' said Madge.

'Next you'll be wanting curtains up at the windows and antimacassars on the chairs.'

Molly took the opportunity. 'That's a good idea, Brian. Will you suggest it to Mr Routledge or should I?'

'They'll be better next year.' Madge beamed. 'Just supposing there is one,' she added.

Mr Routledge raised his eyebrows. 'That's enough, ladies. Leave poor Brian alone.' Turning to Brian, Mr Routledge said, 'I wouldn't argue with them any more. I should think a married man would know better.' Turning back to the women, he continued. 'Ladies, it is very nice and is in keeping with the sentiments of this time of the year. Miss Butler has done a splendid job. Now, it's time we started work for the day.'

–

December was a bitter month, and today was no different. It had been snowing off and on, probably more on than off. Trams made their way through the towns more slowly than usual. Ruth kept her eyes fixed on the window, hoping the snow would get no worse. Moorland Road was quite steep for trams and the snow-covered lines made it doubly so. She certainly didn't want to walk through this sort of weather and was glad to reach the end of her journey without mishap.

As usual, she got off the tram at Park Road to find Walter waiting for her. She smiled her relief that she could hold on to him to avoid skating along the snow-laden pavements in a most unseemly manner. He hooked his arm in hers and they started off, asking each other about their day.

There was a loud clash of metal hitting something hard behind them. Ruth and Walter stopped in their tracks and turned to look back. A car had hit a motorcycle and stopped a few yards away. The rider was lying on his side, not moving. Ruth's heart was in her mouth as she followed Walter to the man on the ground, who was now trying to move.

Ruth dropped beside Walter and, to her utter shock, discovered the man was none other than Stan Bristow from work, Peggy Thompson's young man. He was groaning and holding his leg.

'Stan! Are you all right? Does it hurt?'

When Walter glanced at her with a puzzled frown, Ruth explained Stan worked in the garage at the PTC.

'Can you sit up, Stan?' Ruth needed to hear him say something – anything to show he wasn't in shock.

'Bloody hellfire!' came the answer as Stan attempted to sit upright.

'Careful, Stan – that's my sister you're talking to.'

'Sorry, mate.' He turned to Ruth, saying, 'I'm sorr... Ruth!'

She nodded.

'Let's see if we can get you up. Get hold of him under his arm, Ruth, and let him lean on your shoulder so you can take some of the weight.'

As Stan got slowly to his feet, he groaned again, but he made it. Now his face was closer, she could see he was pale – probably caused by the shock. He was wearing a thick coat with leather pads at his elbows and on his head, a cap tied on with a scarf.

Once on his feet, Stan's first thought was for his motorcycle. He struggled towards it to find the handlebar slightly bent and a few scratches, but nothing too worrying. As soon as Stan could move, the car driver handed Walter his card. 'Be a good chappie and give the young man my card. Got to go. Mater's waiting for me to come home. Toodle-oo.'

Ruth stared after him.

'He left you his card, and now he's buggered off,' Walter said. 'Talked to me as if I was a lackey.'

Although Ruth couldn't feel Stan's body through the layers of clothes he was wearing, she felt a warmth emanating from him. A sudden spark of something. It made her jump. Despite the darkness obscuring their colour, his eyes drew her in.

He tried to lift the motorcycle on his own, but failed.

'Don't do anything, Stan. You need to be careful.'

'Hey, mate. Let me help,' said Walter. He picked it up and held it upright while Stan hobbled around it, inspecting it closely.

'I'll have to get it down to the garage. I conner see anything at the moment. It's too dark.'

'I'll take the motorcycle. Let Ruth help you.'

Stan put his arm across Ruth's shoulders and the group made their way slowly to Hesse's Stores, following Walter and the bike. Mrs Hesse let them use the telephone to call Stan's father or at least call the doctor who lived in the next cottage. Mrs Hesse insisted they wait there and made them a cup of tea. Walter went home to tell Father what had happened, and Ruth needed to pay a visit to the privy.

—

Ruth returned from the privy, blowing on her hands to keep them warm, just as Carla came in, shouting, '*Ich bin zu Hause, Mutter. Das bin nur ich. Die Schnee wird immer schlimmer... Wer bist sie?...* Who are you?' Her voice sounded panicky. On hearing Carla, Stan's eyebrows lifted.

'Don't worry, it's only Stan from work. He's had an accident on his motorcycle in the snow. We're waiting for his father to collect him.'

'I thought Father Christmas had delivered me a late present,' said Carla flirtingly, surprising Ruth.

They all chatted in the back room, where Mr Hesse joined them. An hour later, a knock came on the shop door and Mr Hesse let in an older version of Stan, followed by Walter.

'I think my son's here. Stanley?'

'Yes, do come in.'

Stan was sitting on a chair in the corner.

'Now then, what's been going on?'

'Came off me bike, Father. A car hit me. Dunner think there's any damage done,' Stan said. He'd taken off his scarf and cap and now looked more like the Stan she saw in the workshop.

'I dunner care about the bike, lad. I'm talking about yersen.'

'I'll mend. I'm indestructible.'

Mr Bristow grunted, clearly not believing a word Stan had said. 'And when do you intend to introduce me to your friends here?'

Ruth smothered a laugh, embarrassed for Stan, whose father had determined to take charge, whatever Stan's views were.

Stan cleared his throat. 'Miss Ruth Latham, who works at the PTC. These good people are Mr and Mrs Hesse and their daughter, Carla. This is their shop.' Stan continued, 'I'd like to introduce my father, Jim Bristow.'

'Good evening everybody. Pleased to meet you. Thank you for helping my son.'

Stan turned to Carla. 'I'm sorry I surprised you, Miss Hesse. What were you saying when you came in – it was German wasn't it.'

Carla nodded. 'Nowt special. I was just telling Mother I was home, and the snow was getting worse. Then I asked who you were.'

Stan laughed.

'Everything appears to be fine now. That young chap, Walter, is waiting with the motorcycle – we'd better be going,' said Mr Bristow after several minutes of conversation.

Immediately, Stan took Ruth's hand. 'Thank you for your help today. I don't know what I would've done without you. All of you,' he said, nodding to Mr and Mrs Hesse.

'Thank you.'

Stan gave Ruth one last smile before he left.

–

Outside, Walter was waiting beside Mr Bristow's van and, between him and Stan, the motorcycle was loaded onto the vehicle. Stan and his father bade everyone goodbye as the van trundled away.

Ruth and Walter continued on their way, each lost in private thoughts. As they neared the gates of number 32, Walter spoke.

'You've never mentioned him before, Ruth. He seems like a decent bloke.'

'I don't know him that well. I've only spoken to him a few times in passing. He's walking out with Peggy Thompson – or so I've been told.'

'I hope he knows what he's taking on. She can be very persistent. Remember how she was with me when we were at school? Mind you, I think he likes you.'

Ruth, convinced her cheeks couldn't get any redder, stopped walking, hoping that by waiting a few minutes, the redness would die down.

'How could he? I told you, we've only spoken occasionally.'

'That's all it takes, my girl. You mark my words.'

—

On the journey into work the following morning, Ruth thought about Stan and wondered if he had recovered after last night's accident. She would check at lunchtime. What's more, she'd have news that Pearl wouldn't know.

When she walked into the reception area, Pearl greeted her.

'Good morning. I do like it when it's snowed like this. It looks so clean out there. Hides all the dirt and grime.'

'Morning, Pearl. I agree, although it makes life difficult underfoot.'

'Did you see Stan's motorcycle isn't in its usual place? He had an accident on the way home last night. He's all right. He's at work, but I bet the motorcycle damage upset him. I heard that you and your brother helped him and that he waited for his father in Hesse's Stores.

Ruth's shoulders dropped. How did this woman manage to get all the news?

'I think, my dear, it might be a good idea to keep out of Peggy's way for a bit. When she finds out, she won't be too pleased with you. Administering to her young man and spending part of the evening with him when she only lives a few hundred yards away.'

'Thank you, Pearl, for letting me know.'

'Always pleased to help.'

'You won't tell anyone else, will you?'

'My lips are sealed. I know when to keep a secret.'

Ruth made her way to the office, shaking her head. How *did* Pearl find out all that detail? One day, I'll beat her to it.

Surprisingly, the morning went by without any contact with Peggy. Just recently, she'd taken to sending Iris into the cash office with any completed typing. Ruth thought Peggy must have taken heed of the advice given to her by Daisy and Mr Routledge, or simply Peggy was enjoying having Iris to do her bidding.

Dinnertime arrived, and Ruth decided to check on Stan. The one thing that could be said about the engineers' shop was it was warm due to the forge. She scurried across the yard and opened the office door.

'Good afternoon, Miss Ruth, what can I do for you?'

'Good afternoon, Norman. Would it be possible for me to have a word with Stan?'

'Aye, lass, help yerself. Do you want a cup of tea?'

Ruth wondered whether she should risk a cup of Norman's legendary tea. He had a large metal teapot which he filled first thing in the morning, adding tea leaves and water as necessary during the day, and kept warm on the forge. By the day's end, it had steeped so long it would make a drinker's eyes water. But she liked Norman, and so not to hurt his feelings, she said that would be lovely.

He got a tin mug off the shelf, checked inside it, and poured the tea. 'Do you want three or four sugars?'

'I think one will do for me, thank you.' While Norman was pouring the tea, he informed her that three or four was the usual added by most visitors. Some said it brought out the flavour. He handed Ruth the mug, and she walked carefully into the engineering shop and over to Stan.

'Good afternoon, Stan.'

'Hello, Ruth. What are yer doing here?'

'I thought I'd come across and ask how you were feeling after last night's excitement.'

'I'm okay. Nothing worse than a couple of bruises. I wish I could say that about my motorcycle. She'll need a new head stock and bearings.'

'That sounds quite a big job. Is it?'

'The parts'll be expensive but I'll do all the work meself. I'll get that toff to pay for the parts. Probably got more money than sense any road, driving that bloody great Lanchester.'

Stan wiped his hands on a piece of cloth and Ruth continued to drink her tea.

'That's a pretty colour.'

'What, the tea?'

'No, you nitwit, your blouse. We get little colour in here except for red and cream. What colour do you call that?'

'It's lemon.'

'I have a mind to use that colour when I paint me sidecar.'

'What's a sidecar?'

'It's a way of carrying an extra passenger or two on a motorcycle. It has windows all round. You're protected from the weather and the wind so you can wear normal clothes. I've built all the frameworks and me dad built the body. It's not ready for use yet.'

Ruth felt the effects of the heat and the strong tea, and found it difficult to concentrate on the details.

'Perhaps when it's finished, I can have a look at this contraption?'

His eyebrows rose. 'Er... yes, Ruth. That's a good idea. You'll have to wait until the better weather comes along because I'll have to get used to riding with a sidecar. But

I'll hold you to that. Once it's finished, I'll take you out for the day and you can tell me what yer think.'

'I'll look forward to it.' She finished the rest of her tea, or at least the tea that she could drink before she encountered a heap of tea leaves. No strainer was used in the engineers' workshop; that was for sissies.

—

It was just before three o'clock when Ruth decided it was time to visit the privy. She met Peggy in the corridor. She was about to say good afternoon, but Peggy didn't give her a chance to speak.

'What were you doing across at the engineers' shop at dinnertime? I saw you, there's no point in denying it, you were there for nearly half an hour.'

So Peggy was checking up on her. Ruth tried to reply. 'I... er, I went to ask—'

'I heard you'd had some excitement with my Stan last night and that you were making another date with him today.'

Ruth was truly surprised and shocked. She was about to explain when Peggy started again.

'Now look here, my girl, you keep your hands to yourself. Stan's my man. I don't know what went on last night, but I'll find out. He can't keep anything from me. When I know the truth, I'll deal with you.'

Ruth had almost forgotten the reason she had been in the corridor, but while she was sitting on the privy, she realised Peggy didn't really know about the accident. So, Pearl enjoyed a gossip, but knew when to keep quiet. Ruth realised she couldn't warn Stan, but hoped he would survive Peggy's wrath.

That night, Ruth chatted to Walter about the events of the day. He found the whole thing funny.

'Peggy'll be spitting feathers. I'll say one thing for her. Once she's decided you're her man, she'll defend you with the ferocity of a lioness.'

'She was quite frightening,' Ruth admitted. 'It took me right back to our schooldays.'

'You're a grown woman now. Three years' difference when you're ten years old is a lot, but three years' difference when you're twenty is nothing. She won't dip your ponytail in the inkwell and if she does, then I'll have a word with her like I used to do at school.' He laughed.

'You were just as frightened of her as me.'

'Boys had good cause. Peggy wasn't above telling lies. She knew she could make boys do just what she wanted. Offer them something and then take it away. If they demanded what she had promised, she'd tell the teacher the lad had asked her to do something inappropriate.'

'You mean…'

He nodded. 'Some lads paid a lot for a quick fumble.'

Ruth pulled a face. They both contemplated what they had just heard.

'On another subject,' said Ruth, 'Stan and I got talking about his motorcycle and he told me he was fitting a sidecar so he could take a passenger out with him.'

'Yes, sis.'

'He asked me if I'd like a trip out after he finishes the bike, and I agreed.'

'I told you he was interested.'

'Oh, I don't think it means that. He likes his motorcycle and probably is pleased somebody was showing interest.'

'You're not to go out with him in the winter on his motorcycle, mind.'

'No, it's not finished yet.'

'So my little sister's got some competition, then?'

Ruth's chin went up. 'Oh, you mean Peggy. I'll sort her out when I need to.'

'No, sis, I did not mean Peggy. That's the easy bit. Your problem is going to be coming between Stan and his motorcycle.'

—

Ruth planned to tell Stan about Peggy's reaction the following morning, but she met Mr Routledge on Bowstead Street and they walked in together.

The morning dragged by and every time the door opened, she expected an irate Peggy to march in, but it was an exceptionally quiet morning.

Ruth ran over to the engineers' shop at one o'clock and asked Norman to keep a lookout for Peggy or Mr Routledge. She went straight to see Stan.

Ruth's words tumbled out. 'I'm sorry if I got you in trouble yesterday. Peggy caught me unawares and got hold of the wrong end of the stick. I couldn't get down to see you before you went last night, so I hope it wasn't too bad for you.'

'Hey, slow down, Ruth. You needn't worry about Peggy. We've been over since before Christmas. Only she can't seem to understand it and is determined to get me back. Last night I called in on the way home and told her again we were finished. After a lot of crying and ranting, I think she finally got the message.'

He grinned at her and she couldn't help but grin back.

'Are you still interested in going for that ride on the motorcycle when it's ready?'

'Oh yes. I'm looking forward to it.'

'Then things have worked out the way I want them to.'

Ruth made her way back to the office, trying to hide the grin that had spread from ear to ear. She had a lot to think about.

—

Work had been busy since Christmas and Ruth was surprised how tired she felt. Today was New Year's Eve, and she made her way to work as normal. She walked into the cash office to find only Brian in there.

'Where's everybody?'

'I think Molly and Marge are in with the typists. Peggy came in a few minutes ago and nodded at them and as it wasn't starting time, they all went out.'

Ruth couldn't miss out on what was going on. She opened the typing-room door and walked in. There were Peggy, Pearl, Cissie, Molly, Iris and Madge standing in a huddle. As Peggy's eyes took in Ruth's appearance, her voice became louder.

'So you see, girls, you need to keep yer eyes on yer blokes if yer wants to keep them. Men aren't safe being let out on their own. There are women who don't give a toss about taking somebody else's bloke. They get flattered. That's what's happened to my Stan.' She waited for the gossiping to die down. 'That's why I've told him it's over between us.'

To give Peggy credit, she never once mentioned Ruth's name, but her actions made it quite plain to everyone that it was Ruth she was talking about.

Ruth turned and left, followed by Molly and Madge. Molly leaned over and suggested a visit to the privy.

–

'Was that you Peggy was talking about?'

'Yes and no. As usual, she's only told half the story.'

'What happened?'

'On his way home, Stan had an accident. Nothing serious. Me and my brother were walking from the tram stop. We helped him – and that's it.'

'So you took him home and tucked him into bed and then kissed his wounds better?'

'Don't be daft, Molly. We sat and talked in my friend's kitchen with her parents there until Stan's father came in the van to take him home. Nothing more.'

'Hardly worth the drama.'

'Precisely, and for your information, Stan finished with her a while ago, but she won't accept it.'

'Saucy bitch wants us to think she finished with him. No girl likes to admit that a man's rejected her. Our Peggy has got a bit of a weak spot. I'll remember that.'

'There are always two sides to every story.'

Chapter Eleven

March 1915

By March 1915, many of the men who answered the call to arms in 1914 were now trained and in France awaiting action. The war in Flanders had ground to a halt in the winter. The front comprised a continuous line of trenches from the Channel to the Swiss border. Both sides facing each other and waiting for the next move.

On the home front, people were getting used to the war. The early optimism had given way to a sense of resignation and the famous 'It will be all over by Christmas,' was forgotten.

The anti-German feeling so prevalent at the start of the war had subsided somewhat. The numbers of interned men and women had stabilised and was now falling. After his brief internment, Bertie had returned to work. At the shop, Mr and Mrs Hesse and Carla kept the business going. Edith was at full term, but to her credit, she had worked in the shop until last week when Mrs Hesse insisted she took it easy for the last few weeks of the pregnancy.

Carla had become more reticent about leaving home outside of shop hours and always with the same excuses – her mother needed help, or she wasn't feeling up to it. It was understandable during the week. Now it seemed to spread to Sundays. Last week, Dottie had invited them for Sunday tea, but Carla had declined. Ruth was worried Carla might stop going out altogether.

On Sunday this week, Ruth was working, so her day off was Saturday. Before hostilities and even after Dottie's wedding, the three friends spent their Saturday afternoons in Hanley window shopping and then treated themselves to a cup of tea and a cake at the teashop in Parliament Row. But it hadn't seemed the same of late. There was always an excuse.

There was a knock at the back door. It was Dottie and Carla. After the greetings, they sat down at the kitchen table.

Both Ruth and Dottie talked at the same time. 'I've got some news...' They laughed and Ruth could see that Dottie was eager and so told her to go first.

Dottie didn't argue. 'Donald is home from France! He arrived yesterday. When I got home from work, I had the shock of my life. It turns out that he's been posted to the 2nd North Staffs regiment and is now a sergeant in the regular army for the duration. I am so proud of him.'

'That is good news. What does it mean?' asked Carla.

'We've had hardly any time to talk about it. He had to report to the barracks today. But best of all, he will get regular leave and the journey to Lichfield is short. Donald expects to be at home for the next two months. He has to learn how to ride a horse!'

'Why is that?'

They all burst into fits of laughter.

'I don't know, but he said it had got something to do with his posting.'

It was Ruth's turn for news. 'Frank and Joan have had a girl, six pound eight ounces. She gave birth on Thursday evening to Mary Louise Latham. Both of them are well. I popped up to see them this morning and she's beautiful.'

Carla grinned. 'I don't think it'll be long before Edith gives birth. She's enormous.'

They chatted away until almost teatime. How nice it was they all had some good news for a change. The mental picture of Donald on a horse made Ruth giggle.

—

As Ruth turned the corner from Bowden Street into Dartmouth Street she was greeted by an excited looking Carla. 'Edith had the baby at ten o'clock this morning. She had a long labour, but he was a good weight at eight pounds, ten ounces. He's fine but Edith is very tired. I hope I don't have a time like that when it's my turn.'

'Congratulations, Carla. Let me know when I can come to see him. What are they going to call him?'

'Luther Clement Hesse. Both Edith and Bertie wanted a German and English name to show they're united even if their countries were at war. It was a nice gesture, but I'm not sure Edith's mother will think very much of it.'

It was later that evening when Carla came to see Ruth. She had the house to herself. Walter was on afternoons and Father had gone for a pint.

'I asked Edith and she said call around tomorrow after work to see Luther. She might have caught up with her sleep by then, about seven o'clock. Will you tell Dottie?'

'Of course, I'll go down to Mintons and meet her when they knock-off at midday. Don't want to disturb Dottie if Donald is back home.'

'No, we don't want to do that. Do you think Dottie wants to have a baby?' asked Carla out of the blue.

'I think so. The war started in such a rush many couples must be in that position. I bet people are thankful for the period of leave they get after training.'

'I feel a little bit guilty. Of the three of us, I thought Dottie would have had a baby as soon as she could.'

'We don't know they haven't been trying and she just wasn't ready.'

'Ruth, will you have children?'

'Carla, that's a leading question. I can't say I have any strong thoughts about it. Finding a man you want to marry needs to come first. Me and you are the youngsters of our families, so we have had no experience of babies, but I am a bit surprised because Dottie being the eldest will have had plenty. Perhaps it has put her off. All I do know is what will be, will be.'

—

Ruth waited by the main gates of Mintons when the hooters started to sound all over Stoke announcing the end of the half-day's work on Saturday. The gates opened and a rush of people flooded out. Women in turbans, wrap-around pinafores and white dust on their faces and men with flat caps, jackets and white dust on *their* faces.

Carla soon appeared and Ruth called her over. They walked back to Campbell Road. Dottie seemed subdued and had insisted that Ruth came in for a drink. She was expecting Donald back from the barracks in the middle of the afternoon.

Ruth gave her face a quick swill to get rid of any dust on the surface, removed the turban and pinafore, brushing her arms down at the same time.

'I was going to push a note under the door, but I decided to see you.' Ruth told Dottie her news.

'Have you seen the little man yet?'

'No, Carla is arranging for me to go round this evening. We both wanted to give Edith as much chance as possible to rest.'

Dottie went quiet and seemed to spend several minutes looking into her cup of tea as if composing herself. 'I've got some news for you, Ruth. The 2nd North Staffs are based in India at the moment. They have been there since before the war. Donald has been told that they're likely to stay there for the duration. Once Donald goes abroad he will not return to Britain until the war ends or the regiment returns.'

'What do you think about that?'

'At first I was happy as there's no fighting in India and I was pleased that Donald would be in a safer place, but then I realised that it takes a month for letters to travel one way.' Dottie stopped talking and her lips quivered. 'We are trying for a baby, but nothing has happened yet and if he goes to India then nothing will happen until lord knows when.'

'Oh I see.'

Now she knew why Dottie looked so upset and her heart went out to her friend.

'There's more. Because he's now a sergeant he's entitled to married quarters and he can take me with him – at no cost. There would be no rent to pay and we would be together when he wasn't on patrol. We would even have a housekeeper.'

'That's the solution. You've got nothing tying you to Stoke. Your parents would miss you as would me and Carla, but you would be together. That's the most important thing, isn't it?'

'I don't think it's a good idea. There's the distance; the climate is hot and dusty or humid and wet. There are snakes, spiders and man-eating tigers, all of which can kill you. I'm not suitable for a wife in the army. All the other women would be posh and I'd be totally out of place, even though Donald doesn't think so, as there are plenty of NCO's with their wives out there. But you'd have to mix with the toffs and they would make fun of me.'

'Sounds as if you've made your mind up then.'

'But Donald wants me to go. He thinks it might be a good future for us. Any children would be educated in the same school as officers' children. They would get fresh air and have a lot more freedom than they would get in these dirty streets. But he's said it's up to me.'

'I see your problem. When do you have to make a decision?'

'He's due to leave here on 18 May; he will get twenty-one days leave starting 28 April. They would need to know by 12 April so that my passage could be organised and arrangements made at the other side. I'd travel on a P&O liner to Bombay, probably starting in May. It's normal for wives and families to travel on commercial liners because the troopships carry men, horses and other supplies. So I will have to travel on my own. I've never been farther than Tunstall and they expect me to set off on my own to travel halfway around the world, even if I wanted to that would frighten me, more than the man-eating tigers!'

'Can I tell Carla or is it a secret?'

'Tell Carla but although my mother knows, it's best you say nothing to nobody else.'

Chapter Twelve

7–10 May 1915

Ruth and Carla had arranged a shopping trip to Hanley on Ruth's Saturday off, to get some material to make a couple of outfits. She was keen for Carla to accompany her as she valued her opinion and also she wanted to persuade her to leave the house.

The weather was nice and fresh when Ruth started to walk down to the shop. Her heart sank when she saw Carla waiting for her at the shop door. Ruth knew what this meant.

'Hello, Carla.' Ruth could see her friend was in some distress.

'I won't be going shopping this morning, Ruth. Mother thinks it's too risky. Have you heard about that *Lusitania* being sunk, yesterday?'

'Yes, but I don't see how that affects our shopping expedition. I was looking forward to it.'

'I'm sorry, Ruth, but you know what it was like when we went to Longton Park. I don't think I could bear something like that happening again.'

'You sure you won't reconsider?'

'Yes, Ruth, I am.'

Ruth went shopping on her own, She found a bolt of material in a beautiful lemon colour, similar to her blouse, and treated herself to sufficient for an outfit and the suitable accessories to enhance it. The other outfit would be made from a dark blue material and would be suitable for work at any time of the year.

Ruth caught the tram and settled herself into a seat for the ride home. She was glad that Carla wasn't with her as everybody seemed to be talking about the sinking and what they had to say wasn't very complimentary.

–

When Ruth arrived at Dartmouth Street, she decided not to mention the conversations she had heard on the tram. She was surprised to see groups of people hanging around and talking. The shop was open as normal, but there were no customers when she stepped inside.

'I've got the materials and the pattern for the dresses, but before we look at it, what sort of day have you had?'

'Not very good. The shop's been ever so quiet. A couple of blokes came in at dinnertime shouting horrible things. They left. Mother stopped Father from following them – it was too risky. Walter spent the afternoon here. He's only just gone home. If I was you, I'd keep away from here. If anything happens, a mob won't stop to ask your nationality.'

'That won't happen. I'll use the alley at the back. Nothing's going to stop me from seeing my friend.'

'Let's have a look at the material you've bought. I'm sure Mother'll let us use her sewing machine.'

Ruth opened the parcel and spread out the material on the counter and the two of them concentrated on what was required, uninterrupted by customers.

—

Saturday night was always noisy, especially when the pubs closed. During the week, most people were too tired to be out at a late hour, having started work at six o'clock in the morning. Saturday was a different matter. No work the following day, money in their pockets, and extra time in bed on the Sunday. Even so, by midnight, everything was usually back to normal. The cacophony of loud voices, heavy boots pounding the pavement, shouts and barking dogs had faded into silence.

Ruth lay in her bed, biting her nails, still worrying about Carla. Carla had tried to show interest in the dress material but Ruth detected a difference in her. She couldn't get to sleep.

Walter and Father were still downstairs, probably talking about that day's cricket match. Frank, Walter and Bertie all played when they could. Although Walter and Bertie were not as good as Frank, they usually played for the second eleven. Frank was 'a useful batsman and a competent fast bowler', according to *The Sentinel*. Now there were three little ones to think about. His responsibilities might prevent him from spending as much time out of the house. Joan would see to that.

Bertie may have the same problem with Edith now that they had two-month-old Luther. Edith didn't like to spend too much time on her own at the best of times. What must she be thinking? Her marriage to a German man meant Luther was also German. No wonder Carla's anxieties were beginning to tell.

Ruth gritted her teeth. Now she had even more people to worry about. She tossed and turned, in two minds whether to join the men downstairs. Even talking about cricket would be better than lying there, staring at the ceiling.

She turned over and covered her eyes, hoping that sleep wasn't too far away.

The thud of wood on metal followed by the unmistakable sound of breaking glass woke Ruth. She jumped out of bed and ran downstairs.

'What's going on?'

Silence.

She could see no one. She grabbed her coat and hurried to the front door. Father was standing outside the shop talking to Mr Hesse. They had pickaxe handles in their hands and were acting as if the war had already reached them. Walter appeared with Carla and Mrs Hesse and Ruth hurried towards them. 'What on earth's happened?'

'Someone broke our shop windows and scattered stuff across the street... it's all ruined.' Carla broke off and burst into tears. Her mother did her best to comfort her.

'They say it's really bad,' murmured Walter. 'Mr Hesse's staying at the shop and so is Father. I'll join them later. We'll make sure everything is safe and keep a lookout for more trouble.' The group entered number 32 and Ruth closed the door.

'Edith and Luther weren't harmed, were they?' asked Ruth.

Before Walter had time to answer, Bertie, Edith and Luther entered the kitchen from the scullery. Luther was crying, and so was Edith. Bertie was grinding his teeth, his eyes stormy. 'If I catch them buggers what did this, I'll make them pay.'

'Steady, mate, that's what they want. It wouldn't do for a German lad to attack one of us.' Walter must have realised what he had said and quickly added, 'Not that we think of you as German. Who ever heard of a German playing cricket?' He patted Bertie on the back to make light of it.

Bertie nodded back, then turned to his mother. 'I'll be at the shop. You'll be all right with Ruth for now.' He kissed his wife on the cheek.

Edith appeared to have calmed down, but Luther was still crying. *Probably needs feeding*, thought Ruth. There would be no more sleep that night.

'Come with me. I'll boil the kettle.'

Mrs Hesse didn't say a word, just gently cried, mopping the tears from her face with a pretty lace handkerchief.

—

Ruth lay on her bed thinking about the night's events. She'd never thought the people both she and Carla had grown up with would do something so terrible. She hoped it was a group of drunken men, boisterous and fuelled by the day's gossip, rather than a more calculated individual.

With so many people to house overnight, Ruth had shared her single bed with Carla as they had done a number of times over the years. Ruth and Carla comforted each other and no words were spoken.

—

Ruth sat up. Unaware of the time, she rubbed her eyes. There was no Carla. A quick swill of water on her face made her feel brighter, and she descended the stairs to find a pale-faced Carla sitting at the table.

'Morning, Carla. Did you get much sleep?'

'Not really, but you did.'

'I'm so sorry, I just lay down for a few minutes and then I was gone. Where is everybody?'

'Your father's gone to talk to one of his mates. Walter's taken my father to report what's happened to the police, and your Frank has come down and is helping Bertie guard the shop. Mother's there too, trying to tidy up. Edith has taken Luther to her mother's.'

Ruth grabbed a quick cup of tea and a piece of bread with a smear of jam.

'Right, let's go along to see if we can do anything.'

–

They went out of the front door so they could see what the shop looked like. A man was boarding up the windows, whistling. He sounded a happy soul, but stopped when he saw Ruth and Carla.

'Don't worry, you two, it'll be safe soon. I didn't know Gunter had got two such pretty daughters.'

'Oh, I'm not...'

'Good morning, Mr Yearsley,' replied Carla, not stopping to talk, and continued into the shop and through to the back room.

'Don't you like Mr Yearsley?' asked Ruth.

'No. He stares at me and makes me feel he's undressing me. It scares me.'

'Never met him before.'

'You've missed nowt.' Carla shuddered.

Ruth thought Carla sounded like a real Stokie, and so she should. She was born here. Ruth would defy anyone to suggest she had German in her.

Carla handed her a cup of tea and they stood talking about what had happened.

About half an hour later, Mr Yearsley appeared. 'There you are, my dears, all done. Let's hope these hotheads have had enough now. It's not right. You've lived here for such a long time.'

'Mother and Father won't be back for a while. Is there any message?'

'That cup of tea looks nice.'

'I'd offer you one, but it's the last of the tea. They scattered the tea everywhere like all the rest of the goods.'

'No need to bother, lass. Just tell thee father people are angry and everyone here about knows he's German. Best keep a low profile.'

Was that supposed to make them feel better? thought Ruth. He'd have been better keeping his mouth shut.

At that moment, Walter walked into the kitchen, still carrying his pickaxe handle. 'All finished, Mr Yearsley? I'll bid you good day,' and Walter herded him into the shop, closing the back-room door behind him.

Ruth shuddered. 'You're right – he makes me shudder too.'

Ruth and Walter walked slowly back to number 32.

'What do you think'll happen now?'

'Dunno, Ruth. The lads down at the Corner Pin were furious about the sinking.'

'Where did Father go this morning?'

'To see some lads from the cricket club to see if he could organise a rota of able-bodied men to keep an eye on the shop. He had some luck, but I suppose it depends on what the authorities do. We won't know that until they decide to tell us.'

'It's a mess, isn't it?'

'That's the problem with wars. Some lads on my shift are thinking of joining up. The army's sent men around asking for volunteers with mining experience – don't know why.'

'You won't volunteer, will you?' Ruth pleaded.

'No, sis, I'm staying put with what I know. Never wanted to be in the army or to fire a gun. It doesn't seem wise to start fighting trained men now. They need us down the pit. If the coal dunner come out, then the entire country, and the army grinds to a halt. I'm best staying doing what I do now.'

'Blowing things up, whether underground or on top, doesn't seem that safe to me.'

'Dunner worry, sis. I'm always careful – that's why they've given me the job.'

Later, when the family sat down for dinner, Walter told them that Hesse's Stores would be closed for a few days until they could see which way the land lay. The family would, hopefully, be found temporary lodgings until the matter was sorted.

–

On Monday morning, everybody in the offices was talking about the sinking of the *Lusitania*.

'What an awful thing to do,' stated Peggy in her usual way, when she returned some typing to Madge.

'The Germans had warned people travelling on British ships that they did so at their own risk. It said so in the newspapers,' replied Molly.

'But a passenger liner? The Germans must have known. I'd expect that from you. Your lot are all the same, Molly.'

This is going to be fun, thought Ruth. Peggy, who had an opinion on everything, had gone too far this time. Molly could look after herself.

'Because I'm Irish and a Catholic, I must be against the British. Is that what youse saying?'

'If the cap fits…'

There was silence. Peggy stormed out, presumably to the typing room, where Cissie and Iris were much more pliable and would never disagree with her.

Molly sat down. 'There you go, that's how you deal with the likes of her. She's no longer the school bully now.'

Ruth smirked and continued her work. When Mr Routledge returned to the office, everyone was working away quietly. He looked surprised.

Brian brought over a bank sheet. 'I've checked this sheet. Take Molly with you to count the cash. Better keep Peggy and Molly apart for the time being.' He winked at Ruth and gave a little smile.

—

That evening, Ruth left her desk to get ready for her journey home. They hadn't seen Peggy again, and either Cissie or Iris had returned their typing, much to Ruth's relief.

The sinking of the *Lusitania* reverberated throughout the country. In some cities, riots, fuelled by newspaper reports, had broken out. German-owned shops had windows broken. There was even a petition taken to the House of Commons asking for the interning of all 'enemy aliens' of military age in this country and measures about alien restriction orders on travelling, no doubt to ensure that the police could better keep them under surveillance. Bertie had been subjected to travel restrictions since last August and had to report to the police weekly.

Walter was waiting for Ruth when she got off the tram.

'Everything all right? Has something happened?'

'Just thought I'd walk you home. There are a couple of groups of men loitering on the other side of the street, opposite the shop.'

'Have you seen any of the Hesses?'

'The shop's closed. I called in after me shift finished and they were all sitting upstairs, in the dark looking scared. I don't blame them.'

—

Ruth prepared tea. Once the meal had been eaten, the talk inevitably returned to the war.

'Father, did Bertie go to work today?'

'Yes, Ruth, he did, or should I say he tried to. We had changed into our overalls and were walking to the mould makers' shop. No one we passed spoke to him. When we got to the shop, everyone ignored him. We normally help each other by getting a mix of plaster going for everybody what needs it. But nothing had been done. The foreman came in and asked why there was no work started. One man said that he wouldn't work with a German. The foreman ordered Bertie to go with him. Dunno know what was said, but the next thing we knew was Bertie walking across the yard in his outdoor clothes on his way home, I'll bet.'

'Did you see him when you called in at the shop?'

'No, Ruth, I assumed he was at work. Never asked,' replied Walter.

'The mood in the warehouse was pretty angry,' said Father. 'Most of the blokes were in favour of sending all Germans to internment camps. They said, "Get them out of the way so we can sleep soundly in our beds." Many men wanted to know how our men at the Front would feel if they knew the Germans were living at home in safety while they were fighting and dying for their country. I reckon by the weekend, if the government hasn't taken action, the men will do it for them.'

'I'll pop to see Carla and find out,' said Ruth.

—

Ruth put on her hat and coat and Walter slipped into his jacket, muffler and cap.

'Where are you going?'

'I'm coming with you to the shop to check they're all right.'

The pair of them left through the backyard and arrived in a few minutes at the back door of the shop. They knocked three times. Eventually, Carla pulled back the curtains in the room upstairs. Once she saw who it was, she came down and let them in. They went straight up the stairs to the family's living room. Sitting there were Mr and Mrs Hesse and Bertie. Ruth didn't ask, but assumed that Edith was with the baby, probably feeding him.

'Hello, everybody. We've come to see how you are.'

'We are doing very good, Walter,' replied Mr Hesse.

'Pour yourself a cup of tea – it's freshly made,' said Mrs Hesse.

Walter and Ruth recounted what Father had told them about the feelings at work.

Bertie was quiet while they spoke. He cleared his throat. 'I've made my last mould at Royal Edwards

Pottery. They've sacked me. The foreman told me that the company couldn't continue to have disruptions like this. Even though they'd spent a lot of money on my apprenticeship, it was nothing compared with what they could lose if the men decided to strike because of me. He said I should clock off and go home. Somebody'll settle up me wages.'

'And that was it?' asked Walter.

'I'll not find another job until this bloody war is over.'

The group sat in silence.

'I didn't think when the war started it would be like this. I've lived here all my life, and I was prepared to answer the call to fight for this country – my country. But it appears it's not my country after all. Mind you, if you believe what's said in the newspapers, it looks as though I'm going to be spending the rest of the war as a guest of His Majesty; I don't see how I can avoid internment. Because I am of fighting age, the German Army would certainly conscript me if I went there.'

'It doesn't look a lot better for us,' said Mr Hesse, shaking his head. 'The government will have to pay attention to public opinion and at the moment that opinion isn't favourable to any German. I'm over fifty-five and so I'm a candidate for repatriation under the current rules. If I'm repatriated, Mrs Hesse will have to go with me.'

'Do you think it'll come to that?' asked Ruth.

'They will certainly seek our repatriation if they've a mind to. But I am not concerned about that. We've been in this country for twenty-three years and I am sure that if we appeal against repatriation, they will find in our favour. We have a business and we are a burden to no one. It makes sense.'

'Let's hope it doesn't come to that, Mr Hesse. If it does, there's plenty of people around here who'll give you an excellent character reference. What about you, Carla?' asked Walter.

Carla looked down at her hands resting on the top of her lap. 'That's the unfair part. Because current legislation considers me British, I can't be repatriated. In fact, it would be nigh on impossible for me to gain entry to Germany. Whatever happens, we'll all be split up.'

Bertie chimed in. 'The funny thing is, Edith is now considered to be a German citizen because she is married to me and, of course, my little Luther is British by birth and German by parentage. I don't know how they would work that one out.'

Bertie said his goodbyes and left the room. Ruth thought it would be a good time for them to leave. She gave each of the Hesse family a hug, encouraging Walter to do the same – although he shook hands with Mr Hesse instead.

Chapter Thirteen

14–15 May 1915

On Friday evening, Ruth read *The Sentinel* and the report of Mr Asquith's announcement of new rules for the treatment of enemy aliens on her way home. Walter was waiting for her at the tram stop as usual.

'Has everything been all right today?' asked Ruth.

'Yes, I got home at half past two. The shop has been open as usual, but Mr Hesse closed it at midday. There's no sign of the family now. There's four large suitcases in the front room at our house together with a note addressed to Father.'

'What does it say?'

Walter shrugged his shoulders. 'I don't know, but we'll soon see.'

When they got home, everyone was sitting at the kitchen table.

'Hello, Frank. Has something happened? Where's Joan and the kids?'

'Calm down, Ruth. They are spending some time at her mother's,' said Frank. 'Joan felt it was safer.'

Ruth took deep breaths until she felt calmer – at least on the outside.

'Last night, when me and Frank went to the cricket club to get ready for tomorrow, one of the old guys,

Willie, the one with the Jack Russell, was doing some ratting. He told me there's going to be some trouble over the weekend at the Hesses' shop. To quote him, "They are going to give them Germans a taste of their own medicine." I dunner think he even knows we're friends. Frank and me talked about it and decided to tell the police. I called in at Burslem Police Station. Sergeant Birchall had just come on duty so I told him what I had heard.'

There was a knock on the back door. Ruth jumped and looked anxiously towards the sound.

'That'll be him now. He said he'd call round to tell us what's happening.'

The policeman entered the kitchen and removed his helmet. He looked deadly serious.

Father greeted him. 'Thank you for coming to talk to us. I'm sure you're very busy at the moment.'

'Thank you, Herbert. Good evening, all.'

'I'll get you a cup of tea, Sergeant. Would you like a piece of my cake?'

'Yes, please, Miss Latham. Very kind of yer.'

Once the cake and tea were in place, Sergeant Birchall recounted the events of the day.

'We've heard there may be trouble tonight and the shop'll be the target. I can't say anything. I spoke to the inspector. He agreed we take Mr and Mrs Hesse, Carla and Bertie into protective custody at the police station. That's where they are at the moment. They closed the shop at midday and they each packed a bag, which are the ones in your front room.'

'Where's Edith and Luther? They're not at the police station, are they?'

'One of my constables escorted Mrs Edith Hesse and the baby to her family. We thought they might be safer there.'

'I'm surprised you did that with no one seeing.'

'We didn't hide it. Better people know the score. If anything's going on tonight, at least the family'll be safe.' He stopped to catch his breath and, after another bite of his cake and a gulp of tea, continued. 'The inspector's informed the necessary people and we'll have to see what happens. When the troublemakers find nobody at home, we hope they'll lose interest.'

Father spoke. 'It's reassuring to know summat's been done.'

'Like the prime minister said, it's "for their own safety, and that of the community, to be segregated and interned". We don't want any trouble because no one benefits from it.'

'What do you think the new rules will mean for the Hesses?'

'We only know what was in the papers, but we'll no doubt get detailed instructions soon. Based on our understanding, they will consider Bertie for internment. We'll not repatriate him because he's of military age, and he can't join the British Army for obvious reasons. They will consider Mr and Mrs Hesse for repatriation because of their ages. They never got British naturalisation, more's the pity. Mr Asquith said that a judicial body would look at those seeking exemption from internment and extradition. The round-up will begin when suitable accommodation becomes available.'

'What about Carla?' asked Ruth.

'Miss Carla has no problems. She was born in Britain, so she's British. It takes precedence over where an individual's parents were born.'

Sergeant Birchall took another drink of his tea and a final bite of cake.

'So the shop's empty?' asked Ruth, breaking the silence.

'Yes, pretty much so. There is still the stock left, but Mr and Mrs Hesse have taken all their personal papers. Let's hope that we are looking on the black side.'

Sergeant Birchall finished his tea and took his leave. The rest could only sit and stare at each other, wondering how everything could go so wrong so quickly.

—

They didn't have long to wait. About quarter past nine a racket started, the sound of wood and ash bin lids unmistakable. The whole family rushed out into the street. Ruth thought there were at least a hundred of them, mainly men, shouting and chanting anti-German slogans.

The ringleader, or at least the one with most to say, Ruth immediately recognised as one of Peggy's uncles, Danny Thompson, who lived a few streets away.

'I call on the family Hesse to come out onto the street and face us, not hide away like cowards,' he shouted.

'But they can't because our brave boys in blue have arrested them and they are in Burslem Police Station,' shouted one voice.

'At least we gave them the chance to save themselves, which is more than they did to those poor buggers on the *Lusitania*,' said another.

'Now, lads, we're not savages. We just want to let them know they can't come back here. No fire-setting. Just make the place uninviting,' shouted someone who was obviously concerned about what was likely to happen.

Ruth ran upstairs and opened the front window. She could see the front of the shop.

They threw the first rocks at twenty past nine. Someone ripped off the wood covering the broken windows, and caved in the front and side doors. The noise was tremendous. First, men and women swiftly seized the stock strewn across the pavement. No point in wasting good food. The mob destroyed all the possessions and furniture they found and heaped it in the middle of the street.

'Well done, lads, I think that's unwelcoming enough. What do you think?'

The crowd cheered.

'It's getting nippy outside. A friendly fire would go down well. Don't want to block the street, do we?'

It was then that they heard a vehicle turning from Bowden Street into Dartmouth Street. A lorry and the unmistakable sound of orders being given and boots hitting the pavement silenced the crowd.

'Gentlemen, gentlemen, you do not need to behave in this manner. The government has the matter of enemy aliens fully in hand and as much as you think you are helping, you are not. I would be terribly grateful if you could return to your homes immediately,' shouted the army captain as his men gathered in front of the lorry.

There was a momentary silence.

'Now, gentlemen, be good chaps and do what the officer says.' It was the army sergeant whose voice echoed around the street.

'Who are you to tell us what to do? It's a free country. Ain't that what we are fighting for?'

There were general shouts of approval.

The officer raised both his hands in a gesture calling for quiet. Ruth thought that the one good thing about the class system was that people tended to be compliant when faced with authority. The mob went quiet.

'Sir, I am the man with twenty soldiers armed with .303 short Lee-Enfield rifles. Does that answer your question?' asked the captain. The soldiers lifted their rifles in response.

A hum went through the mob and then men from the back walked down Bowden Street the same way they had arrived. The army had defused the situation without violence. Some soldiers followed the mob down the street, while others opened the road. Guards were stationed at the shop. Sergeant Birchall and three constables got out of their van once the lorry had moved.

Ruth closed the window and ran downstairs and out to the front of their house and to her father. 'I hope everything is over now.'

'Hello, Ruthie, I saw you watching from the bedroom window.'

'Oh Father, they've destroyed everything. I dread to think what the inside looks like.'

'Yes, I don't think Mr and Mrs Hesse will be returning soon.'

–

'Evening, Herbert, Miss Ruth,' said Sergeant Birchall. 'That was not what we expected. That officer certainly had some balls – pardon me, miss – hope he knew what he was doing.'

'The mob didn't lose interest, even though they knew no one was in there,' said Ruth.

'No, they didn't. I'll have to look into that. Off the record, I warned the inspector this might happen, but he called it a "lightning rod". Give lightning somewhere to strike and it goes harmlessly to the ground. I don't know whether he thought of that or whether he was told. In a way, it worked, if all you want to do is to get the Hesse family out. At least there were no injuries.'

'Daniel Thompson, who must be over sixty now, seemed to be the one doing all the stirring. But I noticed a couple of other faces. Daniel's a talented speaker. He used to be a preacher with the Primitives, but there was a problem with the lead on the roof.'

'What was that?' asked Ruth.

'There wasn't any; it kept disappearing,' he said dryly, and bade them good night.

Before bed, Ruth walked to the remains of Hesse's Stores. The street was empty now. Windows were pulled from their hinges and every pane of glass broken again. In the dark, without streetlights, it looked as if nothing had happened. *It'll be a different story tomorrow*, Ruth thought.

How would Mr and Mrs Hesse take it? Their life's work destroyed in a matter of minutes. She remembered what they had been talking about in the Hesses' lounge just a few days ago. Mr Hesse thought that the time he'd lived in this country and the fact he had a healthy business would prevent his repatriation. Now one of those pillars had crumbled. They had nothing in a country that didn't want them – perhaps repatriation might begin to look a more attractive option. It seemed they would intern Bertie. No job and of fighting age. He had little to recommend him.

Ruth recognised something by the front wall. It was Mrs Hesse's sewing machine, or what was left of it. The case was smashed and ripped off its treadle. Ruth thought about the material she had bought. Was it only a week ago?

She wiped her eyes, praying for a miracle to end the war. How could anyone live through such heartache and not be traumatised?

—

Ruth rose early and walked along to the shop at half past seven, not that she expected to see anything differently. A young constable guarded the entrance. Ruth put on her best smile, explained who she was and asked to have a look inside so she could report to the family.

'Dunno if I'd bother if I were you, miss. They made a pretty good mess of everything.'

'I'll take my chance; I've known this family all my life. Whatever damage's been done, I should see for myself.'

'Right you are, miss, go ahead but mind yer step.'

Despite her determined words, Ruth wasn't prepared for what she found. The smell of urine and faeces was overpowering even with all the air blowing through the unglazed windows. How could human beings act in such a barbaric manner? She would have sunk to her knees and sobbed her heart out, but that would've been a messy and uncomfortable experience.

'Are you all right, miss?'

'Yes, thank you.'

'You don't look it; you should…'

But before the constable finished speaking Ruth's breakfast made an unexpected return, missing his boots

– but only just. She had naturally bent over and as she straightened up she felt giddy. The constable steadied her.

'Be careful, miss.' He handed her a handkerchief, which Ruth gratefully accepted.

'I'm so sorry, Constable,' said Ruth, mortified.

'We can just stand here a few minutes and take deep breaths. You'll feel better.' They stood in silence until Ruth realised she was still holding his arms. She let go and took a step back to regain her composure.

'I'll make sure the handkerchief is returned to you fully laundered as soon as I can.' Before she had a chance to ask his name, Ruth heard the familiar voice of Sergeant Birchall.

'Good morning, Miss Latham.'

'Good morning, Sergeant.'

'You don't look too good.'

'I'm definitely not too good. Have you seen the mess that mob made inside? The Hesses will never return. In fact I hope that they don't have to return at all. So much hatred here, I don't think they could bear it. Do you know what their plans are?'

'If it's as bad as it looked last night I've no intention of allowing Bertie or Miss Carla to see the property. Bertie's got a bit of a temper and I'm afraid it might be too much for him. I'll be having a word with this young man,' he said, pointing at the constable who had been so helpful. 'He should've had more sense than to let you in, Miss Latham. It's too much for anyone to take in. No wonder you upset yourself. But what is done is done.'

'Don't be too harsh on him. I did push my way in. He warned me but I was too concerned about seeing what it was like.'

The sergeant looked at the constable. 'Happen you probably acted for the right reasons but mind you learn from this. Not all women are as sensible as Miss Ruth.'

'Yes, sir.'

'Would it be all right if we start to clean the place just in case you can't stop Mr and Mrs Hesse from coming back?' Ruth asked, dreading going back inside but knowing it would be the least she could do for her friends.

'Don't worry, as they're still under protective custody, I can prevent them from coming here for a few hours.'

'I think that might be a kind and humane gesture. They were so happy here and it'd be nice if the last memories of their home were of the place they could be proud of.'

'I'll see what I can do, Ruth. You and some of the other ladies can start cleaning it up. I'll not be bringing Mr and Mrs Hesse up here before three o'clock. You might be able to make it at least presentable if they insist on visiting.'

Ruth hadn't really noticed that half a dozen women from Dartmouth Street and some of the other streets had collected behind her as she had been speaking to the sergeant. Some had mops and buckets in their hands.

One woman said that she was going back home to get her mop. 'It won't take us long to get that place cleaned out. It's the least we can do. The Hesses was always good to everybody. There's plenty of us around here that's been able to put a meal on the table every night thanks to them. They'd never let anybody go hungry.'

—

In the ten minutes it took Ruth to return with a mop and bucket, around twenty women were standing outside the shop talking amongst themselves. These past few days had been emotional and tears were never far away, but seeing her neighbours pulling together was almost too much to take. She sniffed. She seemed to have been put in charge of the clean-up, and she was determined to succeed.

'Where do you want us to start, Ruth?'

Ruth quickly explained the situation, but none of the women were prepared for what they found when they went inside. They got stuck in, some with pegs on their noses, and by dinnertime, it was as clean as they could make it. Ruth thought it could never be clean in her mind. Not ever.

Someone rolled up the rugs and put them in the back-yard while a thorough scrubbing took place everywhere. The absence of glass in the windows ensured good ventilation. Ruth hoped that if Mr and Mrs Hesse did remain, at least they wouldn't be subjected to that barbaric mess left by the so-called 'avengers of the *Lusitania*'.

—

Just after three o'clock in the afternoon, a police van turned into Dartmouth Street and Mr and Mrs Hesse, accompanied by Sergeant Birchall, got out. They spoke to each one of their loyal customers.

Ruth was concerned that they would want to go inside, but after standing outside for a few minutes in what looked like silent prayer, they continued talking to well-wishers.

After about half an hour, they walked to the Lathams' house and Father, Walter and Ruth spent some time talking things over. Eventually, they could see that Mr and Mrs Hesse were overcome and clearly getting more upset and so they said their last goodbyes. When they opened the front door they found more well-wishers waiting and by now the police constable who had been so kind to her that morning had collected the bags from the Lathams' front room and placed them in the police van.

'Feeling better now, miss?'

'Yes, thank you very much for this morning. I hope you didn't get into trouble with the sergeant.'

'No, miss. Four-five-two Merriweather's the name.'

'Yes?'

'For the handkerchief, miss.'

'I see. I'll make sure you get it back. I'll deliver it myself.' Ruth put on her warmest smile and turned to go, still smiling.

Mrs Hesse came up to speak to Ruth. 'My dear Carla will stay with us until everything is sorted. She'll write to you with our address and you'll be able to meet her away from this... dreadful reminder. The sergeant said that Carla was free to leave any time, as she isn't in protective custody. We don't know where we're going to spend tonight...'

Mrs Hesse was near tears as she embraced Ruth before turning away and rejoining her husband. Sergeant Birchall had told them only that he had arranged a place for them to stay while awaiting developments.

Mr and Mrs Hesse gave one last look at the street they wouldn't likely see again. They looked lost and older than Ruth remembered them, with blank faces. All the years of work and achievement had gone in less than a day.

—

Ruth finally managed to get some time to sit down about eight o'clock, just after a heavy shower of rain appeared to wash away the last traces of the Hesse family in the street. Even the weather was against her friends today. Her thoughts were disturbed by a knock on the front door.

Rubbing the sleep from her eyes, she opened it.

'Hello, Sergeant.'

'Is your father in, Ruth?'

'Yes. Do come in out of the rain. He's in the kitchen. Would you like a cup of tea?'

'Yes, please. I've got news for you.'

Father joined them and Ruth handed out the hot tea.

'Thank you, Miss Latham. Anyway, when I got back to the station, I was told that the army had collected Bertie Hesse and taken him, probably to Brocton, on Cannock Chase. Merriweather couldn't stop them. Mrs Hesse was hysterical when she realised he was gone and Mr Hesse was angrier than I have ever seen him.'

Ruth gasped.

'I telephoned the inspector in Hanley and he was aware that three internees were to be picked up, but not who. He was not pleased. Nor was I. Typical of the army to ride roughshod over the civil authorities when they want something.'

'Shall I put a little something in that tea?'

'Yes, thanks, Herbert. I need it.' He took out a fob watch from his breast pocket. 'I'm off duty in ten minutes.'

Herbert poured a generous measure of whisky into the sergeant's tea.

'When we had calmed down the Hesses, I took them in the van to a temporary house in Wolstanton for the next few days. They won't be able to stop there too long, but long enough for us to get our instructions, and for them to think about what they want to do.'

'At least they're spending the night in a house. How was Carla?'

'Carla took it very well. Merriweather said she was forthright in her condemnation of the soldiers taking Bertie away before her mother and father returned. In fact, Merriweather had to restrain her from lamping one soldier with the chamber pot. Its contents spilled over Merriweather's shoes and trousers. The poor lad's had a rough day, what with you being taken ill when you saw the house, then some women were also vomiting at the sight and then finally...'

The group saw the funny side of the situation and they broke into laughter.

'Thank you for telling us. We'll let you get home for your tea.'

'Good evening, Herbert, thank you for the medicinal addition to my tea and thank you, Miss Ruth, for a lovely cup of tea.'

Chapter Fourteen

16–21 May 1915

Ruth tossed and turned, thinking of the Hesses' plight, and Carla in particular. How could one family have so much heartache – and none of it their fault? Now here she was on a half-empty tram with other workers unfortunate in having to work on a Sunday, wondering how to break the news to Dottie, given her current state of mind.

Ruth was the cashier on duty. She made swift progress, clearing most of the work by eleven. She made herself a cup of tea, then sat at her desk, waiting for the hands on the clock to reach twelve o'clock, so she could leave to fill Dottie in with the events of the weekend and say goodbye and good luck to Donald, who was leaving on Tuesday to start his journey to India.

She hurried down Campbell Road and paused outside Dottie's to get her breath back, then she knocked on the door.

Dottie appeared. 'This is a nice surprise, Ruth. I hoped you might be working today.'

'I am, but I have some news and I thought I'd best pop over to tell you.'

Ruth entered the kitchen.

'I've heard all about what has happened to poor Carla,' said Dottie. 'We were visiting my mother and she told us everything she knew. By the time we left it was too late to call on you.' They told each other of what they knew.

Ruth noticed the table laid for two, with one of Dottie's embroidered tablecloths and steaming pans of food on the range. 'I'm interrupting your dinner. Perhaps I should go.'

'No you won't. You're here now.'

'Where's Donald?'

'Over at the allotment, trying to keep up with the weeding.'

'He's at the allotment on your last Sunday? I'd have thought he'd want to spend it with you.'

'I think he's saying goodbye to it.'

As Ruth got up to go, Donald appeared at the kitchen door. Ruth didn't want to intrude on them any longer and wished Donald good luck and a safe voyage. She told him to look after himself. Donald and Dottie came to the front door and her last memory was of Donald and Dottie standing together, Donald with his arm around Dottie's shoulders.

–

Ruth had seen Stan around at work and had several chats with him about his motorcycle and whether the car driver ever paid for the damage after the accident. Stan was nice and friendly, and would chat until the cows came home. He'd make a good friend.

It was Monday. Ruth was sitting in her usual spot in the churchyard in the sun, mulling over the plight of her two close friends.

'Fancy meeting you sitting here looking all pensive. Either that or you've fallen asleep.'

Ruth recognised Stan's voice. She pulled herself together and smiled. 'Hello, Stan. I'm not asleep. I'm thinking about things.'

'I find talking to someone helps.' He sat beside her. 'Before you say anything, I'm not prying, but I'm a good listener. I'll not pressurise you. The offer's open – if you want it.'

He looked earnest and then turned away, giving her time to think. He had removed his cap and was staring over the old grey headstones, not even looking at her.

'Remember the Hesse family? Where you went after your accident?'

'Yes, I do, that.'

'A mob wrecked their shop and ransacked their living quarters on Saturday.'

'Bloody hell. Because they were German?'

She nodded. 'You wouldn't believe what the looters did, the bastards. There was shit everywhere.'

Stan's eyebrows raised, but he didn't interrupt.

She clapped her hands over her mouth. 'Sorry Stan, but they broke everything, and it was strewn across the street, including some of their belongings. It was horrible.' She burst into tears. Stan put his arm around her shoulder, drawing her towards him. Ruth's tears continued, but she felt better somehow, as if she wasn't alone.

'The family are all right, aren't they?'

'Yes, the police got wind of it and took them into protective custody before it happened.'

'Bugger me, I didn't expect that in Burslem, especially involving the Hesses. As you said, they'd lived there a long time. The daughter was born in England, you said?'

Ruth dabbed her eyes. 'But that's only part of it. Donald leaves for India tomorrow.'

'Mm, you know, I really thought Dottie was going out to India with him from how he'd been talking.'

'She had the choice but decided not to go. She couldn't bear to be so far away from her family and home.'

'I'm surprised. It's right she should think about her family, but shouldn't her new family take precedence? Donald and their children – if they're blessed with them?'

'She's been so torn, but in the end I think she chose the safest way.'

'That doesn't need to be the end of it. Can she change her mind?'

Ruth stared at him. It was an obvious question, but had Dottie considered it? If she had, she certainly hadn't mentioned it.

They returned to work. Ruth had learned more about Stan. A nice man and sensitive to both Donald and Dottie but he had raised concerns about Dottie's decision.

'Goodbye Ruthie.' Ruth walked towards the offices smiling to herself. Only then did she realise that he had called her Ruthie, like her father. And she rather liked it.

–

Ruth continued to think about the conversation. She could see Stan's van and decided she needed to talk to him again. She scribbled a note to him.

> *Stan, could I beg a lift off you tonight, I want to talk to you about something. Ruth*

She asked Sidney Wainwright to take it over to him with the afternoon post. A few minutes later Sidney returned.

He whispered to Ruth, 'He says yes, wait for him in the van.' Sidney winked at her and gave a little smile.

Stan was waiting when Ruth came out of the offices. It had started to rain and she hurried over. 'Hello, Stan. Thanks for the lift. I wanted to ask you about something you said at dinner time that made me think.'

Stan frowned. 'Go on.'

'You said you thought both Dottie and Donald were going out to India. What gave you that impression?'

'Me and a couple of the mechanics were having a drink in the Red Lion after work a few weeks back. Donald walked in and we got talking about his reasons for being home and what a lucky bugger he was. He started to tell us all about his posting to India, a promotion to the regular army and he was really excited about the prospect of him and Dottie living over there. They would get married quarters and have a housekeeper, which would be really good for Dottie when children came along. He expected his regiment to stay out there even after the war in Europe is over. He even said if they both liked it, he could transfer to the Indian Army and stay there after the war.'

'Dotty never mentioned anything to me about being able to change her mind.'

'Oh yes, Donald was very keen on that idea. And if she didn't like it, she could always come back. Likewise, if she doesn't go now, she could change her mind and go out later. That's why I was surprised she's refusing to go. I think she might have her priorities in the wrong place.'

Stan must've remembered at that point that he was talking about Ruth's friend and added quickly. 'But I don't know her at all so I can't really comment.'

'I agree with you. I said virtually the same thing to her, but she seemed so adamant that there were too many things against living there that it was pointless in me continuing. I don't think there's any point in talking to her again. After all there's a lot of water to go under that bridge. Donald himself may change his mind and tell her not to even consider going out to India.'

'Yes, Ruth, I think the best decision is to do nothing and see what happens as time passes.'

They arrived in Dartmouth Street and Ruth thanked Stan again for the lift. The rain was heavier now, so Ruth got out of the van and dashed to the front door and let herself in, turning once to wave goodbye. She watched the van as Stan drove away until he turned right and disappeared.

—

Ruth decided to have her tea with Dottie. It would be her first full day without Donald and she wanted to give her some support. They finished their meal and were having a cup of tea. Ruth spoke of their childhood – a sort of do-you-remember conversation – when the five of them, Carla, Dottie, Walter, Bertie and herself would wander off, before a lot of the houses were built, and invent stories to play out, I-dare-you games, and so much more.

'I remember.' Dottie laughed. 'I was always jealous of you three. You got on so well together – Bertie and me were more of outsiders.'

Ruth protested.

'It was how I felt, Ruth. You three had so much to share.'

'I never knew, Dottie. I feel awful.'

'Don't be. I only told you because I can understand a little of Carla's problems. Of course, hers are so much worse. I'm just telling you that being even ever so slightly different can have a tremendous influence on how you look at things – up here.' Dottie jabbed her forehead with a finger.

'We'll not let that happen again. We're all together and that's how we'll stay.'

As those words came out, Dottie's face lit up. 'I've just had the most brilliant idea, Ruth. How about I ask Carla if she'd like to stay here for the time being? If the worst happens and she's parted from her family, the last thing she wants is to find herself in a strange place being forced to live alone too.'

'Live with you?'

Dottie beamed. 'I'll be rattling around in this house on my own now Donald's gone and I'm dreading it. I don't want to move out because I don't know how long he'll be away and we'll need somewhere when he comes back.' She licked her lips. 'I can't see myself going to India, can you? I've got plenty to think about. I've got my job at Mintons and my separation allowance, so I won't be too badly off. All I would need would be a bit of board money, you know, to pay for extra food and so on. We'll both be the better for it. What d'yer think?'

The two women stared at each other. 'It would solve a mighty big problem for Carla, wouldn't it?'

–

The police kept the Hesse family's whereabouts, including Carla's, secret since that dreadful night, so Ruth wrote a letter to Carla explaining Dottie's idea and took it along to the police station. She would plead with Sergeant Birchall to give the message to Carla that she had somewhere to live when she came out – if she wanted it – and it would do her good if she heard the news as soon as possible. Of course, Carla might have already decided to stay with her parents, but Ruth needed her to know she had an alternative.

The very next evening, armed with the unsealed envelope containing the letter to Carla, Ruth hurried along to Burslem Police Station and, as luck would have it, found Constable Merriweather on duty.

Ruth hurried to the desk and took the letter out of her bag. 'Is Sergeant Birchall on duty, Constable Merriweather?'

'He is, Miss Latham. Can I ask what you want to see him about?'

'I want to ask him to pass on a letter to Carla Hesse regarding a possible place for her to live. You can check it if you want.' Ruth offered the constable the envelope containing the letter. He looked unsure, as if he was torn on what to do. In the end Ruth pleaded with him.

'Certainly, Miss Latham. I'll check if he's available.'

Ruth nodded. 'Thank you so much.'

After he'd gone, she paced up and down the small reception office, hoping he was still in the station.

She heard voices and recognised the deeper voice of Sergeant Birchall before he opened the door and beckoned her inside.

'Now, Miss Latham. Merriweather here tells me you have some information?'

'That's right, Sergeant. I know I shouldn't ask but' – she held out the letter to him – 'this is a letter to Carla. I have found her somewhere to live when everything's sorted. It's in Stoke and nowhere near Dartmouth Street. It's with Dottie Spilling, a school friend of ours. They sent her husband to India, and she has plenty of space for Carla to have a room. You can read it if you like – that's why I haven't sealed it.'

Sergeant Birchall took the envelope and stared down at it.

Miss Carla Hesse, c/o Sergeant Birchall, Burslem Police

He flipped it against his other hand, saying nothing. Then, after a moment's thought, he nodded. 'Very well, Miss Latham. I'm sure there's nothing in here of concern to us, but I'll need to check the contents – as much to protect you as protecting me. If you don't mind?'

Ruth let out a deep sigh of relief. 'Of course, Sergeant.'

He skimmed through the letter and folded it up before putting it in his breast pocket. 'Miss Hesse can leave any time if she has somewhere to go.'

'What about Mr and Mrs Hesse?'

'I'm afraid we'll need to keep them for the time being.'

Ruth bit her lip.

'Miss Hesse is lucky to have you as a friend,' he said, smiling.

Ruth smiled back and gave Merriweather a silent thank you as she walked out of the building.

The following morning, Ruth got up to find someone had put a note addressed to her through the letterbox; it was from Sergeant Birchall. Carla had accepted and Dottie had been told. Carla would arrive a week on Friday.

Chapter Fifteen

28–30 May 1915

It was arranged for Dottie to meet Carla in Hanley, after which they would travel together to Stoke. Ruth would wait at Dottie's house to welcome them, as she was at work until six. Her task was to warm up their tea and make sure everything was ready for Carla's arrival.

It seemed strange taking charge of someone else's house, even for a brief time. She kept glancing through the front window to see if there was any sign of them. By twenty to seven, her nerves were taut and her heart was pounding. She couldn't understand why that should be, but deep down she knew – this was possibly the one and only opportunity for Carla to pick up the pieces of her life but if that meant leaving her parents behind, for however long it might be, it would be a tough price to pay. It could break her.

The clock continued to tick in the silence of the house.

Then Ruth recognised the two figures walking up the street, each carrying a bag. She rushed to open the front door just as Carla opened the gate to the tiny front garden. Their eyes met, and they rushed into each other's arms, clinging together.

'Oh, Ruth, I'm so glad to see you,' came Carla's voice muffled by Ruth's neck.

'Come on, you two. You can talk as much as you like when you're inside.'

Carla wiped her eyes with the back of her hand, and Ruth gave a nervous laugh. She had thought their meeting might be uneasy at first because of all that had gone on. But she needn't have worried. To Ruth, Carla was the same girl she had known all her life. Now they would help her to move on to wherever her new life would lead her.

—

The following day, Ruth had worked her way through all the clean laundry and placed neat piles on Father and Walter's beds, a good hint that they needed to be put away. She put aside the handkerchief Constable Merriweather had given to her after she had been sick at the Hesses' shop. She had promised to return it to him – and that was ages ago. Besides, she had told Dottie and Carla she would call in a few days to see how they had settled in.

She remembered Merriweather as a pleasant, obliging and helpful young man. Sergeant Birchall had given him orders, and he had carried them out in a quiet, timely manner. She had a feeling that Sergeant Birchall was not as gruff with him as he made out and the two got on well together.

Ruth called in at the police station after tea when it was likely to be quiet. She placed the laundered handkerchief in an envelope in case Merriweather wasn't on duty and she had to give it to someone else. She didn't want anyone making a joke of his kindness.

She walked in with more confidence this time. Constable Merriweather was behind the desk.

'Can I help... oh, Miss Latham, it's you. What can I do for you? No problems, I hope?'

'Not at all, Constable.' She smiled at him and received one back. He was quite handsome without his helmet on. 'I'm returning the handkerchief you kindly loaned to me on that... awful day at Hesse's Stores. My apologies, but it is quite late.'

Merriweather flushed violently. 'It doesn't matter, Miss Latham. You shouldn't have come all this way to give it to me.'

'It's no trouble, Constable.' Ruth turned to go.

'How is Miss Hesse?' he called.

Turning, she smiled once more. 'She's as well as can be expected, given all she's been through. She's beginning to settle. Thank you for asking.'

He walked out from behind the desk and met her near the door. 'I'm glad about that,' he said and followed her outside. He paused as if, now that he was standing beside her, he had run out of something to say.

Ruth watched him take a deep breath.

'I'm begging your pardon, Miss Latham. But would you mind if I asked you something?'

Ruth looked surprised. 'Of course not, Constable. What's on your mind?'

He glanced up and down the street and Ruth did likewise. No one was close enough to hear.

'Would you like to go for a walk around Burslem Park tomorrow if you are available?'

Whatever she was expecting, it wasn't that. Her face must have given away her feelings. 'I... er...'

His face changed from its normal colour to red and then to near purple with embarrassment.

His words had come right out of the blue. What could she say? She couldn't possibly take up with Merriweather. He was very nice – but suggesting what amounted to their meeting in full view of everyone... She certainly didn't want to give him any impression she would consider it. 'Thank you for asking, Constable. I'm afraid I'm not available on Sunday. I'm very sorry.'

A picture of Stan came into her mind. No, Merriweather wasn't for her.

'Of course, Miss Latham. Do forgive me.'

She wanted to lay her hand on his arm, to show she didn't hold it against him, but she thought better of it.

Ruth returned home in a hurry. Saturday night was bath night. Time was pressing on and she needed to be quick, otherwise the men would be back before she'd finished.

The family had a long-standing routine whereby she had the house to herself in order that she might have the tin bath in front of the fire, topped up with boiling water. Father and Walter knew not to come home until after eight o'clock, by which time she would guarantee to have finished – to save any embarrassment. She locked the front and back doors. Despite the brevity, she revelled in this one time in the week she had to herself. Taking less time than usual, she dried herself with the towel she had warmed by the range and slipped into an old dress she had hung on the picture rail. She rubbed her long brown hair with the towel. It always curled after washing and was less controllable.

Suddenly, there was a knock at the front door. Damn, she had taken too much time. She glanced up. It was a quarter to eight. Who was that? Father and her brothers knew better than to return home this early, but there might be a good reason. At least she had got dressed. Still clutching the towel, she hurried to the front door, shouting, 'I'm coming. You're early; you could have given me a little more time. I've only just got dressed in—'

Expecting to see her father or Walter, Ruth unlocked the door and wrenched it open — to find Stan.

'Oh! It's you! Oh, my word.'

Realising that he was interrupting something, Stan's eyes bulged and his face turned the reddest shade of red she had ever seen. Ruth didn't dare think about the colour of her own face!

Stan stepped backwards. 'Er... You've had a bath.'

If Ruth hadn't been so embarrassed, she might've laughed. Obviously she'd had a bath. Her hair was still wet, and the curls were back.

'Evening, Ruth. I mean begging yer pardon. I shouldn't have come without an invitation. D'yer want me to go?'

Ruth regained her composure. Of course she didn't want him to go. The circumstances made it embarrassing.

'No, Stan. It's just a bit... difficult at the moment. There's no one else in so I can't invite you—'

Stan shook his head violently. 'Of course you can't, Ruth. I understand.'

He turned to walk away.

'I'm happy to talk on the doorstep — if that's all right with you?' she called in a semi-whisper.

Stan turned back with a broad smile.

He cleared his throat. 'I conner say as I was expecting to see yer like that, Ruth. I brought a note with me.

Thinking as I would post it through the door if yer wasn't in.'

'Saturday is time I have for myself. To catch up on… things.'

'I must say yer hair looks fine. I've not seen it down before. I never thought it'd be curly. It looks grand.'

'Thank you,' she said, although she wondered how he could say that and mean it when it was still so damp and curly.

They were both at a loss for what to say next – until Stan spoke up again.

'I called by because I was hoping you might like to come out on the motorcycle with me. Remember, we talked about it when we were all snowed up after Christmas? I said I would take you out on it when the sidecar was finished. Well, it's finished, all but for the upholstery and the hood. So, here I am…' His voice, which had started confidently, trailed away. '…to ask you…?'

Of course she remembered their conversation all those months ago, but she was surprised he had. She glanced behind him at the motorcycle, which seemed to have grown bigger, although it was just the same as the last time she saw it. A sudden rush of excitement ran through her, and yes, she remembered having the same feelings deep inside, too.

'I'd love to, Stan. I'll be nervous. I've never done anything like that before.'

'That's understandable. But I'll look after yer.'

She couldn't take her eyes off him. Those few words held so much meaning.

'Then yes, I should love to.'

'How about 6 June?'

Next Sunday! Agreeing to undertake exciting activities contrasted sharply with completing them. Seeing his smiling face, she agreed.

'I'll look forward to it,' she said, holding her head high.

'I'll pick you up about midday. Mother has kindly invited you for Sunday dinner with the family and, if it's not raining, we can go out on the motorcycle afterwards and I'll drop you back here in time for tea.'

She swallowed. Why did men want to move so quickly? She was going to meet his mother and she hadn't so much as walked out with him once. It was nearly twelve months since she had declined to introduce Jim to her father. This was different – and she did fancy a trip on the motorcycle. To do something more daring than she had ever done. It was something she imagined her mother would do.

'Thank you, Stan. I'd love to.'

'By the way, it may be June, but it can get cold on the motorcycle, so you'll need to wrap up warm. Wear yer outside coat in case of a shower and have a scarf with you to keep yer hat from blowing off!'

–

Ruth waited for a tram on Moorland Road at the Miners' Hall stop. Now she was heading off to have Sunday tea with Dottie and Carla. She couldn't wait to see how her two friends got on together living in the same house. Friendship differed from cohabitation. She also had to admit the more she thought about their arrangements, the more jealous she felt to be the odd one out. Living with her father and Walter was fine, but at twenty-one, her future demanded her attention.

Dottie opened the door with Carla a couple of steps behind. They all gave each other hugs before walking into the front room. Ruth removed her hat and coat and Carla took them and hung them up on the hooks in the hall.

'I am so pleased to see you both. You don't know how much I've been looking forward to it.'

Carla grinned. 'It seems absurd for us two to be together without you, to be honest.'

'I agree,' said Dottie.

Ruth sat on the settee with Carla and Dottie each taking one of the cosy chairs.

'How's it working out? Have you had any arguments yet, ladies?'

The other two put on an affronted look and then burst out laughing.

'Course not. Dottie has looked after me perfectly,' said Carla, nose in the air.

'That's a good start.'

'Seriously, Ruth, it's been perfect. I don't know what I would've done if you two hadn't thought of it. I've got a lovely room, all to myself, and Dottie's an excellent cook.'

'And Carla chips in too and has promised to cook some German dishes for me.'

'What about the neighbours?'

'I'm not cooking for them!' Carla grinned.

'Don't be daft, you know what I mean.'

Carla's joke proved her resilience. She shook her head. 'I don't think anyone knows. So far, nobody has mentioned anything. We'll not be telling anyone.'

'I've got some good news,' said Ruth. 'Stan has asked me out. Remember the gentleman we looked after that night? The one with the motorcycle?'

'Yes, of course I do. He was rather dishy.'

'His mother has invited me for Sunday dinner and then we are to go out on the motorcycle afterwards.'

'You'll have to tell us more. And it's about time, Ruth Latham.' Dottie grinned. 'Have you never thought about Jim since you ended it with him?'

'Now and again. But mainly because I wonder where he is and if he's all right. I may have finished with him, but I wouldn't want to see him hurt.' Ruth turned to Carla. 'Have you heard any more about what's going to happen next?'

Carla's face lost its smile. 'Father's received notification of "intention" to repatriate his family to Germany. He has fourteen days to appeal.'

Ruth gasped. 'I can't believe it. I really can't.' It was obvious that Dottie already knew and, once again, Ruth felt a little out of it.

'We have fourteen days to appeal, but I doubt it'll change anything. I have a big decision to make, possibly the biggest decision of my life,' said Carla, biting her lip. Ruth knew of old Carla's tendency to bite her lip when worrying.

Both women watched Carla as she composed herself. 'I went to see my parents a couple of days ago.' Carla turned to Dottie. 'Sorry for not saying anything, but I really needed to understand it.' She continued. 'They told me everything. Father said I had to decide what I wanted to do, go with them, or stay here by myself. I must do what is best for me.'

'What about Bertie?'

'He's interned until the end of the war.'

Ruth found she couldn't swallow, anticipating the worst, while Dottie covered her mouth with her hands.

'And you've got to do that in fourteen days? That's a tall order,' said Dottie.

'And I do not know what to do.'

'What does your family want you to do?'

'They're mixed. Mother wants me to go because she wants her family around her. Father thinks I should stay here because I would be a British woman living in Germany and he doesn't think he'll be able to protect me. It's my decision and I'm worried I may choose the wrong one, whichever option I decide on.'

They ate their tea in silence. After all, what could anyone add?

Chapter Sixteen

4–5 June 1915

As they'd agreed on Sunday, the three friends met at Dottie's house for tea on Friday. It would be good to get up to date on all that had happened during the week without interruptions from their families. Because the following day was a workday, Ruth had agreed to stay overnight and go on to work in the morning from Campbell Road.

Ruth knocked on the door and tried the handle. It was open. When Ruth went inside, her friends were chatting and laughing in the kitchen about something that had gone wrong with the timing of the potatoes and now they were all mushy and would have to be mashed. Carla had put the tea on, being the one that was in the house all day, but when Dottie arrived, they had somehow got talking and the timing went out of the window. Ruth had laughed when they told her, but when they said she should sit and have a cup of tea while they finished, she felt another twinge of jealousy. She admonished herself for being envious, but still…

They were partway through their meal when Carla said, 'I've made my mind up about what I want to do. It's been very hard and I've concluded that, whatever decision I make, I'm bound to regret it at some point. I decided I had to think about myself and my future. I've decided to stay in England. I think—'

Both forks dropped onto plates. Ruth and Dottie squealed and jumped out of their seats to hug Carla with tears in their eyes, causing tears to flow from Carla's.

'I'm so glad...'

'That's wonderful...'

More laughing.

'Are you sure it's what you want? I feel I might've pushed you into deciding to stay because it's what *I* wanted – not to be on my own,' muttered Dottie.

'I'm old enough to make my own decisions,' said Carla.

Ruth thought back to the Hesses when they were leaving. How upset they were. 'What about your mother and father? What do they think?'

'A few days ago, I had a conversation with them. They asked me to share my plans before revealing theirs. Their expressions brightened when I told them. They were happy that I was ready to make my way in life. However, my father later informed me they were planning to go back to Germany and would not challenge the repatriation decision.'

Ruth gasped. 'Carla! I'm so sorry. Were you surprised?'

'I think I kind of guessed their answer. I think they were relieved. How would they have treated me as a British citizen moving to Germany? How difficult might it be for me whoever wins the war? At least staying here means I'll be with the people who I have spent my life with. My parents have a family in Germany who will care for them.'

'What about Bertie?' asked Ruth.

'We had a letter from him. He's still interned at Brocton camp, near Stafford. It's much bigger than he expected and there are loads of men just like him there with no jobs. German civilians. The entire camp's surrounded by barbed-wire fences. It sounds awful, and he hates it, I can tell, but I suppose he's safer there than fighting in the war.'

Ruth nodded. She thought to herself Carla needed to be told that she should exercise more tact. She may think Bertie was safe in a camp, but she must remember that the person she was talking to may have men at the war and they might react badly.

'It still feels weird to think that my Donald could have been fighting against him. My hands feel sweaty at the thought of it.'

They were silent.

It was Carla who changed the subject. 'Enough of Bertie. Now that I'm staying, I need a job to pay my way.'

Sitting down after the meal, they talked about what work Carla could do. Suddenly, Dottie shot out of the room and disappeared upstairs.

Ruth and Carla glanced at one another. After five minutes, Dottie came back downstairs. She looked as if she'd been crying.

'What's up, Dottie? Are you all right?'

'Yes. It's only my monthly's starting...' Dottie then burst into uncontrollable tears. 'It means I'm not pregnant. I've never been the most regular with that sort of thing. I only had my first period when I was fifteen. You two had already started. I was always a little bit jealous. The thing is, I didn't have a period last month, and I started hoping there would be nothing this month and that would mean Donald and me would have a baby. Now I'm not – and I won't be for ages with this bloody war. Who knows when he'll be back?'

'Dottie, I'm so sorry,' said Carla.

'It's all I ever wanted and now I'll never become a mother.'

'Yes, you will. You've got plenty of time. This war won't go on forever,' added Ruth.

'But if Donald does not make it. If he's killed. Then it will be forever.'

'Don't talk like that, Dottie. We have to believe our men will come back,' said Carla.

'I don't see how you two can say that. Bertie's not in any danger. He's living for free in an internment camp. And as far as you go, Ruth, both of your brothers are tucked up safely in their beds every night. They certainly made sure they were out of harm's way. And neither of you have got a young man to worry about. So if I want to look on the black side, then I will.'

Ruth and Carla looked at each other, horrified at the amount of venom in Dottie's voice.

'I knew it was too good to be true,' said Carla. 'You are like everyone else, Dottie. The mob that destroyed my family's life at least faced us. But you, you resent me for being German but say nothing. You reveal your true feelings only when stressed.' She rushed out of the room.

The front door banged shut.

'Where did that come from, Dottie? You've known Carla all your life. Why would you take against her after all this time?'

'But you heard what she said earlier. "I suppose he's safer there than fighting in the war." People show what they really think when they're angry. It made my blood boil.'

'I don't mean to be insensitive, but I think you should control what you say. Once you say things, you can never unsay them.'

It was Dottie's turn to look shocked. But Ruth did not have time to ponder.

'I'd best find Carla.' Ruth left the room and grabbed her coat. She looked up and down Campbell Road, which was long and straight, and soon picked up the pale blue of Carla's coat.

After a few minutes, Ruth caught up with her. Carla turned when she heard Ruth call her. Her face was pale and her eyes streaming. Ruth fell into step beside her, saying nothing.

'I'm sorry. I shouldn't have said those things to one of my lifelong friends. I didn't mean that.'

'Dottie knows you don't. She was hurting too.'

'She's right, really. I may have lost all my family, but at least they are safe and sound. I can understand now why people can get so angry when they think about internees.'

'Everything about this war is too awful to contemplate, Carla, but we three have each other to lean on and that's worth something.' Ruth let her words sink in. She linked Carla's arm.

After a moment or two, Carla spoke again. 'I don't know what came over me, Ruth. After all Dottie's done for me by putting a roof over my head and I tear a piece off her. D'yer think she'll forgive me?'

'I think so.'

They were approaching number 147, and their footsteps slowed. 'Do you feel up to going back in, Carla?'

After another deep breath, Carla nodded. Ruth opened the door and followed Carla inside.

Upon entering the front room, they found Dottie by the window, anticipating their arrival. With a watery smile, she turned to Carla.

The two stood face to face, saying nothing. Then they darted together and hugged one another as if their lives depended on it.

'I'm so sorry—'

'I didn't mean—'

The hug continued.

'Now look, you two. We've all had just about as much as we can stand, haven't we? So why don't we say we're all sorry and be friends again? I'm damn well certain we won't let this war come between us. Never!'

The stress of the evening had taken its toll on all of them. The third bedroom was a lot bigger than its equivalent in Dartmouth Street. Ruth was pleased to climb into the freshly laundered sheets and let the events of the evening fade.

—

It was soon time for Dottie to go to work. Ruth could hear her moving around downstairs and went down to see if everything was all right now.

Dottie looked up as Ruth entered the kitchen. 'Sorry I woke yer.'

'Not to worry. I'm normally up around now. I don't think Father can do anything quietly and Walter's not much better. They're usually out of my hair by half past five and I have time to get myself organised for the day. Usually cutting veg or ironing.'

'I'm always glad Saturday's a half day. I'll be home by quarter past twelve. That's the best part of living close to where you work.'

'Ever since I got the job at the PTC, the travelling's been a chore. At first, I enjoyed the novelty, but it soon wore off.'

'So why didn't you move?'

'Family and Father. Seemed wrong to leave them so soon after Mother died.'

'And now?'

'I don't know. Everything is great at home. I have a lot of time to myself with Walter's shifts and Father's work and cricket.'

'And what do you do with that time?'

'Housework, mainly.'

Dottie's eyebrows lifted. 'Why don't you come and stay here – with us?'

Ruth's eyes opened wide, but she smiled. 'Here? With you two? After last night!'

'If we promised to be on our best behaviour. All three of us together. We could help each other through this horrible war. After all, we've come through so much already.'

'But who would look after Father and Walter? They're useless when it comes to housework. I'd probably have to spend my Sundays washing and cleaning.'

'You could always get somebody in to do that, there's plenty of women looking for a few hours work and lots of women take washing in.'

'I would need to talk to Father, but I think you and Carla should talk, too.'

Ruth kept the idea of moving in with Dottie and Carla to herself initially, wanting to think through everything before making a move. The blazing argument between her two friends had shown that it wasn't all going to be a bed of roses. She must be perfectly sure it was what she wanted.

Chapter Seventeen

6 June 1915

Stan turned up in the van on Sunday wearing a shirt, a waistcoat and a jacket topped with a cap. Standard dress for a casual Sunday. In contrast, Ruth, dressed ready for the motorcycle ride, was wearing her long winter coat, which she hoped would keep her warm. She had put on an extra vest, a second pair of drawers, together with a woollen pullover of Donald's, lent to her by Dottie. She looked at herself in the mirror and burst out laughing. Her attire did little for her figure. She doubted Stan would notice what she looked like because he would be driving.

He knocked on the door at midday. She had been waiting at the front-room window so that she could shoot out before anyone could speak to him.

Smiling at him, she closed the front door behind her. She couldn't believe the day had arrived. She gasped for breath with the excitement of it all. To her dismay, the moment their eyes met, her self-assurance evaporated, leaving her feeling intensely shy. Shyer than she had ever felt in his presence. It crossed her mind that she wanted the afternoon to go well and her nerves were getting to her.

'Hello, Stan.'

'Hiya, Ruth. You certainly took heed about dressing up warm, I see.'

'It's not too much, is it?' she said anxiously, twirling round.

'No, lass. But you'll be too warm in the van. At least take your coat off.'

She did so, and he carefully folded it up and placed it on the passenger seat. He turned back. 'By gum, that's a pullover and a half.'

'It's Donald's. I have got nothing warm enough, so Dottie lent me this one.'

'It's perfect for Gertie, but far too warm for a June day. Take that off and then you'll be more comfortable.'

'How embarrassing, taking one's clothes off in the street! Can you help to get it over my head and not disturb my hair?'

'Yes, come on.'

He gently raised the neck of the pullover over her head and brought his face closer to hers, closer than he'd ever been. She caught her breath.

'All done. I bet it feels better. I see you're wearing the yellow blouse.'

Ruth tutted to herself. Fancy, he remembered the blouse, and she'd forgotten. She took a deep breath, trying her best to compose herself. She looked at the front window of her home and was thankful no one was watching.

Ruth was relieved to be out of those clothes. The thought of meeting his family looking like she had done had worried her. The van pulled away from the kerb and they drove up towards Smallthorne.

'I'd better tell you a bit about my family before you meet them. Father has his own business as a coachbuilder.

He set it up in the time of horse-drawn coaches, and his carpentry skills were much in demand. Coaches always need some repair and maintenance. Mother does most of the leather and upholstery work. Latterly they've moved into furniture repair and restoration. They have a workshop on the land next to our house. Mother's self-conscious about her hands. The years of leather, canvas and heavy upholstery stitching have taken their toll.'

'That's a shame.'

'Yes, her hands are very tough, so she'll not shake hands unless she has to. Then there is my brother, Mark, and sister, Rosie.'

'I didn't realise you had a brother and sister.'

'Yes, Mark's an apprentice cabinet maker. He's fifteen, very practical, and will be an asset to the business one day. Our Rosie is the clever one. She'll be twelve in a couple of weeks. She takes after Mother, but we don't hold that against her.' He grinned.

'What do you mean?'

'Nothing really. Mother is a lovely person and very generous, but she can seem remote to some people. She doesn't like to make a show of herself. We all love her to bits, but she's undoubtably the boss in the household. You don't want to fall foul of her, if you can help it. As long as she thinks she's won an argument she's fine, but if she feels bested, then she'll not speak to you for days at a time, until she's decided that you have been sufficiently good to warrant normal relations being resumed.'

Ruth's heart sank. 'Er... that's good to know.'

'There's quite a difference in age between me and Mark and Rosie. I had to look after them when we were young. I'd be the one to get into trouble if they misbehaved. I spent a lot of silent times with my mother over the years!'

They turned off Leek Road and headed to Brown Edge. Ruth couldn't believe how fast the scenery had changed. It took no longer than fifteen minutes to reach the Bristows' house at Brown Edge, a village not too far away but not having the benefit of a tram route or a train station, hence Stan's need for the motorcycle.

The first thing Ruth noticed was the number of trees everywhere. Riding into Brown Edge was a delight, as was the smell of the countryside rather than the smoke and soot of the towns.

They turned down into a narrow lane.

Stan pulled up outside a two-storey stone cottage with a country garden full of colour. 'This is it.'

'It's beautiful, Stan.'

The house was built at a right-angle to the road, like many of the others. The front garden was to the right of the house, and there were stone walls all around. The gate led to a path down to the porch and the front door. Over the wall, Ruth could see a large workshop.

She was not really ready to meet his parents and was unsure of what to do. Stan appeared on the left-hand side, opening the door to help her out of the van. Mr Bristow arrived with a broad grin, taking her hand and shaking it.

'Hello, lass, bit nicer weather than the last time I saw you.'

'Good afternoon, Mr Bristow. It certainly is.'

A young girl ran out of the house and grabbed hold of Stan around the waist.

'This minx is my little sister, Rosie. Rosie, this is my friend Ruth. She works for the PTC too.'

'Pleased to meet you. Come in and see Mother.' Rosie grabbed hold of Ruth's hand and led her through the front door into the house where Mrs Bristow was sitting at the kitchen table.

'Mother, this is Ruth. She seems very nice. She's a friend of Stan's.'

'Good afternoon, Miss…'

Ruth quickly filled in the gap – 'Latham. But please call me Ruth.'

'Good afternoon, Ruth. I trust you had a pleasant journey?'

'Yes, I didn't know that places like this existed so close to The Potteries.'

'There's fresh tea in the pot. Rosie, get Ruth a cup. Dinner won't be long.'

'It's so nice to have visitors. Can I sit next to Ruth, Mother?'

'If you're good.'

Rosie clapped her hands together and started to lay cups out.

'My other son, Mark, is visiting one of his friends. He sends his apologies and is disappointed not to have met you.'

Stan and his father walked into the kitchen, his father wiping his hands on a dirty rag.

'Make sure you wash your hands thoroughly, the pair of you. I don't want that horrible-smelling glue on my best tablecloth.'

Ruth looked at it. It truly was a work of art and had obviously been hand sewn. The colours were so vibrant.

'What a beautiful tablecloth, Mrs Bristow, did you sew it yourself?'

Mrs Bristow beamed. 'It's many years old. I made it for my bottom drawer.'

'What's a bottom drawer, Mother?' frowned Rosie.

'It's when a girl is preparing for marriage so she's got all the items she needs.'

There was roast chicken and spring vegetables. It was followed by a rice pudding. Ruth didn't think it was going to be such a spread, but Mrs Bristow was an excellent cook.

She turned to Rosie. 'Stan tells me you'll be thirteen in September.'

'Yes, and I am going into the next class in September. It'll be my last year at the village school. I love it. There is so much to learn.'

'Rosie is really bright and does very well at school. She loves to go to the library in Leek and gets out as many books as she can,' said Mr Bristow. 'She's going to try for a scholarship to a girls school in Macclesfield when she's sixteen. It'll help her to get into university, we're told. In the meantime she will help out at the school and in return she'll have tuition for the scholarship entrance exams from the teachers.'

Ruth heard the pride in his voice. She thought back to her own ambitions to become a teacher and wondered if Rosie would have similar ideas herself.

'Thank you so much for inviting me, it was a lovely meal.'

'Thank you my dear, I hope you'll come again, sometime.'

-

Ruth put her pullover and coat back on outside. Mrs Bristow and Rosie had followed them as they said their goodbyes. Ruth would have preferred not to have an audience to see her contortions to get into the sidecar while retaining her dignity.

'How do I get in?'

'The best way would be to sit down on the seat and bring your legs together and swing them in. Put your feet against that board. It'll stop you slipping forward.'

'Could you turn away, please?'

'Yes, Ruth.'

Rosie giggled as she watched. 'Don't worry, Ruth, it gets easy with practice. Getting out is a bit tricky. You have to be careful not to show your drawers to everybody.'

'Rosie Bristow, you don't talk about ladies' undergarments in mixed company,' said Mrs Bristow, looking horrified. 'I'm so sorry, Ruth, she's at that age.'

'I seem to have been at *that* age all my life,' Rosie replied.

'Don't answer your mother back, Rosie,' said Mr Bristow.

Ruth shuffled inside. It felt as if she was sitting on the floor and everything else around her had grown. 'It's all right, Stan, you can turn around now.'

'You look comfortable in there, just about the right size. Be careful of that contraption behind you. It's the frame for the hood, which is to be made.'

'I told you, Stan, it would be better to take it off,' muttered Mr Bristow.

'After the trouble we had getting it fixed in the first place, I thought it would be acceptable, but I agree, it does need to be removed.'

'Is there anything I need to know?' said Ruth, interrupting.

'You can look around as much as you want to, but try not to move your weight. It makes it difficult for me to control. Look behind you by swivelling your head and not your whole body. Other than that, tap on my leg if you need anything or you want to stop. There's a pair of goggles in that box in front of you if you need them.'

Stan jumped onto the motorcycle, flicked a few switches and kicked the engine into life. It was noisier than Ruth had thought. Stan turned to her and put his thumb up. She said a little prayer to herself and returned Stan's gesture. She was ready.

Leaving Brown Edge, they headed up a steep lane and came out on a road running along the ridge. Stan pulled onto the verge. 'This is Lask Edge. That way is Cheshire and the other ridge over there is Mow Cop and the little town you can see is Biddulph. There's a large pit near to Biddulph and at Mow Cop there's a ruined castle. We could go to it one day. Straight ahead is Cloud End and on the right are the Staffordshire Moorlands and Leek.'

She marvelled at the views spread out in front of them. She hadn't heard of those places. 'I can see now why you like the motorcycle so much, Stan. It gives you so much freedom.'

'When I was a lad, I had a push-bike and used to ride around these lanes. By the way, how's the seat?'

'A bit hard to sit on and the back rest is too low.'

'I'll tell Father so we can make changes on the final one.'

They continued with their journey, through the lanes to Congleton, stopping as required, and then south towards The Potteries and home.

From Congleton, they drove straight through to Burslem. When Stan pulled up outside the Lathams' house, Ruth's body had begun to stiffen up. This was the fourth time she had got out of the sidecar today and she was, as Rosie had said, developing a technique.

She was glad that Stan was there to help her. If he hadn't, she would have ended up sitting on the pavement.

'Yes, I should have mentioned that. It happens to me too. If you don't move around, you can soon stiffen up, especially in cold weather.'

Better late than never, thought Ruth, but said nothing.

Father appeared with two mugs of tea, followed by Walter with another two. 'Thought you two would like a drink of tea. Have you had a good afternoon?'

'It's been splendid. There are so many beautiful places. We stopped to look at the view at one place and you could see the smoke from the factories in Liverpool and Manchester.'

'That would be Lask Edge,' said Stan.

'And how do you like the motorcycle and sidecar?'

'It'll take a bit of getting used to. So low down everything seems to be going so fast.'

Father turned to Stan. 'You'd better look after my girl if you plan to do more of this.'

'Father!'

'Your father's right,' said Stan. 'I'll look after you.'

Ruth looked at Stan and something inside made her catch her breath.

Chapter Eighteen

June 1915

A few days later, Father was sitting in his chair by the range and Walter wouldn't be in until gone ten o'clock. Ruth finished the dishes and put Walter's tea into the warmer. She walked into the kitchen and watched her father. He looked so comfortable, Ruth didn't quite know how to broach the subject.

'Now come on, Ruth. I can see as yer've summat on yer mind. Out with it.'

Ruth could feel her face reddening. Father could read her mind, she was sure of it.

'You're right, Father.' She sat in the chair opposite him and took a deep breath.

'It isn't about young Stan, is it?'

Ruth let out her breath. 'No, nothing like that. It was what happened when I stayed over with Carla and Dottie.'

'How's the lass settling in after all the disturbance of the last few months?'

Ruth told her father everything that had happened. She was surprised at how easily things went once she started speaking.

'Sounds like you had a bit of a time of it, then.'

'Yes, Father, we did, but in the end, we helped each other so much.'

There was a pause in the conversation. Ruth knew the time had come when she needed to tell him what she had in mind. 'What would you say if I told you I would like to move in with them?'

'You should've told me if you're unhappy.'

'No, it's nothing like that, Father. I am really happy here and feel so guilty suggesting leaving you and Walter, but I feel it's time for me to spread my wings. This house and street hold too many sad memories for me and a period away whilst I'm working in Stoke is what I need.'

'Have you really thought it through?'

'Yes, Father. I know it seems quick, but I think the three of us need each other. On the practical side, I am going to save all that time I spend sitting on them wooden tram seats.'

'Lass, you're over twenty-one with a mind of your own. I don't think I could stop you if I wanted to. But I don't want to. You sacrificed a lot of your life to look after your mother, and now it's your turn to make a life for yourself. It can't be a lot of fun living with me and Walter.'

'Oh no, Father, it's nothing like that. I don't want to get away from either of you, but I do want to be with my friends.'

'Me and Walter'll miss yer. But Stoke's not the other end of the country.'

'You'll see plenty of me, I promise. It'll leave you and Walter to fend for yourselves, I know but I'm earning good money doing this job, so we can pay someone to come in and do for you. You know – cook your tea, and clean the house and there's plenty of women who take in washing and ironing.'

'Me and Walter aren't helpless, Ruthie. As long as you leave the recipe for a boiled egg and a cup of tea, we won't starve. I'm sure Joan won't mind extra for some meals and then we can get something to eat after work. It'll be cheaper than paying someone.'

'Yes, but it'll take a lot of organising. This way there's nothing for you to think about. I know Mrs Wheeler takes in washing so that will be easy. I'm sure she can fit you in.'

Father smiled. 'I'm sure she would, been around the block a few times has Beatty Wheeler.'

'Father, she's a very nice lady and will do anything for you.' Ruth went red with embarrassment when she realised what she'd said. 'I didn't mean…'

'Stop digging a hole for yourself. I agree she can do the washing.'

Ruth calmed herself down. 'That would just leave the cooking and cleaning. I'll put a card in the sho—' Ruth clasped her mouth and a tear came into her eye. 'I know, I'll go to see Mrs Scott, she might know someone.'

'I'll give it a go then; I'm sure Walter won't be against it.'

Ruth gave her father the biggest hug she had given him in years.

'And if it doesn't work out, you'll always have a room here. You're a good girl, Ruth, and I know I don't need to say anything, but I will. Be careful and be your own woman. Don't get carried away by others. Know you own mind and keep it.' He smiled. 'I don't think you realise how much like your mother you are. Remember one thing, love. There is no rush. Take your time and you'll know when you've met the right man, like I knew when I met my Millie.'

Later, she told Walter of her plans. He looked shocked at first, and then he sighed deeply. 'I suppose I should've expected something like that, you three being so close, but I never thought that you'd leave home before me, sis.'

'I know. Strange, isn't it?'

'You've lived nowhere other than home. Everyone's going their own separate ways – except me.'

'You'll soon be off yourself, I'm sure. Who could resist my darling brother?'

'Give over. Trust you to turn the subject away from yourself when you're trying to avoid answering.'

'I'm not. I feel the time has come for me to fly the nest. I'm looking forward to becoming myself, Walter. You men can do whatever you want when you want to. It's not the same for women. We're supposed to stay at home until the men who will become our husbands come along. I want to find myself before that happens. Do you understand?'

Reluctantly, Walter nodded. 'I've never thought of it like that before.'

'Can you imagine me, Carla and Dottie living together? We'll have such fun.'

'You will take care, won't you, Ruth?'

'You needn't worry. I promise everything is going to be all right.'

'Promise you'll come straight back home if it doesn't work out.'

Ruth threw her arms around him. She would miss him most of all.

Two weeks later, Ruth was on the move to 147 Campbell Road.

–

Dottie received a letter from Donald towards the end of June. It was short and sweet.

2 June 1915

My dear Dottie,

We have arrived in Alexandria. We travelled out on ~~HMT Saturnia~~ from ~~Avonmouth~~ and arrived on 2 June. ~~Alexandria and Port Suez~~ are very busy with what's going on at ~~Gallipoli~~. We are waiting for transport by train to ~~Port Suez~~ to board another ship for ~~Bombay~~.

Time on the ship drags. I was sick for the first three days and felt rotten, but now I've got my sea legs; I feel much better. The food is good and there's plenty of it, as we stocked up on local stuff when we called in for coal at ~~Gibraltar and Malta~~.

That's all for now. I will write again when we get to ~~Bombay~~.

With all my love,
Donald

Dottie laid the letter on the table. 'Well, girls, that was a lot of use. All I know is he's alive, probably eating too much and has been seasick. But it's the thought that counts, wouldn't you say?'

—

Back at work the following day, Ruth opened the mailbag from May Bank. There were only a few trams based there, and the second electric generator set for the tram wires. There was never much in the way of paperwork, but today, there was an envelope addressed to Stan Bristow. Ruth felt it might be a catalogue or something similar. It would give her an opportunity to speak to him again.

'Brian, I'm popping across to the workshops to take this envelope. It feels it might be something important.'

'What does important feel like?'

'Like this.' She waved the envelope at him.

'Okay, go right ahead. Don't be too long.' Brian nodded towards Mr Routledge's office.

'Yes, Brian.'

It was the end of June. The morning was pleasant enough when she walked into work, but now, just before ten o'clock, the sky had clouded over. Ruth took a gamble that it wouldn't rain before she returned. She arrived at the workshop office.

Norman greeted her. 'What can I do for you, Miss Ruth?'

'I've got this envelope addressed to Stan from May Bank, so I thought it might be important.'

'I'll take it.'

'No, could you call him? There's another matter I need to talk to him about.'

Norman slid open a small window in the office and bellowed, 'Stan, you've got a visitor – a lady visitor.'

A few moments later, Stan walked into the office, wiping his hands on a cloth. He grinned when he saw her.

'Morning, Ruth.'

'Good morning, Stan.'

'To what do I owe this pleasure?'

'I've got this envelope. It's addressed to you at May Bank, so I thought it might have been important. To do with the boilers and things.'

Finding everything above board, Norman strode into the workshop and to the forge.

'Thanks for bringing it across. I know what that is. I've been waiting for that catalogue for a few days.' There was a pause. Stan unsealed the envelope. It contained a catalogue from an engineering company specialising in bearings and joints. 'It's for Gertie,' he said, his face lighting up as he opened it. Ruth should have left, but Stan launched into his plans to improve the sidecar's attachment to the motorcycle. After going into some detail, he got to the point of his story.

'I want one of these special connectors they make to attach the sidecar to Gertie. At the moment I take about two hours to attach it, but with these joints...' he said, wiggling the page in front of her nose, 'it'll take me less than half an hour, I reckon.'

Ruth nodded as if she understood and felt obliged to reply. 'I didn't realise it was such a time-consuming job.'

'It'll be worth it if you can come out with me.' His eyes burned into hers. 'Being on Gertie's amazing, but it can get lonely, too.'

The remark surprised Ruth. Judging by the look on Stan's face, he was, too. 'I'll have to go or else I'll be in trouble.'

Stan nodded but said nothing.

Ruth walked out, saying goodbye to Norman, who was just getting her a mug down for a cup of tea.

'Yer not stopping for a cuppa?'

'I need to get back, but thank you, Norman. Goodbye.'

—

Ruth thought back to what had just happened. Did he mean what he said, including her in his plans, or was it just a poor choice of words? She hoped it was the former. She was still thinking about him when she returned to the office.

Peggy was sitting at Ruth's desk with a scowl on her face.

'I've been sitting here for ten minutes waiting for you. I need the May Bank sheets to type them, but I see you have not started them. You obviously had something more important to do.'

'I've only been gone for ten minutes. Don't make a mountain out of a molehill. Come on, Peggy, you must have something you can work on. They'll be with you presently.'

'Ruth, how long will it take for you to finish the sheets?'

'About half an hour. I will ensure you receive them once approved.'

'I'll be waiting.' Peggy flounced out of the office without saying another word.

'What's up with Her Ladyship this morning?' asked Molly.

Brian replied. 'She saw Ruth going across the yard to the workshops and I expect the green-eyed monster took hold. She has nothing to do with Stan…'

'She says,' said Molly.

'…but I think she doesn't like the idea of anyone else getting close to him.'

'That makes sense. She rarely comes looking for work. In fact, I think that must be the first time she's done that since she started here,' muttered Brian.

Later on in the morning, Molly and Madge were counting money downstairs and Brian called Ruth over to his desk.

'You know what Peggy's like – so don't give her any ammunition to have a go at you. Shouldn't worry too much, she'll not say anything to Mr Routledge. He's already warned her about her attitude.'

'Yes, Brian. I'm sorry.' She returned to her seat, but she couldn't get Stan's words out of her mind.

Chapter Nineteen

July–August 1915

As Father predicted, Mrs Wheeler, a widow herself, was happy to 'fit him in' as she put it. When it came to the other woman it took a bit longer. Dottie's mother said that she knew of a spinster who currently looked after an old lady, Miss Riley from Bank Hall. But Mrs Scott had heard that the lady was going into hospital and wasn't expecting to come out. She was in her eighties.

The upshot was that Miss Latimer was only too pleased to take on the role as housekeeper. She lived in Leonard Street, which was only four hundred yards or so from number 32. She was very prim and proper and they agreed a trial period when she would provide tea and leave a cooked joint for Sundays. She would clean while they were at work. It looked promising. It was only later that Ruth found out she was Madge Butler's auntie.

—

Towards the end of July, Ruth read with interest the advertisement that appeared in the Saturday edition of *The Sentinel* announcing the opening of the new general store, formerly Hesse's Stores, in Dartmouth Street. Following refurbishment, Richard Clarke, and his family from Tunstall, would manage the shop.

She talked it over with her father at Sunday dinner.

'Have you seen the shop, Ruth? It looks…'

'No, Father. You know I always come in via the back door so I don't see it.'

'Yes, I know what you mean. It still seems strange not to have Mr and Mrs Hesse just down the road. You know we moved in around the same time, don't you? I don't know what Millie would have had to say about what happened.'

'When I go back home after tea, I'll go out through the front door and have a look.'

She did as she promised and hurried down the road to catch the tram, passing the shop on the way. Glancing inside, she could see workmen still painting the woodwork. With new windows and doors, and the external paintwork refreshed, Ruth hated to admit it looked more inviting than the old shop. Still, it would be a constant reminder of everything bad that had happened that year, and she was glad she wouldn't have to pass it every day.

—

It was the Tuesday of the Potters' Holiday. The war had been raging for a year now and still no end in sight. Ruth got home from work as usual. Dottie was out with her family for the day. They all had something to do with the pottery industry so they were all on holiday.

A hot and flustered Dottie arrived back about half an hour later.

'Did you have a good day out?'

'Ruth, it's more tiring being on holiday than at work. We did some shopping in Longton and my sisters had to look at every item of clothing on display. Then we walked around the park, which was busy and very warm. We must've walked miles and I'm glad to be back home.'

Dottie flopped onto the settee and removed her boots. She wiggled her toes and looked thoughtfully at them.

Ruth, ignoring Dottie's feet, said sharply, 'The postman's been. It's another letter from Donald. I put it on the sideboard. I'll get it for you.'

'As you're on holiday, do you want a bowl of hot water to soak your aching feet and you can read Donald's letter?' asked Carla.

'That sounds wonderful.'

Carla returned with a bowl of warm water and Ruth followed with a fresh cup of tea and the envelope.

'Thanks, both of you. I've come to the conclusion that I like being pampered.' Dottie sighed deeply and settled back to read Donald's letter.

22 June 1915

My dear Dottie,

We have arrived in ~~India~~. It's hot, humid and wet. The monsoon season has just started, you thought it could rain in The Potteries, but it's nothing compared with the monsoon. It was a spectacular sight when we docked in the early morning, just after sunrise. There seem to be people everywhere. Stoke is quiet compared to here. We now have to wait for orders to move to the barracks, so we are sharing billets with some ~~Indian Army soldiers~~ waiting to go to ~~Gallipoli~~. They're ~~Sikhs from the Punjab~~. They seem a good bunch. They are fierce fighters ~~and wear turbans~~.

I am missing you more than I can say. You have a lot of time to think about things aboard ship and

> *we don't get much news. Hope you are well. I will send you my address and then you can write to me.*
> *Love*
> *Donald*

She threw the letter onto her lap. 'It's a good job I knew he was going to India, otherwise I'd know nothing.'

'I suppose they have to be careful. Better we know nothing than the enemy knows everything,' said Carla.

'I hope his letters are not going to be censored like this all the time, otherwise it won't seem like he's writing them.'

—

Two weeks later Dottie received another letter.

'Let's hope either Donald's got more to say or the censor has run out of ink,' Dottie said as she opened the envelope. Ruth and Carla were sitting at the kitchen table.

'Listen to this, girls…'

> *30 June 1915*
>
> *My dear Dottie,*
> *We have finally arrived at the barracks in ~~Rawalpindi~~. My address will be: 350164 Sgt. Spilling, British Army – India. That will find me. It takes mail about five weeks. Don't write too often as it's expensive for you to send letters out here.*
>
> *I spent my first night in the bungalow (single-storey house) I have been allocated. I am sharing with another sergeant who is currently out on patrol, so I have the place to myself. We have*

a cook/housekeeper, gardener, houseboy and a punkawallah, who operates big fans by hand to keep a breeze going. We pay for the servants ourselves, but wages are so low I feel guilty paying them so little, but they're happy.

I will tell you more in my next letter.
All my love,
Donald

'He won't be wanting to come back at this rate. He told me there would be servants, but I thought he was exaggerating.'

'Perhaps you should go out to him and when Carla gets a job, we can pay the rent of this place until the war's over,' said Ruth, a bit tongue-in-cheek. She gave Carla a wink.

'Oh yes, we can do that for you,' said Carla.

'He's only been in India a few days. Let's see what he says in a few months.'

—

Ruth was still concerned about Carla. She'd heard from Bertie, but nothing from her parents as yet. And she still hadn't been able to get a job. She kept the house tidy and did the cooking and washing, but she stayed indoors most of the time, not wanting to risk any anti-German comments. She left the shopping to Dottie or Ruth.

Ruth had to be at work after Dottie and so she was on her own when suddenly there was a knock at the front door. Ruth hurried to answer it before the person knocked again and woke Carla. She opened the door to find a young boy in a post office uniform holding out a brown envelope. Ruth gasped but quickly realised it was too thick to be bad news. She took the letter and thanked him. He waited a moment, then, disappointed by the lack of a tip, he got back on his red bicycle and left.

She turned round. Carla stood there as white as a ghost.

'What is it? It isn't...'

'No, it's too thick for something like that and it's addressed to you.' They sat down at the table. 'You open it. Shall I stay with you?'

'Yes, please, until I know what it's about.'

Carla read out the words on the front of the envelope.

On His Majesty's Service
Overseas communication
Deliver by hand

Carla's hands shook, but she tore the envelope open – and gave a sigh of relief. 'It's from Germany; it'll be from Mother and Father.' She opened the envelope to reveal several letters in her father's handwriting. One letter was addressed to Bertie, one to both of them and finally one to Carla which she opened and quickly scanned the contents. 'They're all right, Ruth.'

'That's a relief.'

Carla smiled. 'You get off to work now. I'll be fine.'

–

It was a few minutes before ten o'clock that morning when Pearl came into the office and went over to Ruth.

'Your friend's downstairs. She wants to see you.'

'Carla?'

'Yes, come on.'

'Does she look all right?' Ruth crossed her fingers behind her back.

'Put it like this. The lass is positively beaming!'

A smiling Carla was waiting by reception.

Ruth pulled her outside to where they could speak without interruption.

'The letter was from Mother and Father. They arrived in Germany on 15 June, but the post is difficult and very slow. Judging by the envelopes, many people have read it before I got it.' Carla's words fell over each other as she tried to speak quickly. 'But none of that matters, Ruth, and they sound in good cheer.'

'That's great news, Carla.'

'They're staying with my uncle.' Carla didn't say his name. 'At least I know their journey's over. I can get on with my life and put what happened behind me. I'm sorry I came to you at work. You can read it when you get home tonight. I just wanted you to know.'

The two friends hugged, and Carla left. Slowly, Ruth walked back into reception, dabbing a few tears from her cheeks.

—

When Ruth got home, the first thing Carla did was to pass the letter to her.

'You can read it when you're ready. It is all in English.'

'No, I'll read it with you here if I may?' Ruth picked up the letter and read.

> *Bäckerei Hesse,*
> *44 Schuhstraße,*
> *Hildesheim*
>
> *My dear Carlotta,*

We have arrived in Hildesheim and are staying with my brother Friedrich and his wife, Johanna, at their bakery in the centre of the town. Friedrich is a little older than me. We could not contact him until we left Aachen, and we arrived the day after our letter.

The journey was long and tiring. Your mother seemed to travel better than me. We left Newcastle-under-Lyme on 8 June with all our possessions in one suitcase each, and complete with a soldier named Sandy, who was very formal but kind. We got to London and spent the night in a cell in the local police station. It was awful. In the morning, a policeman escorted us to the docks at Tilbury and onto a Dutch ship.

They kept us in our cabin for the entire journey. The sea was very calm and by the time we were out in the North Sea, both your mother and I had got our sea legs. We arrived at Ijmuiden a day later. I overheard a Dutch crew member say the journey took longer than usual because they had to follow a 'safe route' agreed upon by the British and Germans. After what had happened a month ago, I think both sides did not want a repeat.

After we left the ship, we stayed in the harbourmaster's office until two Dutch policemen collected us and accompanied us on the train into Amsterdam and then straight to Aachen. The policemen left us just before the Dutch–German border. We spent five nights in Aachen while the police checked our identities and no doubt communicated with the police in Hildesheim. Both your mother and I were interviewed separately and

> *in both interviews the policeman said, 'Perfektes Englisch, genau wie der König George.'*

Ruth glanced at Carla. 'What does it mean?'

'Oh, yes. It says, "Perfect English just like King George."'

Ruth nodded and continued to read.

> *On Monday morning, officials issued us papers confirming our German citizenship and identity cards; they advised us to carry the cards at all times because the police will demand to see them, and failure to produce them will result in arrest until police verification.*
>
> *A man about our age took us to the station. He was from the German Red Cross and did this regularly, he said. He was with us to make sure we didn't get lost, although by his looks and military bearing, I think he was making sure we were who we said we were.*
>
> *We arrived at Friedrich's bakery mid-afternoon and said goodbye to our escort. Having only written letters to each other for the last fifteen years, seeing him again was just too much for me. I think it may have also been a reaction to what has happened. It seems incredible that five weeks ago, we sat in the living room at the shop talking to Ruth and Walter. I thought things had settled down and we could continue our lives.*
>
> *Still, that's enough of how we got here. We've been here two days now and we're helping in the bakery and the shop. Friedrich has lost two of his regular helpers to the army, and so our arrival was good.*

I do not know how long it will take for this letter to reach you. The Red Cross told us we should address the letter and then put that letter into another envelope and send it to the Red Cross in Aachan. They would arrange for the letter to be passed to the Dutch Postal Service and they would then pass it to the British. Hopefully, you will receive the letter. They warned us it could take several weeks, as many people would check the letter.

I don't think I have put anything in this letter which I shouldn't. But no doubt, someone will cross out anything inappropriate.

We are planning to go to the old family farm at Geisen. And visit the graves of our parents. What we will do after that is, as yet, unknown.

We were so upset when we left you at Newcastle, we never had time to say a proper goodbye. You remember we love you and your brother with all our hearts. Although we're separated now, this war, like all wars, will eventually end, and we will reunite as a family.

I hope you are safe and well and getting on with Dottie. She was wild when you were at school, but I'm sure she has calmed down now she is married. Your mother has asked me to remind you to be a good girl.

I don't know how often we will write to you as the Red Cross will only pass the one letter, so do not expect to hear from us. I think you should assume that no news is good news. I have written a letter to Albrecht, but I doubt it will find him, as we only have the address of the internment camp in Staffordshire. You will be in touch with him, so give him our best wishes and all our love. Tell him to be strong, and not to resent his imprisonment too much. Urge him to work hard, and perhaps he'll be released soon.

Have you been back to the shop? Has the landlord done the repairs? I know somebody else will run it, but in my head it will always be my shop. That is it. I will not mention it again. We have been given a second chance to start a new life and we take that chance with both hands.

We hope to be reunited as soon as possible.
Love and best wishes and take care of yourself.
Your loving father and mother

When Ruth got to the end, tears were running down her cheeks. No wonder Carla felt the way she did. Ruth couldn't imagine all of her own family being out of reach. How lonely she must feel. Perhaps this letter would help her start anew. They were safe – and that was all that mattered.

—

There was a knock on the front door, and Dottie went to answer it.

'Hello, you must be Dottie.'

'Hello. Who might you be?'

'Stan Bristow, I'm a friend of Ruth's.'

'I remember now. You came to the wedding. I'll give her a shout. She's in the kitchen.'

Ruth came to the front door and greeted him. 'Do you want to come in for a cup of tea?'

'Thank you, but I'm in a bit of a rush. I am going to collect some leather and canvas. Once Gertie's trim is added and the hood is made, the work'll be finished.'

'I've never asked, why have you called her Gertie?'

'It's a long story. I'll tell you sometime. What I wanted to tell you, Mother has asked you for Sunday dinner and the grand unveiling of the sidecar.'

Ruth beamed. 'I'd love that. Tell your mother thank you.'

Stan handed Ruth a bag. 'Rosie has sent you these to wear in the sidecar. She thinks you'll be warmer and more comfortable. There's a note inside. I don't know what it says. She made me promise not to read it.'

Ruth took out the note.

'We'll do the same as last time. I'll pick you up in the van. We can have dinner and then go out on Gertie's first journey. How does that sound?'

'That sounds lovely. I'll see you then on Sunday.'

Stan got into the van and drove off down Campbell Road towards Hanford.

—

'That sounds promising, Sunday dinner with the family – for the second time,' said Dottie.

'His sister has sent me some clothes to wear in the sidecar.' Ruth laid out a waistcoat, which was padded, a lovely pair of leather gloves and a fine-looking jacket.

> *Brook Cottage*
> *St Anne's Vale*
> *Brown Edge*
>
> *29 August 1915*

Dear Ruth,

I hope you don't mind, but I borrowed some better clothes for you. The waistcoat will keep your body nice and warm under your jacket and should be worn with a skirt and boots. It will look very smart.

I would also like to advise you woman to woman that a second vest and drawers would be helpful to keep you warm. I've heard Stan say that is the case. The waistcoat comes from Mark and the jacket is my mother's. Don't worry, they know about it.

I look forward to seeing you on Sunday.
Best wishes,
Rosie (Bristow)

Ruth handed the letter to Dottie, who remarked how nice the handwriting was. When she read the letter, she smiled. 'I think you have made a friend there.'

'I think my coat and Donald's pullover didn't impress her.'

'I hope it's a nice day for you on Sunday.'

Chapter Twenty

September 1915

Ruth was ready on Sunday afternoon. Her borrowed clothes fitted her, and did a lot more for her than those she wore last time. The gloves were particularly nice. She wondered if Mrs Bristow had made them.

Stan arrived in the van a few minutes early. Dottie and Carla were waiting with Ruth in the front room.

'Have a lovely afternoon and we'll see you at teatime,' said Carla.

'Thank you.' Ruth left the house and was shutting the gate when Stan appeared from the other side of the van.

'Hello, Ruthie. Glad to see everything fitted. The weather looks set fair. Shall we go?'

Stan helped her into the van and cranked the engine. After a few minutes, they were on Moorland Road.

'Rosie will be pleased everything fits you. Hope you don't mind, but these are more appropriate and you will feel more comfortable.'

'She did a splendid job. I really like the gloves. Did your mother make them?'

'Yes, she makes them out of offcuts of leather. She doesn't like to see waste.'

'So Gertie's finished.'

'Yes. She looks magnificent, if I say so myself.'

'So, let's hear the story of how she got her name.'

'That was Father's idea. Gertrude's my mother's name and when we were having a bit of difficulty building the sidecar, Father decided she was being awkward like Mother is from time to time. The name just stuck.'

Ruth giggled, and her eyebrows lifted. 'What did she say when she found out?'

'Nothing. She just tutted and carried on with what she was doing. You see, it may be my father's business and it might be my motorcycle, but it's Mother that's the boss in our house. If she didn't like it, she would have told us so and that would have been the end. So saying nothing was the highest level of approval she could give about the name, without having to admit she liked it.'

'Do I use it or just call her "the motorcycle and sidecar"?'

'No, you can call her Gertie. Everybody does. Mother is always called "Mother"; even Father calls her that so there's no confusion. I've never heard her addressed by anyone from the village as anything other than Mrs Bristow. Likely as not no one will make the connection. Between me and you, I think Mother really likes it.'

Soon they arrived to be greeted by a gleaming Gertie. Stan had painted her pale lemon, as he'd said.

'What do yer think of her?' Stan said with pride.

'She's beautiful and you're right, the colour looks very nice.'

Rosie came running out of the gate and over to where they stood looking at Gertie. 'Hello, Ruth, I'm so glad the jacket fitted you,' she panted.

'Yes, thank you very much, Rosie. I feel much more comfortable than last time. I have a scarf and the gloves ready, so I'm all set.'

'And the other things?'

'Yes, I have two of them on.'

Rosie looked pleased with herself and her elevated status as Ruth's confidante. 'Good.'

'You've grown since I was last here.'

'Yes, Mother has had to alter my clothes. I'm so excited. I'm starting my last year at school tomorrow.'

'Go and tell yer Mother we've arrived. I want to show Ruth what we've done.' Stan gave his sister a stern look.

'Yes, Stan. I know what we agreed; I'm going.' Rosie left them and returned to the house.

'She's been looking forward to today all week, and will probably not stop talking until she's told to by Mother.'

They walked over to Gertie. 'If you look down between the side of the motorcycle and the sidecar, you'll see those two joints. They were the ones that I got from that catalogue you brought over.'

'Oh yes.' Ruth immediately thought about his parting remark on that day – *it'll be worth it if you can come out with me*. This remark had given her some sleepless nights. What did he mean? Was he testing the water or was it just a slip of the tongue? Come to think of it, he had mentioned about them going out on more than one occasion.

She came out of her reverie.

'…and you remove these safety bolts and then the sidecar's no longer connected. There's nothing left on the motorcycle that might catch on the ground when I'm riding her solo. It's safer for me and faster when I want to take somebody out.'

'Yes, I understand.' She didn't – she had taken in little of what he had said at all. Instead, she'd concentrated on the animation on his face.

The rest of the family had joined them. The last one being a tall, leggy lad Stan introduced as his brother.

'Pleased to meet you, Mark,' said Ruth, shaking his hand. 'Thank you for the waistcoat; it was a kind thought.'

'You're welcome, miss.'

'Call me Ruth.'

'Yes, Miss… Ruth.' The poor lad looked so embarrassed she felt sorry for him.

'The seat looks so nice and the inside looks totally different. You've made a lovely job of the upholstery and leather work.'

'Not me,' said Stan. 'That's all Mother and Father's work.'

Stan then pulled the cloth away from the front of the sidecar.

Ruth gasped. 'Oh, you painted her name on her. That is exquisite. Did you do that?'

'No, that was a friend of Father's. He's a sign-writer, and he happily helped. He normally works on canal barges and delivery lorries and the like. So you like it, then?'

After more chatting, the family and Ruth went into the kitchen.

Ruth whispered to Stan, 'Does your mother approve?'

'Yes, she even said it was pretty, and that she felt honoured.'

They ate their Sunday dinner. As predicted, Rosie was full of herself and even Mark entered the conversations. Mrs Bristow was the quietest and Ruth thought how proud she looked of her family.

It was easier for Ruth to get into the sidecar now the seat was complete and a little higher. She settled inside and soon they were waving goodbye to the Bristows.

They left the village in the same direction as before, but soon turned left down a steep lane. Eventually they arrived at Mow Cop Castle. The view from here was spectacular. They approached the landowner's folly, a mock ruin. All the time they were walking, Stan kept looking at Gertie and she thought he looked relieved once they were back.

The journey continued through south Cheshire and after several more stops they pulled into a little village with a pond at the centre. There was a bench by the side of the pond on which they sat, looking at the scene.

Ruth glanced across the view in front of them. Fancy living in a place like this without the carts and carriages, smoke and the noise of the town.

'This is lovely. Where are we?'

'Betley, south of Crewe.'

'We went to Crewe Park the Easter before the war started. Carla, Dottie and me. It seems like a lifetime ago.'

They sat for a few minutes, taking in the view.

'It's quiet because everyone's mucking in with the harvest,' said Stan.

'It's a different world, but so close to Stoke. It feels like I'm on my holidays, but I've never had a holiday, so can't really compare.'

'We'll have to correct that one day.'

There it was again. The 'we'll', the expectation that the two of them had a future together. She was about to ask him when he picked up her hand in his.

'I want to talk to you about the day you brought the catalogue over.'

'Yes?' She looked him in the eye.

'I meant it, you know. When I had the accident and you and Walter took care of me, I knew from that moment I wanted to ask you out, but I never seemed to get the chance or have the courage. You seemed happy with your life and then there was all the trouble in your street and you had to help your friend.' As if he suddenly realised he was still holding her hand, Stan let go.

Ruth would have been happy for her hand to stay exactly where it was. She just wanted to listen to him talking.

He frowned. 'D'yer want me to carry on?'

She nodded, smiling. 'Yes, please.'

She didn't find out what he had been going to say when the conversation started, because their lips met and they kissed. A kiss like she had never experienced before. Her heart almost stopped. Her body, her whole being, yearned for it. When he finally moved away, she wanted to pull him back. Jim had never made her feel like this.

'Ruthie, I want to hold you, to kiss you, to feel you near me. D'yer think you might feel the same sometime soon? I'm prepared to wait. I dunner want to fo—'

Ruth laid a finger on his lips to stop him. 'I don't have to think about anything, Stan. I know what I want to do.' She leaned towards him, inviting his kiss. His arms went round her and she clung to him, not wanting to let go.

They continued to sit, arms around each other, watching the sun creep across the landscape.

Later, they rode around empty lanes, weaving their way back towards Stoke. The experience had been exhilarating. Ruth's body had never felt so alive. She could see why Stan loved his motorcycle and the freedom that it gave. And the kisses had taken her breath away. There would be no going back now. He felt the same as she did.

They returned to Campbell Road.

Getting out was more difficult than getting in and this time Stan didn't need telling to turn around.

'Did you enjoy that?'

'Yes, I really did. We were going so fast – in every sense.' She felt breathless.

'Not really – about thirty miles an hour, but because you're low down, it feels much faster.'

'It was certainly an exciting way to travel, but rain could be a problem.'

'You need a leather jacket like mine.'

As Stan was about to set off, Ruth said, 'By the way, what were you going to say when we were sitting by the pond?'

'It doesn't matter.'

'Of course it does. What was it, Stan?'

'I was going to ask if you would consider walking out with me – regular like. But I think we've already got the answer.' He grinned and, with a wave, he revved the engine and pulled away.

–

Later that evening, Carla asked Ruth if she had enjoyed her ride on the motorcycle.

'Yes, I really did. It differed from how I thought it would be and it's so comfortable now it's finished.'

'In what way?'

'It felt fast, and I was low in the seat. We met the occasional car and tram and they seemed enormous. You know something, I really enjoyed the time we spent together today. He is such a nice man. So comfortable to be with.'

'I don't think that description applies to Donald. The first time we kissed, I could have ripped his trousers off. But I didn't.'

'Dottie Spilling, fancy you thinking like that,' they both said in unison.

'I can say that now. I married him. What I really meant was that you want a man that makes you go weak at the knees foremost, and then you can think about comfort.'

'Oh, he does that, too. I discovered that today. I never thought a man could make me feel so alive.'

'So long as you love his motorcycle, I suspect,' said Carla.

They laughed.

'You can't say anything to anybody just yet. We didn't exactly say we were walking out, but after the way we kissed, I think we both know that'll be the result.'

'You kissed!'

'Yes, more than once.' She recounted what had happened, even though she was originally going to tell no one. But she couldn't hold back her happiness. No doubt tomorrow she'd be plagued by guilt that she had not thought of Dottie being without Donald, and Carla being on her own. She was sure they'd be happy for her.

—

When Ruth got home from work that evening, Carla was sitting at the kitchen table. Dottie hadn't yet returned from work and there was no smell or sounds of cooking.

'What's up, Carla? Why is there no tea on?'

'I'm sorry, Ruth, is it that time already? I've had a bit of bad news today.'

'It's not your mother and father, is it?'

'No, it's Bertie. They transferred him to an internment camp on the Isle of Man. It's so far away, Ruth. Here, read the letter yourself.'

'I think we should get some tea first.'

The two women busied themselves preparing potatoes and some runner beans from the allotment.

Once that was out of the way, Ruth and Dottie caught up with the contents of the letter.

27 August 1915

My dear Carla,

I hope you are well and putting up with all the changes. I have got some news myself for you.

The authorities moved me to an internment camp, Knockaloe, on the Isle of Man. The island is in the middle of the Irish Sea. I left Brocton camp on the 24 August and travelled to Liverpool. They put me on a boat to the island. There were five other men with me, all of us German, from various parts of the Midlands.

When we arrived, we were feeling ill from the crossing. It is not a bad idea of the authorities to put us here, because if any of us were thinking about escaping crossing that sea again, we would think twice about it.

They built the camp quickly, yet the wooden huts are sturdy, and the camp has a permanent feel that doesn't bode well for us. There's not much I can say about the camp – we get three meals a day which are fine, not like home cooking, but nourishing. Currently, many more huts exist, and I believe Mr Asquith intends to fulfil his promise to intern more aliens. The biggest problem for us is boredom. Pleasant countryside surrounds us, yet we remain idle. One guard said that the British can't put us to work because it's against international law. We even volunteered, but they rejected us.

So we just sit here, playing cards, playing chess and exercising. One guard brought us a football last week and so at least we can get regular exercise and have some fun at the same time. I think you will need to prepare yourself for me staying here until the war ends. There is barbed wire everywhere, a constant reminder we are prisoners.

I would like you to see Edith and Luther and tell them about me. I will contact them soon. We may send letters, but the cost of postage will be prohibitive.

Give my regards to Ruth. And also Dottie. Knowing you have friends and a place to stay provides solace.

I must close now. Please take care of yourself and I will try to write again.

Your loving brother,
Bertie

Bertie had never been a keen letter writer, but all agreed that he sounded depressed. But at least they knew where he was and he was alive. Carla went to bed early that night and when Ruth crept past the door later, she tried not to disturb her friend, who was sleeping peacefully.

—

September ended, and a chill permeated the air. When Ruth got home from work on Monday evening, a concerned-looking Carla greeted her.

'I've had another letter from Bertie today.'

'Is he okay?'

'Yes, as far as I can see. He hasn't heard from Edith since his move to the Isle of Man in August, almost two months ago. They were in contact a few times at Brocton, but nothing since. Bertie's concerned she's lost his address at Knockaloe. He's asked if I'll go to see her to be on the safe side.'

'How do you feel about that?'

'I'm happy to talk to Edith, but I don't know how I'll feel returning to the estate.'

'Don't worry, I'll come with you. I can visit my father and Walter and then we can see Edith. We can make an afternoon of it.'

'I'm not sure I feel up to socialising.'

'It's the first time I've heard my father and Walter described as socialising.'

'Would you be upset if we simply went straight up to Edith's and returned without visiting the estate?'

'Of course not. I don't want to walk up Dartmouth Street, with its memories. We can catch the tram from London Road, which goes straight to Smallthorne and get off at the Miners' Hall. That way we can skirt around the estate to Hamil Road, visit Edith, and then walk back down into Burslem. Perhaps if you feel like it, we can have a cup of tea and a bun at the café near to the town hall.'

'Yes, that sounds excellent.'

Chapter Twenty-One

October 1915

'You'll never believe it, girls.'

In the restroom, Ruth, Peggy, Cissie, Molly and Daisy were chatting and laughing while eating their dinners. The men sat together in the workshop, talking about engines and the two local football clubs.

'What have you heard this time, Pearl Langley? Sit yourself down and tell us,' said Daisy, as if she didn't already know the latest gossip. Of course, she couldn't say anything. Not without Mr Taylor's say so.

'You've heard the chatter about places employing women as drivers and conductors, right?' She stopped, looked at their blank faces and carried on, regardless. 'A journalist has just been in.'

'Yes, I know,' said Daisy. 'He was with Mr Taylor until about half an hour ago.'

'He says that several tram companies are signing up women to be conductors... and some are even employing women as drivers! What d'yer think of that?'

Women – running trams through The Potteries. Now there's an interesting idea, thought Ruth. The war's losses of more and more men had prompted some discussion of the idea, but the PTC appeared unwilling to employ women in traditionally male roles. The unions believed it wasn't a job for a woman, to be working on her own, on a tram during the hours of darkness. Who would protect them from... the inappropriate behaviour of drunken men late at night?

'I don't want no union man telling me what's lady-like and what isn't. Women should have their own say in the matter,' said Molly.

'I don't believe I know of any man what would take you on, Molly, duck,' said Pearl with a laugh.

Molly thought for a moment. 'I think I might have a go at something like that. Would clippies have to wear a uniform?'

'It could be very fetching, don't you think?' said Cissie. 'And make you look intelligent.'

Everyone laughed. 'Who says as we need a uniform to make us intelligent, Cissie,' said Pearl, hands on hips.

'I think the PTC's going to employ women on the trams, otherwise they will have to stop running cos there'll be nobody to operate them.' Ruth shrugged her shoulders. 'It's common sense.'

'The man from the paper said they'd already done it in Birmingham and they've even got a hostel for the women who come from outside of the city,' said Daisy, nodding her head as if to prove a point.

Later that day, someone saw Daisy putting a notice on the restroom board, which caused quite a hullabaloo.

```
          Potteries Tramway Company

      Male Conductors and Drivers, and
               Lady Conductors

       To start now. For the duration of
                   the war.
```

> Gentlemen, if you haven't been accepted into the army but want to serve your country, the Potteries Tramway Company is eager to hear from you.
>
> Ladies, are you looking for something to do to help your country while earning a man's wage? We want to hear from you too.
>
> Advertisement to appear in tomorrow night's copy of The Sentinel.

The notice explicitly referred only to lady conductors, clearly omitting lady drivers. Still, getting women employed in the industry had to start somewhere. She had heard of women going into munitions, the railways and even shipyards, so why not trams?

It sounded exciting and if she'd still been a typist she might have considered it. She might not be interested, but she knew a woman who might be and she couldn't wait to tell her!

—

Ruth bounded into the house. 'I've got the most fabulous news.'

Carla was in the scullery putting a pan in to soak; Dottie was carrying the tea into the kitchen. 'Ruth, for goodness' sake, I nearly dropped the tea.'

'Carla, I might've just found a job for you.' Ruth held her breath, waiting for a show of excitement from the other two. 'At the PTC.'

'And...?'

'I thought you'd be eager.'

Carla gave a nervous laugh. 'I might be if I knew more about it and I wasn't hungry.'

If Ruth didn't know otherwise, she would have thought that Carla was trying to change the subject.

Ruth forgave her. Maybe she was expecting too much. After all, she had said nothing about the job yet.

Dottie was looking at Carla and added, 'I'm sure we're all ears, but do you think we should eat first before the taters get cold?'

Ruth took the hint. Given Carla's rather fragile disposition, her news might need careful handling. Carla didn't speak and spent the time staring at her plate, picking at the food. But Ruth was determined that it would be ideal for Carla.

'So, what did you two get up to today?' said Ruth, smiling at both of them.

'We got some new designs at work today. Makes it a bit more interesting to do but takes longer cos yer has to learn the design,' said Dottie. 'The piece-work rate is the same.'

Carla shrugged. 'I was mainly tidying the house, you know.'

They carried on in silence. It had been such a shame these last few weeks with so much in the air with her family. If they could persuade Carla to take a lady conductor job, Ruth believed it would help lift Carla's current depression.

Before anyone could get up to make a pot of tea, Carla spoke out. 'I can see you're bursting to tell me, Ruth. What sort of job is it?'

'It's jobs, Carla. The PTC are taking on several people to replace the men that have gone to war. They're looking for women and men to be conductors on their trams.'

'Conductors?'

Ruth nodded. 'Yes, conductors, all across the borough. You'd be working on the trams all day, handing out tickets and collecting money. You'd get a man's wage, a war bonus and free travelling. Doesn't that sound worth thinking about?'

'I don't think I could do that – meeting all those people.' Carla shuddered. 'You know what it's like. Supposing people find out about me?'

'Think about it, Carla. You're British... and you have the paperwork to prove it. You can tell them at the interview and if you get the job, there's nothing more for them to find out. Yes, Peggy might gossip, but you've already been the subject of one of Peggy's rants and she's been told to be careful how she treats other people.'

'But, people will still know and what happens if the public find out?'

'Nothing, the public don't care a jot. They use the trams to get to and from work or shopping. They have their own lives. Come on Carla, it makes so much sense.'

'Ruth's right,' said Dottie, 'you'd never be on your own with passengers coming and going. You don't have to talk to them if you don't want to.'

Ruth stared at Carla and could see uncertainty in her face. She pressed on. 'It must be worth thinking about, wouldn't you say? Think of the money if nothing else.'

Carla stared at Ruth.

'Come on, Carla. It could be a great opportunity. You were used to handling cash in the shop – it would be ideal.

No one would ever detect you were not born and bred in The Potteries. Please say you'll think about it.'

Carla gave in with a deep sigh. 'Yes, I'll think about it.'

—

Carla and Ruth had an early dinner on Sunday to make sure they caught the direct tram to Smallthorne to see Edith. At the Miners' Hall stop, which was one before they would normally use, they got off and walked along Park Road, into Sneyd Street and then right onto Hamil Road. The third street up on the left was Leigh Street and number 24 was on the right. It had a wall and gate at the front, giving a small garden only five feet deep, very typical of the newer houses being built in the area. Children were playing, enjoying themselves in the early autumn sunshine.

Ruth closed the gate behind her and Carla was just about to knock when she heard whispering voices -- too low to make out anything said. Carla glanced at Ruth and made a face of concern. She knocked and waited. A few moments later, Mrs Wren appeared at the door.

'It's you. What do you want?' snapped Mrs Wren.

There seemed to be a lot of anger in the voice. 'Hello, Mrs Wren. I wonder if I could speak to Edith, please?'

'No, she's not in and neither is her boy.'

'When will they be back?'

'Dunno. After seven o'clock, maybe.'

Ruth and Carla stood there. Ruth hoped for an invitation, but none came.

'Would it be possible for me to leave a note of my brother's address for Edith? He's now on the Isle of Man and would like to hear from his wife,' said Carla formally.

'So, they've moved him with all them other internees. Safest place for them, I reckon, they conner do nobody any harm.'

'But Mrs Wren – he's your son-in-law,' Ruth butted in.

'And what business is it of yours?' Mrs Wren continued without pausing for a reply. 'I think it'd be best if you ladies return to where you came from. Edith and Luther want nothing more to do with him. They were raised British, and I'm proud to be British. I objected to her marrying a foreigner from the start, and now the baby will always be identified as part German, thanks to your brother.'

'What difference will that make? Most of the people in Stoke-on-Trent come from somewhere else. Miners have come from all over the place, and so have people to work in the potbanks. How in God's name is anybody going to think of Luther as anything but a Stoke lad?'

'You hit the nail right on the head there. His name, for one thing. No matter what you say, he's always going to be known as Luther Hesse.'

'So you just don't like him because of the German implications.'

'You're quick on the uptake, aren't you? Your type's not welcome around here. Our British lads are fighting abroad, while you lot stay here in safety. Your brother dunner have to work and gets a bed and three meals a day. It makes me sick.'

Carla was on the verge of tears when she looked round to Ruth. Although Ruth had learned to always respect her elders and betters, she decided it was time to tell Mrs Wren a thing or two. She was just about to launch into a defence of her friends when Carla handed Mrs Wren a piece of paper on which she had written Bertie's name and address so that Edith could write to him when she wished.

Carla gave one last plea. 'We'll leave you in peace, but please give this to Edith, Mrs Wren.'

Without another word, Mrs Wren took the note and shut the door. A bolt clicked into place as much as to say the conversation was over.

Ruth and Carla were so shocked they couldn't move. Carla spoke first. 'I half expected that. Mrs Wren was never in favour of Bertie, but he was a respectable man and would one day be the owner of a very prosperous shop. She considered the marriage to be advantageous. Bertie always said that his mother-in-law could see herself running the shop one day.'

'I think that might have had some influence on her,' agreed Ruth.

'She was very concerned about her appearance to the neighbours and obviously before war broke out, he was being portrayed to Mrs Wren's friends as a fine man, a good catch.'

'She's changed her mind now. How could somebody say what she said about a child less than a year old? Do you think it's Edith's view?'

'I lived with Edith for a couple years, but I never really got to know her. I remember Edith and Bertie having a discussion one night and Edith saying her mother would come round eventually, but that was when they were first courting.'

'What are you going to do, then?'

'There's not much I can do. I shall write a letter to Edith to explain everything, but I doubt whether her mother will give it to her. But I've got to try.'

'I think Edith was in the house all the time. All that whispering was making sure that Edith and Luther were out of earshot. Let's knock on the back door. She'll not be expecting that.'

'No, Ruth, as much as I would like to, I don't want to make the situation worse. I'll write back to Bertie telling him what's happened. But I shall worry that it'll destroy what little confidence he's got left.'

'Perhaps take a few days before you reply. I'll help you if you want me to?'

'Yes, that sounds like a good idea.'

The two friends walked down Hamil Road, then cut through Burslem Park and into the town centre. By the time they got home, they had both calmed down. When they told Dottie, she was as shocked as they were.

—

Ruth, Pearl and Daisy were sitting in the restroom.

'Have we had many applications for the lady conductor jobs?' Ruth asked, wondering how much competition Carla would have. Ruth had finally persuaded her to apply, and now she felt concerned about whether she had done the right thing.

'We've had quite a few letters – and several women have been in to the reception wanting to apply.'

'So, it looks as if it's going to be successful.' Ruth was glad for the company, but hoped it wouldn't make things difficult for Carla.

'I'm not so sure of that,' said Daisy. 'Being a conductor requires a certain level of education; being able to do simple maths and to write legibly are so important. But we'll see. I'm glad I don't have to interview them.'

'I bet it was strange when you started here, Pearl. All of those men and just you,' said Ruth.

'It was different. I'd worked in a shop before and was used to meeting lots of people. I think that's what got me this job. The company had only just started here. It was 1899, the year we had the boiler house built, and the generators installed.'

'I came in 1909 and was the first female secretary the company had,' said Daisy. 'Now the situation has become acute. I believe that thirty-seven men have left to join the army out of just over four hundred. So far, only Mr Adams, the manager at Goldenhill, has returned. They're covering the men's work by paying overtime or reducing services, but it's expensive. We can't stop men from joining up, but they have to be replaced somehow.'

-

Ruth went back to Dartmouth Street to pay a visit to her family on Sunday afternoon. She wanted to pass on the news to Walter about Carla.

While the family were eating their warming pudding of crumble, she made a general comment for the ears of everyone. 'Carla seems to be feeling a little better now she's heard from her family. I've even persuaded her to apply for one of the lady conductor jobs the PTC are advertising.'

'Well done to Carla, and well done to you, Ruth, for helping her to come to the decision,' said Joan with a broad smile.

The men, except for Walter, cheered at the news. Walter just looked astounded. Before he could blurt out anything he might regret, she added, 'Yes, we talked about it and she thought it would help her to start a new life, and put what's happened this year in the past where it should be.'

'It could be the making of her,' said Frank, devouring another mouthful of pudding. 'Wouldn't you say so, Walter?'

He nodded slowly. 'I suppose it would be a help.'

He didn't say much else, and Ruth was glad.

When they went to sit down, Ruth helped Joan with the dishes and then, noticing Walter on his own in the backyard, she went out to him.

They stood together, neither speaking.

'So she truly is all right about the job?' said Walter in a low voice.

'When I first saw the notice about the jobs, I told her about it, casually. She was nervous at first, but then she picked up and thought it was a good idea. The wage is good and she will be with a lot of people.'

'But how'll she cope?'

'She needs to learn, Walter. She's a grown woman and now her family isn't here, she needs others around her to make up for her loss. You have to support her through this.'

—

Ruth returned from her parents. Carla had waited a few days before she replied to Bertie. Whatever she said was going to crush him, and she admitted to Ruth that doing nothing seemed an attractive prospect. Carla handed Ruth the letter to Bertie, which she had just completed.

13 October 1915

Dear Bertie,

I have been to see Edith, but she was unavailable. Mrs Wren agreed to take your new address, but she did not seem too keen on the idea of you communicating. So what do you want me to do?

There isn't much else I can say. The only bit of comfort I can offer is that Mrs Wren's attitude sounds nothing like the Edith we know, but we also know that Edith's mother was very conscious of what the neighbours thought of her, so perhaps she's influenced her daughter.

Look forward to hearing from you soon.
Your loving sister,
Carla

'What d'yer think?'

'It's short, but you don't want to go into too much detail when he can't do anything about it. He'll feel helpless and, worse, very angry.'

—

That day, twelve ladies attended for interview and ten were chosen to train, including Carla, according to Pearl.

Ruth was over the moon to hear the news and promised to tell no one apart from Carla herself – to put her mind at rest. To be honest, Ruth would've had great difficulty in keeping the news to herself because as soon as she saw Carla, she grinned like a Cheshire cat.

Carla jumped out of her seat as soon as Ruth walked through the door.

'You think I've got the job?' There was a level of anxiety in Carla's voice, and Ruth couldn't keep it to herself.

'Yes! You've got a job! The letters'll go out either tomorrow or Thursday to start on 25 October. I'm so pleased for you.'

Everyone embraced. This had to be one of the best days they'd had for a long time.

Chapter Twenty-Two

October–November 1915

Ruth and Carla walked along Campbell Road and through to Woodhouse Street together. It was raining and not a good start, but Carla didn't seem to care – she was just happy to have, at last, found a job so that she could pay her way.

Last night, Ruth had caught Carla crying in her bedroom. 'Carla, whatever's the matter? Sitting here upset and on your own. Are you worried about starting to work tomorrow?'

Carla shook her head, biting into the handkerchief she had wiped her eyes with.

'Then what is it? Has something happened?'

'No. Nothing bad – quite the opposite, really.'

Ruth put her head on one side. 'Then what is it?'

'I've just read the letter from Mother and Father again and I so want to tell them about the job and all that's happening, but even if I write to them now, they probably won't get it. If I write and tell them, I'll want proof that they've received it.' She blew her nose and glanced at Ruth. 'Do you think I'm being childish?'

'Of course not. Why don't you write it anyway and then you'll get it off your chest and who knows – you might get a reply.'

Carla had been honest with the PTC, too. Because she knew Ruth, she felt honour bound to tell them she was British, born in The Potteries, but her family was German. When asked if her family was still in this country, she said no and wasn't expecting to see them for some time, given the current situation. The man asking the questions had thanked her for her honesty. Later, she told Ruth that she didn't want to be incessantly looking over her shoulders, wondering if she might be reported.

Carla was stronger than Ruth had given her credit for. 'How do you feel today, Carla?'

'Surprisingly, I'm looking forward to it. Nervous, but that'll pass once I've got something to do.' She paused and then said, 'Sorry about last night. This job is the most important thing I've done for myself since deciding not to go to Germany with my parents.'

Ruth linked arms with her. 'I don't blame you. But hopefully, it will be the first of many experiences for you.'

Once inside the PTC, Ruth wished Carla good luck and walked up to the cash office, knowing her mind would be with Carla until they spoke again and she very much hoped Carla didn't make any mistakes.

Ruth waited for Carla at dinnertime and showed her round the building to where they could eat. Carla talked until she went back to work about her new colleagues, and how to use the clipping machines, handling cash and so on. Carla giggled when she mentioned Daisy had told them about the facilities because queues were forming in the yard over the two conveniences available. More were due to be installed, she said. After all, if a tram was late, the lady conductor could hardly say that she had been waiting in a queue for the privy, could she?

'You never told me about that, did you?' The grin spread from ear to ear.

Watching Carla now, Ruth could see nothing of the girl she had comforted last night. She hadn't seen Carla so animated for a long time. This job could be the making of her.

–

Today had been the first time the trainees had been out on a tram with an experienced conductor. The trainers asked each new lady conductor to wear dark clothing and provided them with a red-and-cream sash and a PTC lapel badge until their uniforms arrived after passing the final test. Which was fortunate, as the manufacturers had not yet delivered the uniforms. However, they expected the first delivery of assorted sizes any day.

Ruth caught up with Carla during their dinnertime break. She was desperate to find out what Carla thought of being on the trams. Ruth found Carla sitting with another woman, chatting away. Ruth joined them.

'This is my friend Ruth. She works in the office. Ruth, this is Doris Barlow.'

'Pleased to meet you. So, how did you go on?'

Doris had plenty to say. 'It was good. First two days were like being at school talking about what we were going to do and simple things like adding up cash and the like. Everybody knows how to count, don't they?'

Ruth laughed. 'I suppose it is easy to think that, but when you've got a tram full of passengers clamouring for tickets and nobody's got the right change, it might get stressful.'

Doris nodded. 'Putting it like that, I can see that it could put a lot of pressure on us.'

Ruth turned to Carla. 'What about you, Carla?'

'Being used to working in the shop, I was fine with the money, although I never had the pressure that we might have. But, so far, so good.'

Carla was grinning, and Ruth had no reason to think she was lying and so she relaxed.

'But today was totally different. Spending time on the trams made it all feel real. I think I'm going to enjoy it,' said Carla.

—

Ruth thought the women had settled in well, considering the work must've been so different from what they'd been used to, standing on their feet all day, being pleasant to unpleasant people and being responsible for bags heavy with coins. Aching legs and feet, aching shoulders and occasional headaches often appeared during those first few days. Inside, the trams were cool and full of cigarette smoke. Windows steamed up and had to be wiped.

Over that first week, Carla seemed to grow in confidence, as did the rest of the clippies. She had continued her friendship with Doris, who Ruth had described as 'motherly' to Walter and Father when they asked. Ruth didn't think Carla was looking for a mother substitute; rather, she had spent a lot of her time in the company of older people and felt most comfortable with them.

They assigned Carla to Stoke depot with Doris and a couple of others. The training lasted ten days and as the second week began, excitement buzzed throughout the buildings. The tests, which would confirm them all as lady conductors, would start the next day. For the test, inspectors would observe them working as real conductors on one of the longer tram routes, assessing their performance at any point along the route. Two experienced male conductors did their best to make the test sound even worse than the trainees could imagine, while others said not to be so daft because the PTC needed all of them. If the inspector approved, they would receive their full uniform and join next week's rota.

Ruth found time to speak to Carla and Doris after their tests and wanted to know how each had fared.

'I believe we all knew what we were doing, but it's so scary being watched, isn't it, Doris?' Carla admitted. 'Most things you do naturally because you know it's right. When the inspector's watching, you question yourself over everything and wonder what he would've done. That's when the panic sets in and makes it much worse.'

'And you wonder if somebody'll start playing up,' said Doris. 'Somebody had a go at me. Said I'd given him the wrong change for the ticket he'd bought. As luck would have it, I still had the ticket in my hand. That nice inspector, Mr Caldwell, came to me, asked the passenger for an explanation, but he couldn't explain, so Mr Caldwell told the passenger to leave at the next stop or face being reported as a public nuisance.'

Carla shuddered. 'Thank the Lord that didn't happen to me. I wouldn't be able to sleep at night. I hate being watched.'

From the ten women who had trained at Stoke, one left after a single day, while another failed the test and was required to repeat the training.

The uniforms, in the same dark blue serge as the men, had arrived. Skirts were a regulation ten inches above the ground to enable the lady conductor to move up and down the steep flights of stairs on double-decker trams.

'It's great having more of us women about the place. Show all these men we can do our bit,' said Pearl.

Ruth stayed in the office until Carla finished her first shift. When she arrived at reception, the group of clippies were having their final instructions from Inspector Caldwell.

'So how did you really get on?' Ruth asked.

'Better than I thought. I thought all eyes would be on me, watching me and trying to trip me up. I even wondered if people would realise I'm part of the German family that had all the trouble a few months back. Some are friendly and like a chat, but most of the passengers don't know we're there.'

Ruth nodded. 'I'm so glad you've enjoyed it. You'll find that now you're wearing your uniform, all you clippies will look the same. I've seen it happen with the men. You're going to be fine, Carla.'

Seeing Carla so eager was a real bonus, although Carla's excitement might diminish when she was getting out of bed at four or five in the morning for the early shift!

—

'Right now, ladies. Gather round. I've got your badges here. This badge shows you work for The Potteries Tramway Company, or the PTC – so please don't lose it. You should wear it with pride – every one of you. You lady conductors will go down in the history of this company as our very first clippies.'

He handed out the badges, and chatter erupted as each woman pinned her badge to her lapel.

'There will be a list on the notice board of your placements from Monday. Could I speak to Doris Barlow, please?'

'I'm here, sir.'

'You'll be working at the Stoke depot until 4 December when you'll transfer to Longton.'

Once outside in the chilly darkness of the November evening, Carla linked her arm with Ruth's and drew a deep breath. 'I'll be working at Stoke depot. It's been so good getting this job. I hope I succeed.'

Ruth patted the hand holding her arm. 'I'm so glad you're enjoying it, Carla. A new life beckons?'

'Definitely!'

—

Carla had finished her work for the week and decided that as she had not heard from Bertie, she would give Edith another try. It was a month before Christmas when Carla and Ruth repeated the journey that they had made at the beginning of October.

'What sort of reception do you think we'll get this time?'

'I don't know, Carla; I'd expect it to be a little bit worse and as we haven't heard from Bertie, I think we safely can assume that he hasn't heard from Edith either.'

'We have to keep trying. It must be horrible for him with nothing to do and not able to take charge of anything.'

The tram pulled up at the Miners' Hall stop. Arriving at number 24, the different curtains at the window surprised them. Carla knocked on the door and waited.

'Hello, love. What can I do you for?' A jolly little man in his early forties answered the door.

'I'm looking for a friend of mine, Edith or Mrs Wren?'

'Oh love, you've missed them. We're new tenants. We moved in a week ago.'

'Do you know where they went?'

'Oh no, love – they didn't leave any address. You could try asking the landlord or the rent man.'

'Thank you. I'm sorry to disturb you on a Sunday afternoon.'

The man smiled and shut the door. As they closed the gate behind them, the lady from number 22 popped her head around her front door.

'Are you looking for Mrs Wren?'

'Yes. You don't know where they are, do you?'

The woman stepped out onto the front step. 'They've gone to Bradford, duckie; that's where Mrs Wren came from originally.'

'Bradford?'

'Bradford in Yorkshire. They went a week last Thursday. I said to my husband, Mr Bailey, it was strange. They was all carrying cases and disappeared down the road before I could get outside to ask them where they was going. Then the following day some men came round and picked up all their furniture.'

'Did they say anything?'

'They started at seven o'clock in the morning, woke me and my husband up. They were gone by ten o'clock, miserable bunch, they were, wouldn't tell me nowt. When the rent man came round on Friday, I asked him what was happening and all he would say is that we were having new neighbours.'

'Did the van have a name on it?'

'No, it was blue.'

'Dark blue or light blue?'

'Middling. It was Mrs Corbishley from number thirty-seven what told me they had gone to live with her family in Bradford, or was it Barnsley?'

Ruth scribbled Walter's name and address on a piece of paper and handed it to the woman. 'If you hear anything, we'd be grateful if they could tell my brother Walter.'

'Yes, love, I'll do that if I hear anything. What's your interest in them? I reckon I've seen your face before?'

'Edith's my sister-in-law.'

'You used to own the shop on Dartmouth Street.'

'That's correct.'

'Terrible business what happened to you.'

Ruth and Carla returned home. This time, Carla wrote to Bertie immediately. She told him what had happened and asked what he wanted her to do next and waited for his reply.

Chapter Twenty-Three

December 1915

Carla didn't have long to wait. When she got in from work, she saw the letter waiting for her on the kitchen table. It came from the internment camp.

'It looks as if we've got a reply from Bertie,' said Ruth.

'But that's not Bertie's handwriting.'

'The only way to find out is to open it.'

With her heart in her mouth, Ruth watched as Carla took a knife from the table and slit open the envelope. A single sheet of paper lay inside. She looked at the letter, turned it over to check the signature and then read it.

'I was right. It's from someone called Manfred. Oh my word! I hope Bertie's all right.' Carla's hands shook as she tried to read the contents. 'It's in German, so it'll take me a few moments to translate it.'

'Is your German getting rusty with not using it now?'

'No, but this German's different, not the words but the phrases he uses. He could be from Bavaria.'

'Oh, you have different ways of speaking in Germany then?'

'Yes, it's just the same as here. You can usually tell where a person comes from by the phrases they use.'

Carla got a pencil out of her handbag, along with a small notebook, and worked on the translation. In the meantime, Dottie had arrived with a pan of sprouts from her allotment.

'Donald always said there was no point in picking sprouts until the frost had been on them. He said it brought out the taste.'

'I thought that was celery?' said Ruth.

'Perhaps it was. I see you've opened your letter, Carla. What does he have to say?'

Ruth shook her head. 'It's in German but not from Bertie.'

Dottie sat down at the table and, after a few more minutes, Carla announced that the translation was complete.

'My darling brother has been involved in a fight.'

Ruth's mouth fell open. 'Bertie! In a fight! I don't believe it.'

'He is all right, but unfortunately he fought with a guard, and they sentenced him to three months in solitary confinement.'

'What?'

'That's definitely what it says. His friend Manfred has written to let me know, so I don't worry. It means I won't hear from him until March at the earliest.'

'Poor Bertie,' said Ruth.

'Doesn't sound like Bertie,' added Dottie.

'No. Manfred said Bertie had got my letter and announced that his family had run away to Bradford. He was really angry and ended up hitting the guard who came to calm him down; none of them liked that guard, apparently.'

'What are you going to do now?' asked Ruth.

'Something I wish my brother had done. Wait patiently.'

The shops in Tunstall were busy, which meant the trams were too. Ruth gazed through shop windows in awe at the decorations, encouraging people to spend their money. Only a week to go. A second Christmas at war with no ending in sight.

Ruth was the last one home, and they had their tea almost immediately. They were finished when Dottie piped up, 'What are you two planning for Christmas?'

'I'm going to spend the day sitting by the range with my feet in a bowl of water. They've never ached so much!' said Carla.

They all laughed.

'There are no trams or trains on Christmas Day. So I'm going to stay with Father and Walter on Christmas Eve. We're going to put flowers on Mother's grave and then to Frank and Joan's for Christmas dinner and back to Dartmouth Street in the afternoon, spend the night there and return here on Boxing Day morning. Then nothing. Stan's spending the day with his family and working on Boxing Day. He said he would call in after work.'

'I was planning to do exactly the same. I'm the only one of the family to have left home so far and, like last Christmas, there will be no Donald. But, that leaves you, Carla, on your own for two nights.'

Carla shrugged. 'It's what I was expecting, anyway.'

'I can't leave you on your own, you must come to ours,' said Ruth.

'Or you could always come to mine, you're more than welcome, you know that.'

'Thank you very much for all your kind offers, but I have already made my plans. This is going to be the first

Christmas I have ever spent away from my parents, also the first Christmas away from the shop. I don't want to go back to Dartmouth Street or anywhere near. So I am going to spend it with Doris. She lives on her own and it seems the best thing to do.'

Ruth and Dottie looked at each other with surprise. This wasn't what Ruth expected. 'Are you sure?'

'Perfectly sure, but thank you for thinking about me.'

'That's settled then. By the way, Carla. A postcard came for you today,' said Dottie. 'I've put it on the sideboard in the front room.'

'Thanks, Dottie.' Carla wandered off to pick it up and returned quickly. 'It's a postcard from Edith. I recognise her writing. She says she's enjoying her holiday up north and may stay awhile. She says the landlady is very nice, and it's just like being at home. But she's signed it "Edith and Lionel Turnbull".'

The three of them looked at each other, each of them frowning.

'It's definitely Edith's writing,' said Carla. 'I think she's being careful with what she says in case someone else reads it.'

'She shouldn't have sent a postcard, then,' exclaimed Ruth.

The three women fell silent.

Dottie was the first to speak. 'We know her family comes from up north and I think the landlady she refers to could be her mother or other relation. She says it's just like being at home. And look, she's changed their names. What's up with the woman? Does she think she's a spy or something?'

Carla looked up. 'Edith's telling us she's safe. She must be beside herself with worry to go to such lengths.'

Dottie said, 'Hold on. That makes no sense. Like Ruth said, why use a postcard? Every man and his dog have probably read that.'

'So what are you saying, Dottie?' asked Carla.

'I don't know. All I know is that if I was worried about being repatriated, I wouldn't use a postcard to send information.'

'You can hardly blame her if she's being careful,' said Carla with tears in her eyes. 'If she's repatriated to Germany because she married a man born there when she hasn't even set foot in the country, wouldn't you try to do something different to save yourself?'

Dottie shook her head. 'I don't think she's one bit concerned about repatriation. She knows she could appeal and most English-born women married to German men are being allowed to stay. I think that she's trying to lay a false trail for us, or more particularly for Bertie when he comes out of the camp.'

'So she doesn't want Bertie to know where she lives?'

'I think so, Carla; whether it's her mother influencing her or Edith's own decision is anybody's guess. The last thing she wants now is a German name. Too easy to trace.'

—

The weather had been dry but cold when Ruth set out for work on the Monday of Christmas week and there was a lot of work to be done before the end of the year. She had taken some messages and invoices over to the workshop for them to be checked and stayed as long as she dared. She stepped out to return to the offices to find large flakes of snow falling, muffling the usual sounds of workshop machines and passing traffic. She hoped it would not go on for too long. Trying to stay upright on snow and ice was difficult. Happily, by dinnertime, the snow had stopped.

Unfortunately, the snow started again, and by the time Ruth went downstairs to check, a thick white blanket covered everything. Ruth was glad she was wearing her thickest coat, and had remembered her gloves, the ones she wore on Gertie.

Mid-afternoon, they received a warning that the trams wouldn't be running for the rest of the day. Management sent all employees home except those within walking distance.

This meant Ruth would work until six o'clock. She had been meaning to call into the shop to get a few things for tomorrow's tea – but that would have to wait. Her best bet was to walk as quickly as it was possible to do safely, given the circumstances.

'It's seldom we get to leave early but I think I prefer to be at work than out in this weather,' complained Cissie as she made ready to leave.

'Yes, I know,' said Ruth. 'Still, I like the snow.'

'Then you're puddled, my girl.'

As they neared the gate, they made out the shape of Stan with his motorcycle. He had Gertie's engine running, but the wheels were sliding everywhere rather than the way they were supposed to be heading.

Ruth shook her head, tutting. 'Hiya, Stan. You're not seriously thinking of trying to ride Gertie home, are you?'

Cissie's head went up. 'Gertie?'

'Nobody, Cissie,' muttered Stan, and changed the subject. 'I conner hold her upright. She just wants to go her own way.'

'Can I help?' said Ruth.

'Doubt it. She's bloody heavy.' His head shot up. 'Sorry, ladies.'

'You live out in the country. You can't ride out in this weather. Those country roads will be dreadful.'

'I suppose I could doss down in the offices somewhere.'

'You can't, Stan. You'll freeze to death. Look, come home with me. It'll probably be best to leave Gertie here. You can sleep on the settee tonight.'

'At yours?'

'Why not? It'll be much better than going anywhere else.'

'Won't that be… you know… awkward?'

'I'd best leave you two to it,' said Cissie with a knowing smile.

'Will you be all right?'

'Sure I will. But you two had better be careful.' Cissie picked up her pace and waved over her shoulder. 'See you both tomorrow, God willing.'

Cissie picked her way out of the yard and set off down the road, leaving Ruth and Stan with the motorcycle.

'Right then, it's just the two of us. Can yer help me keep Gertie upright so as she dunner slide across the ice again?'

'Of course,' said Ruth. She took one handlebar while Stan took the other. Between them, they kept her steady until they pushed her into the workshop where she would be safe from the weather and prying eyes.

Having secured the doors, they walked towards the gate.

'Here, let me link you. That way, we'll either stay on our feet or land on our backsides together.' Stan grinned.

Ruth laughed, glad after all that the snow had seen fit to fall.

The snow lashed their faces as they struggled to walk and talk, huddled for warmth. The silence was a companionable one. And so they continued.

By the time they arrived at Dottie's, snow covered them; they walked around to the back alley and entered the house through the scullery, removing their sodden outer clothes where it would do the least damage.

'Are you all right, Ruth? It looks pretty bad... Hello, Stan. Didn't know you were visiting tonight,' said Dottie.

'Stan was going to go home on his motorcycle, but I said it was too dangerous. He was going to camp out in the offices, but I told him he could sleep here on the settee.'

'Of course you can stay, Stan. I wouldn't send my worst enemy out in that weather.'

—

Once tea was over, Dottie and Carla made plans to have an early night. They both had to be at work at six o'clock the following day.

'Do you think they have deliberately left us together?' asked Stan when the doors were closed and there were just the two of them sitting in the front room.

'It feels strange just the two of us sitting here, in someone else's house.'

'Mm, I know. I suppose I'm old enough to look for a place of my own too, but it's never been high on my list of things to do. Dad and I have the same interests – as you probably gathered when you met him. I must get my liking of mechanical things from him. I help him in the workshop when I can.'

The time passed, and they talked constantly, tending the fire, now glowing a dull red.

'What do you intend to do with yourself when the war is over, Stan? Do you have any idea? Or do you plan to stay at the PTC?'

'Ah, now I have been thinking about that a lot. You see, I have spent all my working life on mending mechanical things that break. And I want to carry on with that. Truthfully, I'd like to get into buses.'

'Get into buses? What d'yer mean?'

'Buy a bus – or two. I want to build up a bus company. You see, trams are a problem because they can only move around on tramlines with overhead electrics. They are expensive too, so are found in big towns. Buses can move about; they just need a road. Just think what it would be like if people like me could get a bus to take me from my home and into The Potteries – it opens up a whole new set of opportunities for work for all the people who live there.'

As Stan spoke, his whole demeanour changed; he became alive with excitement as he went through his plans, showing he had put a lot of thought into it.

'There are a few omnibuses around. I've seen them.'

'Yes, but more are needed. Omnibuses'll take over from trams in the future. I wouldn't be surprised if the PTC bought some. I want to get into it soon before every Tom, Dick and Harry jumps on the bandwagon.'

His excitement died down a little. 'It may only be a pipe dream. It's going to take a load of money. Still, I can live in hope.' His eyes burned into hers. 'What do you plan to do after the war's over?'

'Oh, me… I don't really know, to be honest. When I left school, I was hoping to become a teacher, but when Mother was ill, I looked after the family for a time and then, like you, I made plans and I got the job at the PTC.

I like it there. It's so interesting and varied. I'm hoping that I'll keep my job when the men come back from the war, otherwise I'll be back to square one.'

'Tell yer what, Ruth. I'll get me buses and you can run the offices for me. How's that?'

His eyes sparkled with excitement. Sitting with him, listening to him talking and including her in his plans for the future was just what she wanted, but for one thing. Another kiss. Then again, she might've been on edge if he did in case they were interrupted.

Later, in bed, she tossed and turned, wanting to go downstairs to see him, to kiss him, but she knew that if she did, she wouldn't be able to leave him.

—

The following morning, Ruth got up at the same time as Carla and met her in the kitchen as she was cutting up her snapping for dinnertime.

'So, how did you go on with Stan last night?'

'We talked for a while about what we'll do with ourselves if this war ever ends.'

'Did he say what he was going to do?'

'This and that, nothing set in stone.' Ruth didn't want to talk about Stan's plans because she didn't know whether he had told her in confidence. Instead, she changed the subject. 'I told him I was thinking of teaching, but that might not be possible now.'

'It's the same for all of us.' Carla frowned and scratched her face. 'How can we plan anything given what we're going through?'

'We all need plans of some sort, Carla.'

Stan's voice came from the door to the kitchen. 'Mind if I come in?' he asked.

Ruth and Carla jumped at his unexpected presence.

'No problem, Stan. Dottie and I are just leaving,' said Carla, pulling Dottie along behind her. 'Like I said last night, the early trams can't afford to wait around when they've got to get people to work.'

Ruth prepared some breakfast for herself and Stan, neither in a rush to leave. Sitting together in the kitchen was comfortable, a home environment. This was what it would be like if they were married. Being comfortable with each other, talking about anything and nothing. It was the first time she had thought of marriage and a man in the same sentence.

Blushing, she ran upstairs to pick up her bag and came back down again, slowly. She could think of nothing to say to stop them from leaving, except maybe another kiss.

She returned to the kitchen to find he was on his feet, waiting for her. As if she had spoken out loud, he took her in his arms and kissed her. And she kissed him back with as much fervour.

She pulled away. 'We must go. We'll be late.'

'I need to see you again soon, Ruth.'

She nodded, incapable of saying a word.

Chapter Twenty-Four

January 1916

On the first Sunday of the new year, Ruth, Dottie and Carla arranged for Pearl and Daisy to have tea with them. The house was full of loud chatter.

'If you'd have told me a year ago that we would sit here, like this, with Donald in India, I would have never let him go,' sighed Dottie. 'It's unceasing. You're all so lucky not to have anyone in the army.'

Ruth noticed that Carla reddened and seemed uncomfortable at these words.

'How's Donald doing?' asked Daisy.

'He sounds all right in his letters. He's got used to the climate and the routine, even the snakes and other nasty bugs. He said I should have gone out with him. He is sharing a bungalow with another sergeant and they have a cook/housekeeper, a gardener and a punkawallah.'

'What's one of them?'

'It's a servant who operates the fans in the bungalow to keep it cool and the air moving.'

Pearl snorted. 'My word, Donald Spilling, with servants. Bit different from driving trams all day!'

The afternoon flew by, swapping a mixture of gossip and news – mainly gossip. They trusted each other and knew it would go no further. They promised each other they would get together more often. Sharing their lives had relieved some of the stress and anxiety they each carried.

–

Ruth had decided to have Sunday lunch with her father and brothers – it was the best time to catch everyone in. Joan and Frank had left the three children with Joan's mother, who was pleased to have babies to look after.

After exchanging the family news, the subject of conscription soon took over. All the Latham men, except Father, who was too old, fell within the age group, leading to him being teased by his sons. It was frightening. For the first time, men had no choice on whether they fought – unless they were married men or essential workers, or both, and therefore exempt.

Being miners, both Walter and Frank were essential workers, although they could still volunteer. Some men at the pit talked about this when they heard the news.

'I hope neither of you are thinking of doing something like that,' said Joan in her best "you can't go to cricket today" tone. 'It's risky enough down the pit and now we've got children. You need to take your responsibilities seriously.'

'No, Joan. I won't.'

Poor Frank, Joan was a lovely person, but she had him well trained. Ruth speculated he might prefer the army.

'Even if they extend it to cover married men,' said Frank, 'I made me decision to go down the pit and I'll not change me mind. Someone has to dig the coal.'

'Walter, are you thinking about joining?' asked Ruth.

'No, sis, my work is too important. The King will have to manage without me, but at least he'll have a fire at Buckingham Palace.'

Trust Walter to come up with the comical view. She was proud of her brother. He was becoming a well-respected young man in the pit. He was still training as a shotfirer, but the men had to put their trust in him and in return he had to always put safety above everything else. This would sometimes lead to conflict with the managers, but Walter would always stand his ground.

'How's it going to affect you, Ruth?'

'No doubt the PTC will lose more men. There are few men left in the offices where I work. I know Stan will qualify, but he's likely to be needed here. If the trams break down and can't run, who knows what'll happen?'

'In transport, I think it depends on what your job is.'

'Wherever yer work, there'll be lots of talk. But you can bet the boss's sons will all be essential workers when the time comes.'

She had avoided speaking to Stan about conscription until now. But its coming was certain. They needed to talk – soon.

—

Men collected together in little groups and talked about whether they qualified for conscription. Some men believed driving a tram was essential war work, thus qualifying them for exemption. Others were more realistic.

Ruth contacted Stan at dinnertime. He was out in the yard getting some fresh air, so Ruth donned her hat and coat and joined him.

'Now it is official. What do you think will happen to you, Stan?'

'From what I could see, it looks like I'll be in the first draft. Whatever they choose to do, I'll be in the Army Reserve from the beginning of March and liable for call-up. I heard some men talking about exemptions and the like, but I feel it's my duty, once called, to do my bit for the country.'

'I thought the company would say you were essential because of your knowledge of the boilers and generators. If they do, you won't have to go.'

'To be honest, several men with families have my level of expertise, and our two top employees are over forty-one, so the company is well-protected. I was called up to Mr Taylor's office this morning.'

'Had you done something wrong?'

'No, nothing like that. He asked me the same question as you have and I gave him the same answer.'

'Was he disappointed?'

'I don't think so. He said he understood my position, and I had to do what was right for me. But he offered me one thing.'

'What was that?' Ruth feared wrongdoing.

'He said that if I wanted, he could arrange my posting to the Ordnance Corps, which handles the supply and maintenance of transport. It would mean I would serve in France, helping to keep the transport side moving.'

'What did you say?'

'Yes, of course. It's perfect for me. Messing around with all them different vehicles and steam engines, even if the Germans are shooting at me.'

'Don't say that.' Ruth looked away to compose herself. 'You must promise to be careful and to come back. After all, the trams need you. I need you too.'

His eyes smouldered. 'Don't say that out here, Ruth. I might not stop meself kissing you.'

She stared at the ground, not wanting him to see the effect he was having on her.

'There's a difference between doing your duty and being reckless. I shall listen to my training and follow orders and, like my father said, "dunner volunteer for owt". Besides, I've got you to come back to, haven't I?'

With no idea who might look through the windows above, she thought it best to change the subject. 'They'll exempt Walter and Frank. But Frank said yesterday that some men down the pit were thinking of volunteering or not appealing against the call-up when the time comes.'

'All good on them. Every man should decide based on his conscience, but this war is consuming men too quickly. It looks as if the government has made up our minds for us.'

'You're beginning to sound like some of those Labour politicians.'

'Yes, perhaps I am, Ruth.'

Chapter Twenty-Five

March 1916

Ruth had worked late this evening so that she could get a flying start on Monday morning. She'd wait for Carla to finish her shift at six o'clock and they would walk home together. It had been one of those blustery days, and the smoke from the kilns was not too bad.

Carla joined Ruth at the gate. 'Hello, Ruth, there isn't bad news, is there?'

'No, I've only just finished myself and wanted some company on the walk home.'

'I finally had a letter from Bertie this morning.'

'Splendid. How is he?'

'He sounds a lot more subdued than before and I'm worried about him, but I think three months in solitary has made him realise and accept what has happened to the family.'

'That's good. We don't know when the war is going to end and Bertie needs to be at peace with himself.'

'He's decided he wants Edith and Luther to be with him, if they still want to. He thinks Mrs Wren has turned Edith against him. She can be very persuasive. Edith always said it was better to agree with her mother and then do what you want than argue your case in advance.'

'That sounds like a very good idea.'

'He also thinks both of us will have to come to terms with not seeing our parents for a long time after the war ends. Most men in the camp think the British will stop repatriated Germans from returning and a lot of the single men expect to be sent straight to Germany when hostilities have ceased. It's not clear which way the war will go and he doesn't think there'll be a quick resolution either way.'

'That's strange, Carla. I haven't really thought about what might happen if the Germans win. What do you think?'

'I have to assume that the Germans and Austrians have a plan, and that they didn't just start the war for the fun of it.'

'That's the way I feel. I remember everybody said that Britain wouldn't join in and then the following day we were at war. In fact, I'm finding it hard to know what the war's about.'

Coming in the opposite direction was Dottie, complete with another pan of sprouts. The three girls smiled to each other.

'Next year, I'm planting a lot fewer sprouts. I think I'll go mad if I have to peel or eat another one.'

They laughed.

'I didn't know how to break the news to you. I've never liked sprouts, so I wouldn't object,' said Ruth.

'I wish you had told me. The pair of you always seem to eat every one of them, so I put up with them too. I can't stand the bloody things.'

Dottie turned and knocked at the front door of number 149 and handed over her pan of sprouts to the family next door. Then the three of them crossed over the road and walked up Corporation Street to the chippy and had a big bag of fish and chips each. Expensive but a real treat.

—

Stan decided not to try for exemption and on 5 March he became a member of the Army Reserve, like every other single man in the country. Ruth was upset and angry with him, but couldn't show it. He had decided based on his conscience and for her to dictate his actions at this early stage in their relationship, or at any time, for that matter, would be a mistake.

The whole of the depot seemed to hold its breath, waiting for the letters to arrive. Stan told her he would receive a document called a W3236, which would tell him where and when to report. It would also contain necessary train warrants to get him there. Stan said he thought that was nice of King George to give them a free train ride. Trust him!

The news spread like wildfire around the depot. And this time it didn't need Pearl's encouragement. Six men in the company had received their papers, including Gerald Hunter, Charlie's assistant in the ticket office, and Stan. No disrespect to Gerald. It was the fact that Stan had been called up and was going which surprised the depot.

Ruth decided she couldn't concentrate on her work until she'd at least spoken to Stan and so she went down to the reception room where Pearl had just finished sorting out the morning's mail.

'Have you heard the news?'

'Yes, Pearl,' Ruth said with a little sharpness in her voice. She did not want to talk to anybody at the moment other than Stan.

Pearl got the message. 'Can you do me a favour, Ruth?'

'Yes, of course.'

'Can you take this mail across to the garage?'

Ruth realised what her friend was doing and smiled. 'Sorry, Pearl, and thank you.' Ruth didn't put on her outside coat, but hurried across the yard to the garage. She found the office empty. Somebody, somewhere, was hitting metal against metal and making a hell of a noise.

'Hi, Ruth, oh that's me post, is it?'

'Yes, Norman. Pearl asked me to pop it over.'

'I see. Well, if yer want a word with Stan, he's behind number six. He's the dozy bugger what's making all that noise. Mind you dunner slip, lass – there's a lot of sh… oil on the floor.'

Ruth thanked Norman and crossed the floor. As she rounded the front of the tram, she saw Stan. This proved an unsuitable meeting place; the workshop fell silent when Stan stopped hammering.

'Hello, Ruth, what can I do for you?'

'I heard you'd received your papers.'

'Yes, afraid so. I've got to report to the Hanley Recruiting Office on the twenty-sixth of this month, so I don't even get me free train ride.'

They both laughed when they saw the funny side of it. Ruth didn't know what to say now she was standing in front of him.

'Pearl wanted me to bring the post across and I wanted to tell you' – her voice wobbled – 'to be careful and to come back. After all, number six will be heartbroken if you didn't.'

Stan leaned forward and their lips met. Ruth didn't care if anyone saw them.

'I'd better get back. Mr Routledge will wonder where I've gone.' Ruth turned around and as she emerged from the side of the tram, a great roar went up and whistles were heard. To say she went red was an understatement, but as she reached the door, she gave herself a little smile.

Norman shouted, 'Ruth! Can yer tell Pearl to put her glasses on? This letter's nowt to do with me.'

—

Stan worked until dinnertime on the Saturday. With his mates, he had a liquid dinner in the Red Lion. Stan was not a drinker and somehow he had stayed sober. He knocked on the door of the cash office and crossed over to Ruth's desk.

'I just thought I'd pop in to say goodbye.'

Molly and Marge got up from their work and gave him a hug, and told him to take care. Brian did the same – Ruth was not sure what Stan made of it. Her three colleagues made their way out of the office and gave Ruth and Stan a few precious minutes together.

'Well, Ruthie, it looks like this is it. Father's outside waiting to take me home and he'll take me to Hanley in the morning.'

Ruth didn't quite know what to say or do, so she put her arms around him and gave him a hug, which turned into a long kiss. She hung on to him as if she could stop him by doing so. Her cheeks felt wet.

'I've got summat in me eye,' he mumbled, rubbing both with the back of his hand. They were in danger of breaking down altogether. This was what it felt like to have the man in your life go off to war. Imagining heartache was simple, but experiencing it proved transformative.

'You'll write to me, won't you, Stan?'

He nodded. 'Course I will, and I'll be waiting for you to write back too,' he said; his hand touched her cheek slowly, brushing away her tears, as if willing his heart to remember what she felt like. 'I'd better go. I'll see you when I get some leave, whenever that'll be. Take care of yourself, Ruthie. Goodbye.'

Ruth looked at him as he reached the door and turned towards her. 'Goodbye, Stan. Take care. I'll write to you.'

She heard him murmur a few words to the cashiers, standing in the corridor, before she heard his footsteps on the stairs. She ran to the window to watch him walk across the yard to collect Gertie, and then he was gone.

As the cashiers walked back into the office, Molly put her arms around her until the tears stopped.

Chapter Twenty-Six

June–July 1916

The days passed slowly. How strange it felt to look over at the garage and know that Stan wasn't in there. She was only just beginning to realise how many times she'd done it over the last year. She was thankful she had Carla and Dottie to help her through it. She had thought she knew how her friends had felt when Donald went to war and the Hesse family was split up, but she didn't know the half of it.

The three friends spent a lot of time together over the months that followed Stan's departure and felt the better for it. How strange that the very thing that had drawn them together was also the thing that had separated them from their loved ones.

Ruth left the office at exactly half past five and walked down the stairs. When she got to the outside door, Stan was waiting at the roadside gate. She flew into his arms.

'What are you doing here? Why didn't you tell me you were coming?'

She let him go and they walked around the block.

'Forty-eight-hour pass, Ruthie. I've finished my basic training and once this leave is over, I am going to a supply depot near to Brighton. I'll spend a bit of time there – don't know how long – then I'll be off to northern France and one of our main supply depots. Can't tell you which one. It's a secret.'

'That sounds rather mysterious.'

'Not really. I'm told by my sergeant that the depot we'll probably go to is big and deals with motor vehicles, steam engines and static steam engines. It sounds something I might enjoy.' Stan had a little laugh to himself. 'Mr Taylor's been good to his word. At least I'll keep my skill level up.'

'How long have we got?'

'About an hour. I'm sorry I can't spend too much time with you on this leave, but I'm hoping I'll get some more before shipping out to France. Father's picking me up and I'll spend the rest of today and all tomorrow with my family. Would you like to come over? I start my journey to Brighton first thing Monday morning.'

'I'd love to, but I think it best you spend time with your family. We can spend more time together on your next leave. What time's your father due to arrive?'

'About seven. The time my original train should've been arriving, but I took an earlier one.'

'What has the training been like?'

'It's funny really, when you first get there you don't know what's the point of all the marching up and down. You even wonder whether you are ever going to see a gun. But it seems to work and by the time it was at an end we were working together like a team. I'm the only one going to the Army Ordnance Corps. Most are being transferred to various line regiments for active service training.'

'Sounds horrible to think that some of those men you've just spent three months training with might not make it back.'

'You can't think of it like that, Ruth, or you'll go mad. I'm going to be just as much at risk. The Germans aren't daft. They know that hitting supply depots is very effective. So we'll be constantly on our guard. We just have to get on with the job.'

Having decided on enough talk, they leaned against the PTC's wall, preventing themselves from being seen inside. They embraced, content to be in each other's arms.

All too soon, it was seven o'clock. They crossed back over to the PTC main entrance and a few minutes later, Mr Bristow arrived with Rosie sitting in the front seat. When Rosie saw Stan and Ruth, she leaped out and hugged her brother before giving Ruth the same treatment. Stan tossed his kitbag in the back, along with Rosie, who was squashed between her father and her brother.

The van disappeared around the corner, and Ruth wondered when she would see Stan again. She was forever grateful for the hour they had just spent together.

–

Pearl scurried into the cash office and went straight in to Mr Routledge after knocking but not pausing, as was usual. Ruth and Madge glanced at each other.

'What's got into Pearl?'

'I don't know, Ruth, but she had *The Sentinel* in her arms. Doesn't bode well.'

A few moments later, Mr Routledge came out of his office with Pearl behind him – her eyes red.

'Can I have your attention, everyone? I have received some bad news. I'm afraid Jim Wilson has been killed in action. He isn't the company's first casualty, but he's *our* first casualty. Can we just take a moment to think about our fallen colleague?'

The news shocked Ruth. She had imagined this moment and her reaction to hearing about the death of a friend or colleague. But Jim, who she had been close to at one time, was gone. It was hard to believe. They had been together for only a few weeks and had some good times, but he had not been the man for her. She wished now that they hadn't broken up in such a manner, but what was done was done. She didn't know whether he had left a lady friend behind, but hoped there was someone to mourn his passing.

She prayed he hadn't suffered and that his sacrifice would help to win this war.

—

She had decided not to mention anything to Dottie. It would keep until it came up in normal conversation. But, unfortunately, Carla blurted it out as soon as Ruth walked through the door. She walked towards Ruth and gave her a hug and asked if she was all right.

Ruth could have burst into tears at that point, or told Carla to think before she spoke. Ruth didn't know what to do. She was upset for herself and for Jim. 'I'm all right.'

'Can someone mash up those taters? They aren't very good and seem to have boiled away into the water.'

'Yes, right away, Dottie.'

'I'm sorry to hear about Jim an'all,' said Carla. 'I never met him, but I believe you went out with him for a few weeks.'

'Yes, it's sad to think about it now. In the end, we didn't really get on, but we parted on good terms, poor bloke.'

—

It was a Monday morning and Ruth walked to work a little slower than normal to take in the sunny weather. The news from the continent hadn't improved. The British had sustained substantial casualties in the enormous battle raging on the River Somme. For the newspapers to use the word 'substantial', it must've been bad. Casualty lists were getting longer.

When she got to the top of the stairs, Brian met her.

'Morning, just the lady I'm looking for. Dennis Laycock at Goldenhill has been taken ill and Mr Routledge has asked me to cover for him until his return.'

'I hope it's nothing serious,' replied Ruth.

'I don't think it is, but I heard he had received his call-up papers so it's maybe nerves.'

Brian gave a wink to Ruth, who was just getting used to his sense of humour. No doubt he'd find out after he'd been to Goldenhill.

'So, I'm appointing you as senior cashier for the day. I don't want you to make any changes, and please don't put curtains up at the windows. I'd like the office to remain the way it is without a woman's touch.'

Ruth gave Brian a friendly punch on the shoulder and told him that not all women thought about curtains.

Afterwards, Peggy came into the office. 'Good morning, ladies, I've got this typing for Brian. Where is he?'

'Good morning, Peggy. He's standing in for Dennis at Goldenhill,' answered Molly.

'Why has *he* gone? He usually sends one of his lackeys. Is there a problem?'

'You'd better ask Ruth – she's in charge today.'

Peggy put her hands on her hips in protest. 'What, in charge, who says so?'

Ruth could see what Molly was doing, so she thought she'd better put Peggy out of her misery. 'Dennis is off sick, so Brian's gone to keep things going and he's asked me to look after things here. He should be back this afternoon. Is there anything I can help you with? Do you want your work approving?' asked Ruth, attempting a smile.

'It'll keep.' Peggy spun on her heels and left the office. She was not too careful shutting the door.

'It's too easy. She rises to the bait every time. You should stop taunting her, Molly. It's not fair,' said Madge.

They continued with their work. It was a pity that Molly liked to rub Peggy up the wrong way. Things had been running smoothly since they no longer worked together. Ruth thought it was strange Peggy had shown so much interest in Brian's whereabouts when she was told he was at Goldenhill depot.

—

Dennis returned to work on the Wednesday and according to Brian, he didn't look too bad, although he thought he looked nervous.

Brian himself chose not to enlist when the rest of the cashiers did because he was married and expecting a second child. But now, the government had extended conscription to married men, so Ruth assumed Brian might be called up. Strangely, there had been no gossip about Brian, and even Pearl treated him as off limits. It intrigued Ruth, but she was sure if he wanted to talk to anybody, he would.

After dinner, Mr Routledge called them together. 'You will no doubt know, Mr Laycock from Goldenhill is joining the army. I'm sure everyone will wish him the best of luck and a speedy and safe return. He will leave the company for the duration of hostilities, and we have already looked for his replacement. In the meantime, Mr Bertram will cover the depot clerk's job at Goldenhill, working mornings at the depot and afternoons here. It means we'll be one short in the department, but I'm confident you ladies will be able to take up the slack for a few weeks.'

'Who do we go to if we have any queries?' asked Molly.

'I'm coming to that. I intend Ruth to be senior cashier when Brian's not here. It's important that others in the building know who they must talk to. It worked very well last week, so I think there is no need to change.'

Molly and Madge showed their approval, and Mr Routledge looked pleased with himself. He left, and they got back to work.

Brian came over to Ruth's desk. He said nothing about the job, which made Ruth feel confident that Brian felt she could manage.

'I brought a box of summary sheets and other papers from Goldenhill when Dennis was sick and left them with Mr Routledge. He's asked me to ensure they're checked against the ledger and filed in the correct place. I know you're in on Sunday, so would you be so good as to look at them? I expect they're incorrect sheets or duplicates, but also Dennis wasn't the best at filing and might have forgotten to send them down with the cash. Whatever the reason, they need to be checked and filed.'

'Yes, of course, Brian. That will be a pleasant job for the afternoon.'

Chapter Twenty-Seven

August 1916

The one thing Ruth always liked about working on a Sunday was the lack of interruptions. On weekdays, people were always popping in and out, and Ruth found it quite distracting, especially when adding up columns of figures. But on a Sunday, she'd have the cash office to herself, an ideal opportunity to sort out the cash summaries Brian had brought back from Goldenhill.

Both bundles contained depot control sheets. These were preprinted with the route numbers, and name, such as *3 – GOLDENHILL to LONGTON* down the side. Across the top were the days of the week, starting with Monday.

The documents had been rolled into a bundle and tied up with string. Ruth went into the strongroom and brought out two of the large ledgers. She unrolled each bundle and placed them on the table, covering each with one ledger, hoping the weight would flatten them to make them easier to work with.

By eleven o'clock, she had finished her normal duties. Time to look at the mystery sheets – but after a break.

She popped down to the restroom and made herself a cup of tea and ate half of her dinner. She returned to her desk refreshed and ready for action half an hour later.

The ledgers had done the trick, and she could handle the sheets. Her first job was to sort them into reverse date order with the latest sheet on the top. She then made a list of folio numbers, dates and values on a sheet of cash-ruled paper. By the time she had finished, there were four sheets of cash paper with about one hundred and twenty folios.

She turned her attention to the head office. There was a file for each of the depots. She took out a red pencil, sharpened it and checked the first one. A sheet already existed for that date. In the column next to the corresponding sheet from the depot, she wrote the amount and calculated the difference. It was lower on the sheet in the head office file than it was on the corresponding sheet from the depot. It took a few minutes to find the differences, which amounted to two pounds, seventeen shillings and sixpence. She reviewed each sheet in the same way.

It was gone two o'clock when Ruth had the rest of her dinner and more tea. She needed to think, and she needed to eat. Why was there a difference and why always the same way?

Ruth's eyes opened wide – well, bugger me. She drank the remains of her tea and rinsed the cup.

She burst into the office, flopped onto her seat and took the depot sheet out of the head office's file and compared it against the copy from Goldenhill – and they were not the same. Minor differences appeared across the page. Consistently the depot copy was lower than the head office copy.

She stood up and let her eyes run over the two sheets. Comparing them side by side revealed the differences more easily, but viewed alone, the sheets looked normal and would be accepted without question.

The excitement built inside her. Where else could she check? She needed access to the depot's ledgers, which kept each route's individual details and the sheets each conductor had signed. It would be a slow process, but that would prove which one of the two figures was correct – the depot or head office.

Could she be mistaken? No, the facts were there right in front of her nose. Mr Routledge would need to find out the reason for the differences.

–

She finished tidying and walked home; it was eight o'clock. Dottie was sitting in the evening sunshine. 'Hello, Ruth, you're late. I was getting worried about you.'

'Sorry I'm late, Dottie, but I had a special job to do at work and it took longer than I thought. I'm famished.'

'Your tea's between those two plates on the hob. It should be fine.'

Ruth walked over to the range, picked up her meal, and sat down at the table. Once she had finished, she went to get herself a piece of fruit cake and a cup of tea. 'You wanting a cup of tea too?'

'Yes please, when have I ever said no?'

Ruth brought in the tea and two slices of the fruit cake. Dottie never said no to fruit cake either.

–

'So what was the special job you were doing?'

'Brian found some sheets that were at the depot in Goldenhill and he wanted me to make sure that they were duplicates before he dealt with them.'

'And were they?'

Ruth thought for a good few moments, turning over in her mind whether she should say anything. In the end, she decided she needed to tell somebody. Dottie was level-headed and so good at listening.

'Yes, they were all duplicates, but what I found was worse.' Ruth lowered her voice even though they were on their own. 'I think I've discovered a fraud and I don't know what to do about it.' Ruth then recounted her actions of the day. Dottie listened. '…amounting to over eight hundred pounds.'

Dottie's face was a picture. 'You mean someone's had their hand in the till for that amount of money?'

'It looks like it.'

'Who is it? Do you know?'

Ruth felt she'd said enough. 'Not really. But I don't know what to do.'

'You'll have to tell them, Ruth. If it's found out later on, they might think you were involved in it.'

'I hadn't thought of that. I'll tell Mr Routledge first thing in the morning.'

'It might be a better idea to talk to Brian. You know him better, and if you have made a mistake or there is a simple explanation, Brian could prevent you from showing yourself up. If he doesn't want to take it further, you can take it to Mr Routledge at that stage.'

'Please don't say a word to anyone, Dottie, not even Carla.'

What Dottie advised made sense. Ruth picked up the dishes and the two of them went into the scullery and washed them. Ruth refilled the kettle and put it on the hob. It was second nature – nobody ever left an empty kettle because you never knew when you were going to need hot water.

Ruth was considering an early night. As she was attending to the last-minute tidying-up, Dottie walked into the kitchen and leaned against the door, looking pensive.

'Ruth, I've got something I think you should know about.'

'Is it about the fraud?'

'Yes. It's something Donald told me a while ago, just after we got together.' Dottie continued without hesitation. 'A while ago there was a fire at Stoke depot which destroyed a wooden workshop. The carpenters used the workshop, and always locked it overnight. On this particular day, the PTC had a delivery of wooden boxes of tickets from the ticket printers, but it was too late to put them into the correct store, so the next best thing was to put them into the carpenter's store. Just before midnight, a fire was discovered; the shed was ablaze. The fire destroyed the shed. Donald was of the opinion that you never get coincidences and he wondered whether somebody had taken the tickets and set the fire to cover their tracks.'

'There might be a connection – but that was a long time ago. Whoever it was has been very patient.'

'For eight hundred pounds, I would be patient, wouldn't you?'

—

It was raining hard as Ruth walked into work that Monday morning. She hoped it wasn't a portent of things to come. She knew Brian wouldn't return from Goldenhill until around three o'clock and she was glad she had taken that bit of extra time to make sure that the office was tidy.

The day flew by until the office clock chimed three o'clock. Ruth's stomach tensed up. Not long to go now.

He arrived at twenty-five past three. The rain, which hadn't stopped all day, had drenched his raincoat.

'Good afternoon, Brian. Is it raining?' asked Molly.

Ruth grinned. Always trust her to have a witty thing to say.

'Just a bit, Molly, just a bit.'

Eventually, Brian returned to his desk looking less dishevelled, and a lot drier. He sat down to start work.

'Would you like a cup of tea, Brian? I'll make you one,' asked Madge.

'That would be nice.'

'I don't suppose anyone else wants a drink, do they?'

'I will,' came a voice from Mr Routledge's office. The girls always said he could hear the word 'tea' at a distance of a mile.

'So that's five cups of tea, then. I won't be long.' Madge returned with the large teapot and five cups and saucers.

After he had downed his tea, Mr Routledge popped his head around the door to let them know he was going out. Ruth asked Brian if she could see him as soon as Mr Routledge left.

—

They stood in Mr Routledge's office with Ruth holding a pile of paperwork. She took a deep breath and launched into her discovery.

'I needed to see you about that work you asked me to do this weekend.'

'Oh yes, did it go all right?'

'Yes, but I've found something I don't understand. Or at least I hope I don't understand it.'

'That sounds mysterious. When we've had this cup of tea, you can tell me all about it. We'd best go downstairs.'

Twenty minutes later, they were sitting in one of the cash rooms.

'You've got me intrigued. I know you wanted privacy. All the others will be wondering what's going on.'

Ruth gave a nervous smile and handed Brian the sheets she had prepared yesterday. Brian looked at them. After what felt like an eternity, he asked Ruth what she understood the figures meant.

'At first I thought it was mistakes, but I can't see how. I checked all the additions twice and made sure that our sheets were complete – not missing any lines. Once I finished, I concluded that there was a shortfall of cash from Goldenhill to head office of around eight hundred pounds for fourteen months, but we don't have the benefit of duplicate sheets for most of the weeks.'

'It certainly looks like that. It's why we have inspectors and the ticket system. But it appears that someone's worked around that control.'

'I don't know what to make of it. I think we should check the other depots. And we need to go to Goldenhill and check their daily run sheets and ledgers. One of them must be incorrect.'

'Hold on, we don't want to get too carried away. I think the best thing for you to do at the moment is to say nothing to nobody. I'll see Mr Routledge and we'll hand over your work to him. After all, Ruth, we don't know who's behind this and if we say something in the wrong place, we might tip them off.' He looked at her keenly. 'Also, although you will never get me to admit I said this, it might even be a fraud that goes to a high level.'

'I wish you hadn't said that, Brian. If they think I found something and it's the boss who is doing it, they'll sack me.'

'Like as not, they'd sack me too, so you'll be in good company,' he said dryly. 'We'll see what Mr Routledge says before we set any hares running. In the meantime – mum's the word.'

They returned to the office and, apart from a few sly looks, nothing was said. Brian disappeared into Mr Routledge's office and was still there when Ruth left at six o'clock.

—

They didn't have to wait long. The following morning, Mr Routledge called Ruth into his office and asked her to close the door.

'Miss Latham, you seem to have found something. Mr Bertram and I spoke to Mr Simpson, the company secretary, and we're taking the matter seriously. I can't disclose what will happen. I received instructions to give you this letter. If you would be so good as to read it and then sign the two copies to show your acceptance.'

Ruth took the letter, which put into writing what Brian had said last night, except it was in posh language and left Ruth in no doubt that the company was taking the matter seriously.

'Of course I'll sign it straight away. I'll not talk to anybody.'

'If you need to speak to someone and I'm not available, Daisy will organise a private meeting for you.'

Mr Routledge got up and walked around to Ruth's side of the desk. He shook her hand. 'You have acted very professionally, Miss Latham. I won't forget that.'

Ruth returned to her desk and started to work.

'Everything all right?' asked Molly.

'Yes, it was just about work.'

By the day's end, Goldenhill faced a paperwork audit and wage payment review. Pearl was in her element. A juicy bit of news involving people she could gossip about who were no longer there was just up her street. Various rumours began circulating, including one about the tickets destroyed in the fire.

Ruth kept her head down for the next few days.

—

Carla worked a late shift on Sunday and when she got in at ten o'clock, she was full of the news that there had been stock-takes of tickets at all the depots and in the central store. Those involved were strangers, dressed in posh suits and, according to somebody she spoke to, 'they was miserable buggers who wouldn't say nothing about what they were doing'.

—

Ruth went to work prepared for an early Monday morning of gossip and speculation. By the time she arrived in the office, Pearl, Brian, Madge, Molly, Peggy and Cissie were already talking.

Mr Routledge hadn't arrived. Pearl soon told Ruth the details of what had happened over the weekend. Ruth was shocked and avoided looking at Brian.

'Do you know anything, Ruth?' asked Pearl.

'No. All I've heard was from Carla last night.'

'They checked the stock of tickets at all the depots, including opening all the boxes and checking what was inside. I don't know if it was planned, but yesterday, none of the depot clerks worked. So it was just the managers, the bosses from here, and these strangers. Daisy's saying nothing to me about it and when they came for the board meeting last Tuesday, she made sure that I didn't find out who any of the strangers were.'

Peggy spoke out. 'It's unfair of the company to carry out these checks in such a high-handed manner. People will say there is no smoke without fire and blokes like Dennis are having their characters questioned and they conner defend themselves because they are fighting for their country.' She paused for dramatic effect.

'That's interesting, Peggy.' Ruth couldn't stop herself. 'Last year, you were quite happy to question the characters of the Germans living here. *They* couldn't defend themselves. You just hounded them until *they* left the country.'

'That was different! We're at war with them. Why should our money end up in the pockets of Germans? Surely you can see that?'

Ruth glared. 'No, Peggy.'

At that moment, Mr Routledge walked in. 'Pearl, the reception is unmanned, so get down there immediately. And for the rest of you, I suggest you suspend the mothers' union meeting and reconvene in your own time and not on these premises.'

By the time he got to the door of his office, Pearl, Peggy and Cissie had all left.

'Mr Bertram, can I have a word, please? Now if you don't mind.'

Brian emerged half an hour later, appearing chastised.

Ruth kept out of Peggy's way for the rest of the day. Ruth was especially glad to be home that Monday evening.

Mr Simpson called a meeting for nine o'clock on the Wednesday morning. All the staff were to attend. They collected in the cash office and waited. Mr Simpson arrived with a flustered-looking Mr Routledge and two men Ruth didn't recognise.

'Good morning. I called this meeting to inform you that The Potteries Tramway Company has contacted the police to investigate a serious fraud we have uncovered. These two gentlemen are detectives from Hanley and will, over the course of the next few days, interview you all. Your full co-operation is required. Go about your work as normal. It is in all our interests to find the culprits.'

That was it.

For the rest of the day, people were called in to give their statements. When Ruth's turn arrived, she remained calm. She had nothing to worry about, but as she walked down to the cash room, her calmness evaporated, and panic replaced it.

—

'Good evening, Miss Latham. Please take a seat. I'm Inspector Rawlings.' He was tall with a beard like the King's. He had quite a deep voice. She thought he looked about the same age as her father. 'This is Sergeant Phillips.'

Standing next to him was a younger man, clean-shaven, but with extensive burns on the left side of his face when he turned to look at her. Ruth did not know where to look.

'Are you ready to begin, Miss Latham?'

Ruth swallowed and turned her head back to face the inspector. 'Er... yes, Inspector. Of course.'

After summarising the details, her name and address, how long she'd worked for the PTC, he then asked her to recount how she came to discover the shortfall in the cash. Ruth noticed he had the sheets she had prepared on that Sunday.

'Eight hundred pounds is quite a sizeable sum. According to... Mr Bertram, however, it could be as much as twenty-five hundred pounds. Who do *you* think is responsible?'

Ruth's mouth fell open. 'I don't like to say. To my knowledge, Mr Laycock wrote all the sheets.'

'Do you think he had help?'

'I don't know, sir.'

After a couple of further questions, he sat back in his chair. 'That will be all, then. Thank you very much for your help.'

Ruth got up to leave. The inspector asked another question. 'Did you notice anything about the figures?'

'No, they all looked normal. The differences caught my eye. They were all multiples of sixpence. So I would have checked the sixpenny tickets first. But someone else took over.'

'Interesting observation... I hadn't noticed that. Thank you again, Miss Latham.'

Chapter Twenty-Eight

September 1916

Ruth stretched her back to give it some relief. She had stayed late to finish the last summary sheet.

The sun was getting lower in the sky as she entered the yard. This idea of putting the clocks forward in the summer meant you could make the most of the daylight.

'You lying bitch,' screamed Peggy as Ruth walked towards the gates opening onto Woodhouse Street.

Ruth jumped, startled out of her wits. 'Peggy! You frightened the life out of me. What's the matter?'

'You know damn well what the matter is. You getting Dennis Laycock into trouble. How could yer?'

Ah, so word was already beginning to circulate. Ruth decided to play for time. 'I don't understand, Peggy. What are you talking about?'

'Don't give me that bullshit. Everyone knows about Un— Dennis. You know what I'm talking about. Wanting to get on and only thinking of yourself. You could just have shut up and said nowt.'

Ruth shook her head. 'Peggy, for goodness' sake. What are you talking about?'

'Don't give me that innocent look. It's all over the Red Lion. The police are saying Dennis Laycock stole the money and they're asking the military police to arrest him. All because of what *you* told them.'

'The only thing I did was to find a problem.'

'You should have told me.' For the first time, Peggy's face changed as if she had remembered something.

With her head on one side, Ruth said quietly, 'How can it be any business of yours, Peggy? Surely it's what's best for the company? Keeping us all in a job?'

'Did you think through what the consequences would be?'

'I don't understand.' A cool tingling in her fingers grew until her arms and then her chest felt about to explode.

'I should think by now most of the company knows what you've done. Poor Dennis is away fighting for King and country and has no chance to defend himself. His poor wife and two kids have no money. They've probably gone back to Ireland to avoid the workhouse.'

'That's nonsense,' protested Ruth. 'It's the company and the police who've done the investigation. They interviewed me just like everyone else. To my knowledge, they've decided nothing yet.'

'I can't see them giving Dennis a pocket watch rewarding him for his activities, can you?'

'Are you saying he did it?'

'No. No! There you go, twisting my words. You're accusing him of stealing money, but Aunty Kathleen takes in washing cos she's had no money from the government yet. They haven't got two halfpennies to rub together. And you're saying he's stolen that money. You've acted as judge and jury.'

'I think it'd be an idea if you went home, Peggy; you're clearly angry and distraught. We can talk about it tomorrow.' Ruth's skin tightened. She felt sick. She couldn't see what she could've done differently. 'You're talking as if he's guilty and the more you gossip, the worse it'll get. None of us know the facts...'

'And you dunner know what you've done.'

'We'll have to wait until his trial, if there is one, then he'll have time to say his piece.'

'Tell that to Aunty Kathleen. She'll tell you whether it's a chance she wants to take.'

'Aunty? Just a minute – what's your aunty got to do with it?' Ruth felt another wave of tingling flow through her. 'Do you mean you're...?'

'Dennis's my uncle. Him and Aunty Kathleen have two children. Now, do you see what you've done? Probably made them all homeless.'

'I'm sorry, Peggy, but what else could I have done?' Ruth groaned inwardly. Surely this couldn't get any worse.

'You could've found a way. You just didn't try. When he returns to England, prison will likely be his destination, and Aunty Kathleen's money will cease. She'll be better off if he never returns from France. At least she'll get a widow's pension then. What a prospect.' Peggy caught her breath. 'All you needed to do was turn a blind eye to what had gone on in the past. Nobody suspected nothing. All you had to do was to say those sheets were duplicates and that would have been the end. Old Routledge would never have found it. He couldn't find his own arse. If you'd told me then, we could have made a plan.'

'Are you saying you're in on it, too?'

'No. But we're family, and we don't rat on each other to the police. We sort things out amongst ourselves and we don't forget... you mark my words.' Peggy turned and stormed right into the arms of Mr Routledge. Mr Adams, the depot manager from Goldenhill, was standing beside him.

Ruth took a sharp intake of breath. Where had they come from? How much had they heard?

'Sorry – Oh, M… Mr Routledge…' stammered Peggy.

'Yes, Miss Thompson, and good evening to you. Good evening, Miss Latham.'

Ruth could only nod at Mr Routledge.

'Miss Thompson, I think it would be a good idea if you come to my office at nine o'clock tomorrow. We need to talk. Good night… ladies.'

—

Ruth couldn't remember the walk back home. But by the time she arrived, she had composed herself. She hung up her coat and hat in the hall and walked through into the kitchen. Her face must've given something away.

'Whatever's the matter?'

'Dottie, I've just had an almighty row with Peggy. I learned she's related to Dennis Laycock. I don't believe she intended to tell me, but it must have slipped out. She'd been across to the Red Lion and I bet the missing money was the talk of the bar. I don't suppose she had been drinking lemonade either, so she might have been intoxicated.'

'So what happened?'

'She was extremely upset about everybody saying that Dennis had stolen the money and she also told me that his wife and children have gone back to Ireland to avoid having to go into the workhouse. I have to admit that she looked genuinely upset.'

'Be careful with Peggy. She can turn the waterworks on and off on demand. We've seen what she was like at school – teacher's pet one minute, and then a bully the next,' added Dottie.

'She then said that people like the Laycocks stick together and don't go tittle-tattling to the police. She said I should remember they are a large family. It sounded like a threat.'

'You'll have to tell somebody.'

'I don't need to – Mr Routledge and Mr Adams heard the entire episode. The shadow of Mr Routledge's car hid them while they talked. I think they were coming over to stop us from fighting. But Peggy turned round and ran straight into Mr Routledge's arms. Now I think back, it must have looked quite comical. I thought she was going to knock him over. But Mr Routledge soon regained his composure and dignity. He told Peggy to report to him tomorrow morning at nine o'clock.'

'What do yer think he'll do?' asked Dottie.

'She'll be in big trouble because she also said some unkind things about him.'

'What did he say to you?'

'Nothing. He just wished me good night.'

–

Sleep evaded Ruth again. She kept going over in her mind what Peggy had said and worried about Peggy's implied threat that the Laycocks might decide to take it out on her family. She decided she would go up to Dartmouth Street that evening to tell everyone.

–

When she arrived at the offices the following morning, Ruth went straight to the typing room to talk to Peggy.

She was nowhere to be seen. Cissie and Iris were working away and asked Ruth, almost in unison, where Peggy was.

'I was just about to ask you the same thing.'

'Pearl's just been in saying that Peggy had a good night in the Red Lion. Rumour has it she was slagging you off something wicked. She made little sense and, according to Pearl's information, she was as drunk as a lord by the time she left.'

A very dishevelled-looking Peggy staggered through the door, wearing the same clothes as yesterday, her normally immaculate hair looking as if someone had pulled her through a hedge backwards. She made a moaning noise and then threw up on the floor.

Cissie shot to Peggy's side, but well away from the mess. 'Get a mop and bucket, Iris. I'll get some strong tea. You make yourself scarce, Ruth, and try to keep Mr Routledge out of this office for a while,' she finished, sniffing the air. As she was leaving to get a pot of tea, Cissie threw open the windows.

Ruth never discovered what miracles Cissie, Iris and Henry carried out, but by nine o'clock when Mr Routledge arrived, Peggy was presentable even though to another woman she would seem a little frayed around the edges.

Peggy and a very stern-looking Daisy came into the cash office and went straight in to see Mr Routledge. A few moments later, all three appeared and silently left the office, going somewhere more private.

About half an hour later, Pearl came running into the office. 'What's going on? I've just seen Mr Routledge and Daisy escorting Peggy off the premises.'

'We don't know.'

'I heard she was so drunk last night that the landlord tried to put her on the tram. The driver was one of ours and he knew she lived in Burslem and he persuaded another driver, who was coming back to the depot for the night, to let her sleep it off in his tram. When the new driver got into the tram this morning, he found Peggy curled up like a baby asleep on the floor. With the help of a couple of clippies, they got Peggy into the restroom and pumped her full of strong tea. Anyway, I must go – can't stop here gossiping all day.'

It was about an hour later when Daisy came into the cash office and announced that Peggy was no longer working at the PTC. Daisy didn't stop for comments.

Ruth looked at Molly. Neither said a thing.

Chapter Twenty-Nine

October–November 1916

After the sacking of Peggy, things seemed to go quiet on the fraud front. The people in the offices settled back into a normal routine. Daisy, unfortunately, had to find another typist quickly. She had asked Ruth to pop in to see her. Ruth knocked and walked in.

'Good morning, Ruth.'

Ruth smiled. 'Good morning to you too, Daisy.'

'I've asked you to pop in because I want to sound an idea off you.'

'I'll help if I can.'

'I need to find a replacement for Peggy. We have four clippies who are qualified typists and I was wondering what their reaction would be if I offered one of them Peggy's job.'

'What would the pay be?'

'Unfortunately, the pay would be the same as it was when you did the job.'

'I'd imagine you'd not get any takers. The reason many became a lady conductor was to do with the twenty-seven shillings a week. You'd be asking them to part with half their wages. It wouldn't be a very good swap, would it?'

'Even if they knew it was a permanent job?'

'I don't think an offer of a permanent job would make up for the difference in the wages.'

Daisy nodded. 'Mm, that's what I thought. I've made my mind up; I'll advertise the job as soon as I can.'

Daisy scribbled something down on her pad and continued, 'Have you given any thought to what you are going to do when the war ends?'

'Not really, there seems no sign of that at the moment, so I've put it to the back of my mind, to be honest. I know I'll be able to return to the typing room and I don't suppose for one minute Mr Routledge will miss the opportunity of turning the cash office back to a boys' club.'

Daisy laughed. 'I think you're right there. But, Ruth, you can do so much better. You have a nimble and agile mind; you're organised and could become a good leader given the chance. Perhaps that's why Peggy was always at odds with you.'

'Ideally, I'd like to stay where I am.'

'You remember the PTC guaranteed all the men their jobs back?'

Ruth nodded. 'Poor Jim won't be coming back. I think that's the real reason I'm not thinking about what I do. Wherever I work, I'd probably only be getting the chance cos some poor soul hasn't come back.'

'It's upsetting, I know. Women have done lots of jobs very successfully since the outbreak of war. The men are worried that more women working in an industry will reduce their pay. After all, why should the bosses pay more than they need to?'

'Do you think that the company would do that?'

'Without sounding like an anarchist, yes. After the war, things are going to be tough and businessmen – there I go, assuming they are going to be men – will take every opportunity to save money.'

'Daisy, I don't think we can do much about it as individuals. But when we got together before the war, we nearly got the vote. Do you think Mrs Pankhurst will start her agitation for the vote again when the war is over?'

'It may be even worse now women have had a taste of the jobs they can do, but I can't see how they'll be interested in equal pay for working women, except maybe for Sylvia Pankhurst. I think it'll take a long time before women get paid the same as men for doing the same job.'

'So once the war's over, they'll send us back to the kitchen and to domestic bliss, where we'll wait for our husbands to return home with money for bread.'

'On that philosophical point, I've got an advertisement to write and no doubt Mr Routledge will fret where you are.'

Ruth smiled at Daisy and left the office. Sure enough, in Thursday evening's *Sentinel*, there was an advertisement for a typist at the PTC.

—

Unfortunately, Stan didn't get the opportunity for another period of leave. His posting to France came through quicker than expected. Ruth was disappointed she wouldn't see him again before he left, but relieved that she wouldn't have to say another goodbye when she knew that this time, he would be heading for France.

He was as good as his word and she received his first letter towards the end of October. It was very chatty and caused a few laughs when she read it out to Carla and Dottie.

6 November 1916

Dear Ruthie,

As you can tell from the postmark on the letter, I am in France. There's no point in me telling you where, as the censors will remove it. But what I can say is that it's a beautiful country from the bit I've seen.

It is coming up to three weeks since I arrived. We work on lots of different vehicles, so every day it's something new. A lot of the men in the unit have been here since the start of the war. They seem to be a lot like me, working in engineering and the like when they're home.

One bloke I'm working with works for Birmingham City Transport and he's been telling me about how they're extending bus routes in preference to trams. I've met no one else from Stoke up to press, but back in Brighton, one major I got to know was a pottery owner named Matthew Roundswell. He seemed to be something to do with paperwork, and believe you me, there's plenty of that. He'd been based in Brighton for the whole of his service. Nice way to spend the war, if you ask me. He was getting married to a lass from Burslem, but something went wrong, or so I heard.

I don't know how far behind the lines we are, but when the wind is in the right direction, you can hear the artillery. I experienced my first action this week. German aircraft raided the base, but our planes fought them off, only after the German planes dropped their bombs. These bombs hit nothing important, but the raid was unnerving and noisy.

The food is what you'd expect.

I hope you're all right and that your friends are coping. Already, I feel as if I've been away forever. I want this war to be over because I miss you so much. Our journeys out on Gertie are a positive pleasure and I think of those when I'm trying to get some sleep. Father's looking after Gertie, so she doesn't get rusted up. I wouldn't put it past him to give her a run out. He'd be in his element.

My dear Ruth, I think that's the most I've ever written since I left school. I will write to you as soon as I can.

Best wishes and take care of yourself. I'll be thinking about you.

Yours,
Stan

Dottie smiled. 'He doesn't sound too bad, Ruth. He's obviously settled in, although it sounds scary.'

'Ruthie? Stan calls you Ruthie?'

Ruth's face burned. 'He's done that from the beginning. The only other person to call me that is Father.'

'Ahh. How romantic!'

Ruth had thought she'd be embarrassed by Stan's affectionate name for her. Turned out she didn't care a jot! She changed the subject.

'I don't know how you've put up with it for so long with your Donald, Dottie. It's only been a few months. Heaven help me if it goes on for a long time.'

The managing director assembled all the staff from the Stoke offices in the restroom. Mr Taylor had an important announcement to make.

Speculation ran wild between eight o'clock when the notice appeared and now, when it was due to start. Everybody knew that there had been an Emergency General Meeting, in a private room at a hotel near to the station. It must have been to discuss the fraud. All the head office employees were there, except Pearl, who, much to her disgust, had to remain in reception in case of callers. Apart from the sight of managers mixing with staff, the most noticeable thing was Henry. He attended the meeting, not smoking his beloved pipe. Ruth wondered whether that was a conscious choice on his behalf or whether Daisy had suggested that so many people in a confined space might not be too keen on Henry with his pipe in full flow.

Mr Taylor walked in, and, just like school, everybody went silent. He walked to the front of the gathering and started to talk.

'This announcement is being made simultaneously in all our depots. I will read it out verbatim. There will be no questions at the end.

'At an Extraordinary General Meeting held on Thursday 16 November, the Shareholders of the Potteries Tramway Company agreed the following statement. "The Constabulary has informed the company that they are suspending the investigation into the fraud at the Goldenhill depot of The Potteries Tramway Company. The company wishes to inform all of its staff of the following facts: one, the police have issued a warrant for the arrest of Dennis Laycock in connection with a case of fraud. Two, the military police have issued a warrant for the arrest of Dennis Laycock for failure to report for service in the army when ordered to do so. Three, the police have issued a warrant for the arrest of Kathleen Laycock in connection with a case of fraud. Four, I can confirm that Dennis Laycock was not called up until 22 September 1916. He left the company on 29 July and had not, at that date, received any call-up papers. Five, the whereabouts of Dennis and Kathleen Laycock are unknown. Anybody with information should report it to their nearest police station. Six, the police are not looking for anyone else in connection with this fraud.

'"Finally, the company wishes to assure all its staff that their jobs are safe and that the amount of money taken does not adversely affect the financial stability and strength of the company." That is the end of the announcement. Thank you for your attention and now you can return to work.'

Mr Taylor nodded and walked out without another word. Once the door closed, a buzz of conversation started up. Ruth, who had stood next to Brian, looked at him.

'It looks like it's over, then?'

'Yes, Ruth, it does.'

'There are still a few things I don't understand.'

'Stay behind after work tonight and I'll tell you what I know.'

'That's an offer a girl doesn't get very often.'

'Steady on, young lady. I am a married man, you know.'

The two, now firm friends, grinned at each other and returned to their duties.

—

Once everybody had left and just Ruth and Brian remained, they talked about the events of the day.

'Ruth, I'm going to tell you what I know. It's only fair that you're aware of the facts, given your involvement. But you mustn't discuss this matter with anyone else. Mr Routledge has approved that I tell you this.'

'I promise I'll say nothing. You can trust me.'

'The fraud took place probably from 1912 until two weeks before Dennis left, or should I say, absconded. The company thought that the workshop fire in 1912 had destroyed the sixpenny tickets that Dennis then used in the fraud. Now he had a supply of tickets which he could substitute for cash over a time. He just had to be patient and careful.'

'What about the serial numbers?'

Brian shook his head. 'Without logging the numbers, those tickets have little value, and with twenty-four million sold this year, we'd need an army of clerks to input the data, and another to verify it.'

'I still don't understand why he kept those duplicate sheets?'

'I don't and neither do the police. The best theory I heard was he wanted us to find out he'd done it and got away with it. Sergeant Phillips said this was a well-planned fraud, and the perpetrator made no mistakes. No point in being an artist and never displaying your work to the public. The police believe that only Dennis and Kathleen were involved. The rest of the Laycock clan knew nothing about it. The police discovered from their informants that the rest of the family weren't best pleased. They considered part of what Dennis had stolen to be theirs, but he's broken the family rules and kept the lot for himself. No honour amongst thieves, hey?'

Ruth shook her head. 'So the war helped Dennis to be so successful.'

'He was, in effect, depot manager for several months while Stephen Adams was in the army and recuperating. The conductors were changing a lot more than usual and new people were starting all over the company.'

Brian paused for a drink of his tea.

'But the most intriguing part to me was his escape. He may have always planned to disappear. But conscription's introduction was perfectly timed. He could play the part of a reluctant conscript. Leave the depot, nobody expecting to hear from him again. His wife lived a frugal life and took in washing. She complained about not getting her separation allowance and when she was told by the police that he was not in the army, she was suitably angry at her husband leaving her with two children, no money and rent to pay. She had to take in washing, she said. She didn't wait too long after that before she did the moonlight flit, which was consistent with someone in debt with no way to pay it. It took the police a long time to confirm with the Royal Irish Constabulary that Kathleen's parents hadn't seen their daughter for five years, and as far as they knew, she was happily married in Tunstall. Whether we can believe that or not with what went on at Easter, I don't know. It's anybody's guess where they are now. But with money in their pocket, they can live a very nice life anywhere in Britain, the Empire, or the world.'

'Sounds like one of those stories you would read about in Sherlock Holmes.'

'Yes, but this time he got away with it.'

Ruth thought for a moment. 'Dennis set the fire, didn't he?'

Brian nodded. 'That's what we all think, but there's no proof of this and probably never will be. Once he had the tickets, all he needed was time and for the PTC not to change its ticket design. He needed help from no one and his wife could cover for him to give him time to disappear.'

'She must've trusted him a lot. He could've taken the money and run.'

'Perhaps she kept the money and took it to him. Everyone would look for a man and what officials would ask to search a woman with two children in tow? Ruth, wouldn't you trust your husband? They both needed each other. She gave him the time to disappear, and he used that time to arrange her disappearance, and to make the money safer.'

'That was fascinating. Have you seen the time? They'll be wondering where I've got to.'

'Me, too.'

They tidied their desks and walked over to the coat stand. It was November, and it was raining.

'Bother. I've forgotten my umbrella.'

'Ruth, you can share mine. No point in you getting wet.'

'No, it's taking you out of your way. I'll be fine.'

'You know what Peggy said. I'd feel better if I knew you had arrived home safely. I can go up Corporation Street and catch the tram there to Longton.'

Ruth nodded. Together, they walked through the gates and into Stoke.

Chapter Thirty

April–May 1918

Ruth and Rosie had agreed that between them they would keep Stan plied with letters and Stan confirmed he would write to each of them when he could. It was working quite well, although since Stan had gone to Flanders there were longer gaps between letters. Sometimes, Mr Bristow would drop Rosie in Hanley and they would spend time chatting, go shopping or to visit the library and bookshops. He always winked as he pulled away, his way of saying thank you to Ruth for cheering Rosie up. Rosie was developing into an attractive young lady and Ruth hoped that any interest in the opposite sex would not derail her studies and the possibility of a place at a university granting degrees to women. But that dream was still some way off.

At the end of April, Ruth received a letter from Rosie. Ruth smiled as she glanced at the writing on the envelope. The girl was becoming very dear to her. She had taken to writing to Ruth with odd bits of news from Brown Edge and the rest of Stan's family, for which Ruth was thankful.

Today, the letter was not too long and there was an ink stain on one corner where a hand might have tried to brush it away. Ruth's smile turned into a frown as she unfolded the letter.

26 April 1918

Brook Cottage
St Anne's Vale
Brown Edge

Dear Ruth,

Our Mark has received his call-up papers. He was only eighteen two weeks ago and now, because this awful war is still going on, he's having to fight. As if it wasn't bad enough to have one brother fighting over there. It's not fair that Mark has to go, too. There should be a rule that only one man in each household should go. I don't know how I will feel if something happens to Stan and then Mark.

Have you heard anything from Stan? The last time we heard was in February. Does he sound all right to you? I know he safeguards us from the harsh reality of the war. But I thought he might tell you.

Will you come over to see us sometime soon? I miss not seeing you dressed up, ready to go out on Gertie. I'm sure Mother and Father would agree. Please say you'll come. I'll bake you a cake. I'm getting good at it, although Mother would say I still have some way to go.

Love
Rosie x

Ruth sighed as she laid the letter on her knees. Poor Rosie. To have such worry on her hands at so young an age. And now, she would have Mark to worry about, too. Ruth thought back to the first time she had seen Mark on her second visit. The gangly quiet lad who said very little but who took everything in. She tried to imagine him dressed in a soldier's uniform, carrying a weapon – she couldn't. In her eyes, he didn't look old enough. Poor Mrs Bristow, the stalwart of the family, perhaps breaking her heart when no one was around at the thoughts of what might happen to her boys. And what about Mr Bristow? He and Stan were so much alike and he was another one who would let no one see that his heart was breaking. They all knew Mark's call-up would be arriving and yet nothing could prepare them for the desolation that would follow. Finally, had anyone told Stan? What would he feel? He had spent all his life protecting Mark and Rosie. And now…

All the casualties that had been reported over the years of the war – the horrors those men had faced. The war had transformed the men returning home. Mark would lose the last of his youth over there. Of course she would write back to Rosie and arrange a visit. She felt closer to Stan when reading news about his family, but it was even better to feel included as one of their own.

For now, she would share her news with Carla and Dottie, who were constantly waiting for news of their own families. Who would believe that sharing their troubles would help so much.

Of late, Carla had accompanied Dottie to the allotments to give her a hand. They had completed much of the winter tidying and spring planting. Dottie was in her element, feeling she was keeping everything going while Donald was away. Ruth thought about the two of them, with their troubles, and how they had kept going. She was working her way through a pile of ironing, having cooked their teas and done the dishes.

Eight o'clock struck as the two women returned from the allotment. Ruth had clothes airing on the kitchen rack and piles of ironing, one for each of them, ready to be put away.

'I'm glad you're both back. I've been looking for an excuse to stop. We shall have to stop wearing so many clothes, girls.'

The two gardeners laughed as they took off dirty boots and their work clothes, which would start the whole process off again. Ruth gave a sigh. She didn't mind, but, deep down, thanked her lucky stars that working for the PTC had prevented her having to do this all day, every day, as a job for her father and Walter.

'We keep thinking about how long the war will carry on, don't we?' said Ruth with a deep sigh. 'I told you about the letter Rosie sent me. Even young Mark's been called up now. That's him and Stan gone. She's ever so upset. Please God, nothing happens to them. What a horrible time to be a mother. Sorry, Dottie. I know you and Donald want one.'

'I sincerely hope that by the time we have a child old enough to fight, the war should be long over with – otherwise, we'll be in serious trouble,' Dottie joked. She seemed to have become resigned to it recently. Ruth was glad – for Dottie's sake.

Carla and Dottie followed each other upstairs to change into their nightgowns and returned to the front room, where Ruth had a hot cup of tea waiting for both of them.

Carla sat on the settee and squeezed her toes, trying to get some feeling back into them. 'I'm just about ready for my bed! On my feet on the tram all day and then the allotment – it's no wonder I can barely walk, is it?'

'I thought you'd be used to it by now. Who'd have thought you'd still be working at the PTC two and a half years later, for a start?'

'I didn't expect to be there for more than a month or two. I was sure I wouldn't cope after everything that had gone on.'

Dottie grinned. 'I feel fine. I've been sitting on my backside all day. It was just what I needed.'

'At least you both get some fresh air,' muttered Ruth. 'We can change places next week, Carla. To give your feet a rest.'

'It's been three years since the sinking of the *Lusitania*. It feels like forever. Everything you went through, Carla. The horrible things that happened. I still shudder to think about it all. No wonder you were worried about working as a clippie in view of everyone.'

'It's not been so bad. I suppose people learn to get on with one another. Me not having a German accent helped, although my name might be a bit of a giveaway. Surprisingly, I feel better now because I'm *not* burying myself inside. It helped me to keep myself to myself at the time, but, with hindsight, it was probably the worst thing I could've done.'

'Have you heard from your parents recently? You haven't mentioned it. Is Bertie still in that internment camp on the Isle of Man?'

Carla shook her head. 'No news is good news, I suppose. Remember when they put Bertie in solitary and his friend Manfred wrote to tell me so I wouldn't worry? I couldn't believe it. I've never ever seen Bertie fight with anyone.'

'So unfair,' murmured Dottie. 'I wish I'd had news back from India. I know I have less to worry about, but it's because he's so far away. It'd be so much better if I could see him from time to time.'

'When I think of all those who have gone off to war so far, you know, Jim, Dickie and Tom, of course, and then Stan, Charlie and Gerald.' Ruth paused, then said, 'Jim and Merriweather are never coming back.'

The other two looked at her, the only one of them who had lost someone. 'I still think of Jim, even now. I know I wasn't walking out with him by the time he went, but it's still difficult to imagine that he's… dead. Merriweather was so nice to us. He asked me to go out with him, you know – after it was over and I said no.' Ruth felt a tear run down her cheek.

The other two patted her back and waited for her to recover herself.

'You've got Stan now, duck, and from what I've seen of him, he's going to do his damnedest to come back to you.'

'A number have gone from Mintons too. I don't actually know them myself, but I've heard their names a lot,' said Dottie, shaking her head. 'It's awful to think about.'

'Of course, they awarded Dickie a medal for bravery – did you see the news in *The Sentinel*? They're not given out for nothing, you know. He must have gone through something really bad to be given that.'

Ruth looked ahead, her eyes vacant. 'You know something, I can still see the three of them sat in the cash office goading each other about one thing and another. They always had a laugh. I think Mr Routledge looked on them as "his boys". They more or less started with the PTC together and they went off to war together. I sometimes walk into the office and hear the three of them laughing.'

Dottie shook herself. 'That feels weird.'

Ruth smiled. 'It isn't, Dottie. It's memories.'

—

After a long period without news, Ruth was over the moon to discover a letter from Stan sitting in the usual place on the sideboard and beamed as she picked it up. She would take it upstairs and read it on her own.

'Just popping upstairs, Dottie.'

She heard a faint laugh. 'That'll be Ruth off upstairs to read Stan's letter, I'll bet. Best put her plate to keep warm, Carla.'

12 May 1918

Dear Ruth,

Since my last Christmas letter, things have been rather busy here. The Germans attacked in the spring and it got uncomfortable around here, I have to say. So much so that we had to move further west.

Now we're back at our usual depot, which was knocked about a bit by artillery and bombers. One soldier told me his war began near our new location in 1914. It puts the fighting into perspective. Four years, Ruth, and now we are back where we started. How soul-destroying for the poor buggers who were fighting at that time.

Things seem to have settled down now and let's hope we'll see an end to it soon. We have seen more American soldiers in the area. They seem to do more riding and less marching than we do. I heard that some American units further south took part in stopping a German offensive.

One thing I have heard which you might be interested in was about that Matthew Roundswell chap. I told you about him right at the very beginning. I was speaking to a bloke who was his batman in Brighton and he told me that Roundswell's wife-to-be was a suffragette and had been in prison. She hadn't told him, so he left her at the altar. Not a nice thing to do. Her name was Constance Copeland. Weren't they the people that lived at that posh house near to where you lived in Dartmouth Street?

I had a letter from our Rosie last week. She's so pleased that we are sharing our news and so am I. But I couldn't sign off without asking how you are, my dear. I love to hear from you but it makes me realise how far away you are. Every night I think of you before I go to sleep and pray that we will be together before long. Our happy memories keep me going – but don't tell our Rosie I said that!

That's all for now, dearest.
Love
Stan

Ruth lay grinning on her bed. When she met up with Rosie, she would often let her read his letters, but, of late, they had become more… intimate, and she rather thought that Stan would prefer for her to keep those to herself. Also, for her own sake, she wasn't quite prepared to share him with anyone, not even her closest friends, just yet.

Chapter Thirty-One

June 1918

Ruth was sitting reading and eating her oatcakes in the restroom when Carla came rushing in, looking anything but her usual self. Ruth, as usual, was utterly immersed in her book and had to shake herself back into the present. She hadn't noticed the three clippies walk in, nor had their voices disturbed her.

Then Carla's pale face and tear-streaked cheeks caught her attention. She jumped up at once and held her. Ruth had been expecting her any time because Carla was working the afternoon shift.

'What's the matter? What's happened?'

'Oh, Ruth, you'll never believe it.'

'Believe what? Tell me, for goodness' sake? What's happened?' Ruth swore she would've slapped Carla's face if she hadn't spoken at that moment. There's nothing worse than waiting for someone to tell bad news when the person involved is too shocked to speak.

'Come outside. Best to tell you outside.'

Without waiting for Ruth's reply, Carla marched out of the room, leaving Ruth no other choice but to follow past a surprised-looking Pearl as they trooped through reception.

'Carla! Stop! Right this minute!'

They were outside now, and the street was empty.

Ruth grabbed hold of Carla's shoulders. 'I want to know. Now!'

Carla's eyes misted over. 'It's Donald. He's…'

Ruth's heart overturned.

'Donald? Dead? How could that be? He's in India. Nowhere near the fighting. He can't be. He was—'

'He's dead, Ruth. An accident, the officer said.'

'An officer? What officer? When did it happen?'

Ruth didn't hear the reply. The next thing she knew, she was sitting in Pearl's office, with her head between her knees.

'You fainted, duckie, you've had a nasty shock.'

Ruth sat up and looked at Pearl. It all came streaming back to her. 'Where's Carla?'

'I'm here. You gave me quite a shock. I've never seen someone faint before.'

'You two go into the interview room and I'll bring you a cup of tea and tell Mr Routledge what's happened.' Pearl disappeared as Carla urged Ruth to the interview room and sat her down.

—

It happened this morning. 'There was a knock at the door at about nine o'clock. I'd only just got decent. There was a soldier, an officer called Captain Munro, looking for Dottie. I guessed straight away there was a problem. I told him she was at work but it was only five minutes' walk away and he asked me to go with him, so Dottie had a friend with her. He had a car and driver, and after briefly speaking with the lodge-keeper, we went into the reception and someone showed us to a room. A few minutes later, Dottie arrived, and she knew straight away that it was bad news.'

'Poor Dottie.'

'She kept shaking her head and saying, "No. No." Captain Munro was very good and he gave her time to compose herself. I held her hand while he told us all he knew. Donald was out on a mission in the hills near to the Khyber Pass when he fell down a hillside. He broke his leg and returned to the barracks the following day, but he soon developed a fever and the army surgeon realised he'd got blood poisoning. He died on 29 May.'

'So he wasn't killed?'

'It was an unfortunate accident. That's all the captain could tell us. He was reading the official telegraph. Donald's commanding officer will write with more details, but she probably won't get it for a few weeks.'

Ruth covered her face. This wasn't happening. Couldn't happen. They were all so sure that Donald, above all people, would be safe.

'Captain Munro took us in the car straight to Dottie's mother's house and left. Dottie was in a bad way, and I didn't want her to be in the house by herself. I called in to see Donald's mother and gave her the terrible news. She said she would go to see Dottie straight away. I've just got back. I wanted to catch you, so you know what's happened. Look, I'm just about to go on shift, so I'll have to leave you now. Are you all right?'

Ruth nodded. 'Thanks for telling me. I'll go over to see her once I've finished here. See how she's managing. So you'll know where I am.'

They hugged each other, and left, Carla to go on shift and Ruth to work through columns of figures – which now meant absolutely nothing at all.

Ruth had a slice of toast and she even had to force herself to eat that. Just enough to keep her from feeling ill, she thought. She took the tram to her usual stop on Moorland Road and walked over to Gordon Street, knocked on the door, and waited.

Mrs Scott opened the door and bade her come in. Dottie, sitting in a straight-backed chair in the front room, looked up and saw Ruth. The tears flowed.

Ruth rushed to her side and squeezed her tightly, desperate for her to feel the strength of someone else flowing through her.

'Ruth… Ruth… what am I going to do? How can I live without my Donald? He was everything to me.'

Between sobs, Dottie poured out her sorrows about how Donald was going to finish in the army when the war was over and they were hoping to start a family, plans which would never see the light of day now.

Mrs Scott, having left them alone, came back with tea and cake. She sat opposite to them. Her face was pale, and her eyes bloodshot. Ruth thought she may have cried in the kitchen. With a nod, Ruth showed Mrs Scott she understood the woman's part in supporting her daughter through a horrible experience.

By the time Ruth arrived back in Campbell Road, it was dark. She would be lucky if she got any sleep tonight. Her mind was so active. She was exhausted and needed a rest, and faced the prospect of an early rise in the morning.

She walked into the kitchen to find Carla waiting for her, sitting huddled up by the fire. She stood up. One look was all it took for the two to break down in each other's arms, to let go the tears they couldn't shed with anyone else.

They sat down at the table. Automatically, Ruth moved the kettle to boil and made another pot of tea, but she couldn't drink it. Instead, she said, 'Let's go for a walk, Carla. I don't know about you, but it helps to settle me.' Ruth stood up, and they walked down Campbell Road towards Hanford. 'I don't know what it is about being outside. Inside, I feel I can barely breathe but in the fresh air my mind relaxes.'

'Poor Dottie, married to Donald for five years but living together for less than a year.'

'She told me this evening that Donald had made his mind up to return home as soon as he could and they were going to start a family.'

'Do you remember just after I'd moved in and we had that argument the evening she started her monthly? And you ran after me to bring me back?'

'Oh yes, she was so desperate to be pregnant back then and so upset when she realised she wasn't and wouldn't be until Donald returned from India.'

'I wonder if Dottie would've gone with him if she'd realised the war would take so long?'

They lapsed into silence as they continued walking, and Ruth's thoughts turned to Stan facing danger every day. How long before she got similar news? That thought brought more tears with it.

'Damn this bloody war!'

-

When Ruth got to work the following day, people treated the news of Donald's death much like the other deaths. Each news of a colleague being killed faded into the background. People had got used to hearing bad news and although they were sad, everyone seemed to have developed a stoical way of accepting it.

It was probably a good job because, as the war had progressed, the levels of deaths were in the hundreds of thousands. Ruth could not envisage that being tolerated at the beginning of the war.

—

Ruth had been popping home for her dinner so she could check on Dottie. She hoped Dottie would return to work later that week.

'Hello, Dottie, I've been busy this morning, and I fancied some fresh air.'

'I got this letter this morning.' Dottie handed Ruth an envelope containing several pages in beautiful handwritten script. 'It's from India.' Ruth read the letter with some apprehension.

> *Bungalow 15*
> *Majuba Barracks*
> *Rawalpindi*
>
> *22 May 1918*
>
> *Dear Memsahib Spilling,*
> *I have started to write this letter many times, but could not find the words. My name is Seeta Chakraborty. I was the housekeeper of your late husband, Sergeant Donald Spilling.*
> *Although his illness was short, I attended to him every day at the camp hospital. During that time, he asked me to write to you to express his love and devotion. This is what he wanted me to tell you.*

Dear Dottie,

It looks as if India will not be a safe posting after all. We had been on a patrol around the frontier area near to the foothills of the Khyber Pass. The CO will no doubt have told you what happened. It was my own fault. We were moving into an Indian Army border post to spend the night. I went outside for a smoke and the next thing I knew, I was at the bottom of a hill. My leg was broken, I could tell that. I had my service revolver with me and could attract attention. We did not get back to any medical facilities until the evening of the following day.

I started a fever a few days later. Seeta will know the details. I felt poorly and today they told me I do not stand a chance. The infection has gone too far.

I have got little of value, but of course what I own is yours. You will get a pension. You must not grieve for me too long. If you meet someone else, then you have my blessing to remarry.

All my love, as always,
Donald

I tended to him night and day until the end.

Sergeant Spilling slipped into a deep sleep, and he died just before midnight. His commanding officer will send you his personal things, but I want to send this letter myself. I had the greatest respect for your husband. I went to work for him the day he arrived and I worked for him until the end. He was very kind to me and it was a pleasure to have known him.

> *I will close this letter now, but you have my address if you need any more information.*
> *My condolences,*
> *Seeta Chakraborty (Mrs)*
>
> *Postscript – I hope you received the letter I posted on 22 May from your husband the day he left the barracks for the patrol. I do not know its contents. I was allowed to post my letter in the army's official mail, which is given priority, but his would be sent in the usual way. If you have not yet received the letter, then you need to prepare yourself as it might come as a shock.*
> *Seeta Chakraborty (Mrs)*

Ruth looked at Dottie and they both had tears in their eyes, and it was several seconds before either of them could speak.

'That was very nice of her.'

'Yes, she sounds nice, educated. I'm glad Donald had someone to look after him.'

'Dottie, Donald gave you his blessing to continue with your life, and now it is up to you to decide what you do.'

'Yes, Ruth, but I miss him so much and he is so far away. I'll never see his grave. It still doesn't feel real even after reading this letter.' Dottie sobbed her heart out, and Ruth held her friend. She wondered just how many women were doing the same thing at that moment.

'It is strange to think that there's another letter out there, written by Donald, on its way to me. I hope it doesn't get lost, Ruth.'

–

It was two weeks before the letter Dottie was waiting for finally arrived. Dottie didn't give Ruth a chance to sit down before waving the letter in front of her eyes.

'Look at what's arrived. The letter Donald's housekeeper told me to expect,' said Dottie, her eyes bright with tears.

'Have you read it?'

'Yes, I read it as soon as I got home. I couldn't wait. It is an interesting letter, but you make up your own mind. You can read it.' She handed it to Ruth.

> *Bungalow 15*
> *Majuba Barracks*
> *Rawalpindi*
>
> *14 May 1918*
>
> *My Dottie,*
> *We have been preparing to go on patrol up at the frontier. The entire unit is looking forward to some action. We expect to be away for three to four weeks, so you'll probably not hear from me for a while.*
>
> *A group of us could get some leave, and we went to the city of Amritsar. It was a remarkable place. The city is the most holy place for the Sikhs. It has a golden temple that is surrounded by water. I wish you could've seen it.*
>
> *We travelled by train and I am still in awe of the way the trains are packed with people. They sit on the roof of the carriage and have to lie flat when the train goes under a bridge or through a tunnel. Nobody seems to mind and people cook meals in the coaches and pretty much carry on with their lives during the journey.*

> *The brigadier has asked me if I'd be interested in signing up full time in the unit as a sergeant. He reminded me I could bring you out to live here at any time. Mrs Chakraborty has asked me frequently whether you were coming out here. As she says, 'It would be a fine place to bring up lots of little Spillings.'*
>
> *I will not have to decide until the war in Europe is finished, and I'd like you to consider moving out here and we can make a life for ourselves away from the dust and smoke of The Potteries. If the North Staffords are posted elsewhere, then I'd have the option to enlist in the Indian Army and so we could live out here as long as we wished. Please think about this, my darling. It could be so good for both of us.*
>
> *My unit is leaving the barracks tomorrow morning, so I will ask Mrs Chakraborty to post this letter for me. I will write again on my return.*
>
> *I miss you so much, Dottie, and long for the time when we will be together again.*
>
> *All my love forever,*
> *Donald*

Tears streamed down their faces. Dottie took the letter from Ruth.

'I need a bit of time to myself. I was beginning to think it had got lost.' Dottie clutched the letter to her chest.

It must have felt so odd reading it, knowing he was alive and making plans at that time.

'I didn't realise he was still keen on both of us moving over there permanently. Still, I'll cherish it forever.'

Ruth imagined that Donald's plans would certainly have come as a shock. If Dottie had wanted to go, she would've told her closest friends.

'Come on, Carla, get your jacket on and we'll go for a walk. It'll do us good.'

Chapter Thirty-Two

August–December 1918

A sober-looking Mr Routledge walked into the cash office, accompanied by what looked like all the PTC employees, including Norman from the garage. There were looks of dread on the faces of those who had begun to expect the worst. He said he had an announcement to make and cleared his throat and read from the piece of paper he carried.

'My fellow colleagues, it is with great sadness that I have to tell you about the death of Dickie Smith.' Loud gasps circulated. 'Some of us worked with Dickie for many years. He was always conscientious and willing to help anybody. Dickie joined up at the start of the war along with Jim Wilson, who we lost in 1916, and Tom Walton, who is still out there. Our best wishes go out to our fallen colleague. I'm sure you will all remember Dickie received the Distinguished Conduct Medal for his bravery only a few weeks ago at the end of the German Spring Offensive. I'm sure he'll be sorely missed by us all.' He stopped, visibly upset, and returned to his office, closing the door sharply.

'Mr Routledge and Dickie worked together for The Potteries Light Railways, which formed part of the PTC when it was set up in 1899,' added Brian.

Except for the cashiers, everyone filed out to return to work. That August, the news from the Western Front had been positive. After the German Spring Offensive had been halted, Allied forces had undertaken a major counterattack. The German front line near to Amiens had been penetrated and considerable advances made, capturing a lot of the ground lost in the springtime.

Ruth thought about the list of men who had died since the war had begun. Dickie was the twenty-first employee the PTC had lost in this war and she sincerely hoped he would be the last.

—

Ruth dressed carefully, sure that Rosie would want to show her off to her friends as her brother's intended. Satisfied with her appearance, she ran downstairs. Carla was working, so Dottie was on her own, reading.

'Are you going to be all right on your own, Dottie?'

'Of course I am. Besides, you can't spoil the girl's birthday by babysitting me. I wouldn't forgive myself. No, you go to help Rosie celebrate. I've plenty to keep me busy and I'm desperate to finish my book.'

'Very well. I must say that I'm relieved she has taken to me. She was so friendly, right from the beginning. I think she's lost with both her brothers overseas. In her last letter, she told me that Mark was now in France. I'm sure Mrs Bristow's out of her mind with worry and Rosie tries very hard to be there for them. She even talked about giving up her scholarship place so that she could be at home all day.'

'I doubt Mrs Bristow would allow her to do that.'

'Most definitely. And I wouldn't want to get on the wrong side of her either!'

Ruth dropped a kiss on the top of Dottie's head and then stepped outside.

Ordinarily, it would have taken her some time to get to Brown Edge, with Smallthorne being the nearest tram stop. So, not only had Rosie invited Ruth to her party, but she had also cajoled her father into meeting Ruth at Smallthorne crossroads to take her the rest of the way. Ruth smiled to herself. That girl was going places, of that she was certain. Without a doubt, she could twist a man around her little finger!

As the tram pulled up, she found Mr Bristow sitting inside the van waiting for her.

She hurried over to him. 'It's so kind of you to pick me up, Mr Bristow. Thank you.'

'Yer needn't thank me, Ruth.' He grinned. 'Our Rosie was most insistent. I swear that girl gets more like her mother with every passing day.'

They chatted away until Mr Bristow turned the van into the yard and pulled up near to the workshop. They walked towards the house.

Rosie came flying outside, shouting her name, and full of excitement. 'Ruth! Ruth! Come and meet my friends! I've been waiting for you.'

Ruth gave her a hug and pressed a small present into her hands, a book she herself had read when she was younger, and hoped Rosie would enjoy as much as she did.

As promised, Rosie introduced Ruth to each of her old friends from Brown Edge School. They looked nice, friendly girls, and Ruth soon warmed to them. They asked questions, interested particularly in a woman doing a man's job. Even more so when Rosie told them she earned the same wages. One girl wondered whether there would be clippies after the war finished.

'Why are there no women tram drivers?' another girl asked.

'There are, but not in The Potteries. Glasgow, Birmingham and London have plenty of them.'

'Why don't we have them in The Potteries?'

'The bosses say it's too hard work for gentlewomen.' The girls all laughed, and the consensus was that they were every bit as strong as the boys. 'They said that it wasn't the driving, it was work such as reversing the trolley head and turning the tram around on turntables at the end of lines. It sounds heavy work, but it isn't. The turntables are balanced and one man can turn a tram with no bother, so surely two women would have no problem.' Where did that come from? Ruth thought. She sounded like Stan.

They had a fine time, and at one point, Mrs Bristow drew Ruth to one side.

'You seem to have made quite an impression on Rosie's friends. I bet their teacher would have wished they showed the same interest when they were at school.'

Ruth laughed. 'I don't mind at all. I've had a lovely afternoon.'

'You're a good woman, Ruth. I think you'll be just right for our Stan. He can be quite reserved, you know. He only opens up to people he knows.'

Ruth wouldn't have called him reserved. The Stan she knew had appeared outgoing, in fact.

She thought about Mrs Bristow's words on the way back home. His mother knew him better than anyone. She thought back to some of the early days – his accident on Gertie, gradually getting to know him at work and his embarrassment at turning up on the doorstep when she'd just had a bath. He never thrust himself forward and only seemed comfortable when talking about vehicle parts and the dos and don'ts of repairing an engine. On the whole, yes, now she thought about it, he was quiet and kept himself to himself. She found it rather endearing.

—

The day the Armistice was signed, everybody seemed to finish work early, except for the trams. As Mr Taylor said, 'People will still need to get home from their celebrations.'

Ruth and Carla left earlier than normal and walked towards home.

'Everybody looks so relieved,' said Carla.

'How do you feel?'

'I am relieved now we can get back to the way we used to be. Although I think it'll never be the same.'

'Do you remember the night we were walking home, and we finally plucked up courage to tell Dottie that we didn't like sprouts?' asked Ruth.

Carla laughed heartily. 'Yes, I do.'

'That night was the only time I think we've talked about what might happen if Germany won the war. None of us really thought they would.'

'They nearly did. I must admit that in the spring, I thought the Germans were going to break through and take Paris.'

'Yes, Carla, I thought the same.'

'In the end we just fought each other to a standstill and I really can't see what we achieved. All those men died, and even more injured. Henry said that we lost twenty-one men and have at least a dozen with lost limbs.'

'What's happening with your parents? Have you heard anything?'

Carla shook her head. 'Now we have the Armistice, I'm hoping that letters might start getting through. As for Bertie, I doubt the army will want to keep the camp going. I've no idea whether they'll repatriate him or let him stay. I can't feel happy until I know his fate.'

Ruth nodded. 'At least the fighting's over.'

Carla nodded too. 'And we've got to make the best of the peace. Let this be a lesson. We can't make the same mistake again.'

'I agree with that. They wouldn't be so foolish…'

The two of them had walked through Stoke listening to the joyful crowds celebrating, getting slowly quieter as they reached Campbell Road. The sun had set leaving a nice red glow over the Hanford Hills. Perhaps it was a sign.

–

A month after the Armistice was signed, the government finally announced its plans for demobilisation of the armed forces. As a result, letters ending the employment of all the clippies were sent out, causing considerable upset. The demobilisation would take at least six months meaning the women knew they were losing their job, but not when. Those who had relied on the higher wages were now not only looking for another job but also faced the prospect of earning half the wages they had enjoyed during the war years. It seemed unfair, but then again, the bosses were obliged to find work for all the returning soldiers.

Mr Routledge had promised that, once the war was over, she could return to her typing job. The problem was that she had been a junior typist and her wages were almost next to nothing. Jobs were scarce now – men being the first choice for any job to be filled, and women were at the bottom of the ladder. Necessity forced many women back into service; refusing such work disqualified them from unemployment benefits.

So, when Mr Routledge invited her into his office for a brief discussion about her future, Ruth was, naturally, full of dread. She tapped on his door, wearing her best smile.

'Come in, Ruth, and take a seat. We have a lot of work in front of us in filling jobs with our men who will be returning to us over the coming weeks. It'll take a great deal of planning and we will still have to get the trams out on time, as well as keep the company going during this difficult period.'

Ruth nodded, wondering when he was going to get to the point. She smiled again in case it helped. It seemed to. He smiled back.

'Now then, since we lost our young men in the cash office, you ladies have done a grand job. We would have been lost without you. It is a skilled job and not one easily taught. Can I ask you one thing first, Ruth? I know you are walking out with Stanley Bristow. Are you thinking of getting married?'

Ruth sat upright at that point, eyes wide open. 'Why do you ask?'

'I called you in to talk about the possibility of a job, which, of course, you won't be interested in if you're getting wed.'

A flash of annoyance crossed Ruth's face, which she tried her best to hide. 'No.' She wished she had the confidence to tell him it was none of the PTC's business, but she was intrigued.

Mr Routledge blushed and returned to the original subject. 'I've agreed with Mr Perkins that you should stay with us in your current capacity, as, after Mr Bertram, you are our most experienced cashier.'

Ruth beamed at him, but he held up a hand to stop her from saying anything. 'There is a downside, I'm afraid. You won't like it, but there's nothing I can do.'

Ruth didn't care. She was going to remain as a cashier. That was all she wanted to know.

'Unfortunately, the PTC cannot pay you the same rates as you are currently enjoying. That was for the war effort, along with the war bonus. The women's rates will, naturally, be lower otherwise there will be considerable trouble with the unions and we don't want that, do we?'

The smile faded from Ruth's mouth as she took in the implications of what Mr Routledge was saying. She could keep her current job, but would have to take a reduction in pay.

'And what about Mr Bertram's pay? Will his remain the same?'

'Of course, he will be the senior cashier and, as such, will be in charge.'

'You could always give him more money so you won't have to reduce the women's rate.' Ruth was surprised when the words left her mouth, but it was unfair.

'The company will pay you at eighty per cent of the men's rate, considerably more than your typing post would pay. I'm disappointed in you, Ruth. I thought you'd be pleased.'

'Of course I'm pleased, Mr Routledge. It's what I was hoping would happen. Thank you for the opportunity.'

'Very good. Now, will you ask Molly and Madge to come in?'

Molly and Madge came out beaming. They had also been offered permanent jobs, and the four of them would continue to work together. The three women hugged each other, delighted with the outcome, while Brian smiled but refused the invitation to join them.

The PTC was confident that the new jobs as checkers, agreed by the directors after the fraud, would need to be filled by men and that sufficient jobs would be available, so they hoped they would have no problems offering the cashier jobs to women.

Even though their jobs would not be as well paid as before, they felt they had cause for celebration.

Chapter Thirty-Three

January–March 1919

January brought a period of the kind of rainy weather that makes everybody miserable. Added to the smoke of the factories which was trapped by the rain clouds, the whole of the city seemed to be in a permanent fog. Ruth walked home from work, not thinking about anything, and arrived at the door without taking in how she got there.

Once inside, she peeled off her heavy coat and removed her boots. Then she saw the letter addressed to her. It was from Stan. She opened the envelope.

> *7 January 1919*
>
> *Dear Ruth,*
>
> *After all the excitement and the fuss about the Armistice, things have gone flat over here. Many men expected a quick return home. Quite a few were talking about being home for Christmas. The CO informed us that demobilisation of the conscripts is unlikely before March, and it will be a staggered process. They said that they are expecting it all to be completed by June.*
>
> *I have heard from Mark. He is near the German city of Cologne as part of the occupation*

force. I hope he is careful, as the British are not likely to be popular. I do not think Mark will be back until June at best.

We have still got plenty of work here. Whilst I am writing this letter, I have paperwork on my desk for 127 lorries which are to be checked over and returned to Britain. The lorries are sitting in a nice straight line, all neatly parked. A few weeks ago, such a sight would have made a German pilot believe his prayers were answered. Most of the lorries are new. There is an awful lot of equipment out here which needs to be returned to Britain.

We have been told that when the Armistice was declared, the Germans could not take any armaments or vehicles with them. They had to march away from the Front to assembly stations. There are a lot of German vehicles which now belong to the Allies.

We're no longer under fire, but unexploded ordnance is everywhere and requires cautious movement. So we still have to use the cleared routes only. The officers urge us repeatedly to be vigilant. As one said, just because it looks like a can, it doesn't mean you can kick it.

It is nice to think I'm coming home this year, even though there is a lot of the year left. You don't know how much that means to me, to know you will be in my arms, and I yours. Thank you for waiting for me. My heart is so full, it might well burst before long.

Once I know what I am doing, I will send you a telegram. But until then I hope you keep well

and look forward to seeing you again as soon as I can. I can't wait, my darling.
  Your loving,
  Stan

Ruth smiled as she thought about Stan, surrounded by all the lorries he was talking about. If the circumstances were different, he would have been in his element. It was unfortunate that it would be at least the spring before he'd return, but he was safe.

She was shocked to read about all the unexploded stuff, but it looked as though Stan was aware. She remembered his promise to be careful. She decided she would not tell his family until they told her.

Carla and Dottie arrived, and they stoked up the range to cook their teas. The house soon warmed.

'It's a shame that it is going to take so long for the men to return after all they have been through,' said Dottie after Ruth had read out Stan's letter to them.

'It's taken us over four years to get all those men, guns and machines out there. We can hardly expect them back in a few weeks, what with everything having to be loaded onto ships,' said Carla.

A subdued Dottie took the potato peelings out to the ash bin. Ruth and Carla looked at each other and changed the subject for Dottie's return.

—

Towards the end of the month, Ruth had a visit from Rosie. She'd been to Macclesfield to sit the second part of the entrance examination for the scholarship and had caught the train to Stoke so she could tell Ruth all about it. Ruth was so pleased she'd done well and proud that

Rosie had taken time to visit her. Now the waiting started, poor Rosie wouldn't hear she'd succeeded until 1 July. Five months is a long time. For a sixteen-year-old it must be an eternity.

-

It was the beginning of March when Carla finally had a letter from Bertie. Ruth was the first to see it as she took it out of their letterbox. She would have loved to open it, but it was none of her business. Instead, she stood it on the kitchen table so Carla would see it the minute she entered the kitchen.

'I hope he's got some good news for Carla, although I'm not sure what good news would be,' said Dottie. 'I read in *The Sentinel* last week that many internees are being returned straight to Germany.'

'There's nothing we can do about it. She should be here soon. Do you want any help with the tea?'

'No, but can you take the washing off the clothes maid and fold it into the basket, then we'll have a bit more room? I didn't put them out to dry because there was no wind round here.'

A few minutes later, Carla came in through the back door and kicked off her boots in the scullery. 'Hello, where are me allotment shoes? I trod on something unmentionable on the way home. I'll take them straight out and clean them.'

Carla disappeared outside with some newspaper, a brush and a bucket of water. She soon returned and poured some hot water from the kettle and washed her hands in carbolic soap. Ruth quickly moved Bertie's letter. No point in spoiling Carla's tea, was there? 'Tea's ready,' shouted Ruth.

'On my way.'

At the end of the meal, Ruth passed Carla the letter. 'A letter came for you today, from the Isle of Man.'

Carla shrieked and made a grab for it, grinning from ear to ear. She opened the letter and read it out loud.

28 February 1919

My dear Carla,

At last, I have received my papers instructing me I will be released from the camp and repatriated directly to Germany. When I asked if that was the final decision, the officer conducting the interview said that I would have seven days in which to lodge an appeal. He gave me the appeal form and some advice about what to include.

I wrote the appeal that evening and handed it in on Thursday last. I said I had lived in Burslem since I was two years old and that I had a sister living there who was born in Britain and a wife and child who are English. Part of the form asked me about my education, trade and skills. I have a trade and I can support myself.

Unfortunately, there was a section about criminal convictions, which included any imposed during my internment at the camp. So I had to mention my outburst, which cost me three months' solitary when I found out about my Edith and Luther.

The officer said to me that a criminal record of any sort is not good as Britain can raise enough criminals of their own, but once I told him the circumstances and he checked my file, he seemed more optimistic.

I don't know how long the appeal will take, but the form stated that they would not take action against me until the appeal is decided. I am now left waiting to see what is going to happen.

As I sit writing this letter I have realised, if I am granted a licence to stay in Great Britain, then I cannot see our mother and father again. Once I leave Britain, the licence is automatically revoked and I may not return. If they repatriate me, then I shall never see you, my dear sister, and my wife and child again. I don't know if you appreciate that Mother and Father may not return to Great Britain in the future as the law stands. Even though the war has ended, the powers that be are still determined to make our lives a misery.

I could decide to withdraw my appeal, but I cannot abandon my little Luther. So I am desperate for my appeal to succeed. I will still have my German nationality and could return to Germany along with my wife and child should I wish. I know that would leave you on your own, but Mother and Father told me in one of their letters that you were happy where you are and I respect that.

It is crucial that we get information on the location of Luther and Edith.

I will write to you again when I know the result of my appeal.

Your loving brother,
Bertie

Ruth and Dottie listened quietly as Carla read out the letter. When Carla finished, Dottie got up and went to the privy.

'I think that might have been a bit overwhelming for her,' said Ruth.

'We can't stop mentioning what has gone on. She'll just have to get used to it.'

'That's a bit harsh, Carla.'

'It may be, but it's true.'

'Just give her more time. She'll come around, eventually. She might not like it, but she'll understand.'

—

On a cold and blustery day towards the end of March, Tom Walton returned to his job in the cash office.

'Tom's returning to work today and you don't need me to tell you it will be a big thing for him. We must remember he's lost two close friends and work colleagues and is returning a changed man. I have spoken to him. He seems withdrawn and we are hoping that him coming back to work, and familiar surroundings, will aid his recovery.'

Brian shook his head. 'I must admit I'm worried about how he'll react returning to this office.' Mr Routledge glanced up at the open door to the cash office. 'Even I have moments when I can see the three of them sitting in their places, working away. It upsets me to think of those times.'

Ruth's whole body turned icy at Brian's words.

'It might be like walking on eggshells, ladies. We just don't know. I've learned that many returning men have faced considerable difficulties in adjusting. And who could blame them, poor buggers?'

It was the first time Ruth had heard Mr Routledge swear in all the years she had known him.

'But we have a job to do and I spoke to Miss Butler a few days ago, and we have agreed that she moves to the wages office and works in the ticket store helping Mr Baxter. With all the changes resulting from the fraud, there will be more than enough work for her.'

When they walked back into their office, Molly blew out a sigh. 'God almighty! The poor bloke must be in a bad way for old Routledge to tell us all that. I thought he was going to break down himself.'

Tears gathered in Ruth's eyes. 'Molly, you don't know what it was really like here before the war. There were four cashiers. Young men in the prime of life and all their lives in front of them. Happy-go-lucky, they were. One of them was my beau for a time.' She felt her face reddening and more tears as a picture of Jim flashed before her.

Molly's eyes were agog.

'It ended before the war started. Unfortunately, Tom Walton's the only one who has come back.'

Ruth realised afterwards that Molly must have heard her words before, but she acted as if hearing them for the first time.

Ten minutes later, voices echoed in the corridor. The two pale-faced girls rose. Ruth walked towards the door to welcome Tom back. Mr Routledge opened the door and stood beside him.

Ruth smiled. 'Hello, Tom. It's good to see you.'

Tom was rooted to the spot in the open doorway. Ruth looked nervously at Mr Routledge. He pursed his lips but kept quiet.

'I don't think you've met Molly here.' Ruth beckoned Molly forward.

For a moment, Tom looked startled. Then he gave her a slight nod, but remained standing in the doorway.

Ruth moved forward very slowly, talking to him, asking which seat he would like, a window seat or one in the corner at the back. He walked slowly towards his old seat by the window and sat down, staring at the desk. Ruth watched as Tom lifted his head and stared in front of him, eyes wide open, looking horrified, just as everything seemed to be progressing. It was as if he was witnessing something – something playing out in front of him he couldn't get away from.

It was Ruth's turn to be anxious now. She turned to Mr Routledge. He moved across the room. Ruth reached Tom first.

'They're here! For Christ's sake. I can see them. They're in my head. Get them away!'

'Who is it, Tom? Who are you seeing?'

For one moment, Tom stopped and turned to look at Mr Routledge, his eyes blank.

He tried again. 'Who is it, Tom?'

'Jim and Dickie. It's Jim. He's laughing at me. I can't take it.'

Tom jumped up out of his seat and made a dash for the door, nearly knocking Molly off her feet.

'I'm so sorry, ladies. I'd hoped for something better.' Mr Routledge shot after Tom, leaving the office in silence.

Ruth's tears were uncontrollable. Molly kept blinking, but it was no good. They clasped each other and let go a sorrow too painful for further words.

Mr Routledge returned an hour and a half later, his face pale and unsmiling, to tell them that someone had taken Tom home and that he would not be returning for the foreseeable future.

'But he was ready to come back!'

'Not as ready as we thought. I'll put it another way. He was ready to return to work, but it was a mistake putting him back in the office where he worked with two friends who have not come back. It's the guilt of being the only one to return.' Mr Routledge shook his head. 'Poor boy might never forgive himself. Anyway, we'll give him another month and then put him to work somewhere else – wages or with the checkers, possibly.'

'And if that doesn't work?' asked Ruth.

Mr Routledge's shoulders sagged. 'From what I've seen, he'll not be the only one who can't settle when they return to their former life. It's all right for the government to promise these men will get their jobs back. But how can anyone witnessing such scenes come back to carry on as normal? I'm damned if I know.'

He walked back into his office and slammed the door behind him.

—

Ruth and Carla walked home from work together. It had been three weeks to the day since Carla had received Bertie's letter and since then she'd heard nothing. They knew from the papers that the numbers of internees being processed had increased considerably and there was a backlog.

'All I want now is to hear from my parents. Is it too much to ask? When you read in the newspapers how bad things are in Germany, I suppose getting a postal service between the two countries is probably not high on their list.'

Dottie greeted them. 'There's a letter for you, Carla, and this one is from Germany.'

Carla gave a shriek, and they all went into the kitchen. Carla opened the letter, which still seemed to have many official stamps on it, but this did not bother her.

'It's from Mother and Father. They're all right. Thank goodness.' Carla sat down and continued to read the letter. When she had finished, her eyes were tearful and her voice faltered.

'You can read the letter if you wish. Please, can you keep my tea warm? I just need some time to myself.' Carla put the letter down on the kitchen table and went up to her room.

Ruth picked up the letter. 'Look at the date, it has taken five weeks to get here,' she tutted and then began to read out loud.

Bäckerei Hesse
44 Schuhstraße
Hildesheim

19 February 1919

My dear Carlotta,

This is my second attempt at sending you a letter. I sent one just after the Armistice, but since I have heard nothing back from you or Albrecht, I expect it never arrived.

Both your mother and I are in good health despite everything. We are thinner and older. We are still living over the bakery in Hildesheim. My brother, your uncle Max, died at the beginning of 1918. He had always suffered with asthma and one day it just got too much for his heart. Your aunt Louise now owns the bakery, but between the three of us, we do all the work.

Conditions in Germany are terrible. There is not enough food and not enough coal for heating. It is not as bad for us in the west, but winters in the east are very cold with snow on the ground for many weeks. Even during the war, many people died of cold and starvation and are still doing so.

We asked at the immigration office in Hanover whether we could get permission to return to England. Apart from a very frosty reply and a lecture on how we should remain to rebuild the Fatherland, the answer was no.

We have heard that the internees are going to be released and many of them are being sent back each day. Men with English wives and children are being returned to Germany, but their families remain in England. It is not clear whether these are the rules or just unfortunate circumstances.

Neither you nor Albrecht should travel to Germany. Especially you. You are English by birth and would not be welcome here. Albrecht might fare a little better, but I would not risk it. He must stay with his son and wife.

The one thing that does concern me is that our industries are so rundown there is a shortage of jobs, but no shortage of soldiers returning from the Front with nothing more than their uniform. If you consider the plentiful supplies of beer, it is a recipe for chaos.

I shall wait until the end of April and send this letter again. Please reply and tell Albrecht wherever he is to look after himself and contact us soon. And Carlotta, we know you're with Walter and your friends; your safety is paramount. Please stay there.

All our love,
Mother and Father

There was a similar letter enclosed for Bertie, she guessed, in another envelope which Carla hadn't opened.

'Poor Bertie, how desperate he must be. If only Edith would get in touch with him and tell him how she feels instead of keeping him in the dark. It's not right.'

'It's bound to take time, Dottie. I know it's not what Carla wants to hear. Keep believing. That's all we can do.'

—

Throughout the week, there was a quietness about the offices as word spread about poor Tom. Chattering about whether he had come back to work too soon or shouldn't have come back at all. Ruth didn't know what to think. It was nobody's fault. He was as much a casualty of war as any other soldier. Just because it was his mind affected didn't make it something to get over quickly and move on. She was pleased the PTC hadn't given up on him.

—

Ruth was the next one to receive some news. When she got home from work there was a letter waiting for her. It was from Stan and post marked Grantham.

Saturday, 29 March 1919

Dearest Ruth,
I'm back in England! You don't know how happy it makes me to say that. There are so many

of us and demobbing is taking an age. There are queues for everything. As soon as I have my paperwork I shall be on my way. I'm planning to go straight home to see my family and I hope to see you at two o'clock on Sunday 6 April. No point in you writing back to me because I won't be here, fingers crossed.

See you on the 6th
Love, your Stan

Ruth gasped, and she covered her face with her hands, choking back the tears that threatened.

'It's a letter from Stan. He's waiting to be demobbed. He'll be here on Sunday!'

'Darling! I'm so pleased for you,' cried Dottie jumping out of her seat to hug her.

'I'm so sorry, Dottie. I can't help it. I'm sorry.' Ruth's voice raised and sank by degrees. Full of happiness, followed by heartbreak that Dottie was trying her best to be happy for her.

In tears too, Dottie shook her head. 'Don't you ever think that, Ruth Latham! I'm not expecting everyone to tiptoe around me. How can we ever get over it otherwise? The enemy will have won and I won't have that – do you hear me?'

Ruth nodded.

Sharing pain and heartache, joy and excitement. The war may have ended, but the recovery could take years.

Chapter Thirty-Four

Sunday, 6 April 1919

The day had finally arrived, and Ruth was looking forward to being reunited with Stan. At last, she could stop worrying about his safety. But, after seeing Tom, her thoughts turned to what effect the war might have had on him. There were stories of men afraid of the dark or waking screaming and covered in sweat, some even attacking their wives in bed.

Ruth had the house to herself. Carla was working from eight o'clock in the morning to six o'clock in the evening and Dottie had gone to see Donald's mother. Both had promised to stay away so that Ruth might give Stan the 'welcome' he deserved!

Ruth heard the clock on St Peter's Church strike noon. She finished her tea and walked into the scullery to swill the cup and put it away. She topped up the kettle and replaced it on the range. She sat down at the kitchen table and opened her book. Time seemed to drag by this morning. What would he be like? They had been apart for the last three years. What would they feel about each other? She would have her answer either way in a couple of hours.

There was a knock on the front door. It gave Ruth a start. She hoped it wasn't someone who paid a quick visit that lasted for hours.

Ruth opened the front door. It was Bertie.

–

They both stood there for a few seconds looking shocked and then gave each other a big hug.

'Bertie! Oh, Bertie, do come in.'

She guided him through to the kitchen. 'I didn't expect to see you today. But it's an absolute pleasure. At last, you are out of that horrible internment camp and back home. You should have sent a telegram to say you were coming. Carla could have swapped her shift.'

'When will she finish?'

'Six o'clock, so she should be here about half past.'

'Once things started to happen, everything moved quickly. They never tell you anything until you need to know. I'm sure they took pleasure in the uncertainty they created. Carla would've told you about me being earmarked for repatriation directly to Germany and that I was going to appeal. As you can see, I was successful. They told me Friday evening. I received release documents and was told to present them on arrival in Liverpool to receive a licence to remain in Great Britain. The soldier handling the paperwork suggested that I try to get naturalisation – I would certainly qualify for it using the rules before the war. That would have made my whole life a lot simpler. I still have to register with the police and if I don't do that within seven days, I'll be arrested.'

'But you are free now and can restart your life?'

'Yes, I suppose so. It'll take a bit of getting used to.'

'When did you leave?'

'Yesterday afternoon. They put me on the overnight ferry to Liverpool and checked my papers when I got there. That was it. They gave me other papers and told me to keep them safe. I was a free man, with a licence to remain in Britain, that's the best I could hope for. I went to Lime Street station and got the first train to Stoke.'

Bertie excused himself for a few minutes to visit the privy.

Ruth's mind snapped into planning mode. She needed to tell Bertie about the impending arrival of Stan. Where was Bertie going to stay tonight? The settee was the most likely. She thought back to the Christmas before Stan's conscription, but she stopped daydreaming – there wasn't enough time. She needed to warn Dottie.

Bertie returned and sat down at the kitchen table. It was then that Ruth remembered the poor bloke would be thirsty and hungry after his journey. She sprang into action, making a fresh pot of tea and some cheese sandwiches.

'What was the food like in the camp?'

'Very basic, but it kept us alive. How's Dottie getting on?'

'I'm not sure whether she's fully accepted… about Donald… yet. She feels cheated. He wasn't killed – he died of blood poisoning. His commanding officer told Dottie in his letter that he fell down the side of a hill, breaking his leg and badly bruising himself. They couldn't get him back to medical facilities for a couple of days and although his leg would have repaired satisfactorily, he developed a fever and… that was it.'

'How awful, to spend all that time fighting and then to die from a simple accident.'

Ruth poured them another cup of tea. 'Where are you staying tonight?'

'I don't know. I suppose I can book into a boarding house or something like that. I've got a bit of money.'

'I'm sure Dottie wouldn't mind you sleeping on the settee.'

'I'm sure she wouldn't, but I'd feel better for the first few days until everybody gets used to the situation of being somewhere – neutral.'

'There is one other thing that is happening today.'

'What's that?'

'Stan, Stan Bristow, is coming to visit me at two o'clock.'

'That should be interesting, what with me just being released from internment.'

'That's what I think. We grew... close before his conscription. I don't think he'll be too concerned about you being German, Bertie. He never showed that in the past and although I can't vouch for what's gone on over the last few years, he's too nice a bloke. However, I have no idea how he will react to another man in the house.'

'I'd rather not take the chance. We might say things hastily that would take a long time to recover from. Much better, I think, if I go to a commercial hotel.'

'I've got a better idea. Two of the women from work, Pearl and Daisy, have a spare room and are looking for a lodger. I'm sure they wouldn't mind putting you up for a night or two. Home cooking and you can sleep in as long as you want to as they both work. You might remember Daisy Simmons from Gordon Street, lived opposite to Dottie.'

'Yes, vaguely. She was a lot older than me. I don't know whether I would feel comfortable with that.'

'I don't see why not.'

'They might be afraid of having a bloodthirsty German under their roof. They might think it'll be too risky!'

'I think you're being a bit too sensitive, Bertie. They're good sorts and I'm sure they wouldn't see their friend Carla's brother with nowhere to sleep.'

—

Ruth, ever conscious of the time, put her coat and hat on and they took a brisk walk up to Corporation Street. As they walked along Campbell Road, Bertie asked how Carla was taking the lack of news about their parents.

'Carla heard from them two weeks ago. She has a letter for you from them, but she can tell you everything later.' They turned into Corporation Street and then up to Pearl and Daisy's house.

Pearl opened the door with Daisy standing behind her.

'Hello, girls, it's me. I've got a little favour to ask of you.'

'Yes, I see, Ruth. Good afternoon, do come in.'

'I've got somebody with me – remember Bertie Hesse, Carla's brother? He's just come back from a stay on the Isle of Man.'

Bertie greeted the two ladies with a kiss on the back of their hands.

'I'm Daisy. I knew your family as I used to live near the shop a few years ago.'

Ruth pressed on, aware of the time. 'The favour I want to ask is, can Bertie stay with you tonight? He's only just arrived from Liverpool and has nowhere to stop.'

'Of course,' they both said in unison. Daisy then chimed in, 'He can stay for a few days until he and Carla get their bearings.'

'That is very kind of you to offer, but I feel I am imposing on your friendship with my sister.'

'Don't worry about that; as far as we're concerned, you're a Stokie lad, Bertie – been here since you were a baby. I think we can trust you!'

'In that case, Pearl, Daisy, I would be glad to accept.'

'Right,' said Ruth. 'I need to get back to meet Stan. I'll come back up after he's gone. Then we can decide how you want to meet your sister. But now, I must go. See you later.'

When she rounded the corner into Campbell Road, she half expected to see Gertie parked outside of their house, but there was no motorcycle to be seen.

Ruth unlocked the front door and dashed into the scullery, where she doused her face in cold water to cool her down. Luckily, she had not sweated too much and, with a few dabs of cologne, she was ready to receive her most important guest.

It was wonderful to have Bertie back but fancy him turning up on the same day she was expecting Stan, right out of the blue like that.

Her heart was all over the place. She closed her eyes, taking deep breaths, with her hand covering her heart.

First, she must smarten herself up. She had been planning to wear the new dress she had made in anticipation of their meeting, but she hadn't even had time to change as the hands on the clock approached two o'clock.

She was about to nip up to her bedroom when she heard the sound she hadn't heard for some time – the sound of Gertie's engine. He was here, and she would have to make do with what she was wearing. Thankfully, it being Sunday, she was fairly decent, wearing a dress she had bought two years ago, which Stan wouldn't have seen.

She rushed into the front room and stood in front of the mirror, patting her hands through her hair to smooth it into some sort of order. If she had run upstairs as soon as Bertie had gone, she would have had a little time to collect herself.

She wet her dry lips with her tongue and, with nothing left to do, she walked steadily towards the front door and opened it with a smile.

There he was, definitely Stan this time, pulling the motorcycle onto its stand. He heard the door and looked at her.

'Hiya, Ruthie. Have yer missed me?'

He took off his gloves and thrust them into his pocket before taking off a leather coat. Ruth watched every move, her heart skipping a beat. Her eyes took in their fill. He was here, and that was all that mattered.

He walked towards her and stopped, gazing into her eyes. She was concentrating on him so hard she hadn't answered his question.

'Of course I've missed you.' More than I could say, she thought. It was as if she was mesmerised. His arms went round her, tightening with the emotion of it all. Her arms encircled him. She never wanted to let him go, not ever.

She lifted her eyes to meet his, and there was a light burning in them. Now all she wanted was to take up where they had been when they were interrupted by Mr Asquith. An urge growing inside. An urge to kiss him. To show him how much he meant to her.

Then, what she had been longing for happened. His lips descended onto hers, just the lightest of touches at first and then deeper with more longing. She kissed him back, and she thought her heart would explode. He pulled away first, but it was to look at her with the same longing that must have shone in her eyes.

'Welcome back, Stan,' she said simply.

'I've bin looking forward to this for a long time.' The whisper in her ear told her everything she needed to know.

Ruth heard a noise and pulled away. Two women stood across the road, staring at them. One of them shouted, 'Good on yer, duckie. The lad deserves every bit.'

It was then that Ruth realised Stan was still wearing his uniform. Together, they laughed. Before the war, their actions would've been frowned upon. Today, everyone wanted to celebrate with them. They waved back and together, they walked into Dottie's.

Ruth was thankful they'd arranged everything so she would be alone when Stan arrived. The thought of meeting him with everyone watching was beyond her. She had thought she'd be happy, even ecstatic, but she couldn't have thought her emotions would have run wild within her. She felt as if she could burst into tears or shout for the sheer joy of being alive and with the man she loved.

They stood in front of the fire, staring into each other's eyes, unable to stop.

'Would you like a cup of tea?' she asked breathlessly.

'I'd prefer to kiss you again – if that's all right with you?' He moved slowly towards her and they fell into each other's arms.

That kiss went on and on, but she wasn't complaining. Not one bit. And then it was over and she was resting her head against his chest, listening to the thumping of his heart.

'Maybe we could have that cup of tea you was talking about. All that kissing's been thirsty work.'

She laughed. 'And how will a couple of slices of cake do you?'

'Yer know a way to a man's heart, Ruthie.' There it was – his special name for her. She was still holding his hand until, eventually, she pulled away reluctantly, it must be said.

'It's been a very busy day. Bertie came home this morning.'

Stan's eyebrows shot up.

'Yes, he's free now. Carla doesn't know. I'll be taking him to meet her at the end of her shift, at around six o'clock.'

'I'm glad for her. She deserves something good in her life. Where have you hidden him?' he said, glancing around the room.

'He's at Pearl and Daisy's for a night or two until he gets sorted.'

Ruth got Stan to say a few words about his war effort. After spending three months in Sussex, his unit moved to France and the main supply depot in Amiens. He seemed to spend most of his time preparing and repairing anything with wheels for active service, which he'd talked about in his letters.

He said he also spent time in a place called Rouen in the spring of 1918 when the Germans threatened a breakthrough. They were told to retreat to Rouen with a lorry apiece. Any that couldn't be driven were to be destroyed. That was the closest he came to fighting. He made light of it, but she didn't believe it was all so simple and couldn't bring herself to laugh – not yet.

Ruth sat in Stan's arms as he told her about some of the better things that had happened to him. Ruth knew he heavily censored them, but she happily listened to his voice.

'The closest I came to actual injury was one day in 1917. I was in a convoy of four lorries driving supplies to a forward store. We were carrying corned beef. Them big seven-pound cans. Although the road was marked safe, it actually wasn't. The previous night, the Germans put an observation unit behind the British lines. This unit would have had a telephone to direct the artillery fire.'

'Why would they do that?'

'Artillery is no good unless you know where your shells are landing and you can make adjustments. This post would tell the gunners how to correct their aim.'

'I see.' It was surprising how many things she would have known nothing about before the war started had become general knowledge.

'The first barrage of shells screamed over my head, bursting in the fields. I wondered what the hell it was. I didn't know whether they were ours falling short, or theirs. The next thing I knew, there was an almighty bloody flash and I'm sitting in the ditch, with me steering wheel in me hands and nowt else. The lorry was in bits and tins of corned beef were dropping back to earth after their unexpected flight. It would have been funny if a can of corned beef had killed me by falling on me head. Hardly a hero's death.'

Stan got up to leave. He had promised his mother to be home for Sunday tea. She lifted the heavy and very expensive-looking full-length leather coat with wide lapels, fur collar and fur-lined.

'This is beautiful. You said you would get yourself a better coat...' She looked at the coat's label. It was then she saw it. Inside the jacket was the unmistakable German insignia and a maker's label in the typical German Gothic script:

Luftstreitkräfte
Handgefertigt von Franz Neymeier in Bremen
Das Eigentum von Major Erik von Stürm

Ruth froze. It was a German Air Force major's coat. Handmade and probably paid for by the wearer. And it was here, in The Potteries. She could guess how it came into Stan's possession. She didn't know how she felt. All the elation of the afternoon's events had gone.

'Where did you get it from?'

'The story behind that coat is the first time I spoke to a German.'

'Do tell.'

'It was in the summer last year when the British offensive got going and the Germans were retreating. Like I said before, the Germans couldn't reach our base with artillery and so they used to send planes over to bomb us. At the beginning, it was just a man in the back throwing out artillery shells. But as the war went on they got more sophisticated, like we did, and it was on one of these raids that I was given this coat.'

'Given?'

'Yep, we was in the slit trenches and the raid had finished. Some soldiers guarding the depot had taken potshots at the planes. One plane, a really bonny-looking Fokker, flew over the top of the trench and I heard the unmistakable sound of the engine misfiring and a few seconds later, it went silent. I thought that the daft bugger had run out of fuel. He made a landing in the field behind us and the eight of us in the trench picked up our rifles and charged across the field. Usually, the German flyers, who were nearly always officers, would put up a fight. They felt it was better to die than to be captured. But this was not the case with Erik. He jumped out of the plane, lit a cigarette and put his hands up. He spoke perfect English. I found out later he had been to university in Cambridge and that he was actually a distant cousin of our royal family. We had to stay and guard him and the plane until the MPs came to take him prisoner and no doubt the Royal Air Force would want to look at the aeroplane.'

'So you took his coat?'

'No, nothing like that. He seemed a decent enough chap. He handed over his revolver and knife to the lads and then I talked to him about the engine, expecting him to tell me nothing, but he opened up the cowl and I was looking at the most beautiful eight-cylinder radial engine. I said to him I could see what was wrong. One of our lads had shot a hole in the fuel line, so he'd run out of fuel. He was an unlucky bugger, as our lads could hardly hit a barn door.

'It turned out that he also was keen on motorcycles and we chatted about each of our machines. I think he might have had a few more than I'll ever own.

'When the military police arrived, he took it philosophically and said, "My war is over now, Stan Bristow, and good luck with the rest of your war." The MPs were putting him into the back of the van and I saw this coat tucked behind the seat on his aeroplane. I shouted to him he'd forgotten his coat, and he shouted, "Keep it... for your motorcycle."'

'So that's how you got it?'

'Yes, all above board. We're not supposed to have brought souvenirs back, but a few fags usually did the trick with any guards.'

'Do you know what this label means?'

He nodded. '"Air Force. Handmade by Franz Neymeier in Bremen. The property of Major Erik von Stürm." And I'll never forget him, Ruth.'

She was relieved that someone had given Stan the coat and that it hadn't been looted from a dead German.

Chapter Thirty-Five

6–7 April 1919

Dottie arrived back from her mother's just after half past four. It had been a long day for her and she looked shattered, but was eager for news.

'So, how did it go?'

'He came round on time and everything was just – wonderful, Dottie. He even kissed me outside – for everyone to see. Two women from further down the street, on the opposite side, cheered him on. Said he deserved everything he got. He was in uniform, you see.'

Dottie squealed with laughter. 'Never! Oh, my word. Whatever will Mother say if she gets wind of it? I don't suppose there's any point in asking *if* you'll be seeing him again?'

'He only has to say the words, Dottie. I want him back in my life again. I want to be there for him. For as long as it takes.'

'You love him, don't you?' said Dottie, softly.

'I can't stop thinking about him. He's like no one I've ever met.'

—

Ruth said goodbye to Dottie. She needed to find out what Bertie wanted to do. She hoped he would want to meet

Carla at the depot and then the two of them could talk on their way back to Pearl's.

Ruth went around to the back of the house. She expected they would be in the kitchen and when she looked through the window, there was Bertie, fast asleep in a chair by the range.

Pearl and Daisy joined Ruth in the yard.

'How did things go with Stan?' asked Daisy.

'Wonderful. We're going out for the day next Sunday. Stan doesn't have to return to work for four weeks, so we should have time to get reacquainted. How's Bertie?'

'The poor boy's shattered. He told us he didn't get any sleep on the boat because of seasickness. We gave the lad a meal and a cup of tea and he sat down in that chair and that was it. He's sleeping like a baby,' said Pearl.

'Now, you're sure you're happy with him staying for a few days?'

'Of course, we wouldn't see Carla's brother messing about trying to get a place to stay. We had already discussed the matter when we knew Bertie might be released and allowed to stay in this country,' added Daisy.

'That's a relief.'

'We've prepared his room. Fresh sheets and an extra blanket, just in case. Mind you, I think if he slept on the floor it would be better than he has been used to,' said Pearl.

A very sleepy Bertie joined them in the yard. 'That was the best sleep I've had in ages, and it was lovely to be woken up by the sound of women's voices.'

'We've got a little time; where do you want to meet Carla?' asked Ruth.

'Could we meet her at where she works and then we can walk and talk as we want?'

'Yes, that's fine. So get yer togs on, we'll need to hurry to make sure we don't miss her.'

—

Ruth and Bertie talked on their walk to the depot about general things. Ruth was careful not to bring up the subject of Edith and Luther. Many issues plagued her, making conversation difficult.

It was Bertie who broke the impasse. 'Have you spoken to Dottie yet?'

'Yes, I had a chance after Stan left.'

'How did she take it?'

'Difficult to say. She said the right things, but I could see that it stirred up emotions. We shall no doubt see what effect you being back has on her. I'm sure she doesn't blame you – as a German – for Donald's death. After all, he was in India. He wasn't even fighting the Germans. Besides, he could easily have been injured or killed on a tram here and had the same result.'

They walked in silence for the last bit of their journey and turned in to Woodhouse Street.

'That gate there is where we will come out. I'll find out if she's there – let's hope we've not missed her.'

Ruth entered the depot office and, to her surprise, Archie the depot clerk was working today. It was something they had started in order to reduce the workload on a Monday. Carla and two other clippies were putting their bags and ticket machines into their locker. Carla rushed across to Ruth as soon as possible.

'How did it go?'

'Stan arrived on time and we spent the afternoon together.'

'I was thinking about you at two o'clock. Come on, then, I could eat a horse between two rounds of bread and no doubt my dinner is waiting for me. Best part of a Sunday dinner is when you reheat it in the frying pan.'

'I need a word with Archie. You go ahead. I'll meet you at the gate.'

'I'll have time to pop into the privy.'

Carla disappeared and Ruth walked across to Archie.

'What can I do for you, ma'am?' Ever since the affair with Dennis Laycock, Archie always referred to her as 'ma'am'. He said he didn't want to get on the wrong side of a powerful woman like Ruth.

'Nothing, Archie. Come over to the window. I want to show you something.'

'Yes, ma'am, your wish is my command. What are we looking at?'

'See that man stood by the gate?'

'Yes.'

'That's Carla's brother.'

'Oh, the one who's been interned. The German one.'

'That's him.'

At that moment, Carla appeared out of the depot door and walked briskly across the yard. You could see the moment she saw Bertie. She stopped in her tracks and then ran into his arms.

'Thanks for the chat, Archie.'

'You're welcome, Ruth.'

Ruth joined Carla and Bertie at the gate.

'You could've told me, Ruth. I nearly fainted when I saw him,' said Carla, with tears streaming down her cheeks.

'You wouldn't have wanted me to do that.'

'No, I suppose not.'

'Listen, Pearl and Daisy have kindly agreed to put Bertie up for a few days until you get things sorted out. You'll no doubt have lots to talk about, and so I suggest you walk straight back to Corporation Street and I'm sure Pearl will find something to stave off your hunger.'

'What about Dottie? Does she know?'

'Yes, I told her when she came back from her mother-in-law's at teatime.'

'How did she take it?'

'She seemed to take it in her stride. After all, we knew this would happen one day and have spoken about it. But Bertie and I thought it'd be better that we didn't put too much pressure on Dottie and gave her time to get to grips with the new situation.'

'You seem to have got everything organised.'

'I'll start on my way back to Campbell Road and we'll see you later on.'

'Thank you again, Ruth,' said Bertie, 'for everything that you've done today.'

'You're very welcome. I'll leave you now. You two have plenty to catch up on.'

Ruth walked briskly back towards home. Yes, she called it home now.

—

When Ruth entered the kitchen, she could see that Dottie had been crying. She'd expected this. Dottie turned away and dabbed her eyes with a handkerchief.

'How are you feeling?'

'I have felt better. I have to be honest with you, Ruth, I hoped Bertie would get repatriated directly to Germany. Then, I wouldn't have to meet him again. Carla and I are getting on very well, but I will find it difficult to hold a conversation with a German man. He will be nothing like the lad we used to play with at school. We have nothing in common.'

'Come on, Dottie, he had nothing to do with the fighting anywhere. He was in internment.'

'He might've. He could've returned to Germany and fought. His parents were only too happy to return and if he hadn't been put into internment, he would probably have gone with them.'

'You can't say that any more than you can say that Jim died because I finished with him.'

'That's not the same, Ruth. The Germans started the war. If they hadn't, then my Donald would still have been driving his tram, but the Germans made sure he didn't.'

'So why should Bertie suffer?'

'Because... because... he's the only German I can get to.'

'You can't go through life thinking like that, Dottie. Like you said, you both decided. But why take it out on Bertie?'

'Bertie will be a constant reminder. If the Germans hadn't started the war, everyone would be a lot happier. That's why.'

'That's not rational.'

'I know, Ruth, but I am just telling you what I feel. Time may change things, but at the moment, I want nothing to do with Bertie Hesse. I do not want him to come into this house at all.'

'You realise you might force Carla to move out? Don't forget that blood is thicker than water.'

'If that's the case, then so be it. This is my house and I make the rules. If anybody doesn't like them rules, they're free to leave.'

Dottie then climbed the stairs, and Ruth sat at the table, disbelieving what she had just heard. That's you told, Miss Latham.

—

It was around ten o'clock when Carla returned. Ruth and Carla talked about what things had been like for Bertie in the camp. Ruth walked across to the pantry cupboard and got out the bottle of whisky that was left over from Christmas. She put two glasses down on the table and poured out two not-so-small measures.

'What's this, a celebration?'

'No, I need a drink and after what I'm going to tell you, I think you will.'

'That sounds ominous.'

'Carla, I want you to promise me one thing. Promise you'll sleep on what I have to tell you before deciding?'

Ruth recounted to Carla everything that Dottie had said. At the end, Ruth downed her glass of whisky in one gulp and Carla was not far behind her.

'I didn't expect that. I'm not too sure I really understand.'

'I don't think Dottie understands. That's the problem. She's blaming herself for not going to India with Donald, she's blaming Bertie because he's a German, she's blaming the Germans, she's blaming anyone, when all that really happened was fate. But I'm sure we would feel the same.'

'She should try having a mob wreck her home and her mother and father sent to another country. Unpleasant events happen in life, and you just have to live with it. She could do with growing up a bit. We don't live in a fairy-tale world.'

'Will you think about it before you say anything else?'

'Of course.'

'We three have been good friends through the adversity of war and now the peace is here. We should look forward to the rest of our lives. Granted, they won't be the lives some of us expect or want in a country that's different and will never be the same. But these are our lives, and we should be thankful to have a life to live.'

Carla went upstairs, leaving Ruth to ponder the events of the day. At least Stan didn't seem to harbour any ill feeling towards the Germans.

Ruth made sure all the doors were locked and jobs were done for the night. She moved the kettle off the hob and riddled the ashes out into the pan. She applied the damper to keep the fire burning until morning, poured herself one last glass of whisky before climbing the stairs. At the top, she could hear Dottie crying. Carla was in her room, also crying. Ruth turned around and went back down the stairs, picked up her coat, hat and put the whisky bottle in her bag. Even though the depot would be working, she would get a better night's sleep there.

–

Ruth was awoken by one of the mechanics. She couldn't remember his name, but she had seen him with Stan frequently.

'Time to wake up, my dear.'

'W-What time is it?'

'Half past five. The drivers and conductors'll start arriving soon. You dunner want them to see yer like this.'

Ruth's head spun as she tried to get to her feet. She'd never felt like this before. She couldn't remember all that happened last night, but she was still fully clothed and wearing her coat. She had no hat, but then she saw it on the table. Someone had covered her with a blanket that had seen better days. But it was warm. She sat upright and her head followed a few seconds later.

'When yer feels like getting up, there's a cup of tea in the mechanics' office and a fire. You can get yerself sorted out and then I take yer home in the van.'

Ruth groaned as she got to her feet. The events of last night flashed before her. She had been exasperated with her friends and she had sought the emotional peace that the depot offered.

'Thank you, Reg, that's very kind of you.'

They made their way across the yard to the workshop. It must have been that second glass. She wasn't used to alcohol, let alone whisky. It must've gone to her head.

They arrived at the mechanics' office and within seconds, a tin mug of strong tea was placed into her cold, shaking hands.

'Most of the lads like three sugars in a mug like that, but I left yer to put yer own in it.'

'Thanks.' Ruth rarely took sugar in tea but, having experienced mechanics' tea before, she added two sugars. It was heaven. She was thirsty and the strong tea hit the spot.

Once she had finished her tea, Reg brought the van around to the door and Ruth was stepping out at home within minutes. She put her hand into her bag and fumbled for her keys. Instead, she found an empty bottle. No wonder she slept so well, and had a thumping head.

She let herself in and walked through to the kitchen. It looked, sounded and smelled like a normal morning. When she entered, Dottie and Carla were chatting to each other as if nothing had happened. Carla was toasting some bread on the fire in the range.

'Here you are,' said Carla. 'Where on earth have you been? You look awful.'

Ruth told her friends of her overnight adventure.

'Good job it was Reg that found you. He's a good friend of Stan's and won't tell a soul. And if you've had a cup of mechanics' tea and survived this long, you're probably going to be all right.'

'You two look as if yesterday's argument never happened?'

'No, it happened. What I told you hasn't changed, but Carla and I have decided that our friendship isn't worth losing. When I see Bertie, I'll be perfectly civil to him, but what I said still goes.'

'And for my part, I've also talked to my brother. Yesterday, we discussed potential outcomes with people and he accepts things are unlikely to revert to their pre-war state. He's ready to make the effort, so we'll see how it goes.'

'Good. I'm so pleased. I must admit that when I went up to bed last night and heard both of you crying, my heart sank. But it looks as if you've worked things out. Now, I must visit the privy and get ready for work.'

Ruth looked as neat and tidy as usual when she returned to the office. The conversation was, as she expected, about Stan's return. According to Henry, that now left three men to come home, and fourteen of the twenty-one replacements were in place. The last of the clippies would be gone by the end of the month; that included Carla. In a few weeks, the company would employ male checkers, as agreed upon after the fraud.

Chapter Thirty-Six

April 1919

Ruth and Stan's first day out was to have a celebratory meal at the very smart-looking North Stafford Hotel in Stoke. When Ruth said she had put some money by for the future and that she would pay, Stan said he had been saving up his hard-earned cash for such a day as this and there was no way a lady was going to pay for him. He said he may be a little rough around the edges, but he was a gentleman.

He was picking her up in the van, so Ruth could wear her nicest dress and look her best for him. He dressed in his suit and looked smart, but thinner than she remembered. She'd never seen him in a suit before and found it difficult to take her eyes off him. He couldn't stop smiling. It was a long time since she had been so happy.

A young lady in a black uniform with a white frilly hat showed them to their table and gave them a menu; they both studied it as if their lives depended on it. Once they had chosen, there was nothing left to do but to look at each other. Stan was watching her and when her eyes caught his, his face turned a little pink. It was enjoyable to be out with him, but her mind kept returning to the kisses they had exchanged and her eyes were on his lips. Stan's eyes smouldered as if his thoughts weren't too dissimilar.

As always, it was Stan who put them on a lighter plane.

'Hope yer dunner mind, Ruth. I can't believe I'm here, sitting next to yer and eating food cooked by somebody else, as if I've got all the time in the world. And I'm clean an' all!'

'You've got to relearn how to enjoy yourself again.' She laughed. 'And I think Gertie's going to help you do just that.'

His face clouded. She reached across the table and took his hand in hers. 'How's things generally, Stan?'

He nodded. 'Good, really good.'

His beautiful eyes were bright. She could look at him all day – and night. Her cheeks burned at the thoughts that refused to leave her mind.

'Anyway, enough of me. What are you doing with yerself now? Yer made little mention in yer letters.'

'The PTC kept me on as they promised. They gave me, Molly and Madge permanent jobs in the cash office. I don't know if you'd remember them.'

He shook his head. 'So you should be quite knowledgeable about the money side of things by now.'

'I suppose I am. And the job's better paid than being in the typing room. What about you? Will it be business as usual in the workshop?'

'Aye. But I've had a few ideas that I'm mulling over. But that's all for the future. I don't intend to stay at the PTC forever.'

She looked down at their hands on the table. His other hand appeared, and he placed it on top.

'You don't know how long I've waited for, longed for this moment, Ruthie. I never thought I could feel like this.'

He lifted her hand and kissed it. Bolts of fire spread through her body in seconds. She couldn't look away. She almost wished they weren't sitting in the posh hotel, but outside, somewhere they could be together without the world as a witness.

The arrival of the food interrupted her reverie. She had never seen anything looking so delicious. They ate in silence with their eyes fixed on each other.

Once they had finished their meal, it was Ruth who spoke first. 'It's been a wonderful evening, Stan. Thank you so much for bringing me.'

'I thought we might go out on Gertie a few times while I'm on my leave before I have to return to my job.'

The fluttering in her chest grew in anticipation. She watched his Adam's apple move up and down in his neck as he was building himself up to speak.

'Not at all, Stan. I was hoping to spend more time with you,' she said, provocatively. 'I have several days due when I've covered for one of the other cashiers. Mr Routledge wants me to take them before the end of the month. I think he wants to give us time together. He's good like that.'

—

Carla finished at the PTC on Good Friday. She had talked a lot about it. It had taken her out of herself, in Ruth's view. Now Bertie was back, Ruth hoped Carla would spend some time with him before finding another job. They needed to get to know each other again after all the time they had missed. Ruth noticed Bertie had become withdrawn and introspective from the man he used to be. Carla had told her he would spend hours sitting on his own, thinking about things, because that was how he had learned to cope during those years of internment. How much healing needed to be done before people could believe they had a life to build?

—

The story of Tom Walton's first day had spread around the PTC. Everyone had been so pleased to welcome him back. Unfortunately, it hadn't worked for him. Four weeks after his failed return, he tried again, this time in another office, with the possibility of moving to one of the depots to see if the new location would make it easier for him — but it was to no avail.

The whole experience of working in the PTC was too much for him. Twice he went missing for hours and when he finally returned to the cash office late in the evening, he could not leave and would cry like a baby sitting in his former chair.

Brian took him back home again, talking to him all the way. Tom's mother was at work. Unable to leave him alone, Brian sat with him until Tom's sister, who usually got home first, returned. She worked in the Voluntary Aid Detachment in the hospital and knew how to talk to men like Tom. She put him to bed and then came downstairs and cried on Brian's shoulder until she felt able to cope and then carried on as if nothing had happened.

Four weeks after this episode, Tom left the PTC with everyone's agreement. Ruth hoped that, with help and understanding, he might come to terms with the loss of his friends and live again without blaming himself that he was the only one who came back.

Dottie sat in the upright chair beside the fire in the front room, stitching a sampler she'd started during the winter to keep herself occupied. Ruth lay on the settee, reading and feeling incredibly comfortable. Although it was the end of April, nights often turned chilly, and tonight was one of them. The only sound was the occasional spitting of the fire. Under her eyelashes, Ruth noticed Dottie look over at her from time to time.

'Something on your mind, Dottie?'

'Sorry. I didn't mean to drag you from your book.'

'If you want to talk about anything, I'm all ears.'

Dottie laid down her sampler. 'It's something and nothing, really. I've been thinking about the future.'

Ruth put her book down. 'Anything in particular?'

'Everything, really. You and Stan are getting very close these days. I'll be very surprised if the pair of you aren't married before the end of the year. Now that Carla has Bertie back, she'll want to spend more time with him and might even find a new bloke. I need to think about how I'm going to live when you two have gone.'

'But it might be ages before Stan and I... I mean, we aren't even engaged.'

Dottie held her hand up. 'No, Ruth. Don't say that. I need to be prepared. It'll happen, and I will be thrilled for both of you. After all Stan's been through, he won't want to wait any longer than he has to. And you' – Dottie smiled as Ruth's face burned – 'I've seen the way you look at him. Just like I used to look at Donald.'

'Oh, my dearest Dottie—'

'I've thought of various possibilities – taking in new lodgers, going to lodge with Pearl and Daisy, and then there's moving back to Mother's, although I doubt there'll be enough room. Even little Eliza is nine and Roy will leave school at Christmas. Brenda is twenty-two and has no sign of a chap in her life.'

'The things you mention, Dottie, they're all about where you want to live. But what do you want to *do* with your life?'

'That's just it – I don't know. I feel I need a fresh start. Doing something different. I don't want to stay at Mintons – or any potbank. Staying there would be like living in the past, and I need to look to the future – a future without Donald.'

It was probably the first time Ruth had heard Dottie admitting that there was a future for her and it was without Donald.

'I'm afraid I'll be at the bottom of a long list, behind all the men looking for work.'

'You've taken a tremendous step forward, Dottie. I'm sure you'll find something. It's good news that you've decided the time's right.'

Dottie smiled sadly. 'I shall never stop thinking about Donald, but I know he would want me to decide for myself, wouldn't he?'

You could hear a pin drop.

The fire spat.

Ruth smiled warmly. 'He'd be so proud of you and how you've looked after the house – and us, for that matter. You can do anything, Dottie, if you've a mind to.'

Chapter Thirty-Seven

May 1919

The more Ruth thought about the current state of affairs, the more she realised that something needed to be done about the relationships between her friends, otherwise they might drift apart. It had been nearly six months since the ceasefire and a lot of the men had returned, although the demobilisation was still in progress.

Carla had reached a low point in her life, but getting the job with the PTC had given her purpose and she had thrived. Walter had remained determined to get his mining qualification and get promotion at the colliery.

Dottie was slowly recovering from the tragedy of losing her husband but it was the guilt she felt because she'd refused to go out to India with Donald that had hurt most.

Bertie's sense of being shunned by people he had known all his life and his internment gave Dottie the opportunity to push the blame onto Bertie and his kind.

Action was called for, not in the future, but now. Ruth had to bring them all together, for their sake. If she could get them to open up about their feelings, they could help each other, as they had always done. She would invite them to Campbell Road for a long overdue get-together and she wouldn't let them leave until they had thrashed it out.

Ruth told everyone that she was inviting them to welcome in the future, whatever it might hold, while putting the past where it belonged – in the past. After some cajoling, Dottie agreed – and so did the rest. The get-together would take place on the following Sunday afternoon. If they were curious about the invitation, no one spoke up.

–

Bertie arrived just as the three women put the final touches to the food and Ruth sent Dottie to let him in. It was the beginning of her plan for the day: Dottie welcoming Bertie into her house and Bertie accepting the invitation. Although things had moved forward since the day of Bertie's return and Dottie had relented on her decision to ban Bertie from her house, the relationship lacked its former warmth.

As instructed by Ruth, Walter waited until Bertie had entered the house and followed a few moments later.

They all stood talking, clearly on edge, as Carla handed out small glasses of whisky and it was time for Ruth to put the next part of her plan into action. She shuffled them all into the front room and raised her glass.

'I'm sure you'll all be pleased to see our little band together once more. We've waited four long years, but we're together again, so let's make a toast.' They clicked their glasses together.

Ruth smiled. 'Sitting in this room are my most treasured friends. Our hearts go out to Donald, who was what you might call an honorary member.' She raised her glass towards Dottie, who was tearful but who raised her glass too, followed by the rest. 'We go back some way.' There were nods all round. 'Remember the vows we made all those years ago to be there for one another?' More nods. 'Those vows have been tested during these war years, but we have pulled through – through everything that has been thrown at us.'

Ruth sat down next to Carla and signalled for her to speak.

Carla gave her a nod and stood up. 'I have been so frightened since I…' She glanced at Bertie. '…since we became enemies in this country. If it hadn't been for the people in this room, I would never have got through it. When I got the PTC job, I almost gave it up because I thought people would come after me. They didn't. Ruth persuaded me to accept the job and Dottie gave me a home. I could depend on Walter if I needed help. He always made me see my way through a problem. I thank you all.'

Walter's face burned as Carla turned to face him. Ruth watched his lips as he sent a silent thank you to her as she returned to her seat.

Surprisingly, Dottie got up next. Ruth could see her friend swallowing hard to speak, and she had difficulty in raising her eyes from the floor.

Dottie took a large breath. 'There was a time, not so long ago, when I thought I would never come through the loss of my Donald. He was my world, and he was taken from me too soon. I wanted us to spend the rest of our lives together, to have… children. That's all. Then the war started.'

Dottie paused. She tried to smile, but it soon faded. 'Carla and Bertie – I hated everything that came between us. You took the blame, Bertie, because Donald had been killed in a war started by the Germans. He wouldn't have gone back into the army, but for the Germans. I couldn't cope and I thought someone should suffer. So when talk turned to repatriation, Bertie, I thought that would solve everything, that you'd be gone. But the authorities interned you. You had food, somewhere to sleep – and I thought you were so lucky. No prospect of *you* being killed. Even when you came out, you just had to appeal against repatriation and you'd be allowed to stay.'

She turned to Carla. 'I could forgive you, Carla, because you were English with German parents, but Bertie was born a German and I couldn't forgive him for being on the wrong side. Then Bertie came back and life seemed to carry on as if nothing had happened. I know different now. I'm so sorry I took my anger and heartache out on you, my dearest friends. Bertie, I saw that you and Carla had lost so much – your family, your job and then your wife and child. I hated how I had treated you and I never apologised for it. Well' – another deep breath – 'I'm apologising now. I'm so sorry for what I did. I hope that both of you will forgive me.'

'Dottie, you don't need to—'

'Believe me, I do, Carla.' Dottie turned to Ruth. 'That's what this day is all about, isn't it?'

With tears brimming, Ruth could only nod.

Bertie stood up, moving his glass from one hand to another. And wiped an eye.

'This is a day for laying out our confessions. I have to say I've been through the worst years of my life – all for living in a country where, overnight, I became the enemy. Through that time, I discovered who my genuine friends were, even if I didn't know many of them very well. I took out my frustration on some… individuals at the camp, and I've probably lost my wife and my little boy as a consequence.' His voice stumbled.

The room was silent.

He turned towards Dottie. 'Dottie, I was nervous when I came back from the Isle of Man. I feared everyone knew about my imprisonment as an enemy of Great Britain, and I may have seemed surly or uncommunicative at times. I'd heard Donald had died, and I was embarrassed at being on the wrong side. But you... you had taken in my sister and given her a home.' He looked at each of them as if he was talking to them personally. 'You are all my friends and, with your help, I'm sure I'll succeed again. I'm going to look for Edith and Luther and I'm going to bring them home. I'm sorry, Dottie. I don't know how to put it right.'

His eyes filled with tears, and he stopped talking. Nobody said a word.

It was Dottie who got up first. Dottie who put her arms around Bertie so he might weep on her shoulder before the rest joined them.

'You just have.'

The closeness they had built up since their schooldays had nearly been lost, but today, it was found again.

—

Ruth and Stan spent some time together enjoying the sights around Staffordshire before Stan had to return to work. Ruth saw little of him after his return, for there was a great deal of work for him to catch up on. He told Ruth that three of his former coworkers were missing, presumed dead, and one had been killed in action. New men who were doing their best had replaced them, working hard to impress the bosses so they might keep their jobs – so precious these days.

The next time he saw Ruth, he told her that even though he never had much to do with the clippies, he'd got so used to having them around. Only male conductors were left now. Ruth agreed with him wholeheartedly. She missed the camaraderie of working with so many women.

'I know the government were in a difficult position when the men came home from the war, but I feel it was sad that the women, who had done so much to keep the country going for all that time, were cast aside,' said Ruth one evening when they were sitting together on their own. Carla was off somewhere and Dottie had gone to visit her mother, who was ill.

'Women have done so much, I agree,' said Stan. 'It may not be too long before the politicians see the error of their ways and give women more opportunities. Now some of them have got the vote, those blokes in London had best watch out.'

'Only rich women have got it, though, Stan. Women like me will, likely as not, wait until the cows come home before we get anything.'

The conversation drifted back to where Stan felt most comfortable. Buses, lorries and cars. 'You know, I thought about buying a bus or two when I've sorted meself out, Ruth. I've spoken to Dad, and he is all for it, too. He says as he'll be part of it. And we can build up some routes across the borough that the PTC doesn't serve. I reckon as it'll be a godsend to people cos they'll be able to look for jobs further away and it'll give them more choice. Omnibuses can go anywhere. It makes perfect sense. Several buses what we've brought back from France are going to be auctioned soon and I'm thinking of buying a couple – just for starters. What d'yer think of Bristow's Buses? Starting off small and growing.'

'It sounds… perfect for you.'

'Of course, once it gets going and we start earning some money, you'll be in charge of the office. Don't yer think it would be exciting and we'd be…'

'You really want me to be part of it, Stan?'

'Course I do. Haven't I said so before?'

'Yes, but—'

'That's right. A bit like the PTC, but what they call diversifying. Having a range of vehicles for different work. Now that the PTC have bought a few buses, it'll give me plenty of experience for when I set it up.'

She stared at his earnest face. He showed genuine commitment to this.

'How exciting, Stan. Something to look forward to.'

'I know it's early days, but thinking about it was what kept me sane out there. I was planning it – up here.' He pointed to his temple.

Ruth smiled as a sudden vision flashed through her mind. It was Stan sitting on a rock, writing his ideas down while the war went on around him.

-

Ruth had spent a bit of time with Carla, helping her to put herself forward for jobs. Now that her family matters were settled, she decided to make something of her life instead of feeling sorry for herself. She had scoured the newspaper to find unskilled pottery jobs, shop assistants and jobs in service, and was running out of ideas.

'You may have to actually call in to some places. When they see how well-brought-up you look, how smart and so on, you might persuade someone to try you. But you may find you have to make do with anything that pays a wage. At least you're trying and that shows you're willing.'

'I suppose.'

The one thing that Ruth had noticed about Carla over the years was that she wore her heart on her sleeve. The world knew when she was happy and also when she was sad. This time, she was sad. 'You've got shop experience and you've worked as a clippie, so you've got skills to offer. And once the returning men have been fixed up, then you'll show them what you can do.'

'It's unfortunate that everything you want to do in life means waiting for something to happen.'

'That's life, I'm afraid.'

'Just a moment...' Carla lowered her head and read something she had just discovered. A job. In the Free Library.

Carla's eyes lit up. 'That's the job I want.' Immediately excitement grew on her face again. Ruth almost advised Carla not to get her hopes up, but then changed her mind. This was for Carla to sort out for herself.

By the end of the week, she had got the job and Ruth, for one, was thrilled for her.

Chapter Thirty-Eight

June 1919

Stan had returned to his old job at the PTC. It all seemed back to normal. He had been lucky during the war and had avoided the horrors of the trenches. Apart from a couple of stories, he rarely spoke of his personal experiences. She hoped he'd settle back into his old life without some of the trauma other men were going through. However, his sudden arrival in the cash office surprised her. He rushed in, making everyone jump. He shot over to a startled Ruth and pulled her out of her seat.

'They've demobbed him. Our Mark's on his way back. He says he should be home in time for Sunday dinner!'

Ruth threw her arms around him. 'I am so pleased for you all.' She drew back. 'When did you find out?'

'Father's just rung the workshop to tell me. Mother's so pleased and no doubt our Rosie'll do cartwheels when she gets home from school.'

'Does that mean we'll cancel Sunday tea to give you a chance to have some time as a family?'

'No, it doesn't. You're part of the family. My mother would never let me hear the last of it if I told you not to come along. It'll be the first time we've all been together since 1916. You don't need to make a picnic, mind. Mother'll have all that in hand.'

Ruth realised that the whole office was waiting with bated breath. 'Of course I'll be there, Stan. I wouldn't miss it for the world.'

'That's a date, then, usual routine – I'll pick you up in the van around noon. See you Sunday.'

Stan strode out of the office in very much the same way as he'd arrived. Even Mr Routledge was standing in the doorway to his office with his mouth open in surprise.

'Hello, Mr Routledge.' Stan beamed. 'Splendid news!' And he was gone.

Molly said, 'I thought he was going to propose to you, Ruth. I'd got my handkerchief all ready.'

'My money was on Mr Routledge,' said Brian wryly.

'Now, now – settle down. Miss Latham, I for one think it won't be long until you're celebrating.' But Mr Routledge was grinning as he turned back towards his office.

Ruth grinned. 'Don't be daft, Molly. He was just over the moon that his brother's coming home. He wanted to make sure that I was going to be there for him.'

—

Ruth finally sat down. Everything was ready for tomorrow's outing with Stan and Gertie.

A lot had happened during the last week. Mark had arrived on the Saturday evening as planned and she'd so enjoyed Sunday dinner with the Bristows. Mark looked much fitter and stronger. It had done him some good.

On the Saturday morning, 21 June, news came through that the Germans had scuttled their fleet interned in Scapa Flow, Scotland. *The Sentinel* said that it was because a peace treaty hadn't yet been signed and the Armistice had not been extended for a fourth period.

Saturday's big news had come from Paris. The peace treaty had been signed and this awful war was officially over. She and Stan would have a lot to talk about tomorrow.

—

Stan arrived just before nine o'clock on Sunday. To be on the safe side, Ruth put some apples in a box – just in case hunger struck. She placed them in a biscuit tin which fitted nicely behind and under her seat in the sidecar. Stan had also placed a steel can with a supply of petrol should they need it.

'There's another place I'd like to take you. It's a favourite of mine. North of Leek in the Staffordshire Moorlands. When I was a lad, a group of us used to cycle there once or twice in the summer. It's a beautiful part of the country. A perfect destination for today.'

'Sounds lovely. I've never heard of it. Is it a long way?'

'No. To be honest, it's only just out of The Potteries. Sit tight, Ruthie.'

They left Stoke and travelled along the road to Leek. In places, the road bordered the Cauldon Canal, which carried shipments to the pottery manufacturers in and around Stoke.

They arrived in Leek, a town on the border with Derbyshire, an hour later. It was like another world. Ruth couldn't believe there were such beautiful places so close to The Potteries. Her travels with Stan and Gertie had opened her eyes about the area in which she lived and she loved it.

After walking along the main street through the town, they returned to Gertie and continued their journey to an outcrop of rock called The Roaches. They parked the motorcycle inside a gate and walked up a pathway, made by the tread of thousands of footsteps over the years, to the top of one hill. Ruth carried the box of apples and Stan carried what looked like a cream-coloured blanket, in case the grass was damp, he said. Behind them lay the town of Leek, with its cloth mills and dye works, while in the distance was the pall of smoke over The Potteries. It sounded horrible when she thought about it. But the view was breathtaking, a popular destination for those who lived in the towns.

At the top of the climb, they found a place to sit where they might be undisturbed and could talk, but it wasn't too long before more people joined them. They had found plenty to talk about when they had the meal at the North Stafford Hotel. To be truthful, Ruth was happy just to sit there with him. It was all she wanted.

'I can understand why you like it here so much, Stan. If I could ride a motorcycle, I'm sure I'd be coming here every weekend.'

'There's nowt stopping you. Can you ride a bicycle?'

'No, I've never tried.'

'It might be safest to start with a push bicycle.'

'Yes, several of the clippies used bicycles to get into work for the early shifts. They looked very brave.'

They ate an apple each on a seat outside the church in the village of Butterton, and in the afternoon they rode through the Manifold Valley to a largish village called Hartington. Everywhere there were trees, fields surrounded by stone walls. Sheep grazed.

Stan then took several smaller roads through various villages and eventually they turned onto a larger road which took them back to Leek, heading across a place called Axe Edge, where, again, the views were magnificent. Eventually they retraced their route back towards The Roaches.

Stan turned off the road and held out his hand to her. 'There's summat I want you to see, Ruth. There were too many people around when we were here earlier.' She smiled and, together, they walked back up the hillside. There were fewer people around now. Many had made their journeys home. It was quiet and peaceful, with the sound of birds singing in the late afternoon sunshine.

When they reached the first outcrop, Stan, still with her hand in his, pulled her towards him and placed a kiss on her lips, barely touching, but leaving her wanting more. Slowly, he spread out the blanket again and invited her to sit. Then he gently pushed her back on the blanket while her heart thumped with expectation. The look in his eyes told her he was going to kiss her. Not a peck on the cheek this time, but a proper kiss that meant everything. She stopped breathing as his face drew closer and his lips met hers.

That kiss was unlike any other – her body felt as if it would explode and that she had been waiting for it for so long. Her place was there. She closed her eyes to concentrate on the feel of his skin next to hers.

Slowly, they drew apart, their eyes full of each other, unable to tear their eyes away.

'What if someone sees us?' she murmured, though it didn't really bother her.

'I checked first. There's no one on this side of the outcrop. There's no better place.'

After several kisses, they sat together, arms around each other. Happy to be together.

'Damn it, Ruthie. If it hadn't been for the war, I'd have said summat sooner. You must know how I feel about yer. Ever since you and Walter helped me with Gertie in the snow, you've never been off my mind. Over the last three years it's nearly killed me to spend so much time away from yer and I conner wait no longer. I want so much more than that. We're meant to be together, Ruthie, you and me, and I want the world to know that. My darling girl, will you marry me?'

Ruth's eyes popped open. She had got used to hearing him talking of his plans for the bus company and he always included her in his plans, but they had never included marriage. She stared at him, his anxious eyes, his faintly pink cheeks, his soft lips. How could she not fall in love with this man? She had felt jealous of Peggy for being with him. How relieved she'd been when Stan said that it was over. They had grown close until conscription had put a hold on their relationship. But those years without him had only served to show how much she missed him.

'Well, Ruthie? You have said nothing. Put me out of me misery!'

Taking charge, she covered his cheeks with her hands and drew him towards her, kissing him, gently at first and then with more urgency. She lifted her head. 'I love you, Stan Bristow, and I don't care who knows. Of course I'll marry you.'

His eyes lit up, and he hugged her until she had to tell him to stop because she couldn't breathe.

'I was going to ask you earlier, but there were too many people to witness my embarrassment if you had turned me down.'

'I could never do that, Stan. Not in a million years.'

'I wouldn't have had the confidence to ask you if it hadn't been for your father.'

'What do you mean?'

'I asked him what he thought about the two of us getting together.'

Ruth's eyes opened wide. 'And what did he say?'

'He told me I would never find another woman like you and that I'd better ask you sooner rather than later.'

Ruth burst out with laughter. 'He never said a word to me.'

'Ah, that would be my fault. I asked him not to – in case I couldn't go through with it. And I don't know if our Rosie could've kept quiet any longer. Today had to be the day.'

'So I'm the last to know, Stanley Bristow?' she said, hands on hips.

'It seems I'm the only one with me eyes closed. When I mentioned I was going to ask you to Mother and Father, they didn't look a bit surprised. Our Rosie said that if I didn't hurry and ask you, she would ask you on my behalf.'

'Is it so obvious?' said Ruth.

'Only to those who love us.'

He leaned towards her again. They lay back on the blanket. She had never seen so much sky. She would remember this day, and this place, forever.

Yes, everything was going to be just perfect.

A letter from Lynn

It seems a long time since I penned my last letter to you, but it gives me great pleasure to include this letter with the fifth book of my Potteries Girls series. Those of you who have read my previous books will know that each book tells the story of a group of girls/women as they battle through the war years. *Heartache* tells the story of Ruth and her friends Carla and Dottie. Of course, there has to be some romance and the three friends are all affected in very different ways when the war and love come calling.

Throughout the centuries many people chose to live their lives in a country other than that of their birth. When any war broke it could put them at war with their former people. This was particularly prevalent during the Great War when lots of people found themselves on the wrong side. I was particularly keen on exploring the issues of German men who had lived most of their lives in Great Britain, who had married British women and who became interned or were repatriated back to Germany.

I was particularly keen to show how long-term friendships and relationships can be devastated by suddenly being placed on the wrong side in a war. Ruth, Carla and Dottie were faced with huge change as the war gathered momentum and each had major decisions to make which would impact on their lives for ever.

As usual the characters are all fictional, but I have included real street names, towns and villages which some readers, particularly those living in the area, are happy to follow.

I can also tell you that the publication of *Heartache for the Tram Girls* in 2025 marks the centenary of Stoke-on-Trent's city status, which pleases me no end!

I do hope you enjoyed this journey with our friends and I would love for you to write a quick review.

Best wishes

Lynn xx

Acknowledgements

I am pleased to send my thanks once again to Keshini Naidoo at Hera Books for the patience and support shown during the writing of *Heartache*. As is often the case, characters and writers can be at odds with each other and intervention can be required from a third party and Keshini fulfils that role perfectly.

My research on internment and repatriation of prisoners has benefitted from information I gleaned from *Prisoners of Britain: German civilian and combatant internees during the First World War*, by Panikos Panayi, for which am grateful. The towns, villages and street names are real and I enjoyed searching through The Godfrey Edition: Reprints of Old Ordnance Survey Maps of the period. I know readers have been happy to see names they recognise from their lives. The internment camps at Brocton, near Stafford and Knockaloe, Isle of Man, were in existence throughout the war.

Once again, I have called on my faithful beta readers for their advice and I am indebted to Jacquie Rogers and Lesley Colclough, who have been with me throughout my writing journey.

As always, my husband, Michael, has been a tremendous supporter and has helped in so many ways when I have needed a sounding board. He enjoys research and digging up information, as do I, and revels in working on all things digital and all those horrible things relating to computers. He is my 'go to' buddy and the first person to read and comment on the latest version of my manuscript. In fact, I think he might know the ambitions of all the characters as well as I do – probably better because he has the better memory!

Once again, I would like to send a heartfelt thank you to you, the reader, for your kind words and support as the friends I have created come to life for you too.